Speaking With Strangers

I0636495

Susan Fairfoot

chipmunkapublishing
the mental health publisher

Published by
Chipmunkapublishing
PO Box 6872
Brentwood
Essex CM13 1ZT
United Kingdom

http://www.chipmunkapublishing.com

ISBN 978-1-84991-939-5

Chipmunkapublishing gratefully acknowledge the support of Arts Council England.

Oxford Dictionary: "Dissociation: Psycol. cause (a person's mind) to develop more than one centre of consciousness."

"Dissociation is the ability of the mind to develop more than one centre of consciousness. It is the pathological coexistence of two or more distinct personalities in the same person."

Speaking With Strangers

INTRODUCTION

I have had the experience of being with people showing extreme forms of schizophrenia and people who have shown outstanding clairvoyance. While the first often showed symptoms of fear or agitation, and the second were at peace, there seemed little difference in how they described the visions they were receiving.

The thin dividing line between psychotic behaviour and deliberate acts of evil are often questionable. What is evil? Where in the brain does psychosis lie? Is man predisposed to both, why and where does it stem from?

The Christian church would have us believe that our propensity for evil is the hereditary stain from the sin of Adam. Now we talk of inherent dispositions as moulded by a genetic blueprint.

But what makes us carry out deliberate acts of evil we knowingly, purposely and with self-justification commit upon each other?

The questions I raise in this story are: why some react so aggressively to trauma, some become delusional, and some become logical thinkers from it? Is the way we react genetic heritability?

What if, through the mind only, another dimension can be perceived that is incalculable through our current scientific knowledge? What if evidence of this undefined phenomenon is so sporadic and random that it cannot be called upon with carefully planned deliberation for scientific scrutiny? Could it be, that this very distinctiveness makes us each respond differently to whatever life offers?

Speaking With Strangers

SPEAKING WITH STRANGERS

Gospel of Thomas:
"I shall give you what no eye has seen and what no ear has heard and what no hand has touched and what has never occurred to the human mind."

Chapter 1

Number 63 McDonald is at the end a sedate Georgian terrace.

There is something settled and solid about the symmetry of that row. It exemplifies the perfection of Georgian architecture. Each unit, with its exact proportions, is separated by a decorative front door topped with an elaborately moulded Corinthian capital supported by substantial pilasters to each side.

That day, when I saw it for the first time, the windows had caught and reflected a fire-sparkle of sunlight as if beckoning me in its direction.

A sign in a window on the ground floor proclaimed in large letters: "ROOM TO LET."

I paused in front of the black wrought-iron balustrade which separated each house from the public pavement and looked up. It was what I had been looking for all morning. What chance did I have here? None of course, but I would try anyway.

I had so far, in my short experience of life, lived very much on my own with a pattern of mundane events that led each day towards a future with no great expectations.

I had just finished school and battled, with borrowed confidence, struggling to present myself while searching for accommodation in a bewildering world of indifference.

There is something daunting about that crust of London's outer suburbs. I always felt as if I was trespassing there. It seemed to be a place where those select natives lived an exclusive life, to the exclusion of anyone not born there. People walked about in absent minded anonymity on pavements white spotted from disgorged gum and littered cigarette ends. An impression of sleaze, tidied away by men in council uniforms brushing and sweeping night's offensive litter still traced its suggestion into lukewarm day. It seemed that man's refuse was insurmountable piling up everywhere. Torn refuse bags and upended bins were blamed on the unseen urban fox, living secretly amid the density of human development, adding to the unclaimed refuse of the night. "Vermin" – people say, of creatures trying to re-establish old habitats where humans have staked a supreme claim. Now I was adding to their encroachment and I was swallowed up, like all those insignificant beings that lost themselves there, awed by its reputation and legendary distinction.

They say that children adapt more easily to change than adults. They don't. It only seems that way because they are less capable of vocalizing how the change has affected them. They simply reinvent themselves. Some become aggressive, demanding - even scheming. Some become withdrawn and isolated.

I was one of those.

'Find a decent neighbourhood with a smartish looking house as close to your college as you can then look out for a room-to-let sign,' Peggy had said with her typical optimism.

'What then?' I asked gormlessly.

'Go in and ask how much the rent is you ninny.'

'Oh Peggy I do wish you would come with me.' I begged for the umpteenth time.

'I have told you Anna that it is high time you learned to stand on your own two feet. I have mollycoddled you since you were a baby and now you have left school you need to look after yourself. No one else is going to.'

She made it sound so easy.

I had walked a dozen streets and passed a hundred blocks. There was always a negative response; "no young girls" or "no females" or "no students" or "no permanents".

My toes pinched themselves up to my shoe tips driven by heels too high for all that walking.

I found a road where street cafes abounded on each side and I chose the least imposing one with plastic chairs at plastic tables outside. Two Polish waitresses staffed the cafe. One polished the abandoned tables while the other handed me a menu and waited. 'Cappuccino please?' Cappuccino was the fanciest coffee I knew beyond "filter, hot or cold milk".

Customers came and went, ordered, drank and ate and left in the space of minutes. I occupied my space for twice as long, resting my sore feet. I sipped the coffee through a moustache of foam and negated myself into invisibility as I watched people come and go. I was fading more and more into insignificance, a statistic of little value or consequence as I had always been. It would be easy to lose myself here. If I were to die right then and there, I would be a short term sensation, just for the act of dying; then I would be forgotten.   There is that kind of forgetting.   I was well acquainted with it.

'Will there be something more?' she asked removing my cold, empty cup and cleaning the table vigorously where it had been.

No, nothing more.

'What am I doing here anyway?' I was thinking as I headed once more for the long hard pavements.

Once more I found myself standing on my own two feet as recommended by my older sister and now I was looking up at a house that filled all the requirements I was looking for.   But, without her by my side, I felt intimidated and rooted to the spot.   I stared up at the window with the sign, hesitant and vulnerable. Someone was moving about inside.   I saw the figure of a young woman move from behind the curtain.   She was wearing a bright red top.   Her long blond hair stretched out over her back like a waterfall of silken movement. I noticed how slender and graceful she seemed.   Was she the owner or owner's daughter perhaps? Encouraged by her youth, I walked up the steps and rang the bell to what was marked "Ground Floor Flat".   I heard footsteps coming along the passage and my heart beat faster while I thought of the questions I was to ask.

She opened the door a few inches while first bending down to retrieve the mail that had been posted through the door and had scattered to the floor.   Her hair tumbled carelessly about her shoulders, a mask to her face.

'I have come about the room.'   I said.   Then added as an afterthought; 'The room you have advertised in your window.'

'Yes,' she replied.   'I guessed as much.'   The voice sounded surprisingly older than I expected. She straightened up and opened the door further, whilst clasping envelopes in a white-gloved hand.

I opened my mouth to ask if it was still available to a female, a young one and a student but I shut it again in a state of surprised shock which must have shown on my face.   This was no young girl, or even a young woman.   An old creased face stared back at me like a crumpled shirt left too long at the bottom of a clothes bin. Concealment of thick pancake make-up gave the wrinkled skin an almost grotesque look; added to which, heavily defined eye-brow pencil clowned her expression into one of surprise.

'My God,' I thought to myself, 'she must be a hundred, if a day.'

It was that first impression of her that stayed with me for a long time after, like those little snap shots you make in those pertinent first moments that impress the mind and are the hardest to eradicate.   Right or wrong, judgements are made in those first moments and a super-imposed nature is manufactured by the imagination.

'Come in,' she said. 'I was expecting you.'

'You were?'

'Yes, you are Anna Lockhart? You have been booked into the college,' she said with the authority of fore-knowledge.

How on earth my sister knew I would come here of all places completely baffled me. Why had she not just given me the address and spared me miles of fruitless asking?

'Follow me, I will show you the room. It is the one on the top floor; you will share a bathroom with another student - male. He is out right now. No doubt your paths will cross. He is a music student and out most of the time. I won't have practising here, too much noise, bad enough with the young people in the basement flat with their noise.'

She spoke as if she was dictating a letter. Her voice was flat, without tone or inflection that might indicate some kind of recognition or enthusiasm but there was even less expression in her face. She discussed the rent and the deposit and told me the room was available immediately but she was already aware that I would only be ready to move in a week's time. That was when Peggy was going off to Canada and leaving me alone. The thought of it sent a shiver down my spine.

'It won't be so bad,' she said as if reading my thoughts. 'You will find plenty of friends here - you won't have time to miss anyone or feel lonely.'

I wondered what on earth Peggy had been telling her about me. Not too much I hoped. Peggy had a way of smoothing the path before me and arranging things to make life easier to bear. I only wished she had been more explicit earlier.

It was a small room.

A window looked out onto the street below and beyond that, the garden of the house opposite with large macracarpa trees blocked all other views.

There was an old-fashioned hand-basin against one wall and next to it a large, plain, free-standing cupboard. On the opposite wall was a single bed with a small chest of drawers at its head.

It felt strange and uncomfortable. Not home. No – certainly not home.

I thought that as Peggy had arranged it all that I should accept the terms and the room without any further questions. It all seemed very reasonable, in fact a lot cheaper than I had been led to expect.

We talked a while about arrangements with keys and the deposit and the rules of the house and little else.   This was clearly not someone who wasted time on idle chatter. She got down swiftly to the formalities of what was expected of me, appointing the date and time that I would be moving in.   She had not even asked for references for my character which Peggy had suggested a landlord would do but then she seemed to know about me already so there was nothing left to say.

We walked back to the front door without exchanging further unnecessary words.   Absent of smiles or handshake we said goodbye to one another and I left. I had not even asked her name nor had she taken mine down, but then, she had known it already. Everything was assumed.

It was only when I got outside that I remembered that I had not left a deposit but I reasoned that if Peggy had already made arrangements, that must have been taken care of. I walked back to the nearest tube station, thinking only of the sanctity and refuge of the journey back home.

Home was a small cottage that Father had rented for us when he was with Eleanor our stepmother.   We had never got to know much about Eleanor and we had never been invited to her house. All I knew was that it was somewhere in the country.   When she met Father she made it quite clear that she was not interested in step-children entering her life.   It was a status quo that made little difference to our lives as my sister Peggy and I had become detached and independent from Father for as long as I could remember. We lived in a kind of mental waste-land of coherence where security might at any moment come to an abrupt end.

It has taken a long time to reconstruct those early years of our lives.   It was a traumatic time.   The mind has a way of closing off areas of the past that are too painful to reconstruct and it seems that I had bypassed those years in my own mind. Perhaps it was for the sake of survival, perhaps it was because I was persuaded to forget, who knows. I only knew much later that remembering would answer the tormented questions of its outcome on our lives.

All I carried through childhood was the offered knowledge that Father had acquired sole custody of his two daughters and had fought to get it, only to leave us a few years later in the care of a housekeeper. Contact with our mother and grandparents was a forbidden subject.

Grandparents, Father said, were people who interfered and were therefore circumvented and shunned.

Strange, isn't it, how parents change in attitude when another partner comes on the scene! Even the most diligent parents become insensitive and indifferent to their children's needs when they are aggressively seeking a separation from their partner. Somehow the children always seem to get in the way; that is, when they are not being used as a bargaining tool or a weapon. The stress and aggravation caused by impending proceedings bluntens them from what was once care to a distanced inattention to anything that does not relate to their own immediate emotions.

It was shortly before my fifth birthday that Father announced to Peggy and me that we were leaving our mother and our home and moving to a flat in one of those high rise apartments overlooking the sea in Portsmouth. Peggy is almost six years older than me and managed to take it all in her stride as she does with everything in life. She explained it in simple terms to me.

'Daddy says Mummy has become a lesbian,' she announced with the authority only an older sister is able to command over a gullible and un-launched younger sibling. 'She wants to live with her girlfriend in Bermuda.'

'What is a lesbian,' I asked.

'I think it is some kind of leprechaun,' my sister answered. 'But I am not sure.'

'Well, I have seen pictures of a leprechaun in my story-book and they wear a lot of green and look funny and I don't think it is that.'

Peggy hated not to know something so she added rather sharply, 'Well Daddy says it's not nice for us to be with her now she has become one.'

I remained confused. I did not want to leave Mummy. It was alright for Peggy, she and Father had always been intensely close. I was close to Mummy. The girl-friend bit I understood, we all had girl-friends at school; boys were not the sort you played with. Bermuda was another thing. It sounded like some kind of pudding. Why would Mummy and her friend want to live in a pudding without us? When I put that to my sister she sighed deeply and told me I was a child. Being a child was a fact I was made constantly aware of.

For a long time after Mother had gone I could remember so little. There were of course the nightmares. They came every night and they came with a strong and violent flavour of reality. Peggy would tell me I was only having a bad dream. They were not real. I was to forget what I dreamt. She refused to listen to them. She refused to talk about Mother. I was a silly baby for even thinking as I did.

I learned to forget.

I came to realize later in life that there are numerous categories of ill-defined truths which are religiously adhered to because of the source from which they come. Mother's disappearance was one such tenuous and imprecise truth. Trying to piece together the reasons for her disappearance only confused me more. There had been no doubt that she had been over preoccupied with long phone calls and she had always seemed to be crying for no reason. It seemed that weeks and weeks went by without her coming to read a bed time story. Peggy took over that job, as she did with most of the things in our life.

It was the very fact that Mummy had found this special friend that Father was able to keep us all to himself he told us constantly. He told us that the courts agreed that being a lesbian would harm children. Why they should imagine he was the better parent baffled me. It made no odds that we seldom saw him. He was out most nights and when he was home there was always some female with him that we had to be polite to.

Peggy became morose and rebellious and Father responded by giving her anything she demanded. I simply became more and more dependent upon her and she reluctantly took on the role as my guardian and protector.

Our mother had simply disappeared one day without even saying goodbye and went to live in some remote part of the world. That was how I remembered it. That was how I was led to remember it and led to believe it. Yet the conflicting nightmares continued to infect each night's sleep like the ricochet a sharp and painful wounding, a haunting remnant of something I could not shake from my mind. I would wake at night and find my older sister also wide awake, just standing in the dark as if to rid herself of something she could not come to terms with. I remember crying a lot. That was all. All other memories after Mother had left had simply vanished from my mind. We never saw her again.

What few contacts she made with us via letters were read briefly to us by Father. I guessed later that he was still rankling over the fact that she had left him for another woman. We were never allowed to see the letters or read them for ourselves so I imagined by their very curt content, it was because she had lost interest in us.

What I found most strange about her disappearance was that she had left behind her precious violin. She was always playing. She never went far without it. I secretly took the violin for myself, trying to remember all that she had taught me. She had promised me a small one of my own for my fifth birthday but it never came.

When Father decided that it was the worthy Eleanor that he must have for his partner he was faced with a choice: children or wealthy widow? No guesses as to who won!

In our eyes Father could do no wrong.

In religious teaching we are taught to love God and fear him at the same time; a duality that in no way involves any condemnation of the deity who must remain 'perfect' and always 'right', punishing those who have done wrong, making out of life a kind of preordained value system. I suppose one could say we valued our father in much the same way. We never questioned. We began to see our mother as someone who had let us down, deserted us and he was the saint who had come forward for our protection.

I spent my childhood trying to figure out what I had done wrong that God had seen fit to distance my sister and me from both our parents. In my convoluted child's logic I guessed a terrible sin must have been committed, even though I was unaware of what it was I had done wrong. It became my duty to search deep enough until I found the flaw inside myself and then I would understand the perfect judgement God had rendered.

Peggy had just turned twelve and I was in my second year of school when we moved to a cottage in Hayward's Heath. Later on when Father married Eleanor, it was his original reason for not taking us with him. He said it would interrupt our education and we were not at schools where we could board.

Francis, our housekeeper, was one of Father's old girlfriends. She was under the false impression that she would be living there with him. It took her a full year to realize that his short visits to us would be no more than she could ever expect and that he was in fact living elsewhere in a house he had bought for a new wife.

Poor thing, she suffered terribly when she knew but she stuck it out with us for a further year till Father's wife insisted that it was high time she left and by then Father thought we were quite capable and old enough to look after ourselves. Besides which, there had been growing tension between her and Peggy which had become so bad that she was very ill before she finally left.

I never saw her again after that bitter day when she left in tears, amid groans and complaints of stomach cramps and acrimonious accusations, followed by Father's feeble excuses. She simply took her things and left while I stood by helplessly imploring Father to beg her to stay. She did not even turn her head to say goodbye but charged into the waiting taxi and was gone.

Chapter 2

Crafted by neglect and early responsibility, Peggy became fiercely strong as a character and powerfully independent.   I was left feeling isolated, unworthy and easily intimidated.

Peggy was twenty one when she started working for a large law firm, having majored in international law.   From there she marched ahead in her profession.

I clung like a baby monkey onto the hem of her skirt at every opportunity.

I was so unlike my sister.   She had this wonderful chocolate-coloured hair with a natural curl which released a life all of its own to bounce about her shoulders, showing off her warm olive skin.   I have bright red hair, dead-straight, which I kept in a long plait down my back.   My skin is that shade of white that goes red in the sun and freckles.   I was told that I inherited these genes from a grandfather I did not remember meeting.

Where I lacked confidence, Peggy bubbled over with enthusiastic fervour which she showered over everyone. She loved parties and would stay out all night sometimes. I hated parties and seldom went to them. Where I was always dumped by the few boy-friends I had, she had men falling about her ears wanting to take her out or away on exotic holidays. She seldom went away.   She said she had me to look after which did not bode too well with the men in her life.

I was not an academic match for Peggy either. I struggled through school. My main interest in life was music. I battled away with Mother's old violin, trying to remember what she had taught me.   At school I was given music lessons, starting with the piano, until Father got rid of Mother's old piano, too big for the cottage he had said.   I reminded him that Mother had promised me a small violin that I could handle and he dutifully got me one.   Neither he nor Peggy enjoyed the noise I made on it so I played in what had been named by Francis as the "sewing room" at the back of the cottage. By the time I had progressed to Mother's violin, music had become my solace and sole entertainment.

Peggy was always telling me that I allowed myself to become a natural victim - whatever a "natural victim" is, and I guess I just fell into that niche, hiding behind my music.

'Don't let people get in your way,' she would say. 'It would be so easy if one could just point a finger and rub out difficult people.

When I think of some of Daddy's girl-friends, especially this new one...'

Her eyes would wonder off into a distance of elimination and control. One never took her too seriously. It was Peggy's way.

I think of those threads of our DNA coiling on their double helix, two strands in every cell of our body with our father's dark genes and our mother's fair genes encoded in them. Nature had never been so diverse from its reservoir of genetic blueprint in connecting us as sisters.

When I got back to the cottage after finding the bed-sit, Peggy was on the phone, talking to Father. He was making sure that all the arrangements had been made with the cottage letting agents for handing over the house keys and confirming that my educational requirements had been organized.

'Yes, yes all done,' she was saying. 'She has just been out looking for accommodation near the college. Of course she can do that all on her own. Yes, she has just walked in; do you want a word with her?'

Father went into a long monologue about his busy business life and how he was unable to be there when we moved out and I would be moving into digs.

'Yes Father, it's all been arranged. Yes, really close to the college. Peggy already knows all about it. Yes, yes of course...'

Secretarial school was Peggy's idea. She said the name of the college simply occurred to her one day. Someone had spoken of it and said it was good. I had no inclination towards being a secretary, but as my sister said, I had to be something.

Peggy was busy packing books away into a cardboard box when I turned away from the phone.

'So, you have found somewhere. Any good?' she asked.

'Well, Pegs, you know that already,' I said. At that point the phone rang and she answered it. It was the house letting agent wanting to know when they could come and inspect the house before we moved out.

The move had all been very last minute. Peggy had been offered this wonderful promotion working in Canada but she had to make up her mind about it in rather a hurry. It all fell in quite well with the plans to find digs near my college. Everything was so rushed we had barely time to talk to one another let alone to discuss plans about what was happening.

That last week was so full of Peggy's social arrangements and parties thrown for her or by her that I had no time at all to thank her for finding the bed-sit for me. It was only on her last day as we were on the way to the air-port that she said. 'You must give me that address where you are going. I am so sorry I have not had time to check it out for you. Don't forget Eleanor has arranged to take you there at three tomorrow. Only one night on your own here, then you are free Anna, just think of it.'

I had thought of it and the appeal was far less that the expectations she had for herself and her freedom.

'But Pegs the landlady already knew about me when I got there. She said she was expecting me. I thought you had arranged it all.'

'No, not me. I thought you said you had wondered about not knowing where you would end up?'

'Yes. Pure chance I found myself right there where they seemed to know I was coming. I thought you had...'

'How very odd. Yes it must be pure coincidence. Perhaps they thought you were someone else.'

'I don't think so. She knew my name and has phoned me since to find out what time I will be arriving.'

'Oh, I am sure Father has had something to do with it.' She said dismissively and we left it at that. There was far too much else to think about at that point. Nevertheless on the train journey back from Heathrow after saying good-bye to her, I gave the coincidence more thought, without arriving at any conclusion from current knowledge, so I put it to the back of my mind.

Speaking With Strangers

Chapter 3

The letting agent had checked the inventory, taken the keys and left me waiting outside, feeling more than a little sentimental about leaving what had been home to Peggy and me for so long. I was ready and waiting outside when my step-mother arrived looking impatient and full of self-righteousness at the generous act she was performing in taking me with all my possessions to my new place of residence.

I could not remember another occasion that she had done anything to help either of us. I therefore went perhaps a little too overboard with effusive thanks which she took to her condescending self with a look of self-righteousness.

'Yes, this is the road. McDonald Road, there is the sign. Right at the other end. Number 63,' I said, craning my neck forward to find the row again.

'I hope this is not too expensive for your poor Father,' she said rather tartly.

'You girls have cost him a fortune these past few years.'

As we had never been taken on holiday with them, had gone to state schools and given just sufficient money to live on I could not imagine where the expenses could have been incurred. However, true to the silence of humility I had learned from early on, my thoughts remained unvoiced and my actions compliant.

I told her what the rent was and she seemed not to believe me. 'Well, for that money it must be the broom-cupboard they are putting you in.'

'Actually it is a small room, and I am to share a bathroom with another tenant,' I said apologetically.

I rang the door-bell. This time I was met by an elderly man with an almost bald head crowned with wisps of grey at the sides. I was at once captivated by his eyes that seemed to stare out of a great depth. He held out a hand to greet me with a most wonderful smile.

'Malachi Mahoney,' he said. 'Agatha had to go out. I will help you with your bags.'

My step-mother never budged from her driving seat while the old man helped me to haul out all the cases and boxes of books and bits and pieces from the back of her large Land-rover. When everything was out and on the pavement, I again thanked her profusely and she drove off with a recommendation to behave myself at college. An absurd substitute for anything better to say, assuming that it had not occurred to me before then that I should do anything else.

'Who was that sour-puss?' he asked.

'Stepmother,' I answered.

'Keeping up with the old tradition of step-mothers.,' he said with a wink.

I decided then and there to like this man.

The heavy weight I had carried about in the pit of my stomach all morning was soon neglected as the old man chatted away as if speech were the balm of all forgetting. He seemed to have an endless repertoire of anecdote and comment about anything and everything as we lugged cases and boxes up to my small room. It was soon cluttered with all my accumulated possessions and I dithered about, not too sure where to put anything.

I was being mesmerised by the old man's voice, a soft Irish brogue which charmed and eased the aches of parting from all the security I had ever known. I think it was from that moment on that he began to replace my sister's absence with a new and immediate friendship.

He came from Galway - a life time ago, he said without enlarging upon the years belonging to that period - an arbitrary time of a random existence. He was one of a large family that had packed themselves into a small terraced house close to the Catholic Church where they spent a good deal of time, more to expand a sense of space than anything, he joked. He laughed as he spoke but beyond the lightness of humour, there was a sense of sincerity about him. Perhaps a reverent nature brought with him from that church. Not that pious sort, but a sentiment of something indefinable and good. He talked of pasts and people that affected those pasts and I found myself listening spellbound, yet not quite knowing how it was that I found myself absorbing everything he said. He seemed to reach me on a kind of subliminal level that affirmed innate thoughts not yet aired. Then all of a sudden he zapped back into the present and current.

'An old feller, like meself lived for a good few years in this room before you,' he said breaking a narrative of the past to the more immediate attention.

'Oh yes,' I answered, 'and where is he now? I hope not wanting his room back too soon.'

'Passed away he did. Lived here since the war, but he was seldom here. Let's say he had interests in other countries and when he returned he always came back to this little room, now yours.'

'That's a long time,' I said. 'Did he have no family? I mean, there is no kitchen that goes with this room. How did he manage?'

'Oh, he came over to me and we cooked together in my flat.' Malachi's eyes twinkled as he spoke as if there was little to be taken seriously. There was now something distant about him. It was as if he had stepped out of another world. One to which I did not belong. It was as if he had come from a time and a place that had no bearing on the present.

'Ah, those days we did things different,' he would say in later days. Then out of blue he would say something odd, like: 'There was no transport like today.' Then as if in some reflective reverie he was telling me how many people after the war were left with no families, especially those who had been away or had returned from exile.

I remember how, that first day at Number 63, his presence and chatter, although a complete stranger, was companionable and friendly, it began to permeate those desert places within me and assuage my fears. I felt comforted and sheltered by him. Yet I recognised even then, that there was also something indefinable about him. It was as if he was wrapped in many impenetrable layers that could not be brought into focus. The room took on a different aspect with him there. He became an extension of the room and all the strangeness of the house and finding myself there, so inexplicably circumstantial.

He talked his way to the door and out of it, telling me I should now be left to sort out my things. I felt the loss of his relaxed and tranquil manner as soon as it was gone. I wanted to call after him and tell him not to go, but this was the time I had grown towards, that dreaded, independent, self-reliant time, and I battled with it.

I finally closed my door and began to arrange clothes and possessions in drawers and on scant shelving. A sudden desperate loneliness gripped me unawares. I looked into a going past of empty and solitary spaces, and I tortured myself with my lack of worth.

I sat down on the small, narrow bed after an hour or two of sorting things out and took a look around me. Despite my clutter, the room seemed lifeless, devoid of any life-trace of someone who had spent all those years living there. An uneasy feeling worked its way under my skin, as if its last tenant had hollowed out an empty resonance leaving a kind of abysmal silence.

If I had not been told about him would I be noticing it now I wondered? All the same there was something about this room that felt sad. It echoed the loneliness that had always been a part of me for as long as I could remember. I had always been able to detach myself from it in the way that my past had required, but now it overwhelmed me.

I straightened up and told myself sternly that there was nothing of that silent loneliness of childhood here that could scare me. I had always managed to accept isolation as part of the structure of my universe and now faced with this new extension of solitude I was becoming a little shaken by it.

I examined the room to see what remnants could be identified as someone else's home, not mine.

The wallpaper was old and had begun to come away from the walls especially under the window. It had pale blue stripes with little forget-me-nots in tiny sprays of measured spaces. A dado-rail divided the lower wall-papered part of the wall from the dusty white, upper part which was framed with ornamental cornices curling up to meet the high ceiling. A single picture was suspended from a copper hook on the rail. It was a colour print, behind glossy, reflective glass of a young girl in old fashioned clothes sitting on a log with a mass of unreal foliage around her. Suspended from another hook, near the basin was a bevelled mirror without a frame. It was frosted by age and reflected a distorted image of whoever stood before it, lending affirmation to my lack of confidence.

I turned my mind to my sister and how awful life was going to be without her. For one desperate and unbearable moment that emptiness that life sometimes offers, surrounded me in a dark mist. A slight knock at the door brought me to my senses and broke the blind panic I had allowed myself to dwell in. It was Malachi, right on cue.

'I thought you might like a mug of tea and a biscuit,' he said.

He came in with a small round tray with two mugs and a few biscuits without a plate to hold them.

'Oh, how kind. How very kind. Thank you so very much. Here let me make room on this chair.' I shoved all the clothes that I had draped over the single upright chair in the room and offered it to my guest in one single movement of sheer relief to have company.

'Nice, very nice,' he said. 'Well tell me now; what would a pretty young thing like you be doing in this part of town?' He began as if starting from scratch getting to know me. All previous chatter had been random and about himself; I think to gain my confidence, now I could see, it was going to be interrogative.

'I start at the college next week.'

'Yes? And what would it be that you will be studying?'

'I wasn't too sure when I left school. I thought I would love to have done music but my sister said I was not good enough. Then I thought something with art but she said there was no money in that. She told me I must try the secretarial course. She said there would always be a job as a secretary somewhere and of course that is what I have been booked in for.'

'A good practical girl, your sister.'

'Yes, very much so. Clever too. I am afraid I did not inherit brains like her.'

'Well, I expect you got the looks,' he smiled kindly.

'Oh no, Peggy got all those too. She looks like our mother.'

'And your mother? Why - was it not she who brought you here today?'

'She lives a long way away. We haven't seen her for years but she writes. Yes she writes and says she misses us but she has chosen another life,' I explained as neatly as I could without disclosing all the details of Mother's rather extraordinary life in Africa now, teaching at a mission school somewhere out in the sticks, Father had told us. It had been years since we had a letter from her and we simply never spoke about her. The subject made Peggy bad for days.

'It takes all sorts now does it not?'

'Yes, I suppose it does,' I said, not knowing how else I could respond to that.

'Well now,' he said, rising to his feet. 'I hear Agatha come in and she is calling.'

I heard nothing but then I was not listening out for anyone. He took the mugs away on the tray and said goodbye and hoped I would be happy there.

There were no facilities for cooking in that room. Only a tiny bar-fridge near the door suggested a place to store food. I had brought sandwiches and later in the evening I unwrapped them while making a note of what I would need. A microwave, only a small one would help and a kettle of course and there near the window was a plug for a television aerial. I could hire a small set; it would allow some companionship for the evenings when I was not busy with work.

About an hour later another knock at the door and I was surprised to see "Agatha" the old long haired blond, standing there and it was just "Agatha" as she introduced herself. There was no other prefix or formality about her name as to how else I might address her.

She was wearing a lot more make-up than the last time I had seen her. Deep pencil lines cut macabre contours above her eyes and her eyelashes blinked at me like two butterflies let out into the sunshine. The lines on her face were pan-caked furrows that had attempted to mask what was beneath.

'I told one of the students to let you in,' she said. 'I had a bit of a migraine and slept all afternoon. I have brought you your keys.'

I told her that Malachi had let me in and helped me with my things. She looked strangely at me and sighed deeply. I handed her my deposit and first month's rent. In advance she had said. She counted it and put it into a pocket in the long gown she was wearing. She was far less talkative than Malachi. She had an air of grace about her that absented her from the world about her and seemed vague about Malachi and irritated that the student had not helped.

'I might have known,' she muttered and then left me to go back down-stairs, her long hair slithering around her shoulders, at once shutting off her age to anyone who did not see her face.

Chapter 4

Days followed days of those life-changing experiences, getting acquainted with my new environment around the college, my small bed-sit and trying to discover my new self, with the appointed career ahead of me. I thought of how man becomes identified by his job or profession which he wears as a badge of prestige; he is no longer a name but a stamp of what he does and he is known as such and not by who he is.

I went about those enrolment formalities, meeting fellow students and discovering what my future was going to be like. All the while, I wore a heavy heart knowing inside that I was not doing what I wanted to do.

Meeting strangers was something I shrank from, in the expectation of becoming dismissed as the outsider once again. I felt sick with nerves, although I couldn't have said exactly what it was that I was afraid of.

We were massed together in a hall before being allocated a classroom. I kept my head down listening to the groups of more confident voices speaking in louder tones than those, who like me, shifted uneasily from one leg to the other, awaiting instruction.

When I took the trouble to look up, everything was as commonplace as it should be and the physical appearances behind the voices begin to resolve themselves into young women, all much like me but unidentifiable with myself.

I think maybe it was my own future I was afraid of, as if becoming a part of that group I would for ever become run of the mill, average, mundane and this would be the final irrevocable step. My music would be lost to me for ever and a part of my soul would shrivel and die. I knew that I must accept my destiny and forego all my past dreams of what I really wanted, for as Peggy said, they were only dreams, impossible dreams. There I was, surrendering my life to something that had already been ordained, somewhere far back beyond memory.

I felt a desperate urge to escape, but how? Time dragged her long and empty feet across the floor in an agonizingly slow motion. It was as if this was a test to see how long I would last till I cracked under the strain. I wanted to weep for the loss of the career I had always hoped for. I missed my music and grieved over its loss in my life. It was a bereavement.

Peggy had insisted that I leave my violin behind, that I start a new life without it. It got in the way, she said. It stopped me from growing up, she said.

How I wished that I was more like my sister and was able to make friends as easily as she did. Instead, I agonized over encounters with those enthusiastic students exchanging familiarities about their lives, my own life was always so dull compared with theirs.

I found myself huddled away from everyone trying to work out where I should go and what had to be done. This new life was crammed with so many and various people coming from different corners of the world. Whatever identity I once had was now thrown into a melting-pot of a million pebbles on a beach all striving for the prize of the perfect job, the perfect partner, the perfect life. I wanted to reach out and touch a single soul and know it was to separate it from all the pebbles of all the beaches, one from another.

Chapter 5

Peggy emailed me often with exciting news about her new job and a whole new world opened to her. She had been so eager to get away, right away. Now her life was something else. She sounded so happy there as if she was free of something she had carried for so long. She no longer had the irksome burden of a dependent younger sister.

I, on the other hand, had scarcely anything to say. The course I was doing was horribly boring, it was not what I wanted to do but I could not tell her that. I was missing my music. I felt as if I had lost a limb and battled to cope without it.

I continued as my school days had been, feeling savagely inferior to everyone around me and filled with self-loathing. Escape, a need to retreat into a world of my own was ever present in my mind. I was then, as I had always had been, the outsider, looking in, or, so I had convinced myself. I needed to hold all those unhinged pieces of myself together or I would cease to function.

I had spent a childhood doubting myself. Of course, I feel differently now, changed even, through much anxious exercise of will. If I had any aspirations for music before they had been replaced by a desperate need to start again, to stand firm in a complex world, to live valiantly among uncertainty and have the courage to speak up for myself, which was exceedingly difficult. The slide from an isolated and introverted childhood into solitary adulthood was a lesson in humility and loneliness and one which I battled with. It taught me to try to understand my fellow man and force me to learn to communicate more. The world seemed immense and my significance drowned in a sea of strangers who had long become lost in a miasma of subterfuge and invention. I imagined people scrutinizing me from behind watchful undercover spy lenses while they kept dark secrets behind eccentricities that made them strange.

While Peggy was in the back ground of my life and music filled those haunting times of jagged memory, I managed to cut out those nagging thoughts of my mother. Now they flooded back at me, submerging me with a longing to see her again.

I suppose I could say that everything in those days appeared larger than life and life became a kaleidoscope of surreal, exaggerated images in which I was horribly lost, sorting through the distorted truths I had been fed. I wanted to untangle my isolated and lonely childhood and I began by looking at secrets kept from me, removing the wrappings one by one to look more closely at things that I had not understood.

I imagine most adolescents, at some time or other will question that sacrosanct distinction that parents give themselves. Just as we adhere to the knowledge of the scientists of the day, often against all instincts, so will a small child see its parents as the arbiters of all truth and authority of all knowledge.

If the scientist says something is so or not so, it has to be right by a simple deduction of known, visible fact. If a parent says something is so or not so, it has to be right for the very trusting direction from which the information came. We simply exchange one set of direction with another.

The information that I had been fed for so long that my mother had gone way lodged itself into that maturing doubt area of my mind.

I had come to a cross roads in my life where thoughts and feelings began to be re-examined. I found myself calling out to my Mother with a gut feeling that she would somehow respond and come to me. Of course she never came. Sensibility alone would teach me that unless I had made a contact with her in some concrete way, by letter, phone or visit how else would she know that I was summoning her? Yet I had the strangest, inherent feeling that she could hear me. What would the scientist think of that – madness?

At night and in the early morning the world would creep in from an unseen life of sound and movement beyond; a door opening, footsteps on stairs, hands brushing a wall, a curtain pulled and those muffled voices beyond my vision.

Without Peggy there to reassure me it took on a frightening almost threatening tone. I would lie awake trying to imagine what was going on in that house. Where for example did Malachi sleep? Did he share a flat with old Agatha? Why was the music student who was supposedly on the same floor as me so quiet? Then those steps that went up to an attic floor, Agatha had said nothing about that.

I tried to imagine the layout of the basement flat and who lived there. It seemed to pulsate with a mysterious life of sounds and laughter. I could sometimes smell their cooking and wished that I had a larger place with a kitchen. But what would Father say to that extra expense?

If I had known where Malachi stayed I might have knocked on his door some evenings. I had been so comforted by his presence. I looked forward to our next meeting.   But the thought of being confronted by the formidable Agatha deterred me from asking at her door.

So the days went by without much happening in my life.   I came back from the college each afternoon, made tea with my new kettle, micro-waved an instant meal and read or switched on the television and longed for my music.

Chapter 6

I hated that cloistered, closeness of London, that lack of country freshness that had always filled my life. I sometimes took a walk through a park or caught a bus out to some playing-field and watched boys kick a ball about. I liked to catch the sight of birds overhead that had flown in from somewhere perhaps greener and fresher than here.

Without my music to fill my mind, I began to read. I started to explore significance and meaning in questions that philosophers pose. My own life was so full of unanswered questions of unfounded childhood fears that I began to explore those distant unspoken memories that had never left me.

I hungered for fact, exactness, because it moved away from that tendency for hallucination and fantasy of torturous nightmares. Impenetrable extracts from my mind smacked at each turn into a blank wall of dead end. I had come only so far as offered fact that had been told me. But those overriding issues of my brain kept returning without reason, bringing up broken images, leaving a distortion of memory and a matted web of confused feelings without conclusion. I was searching for answers and never certain where to begin.

I even prayed, but was never sure of the reception of my prayers or if I was simply talking to myself. Prayers were, nonetheless, a comfort. They had become to me, a kind of journey into consciousness. Praying took me away from where ordinary thought mattered, where the boundaries of the body and ego no longer counted. I guess it is that invisible and unreachable source of God that makes praying so much more powerful.

I was in search of meaning, significance.

The quantum Physicist was always there, ready for argument that we are all part of the same matter; talking incomprehensibly to the listening layman, like myself, in terms of nanoseconds of time, of the insignificance of our little life. The religious fanatic responds with his incontestable proof that God is in control of these short term bodies of ours, whose souls will abide in suspension for an epoch of time awaiting resurrection. The philosopher speaks in defence of the soul, using the equations of quantum physics as proof of the soul's existence. Then the scientist steps forward again to say that life originated two billion years ago from a glob of organic chemicals from which self-reproducing nucleic acids started the long chain of evolution, thus proving that we are no more than self-perpetuating matter grown intelligent.

Somehow, proceeding from this raw creation we have fitted in the soul somewhere and attributed to it the duality of pain and pleasure which appears to keep us going.

The very structure of these soul defining metaphors confused me with dimensions of time and space and relativity which are meaningless in a current life of survival for existence in an increasingly competitive world.

I continued to search. Never quite sure of what it was I was searching for and I seldom understood the complex answers. I only knew that something inside me was missing.

Searching implied some kind of self-imposed, tortuous conflict because it involved so many contradictory and inconsistent theories, when in the end, after time, the answers come from within. But by then I realized that the search I was after was something more fundamental, and that too was revealed – in time.

Father made those duty calls to my mobile phone once in a while. We had nothing to say to each other. Conversation was full of those little platitudes that placate and appease the conscience with little real sentiment about them. I would hear about how busy he had been, how Eleanor was, and how they were getting ready for some trip they had planned. It was followed by, 'How are the studies?' – 'Fine, just fine thank you.' 'That's good, well keep up the good work.' And that was it. It must have been as painful for him to phone me as it was for me to receive his calls.

I often wondered why he had tried so hard to claim custody of us when he had no idea what to do but leave us in the care of someone else and then go to such lengths to avoid contact with us. I imagined it was how he reacted to his many girl-friends. He chased them furiously then deserted them after he had won them over.

We had never been close and he had never made any pretence at being the loving Father. Mother was the loving one. I remembered that. I had long since stopped missing her any more, but I was for ever thinking about her and wondering at her silence. That unspoken gap of silence had widened but my mind still battled with all those subconscious issues about her.

Coming back to an empty room each evening, I began to think more and more about her. There was no Peggy to tell me what to do or what not to think any more. I watched endless television to try and stem the thoughts, but it only drained me. I was feeling suddenly so alone and vulnerable in this new environment, without my violin to take my mind into another dimension. I tried instead to force my mind into the consciousness of existence, or whatever it is one calls being alive. I read somewhere that it channels the mind to greater things. I would stare into the square of window sky hoping for some wonderful revelation that never came. Then I would fall asleep exhausted from my thinking only to wake in the night with thoughts spilled from nightmare and dream, like an old wound that has bled through its band-aid upon the darkness of night. It was at those times that I became aware of that other part of being, of existing in a discarnate sense. What, when I am dead? When I am here no more? Would I go on seeing and hearing the things that were there? Would it be as if things were seen and heard through some other sense?

Being alone I was beginning to open my mind to all those unspoken of things. I became acutely aware how much I had relied so heavily upon my older sister to put things right that I had become this timid and incapable thing.

I woke one midnight from a dream. It was one of those old evocative dreams full of moments of regret. The details of the dream were not coherent only the emotions that they had drawn from me and I lay there full of shame at my lack of sophistication and artless naivety. What cue had planted it there from the day? I don't know, but it was sharp and pertinent and I got up to write it down. The next morning none of what I wrote made sense. I only know that the dream was about my Mother and the last time I saw her but it was unreal, as if something strange and horrible had been planted in my mind.

There was something missing in my life. I felt a desperate urge to reconstruct my past, to try to remember where and how it all began, this strange and tortured inner life I had been leading. I felt like the over wrapped chrysalis lost in dead leaves fighting for some other brief life before I became nothing once more.

I began to look back. Peggy had always answered questions for me and I had accepted what she told me. Now I began to ask myself those same questions all over again but without a voice to put answers to them.

For one thing, Peggy would not allow me to ask questions about our Mother. It was a subject she had closed from her mind and no amount of persuading would allow any mention of her, in fact, the only time I found Peggy agitated and annoyed was when the subject came up.

Yet, when I thought of my Mother a reminiscent sweetness filled those hollow spaces of my mind. I could never remember what it was about those thoughts or why they were followed by a sharp trace of unhappiness. Was that from a lost memory or perhaps it was for those unfulfilled times after she had gone. As Father had begun to extricate himself from us almost right away after she left there was only Peggy left to fill the gaps of what had happened.

There was, of course, my music which had shielded me from retrospection and there was some kind of comfort from those brief few years when Francis was around, but even then it was a borrowed security given by someone trying to impress Father, rather than a kindness to make our lives more comfortable.

Over time my mind had become totally absorbed in music to the exclusion of all else. I had stagnated in a repetition of endless daily necessities and duties. There had been no outside influence of an extended family; no aunts or uncles or grandparents or even family friends. No one visited except Peggy's friends who regarded me as inconsequential. For me, music alone filled the precious times. Futility had seeped into life like tar that fills the cracked timbers of an old ship and holds it together till its original strength is taken over.

I simply followed orders, afraid that if I did not, my sister too would desert me, as I felt everyone I had known from my infancy had done.

Now that my music had been left behind, my life reared up before me, a stagnant wasteland, devoid of bright memories or hopeful future.

Chapter 7

As the weeks began to separate us with distance and time, Peggy's phone calls became reduced to once a fortnight and her emails became sporadic with excuses that she had been worked off her feet and so busy with social engagements. Deep down, I sensed that she too was deliberately disengaging her ties with me. I was a reminder of a past she had tried hard to be rid of and now she was free of it. It left me feeling even more isolated than before. And somewhere deep within I was carrying a burden that I had been shielded from, that had been blocked from me.

I came back to my room every evening ready to lock myself away, feeling a sense of relief that the day was over. That heavy presence of irrelevant self was full of doubts, self-distrust and a sense of worthlessness.

I looked out for Malachy but he seemed to have vanished into a world of his own. Agatha was sometimes in evidence and when she was not, I heard her talking the other side of her door to someone or other.

The young students passed me often in the corridor and gave a friendly nod or a muttered hello. I had not yet seen anything of the music student. Though we were purportedly sharing a bathroom there was little evidence of his use of it.

I had been living there a few weeks before I met him.

He was there, half way up the stairs and talking to Malachy.

'Well I'll be blowed, and there she is, the very one I was talking about. Here my pretty one, come and meet the great maestro himself. Lorenzo, this is my friend sweet Anna Catherine.'

I was startled. How had he found out my full name? Only my mother had called me Anna Catherine and after she had left us the Catherine part was dropped, entirely. I was feeling so startled that I looked up at the music student with a hesitant and perhaps less eager curiosity than I imagined I would for this moment.

For a student, Lorenzo was unexpectedly old. Perhaps in his thirties even I guessed. He had a head of thick black hair almost to his shoulders. Black eyebrows and dense sideburns and an overgrowth of black stubble about his face. He was tall and willowy with a slight stoop to his shoulders that gave him the air of someone stooping down to meet his fellow man from a lofty isolation of himself. All in all he was remarkably handsome. There was a furtive look about him as if he was unused to being drawn into a public scrutiny by anyone. I could see that his acquaintance with

Malachi seemed to be a firmly established one by the way they had been in deep conversation before they spotted me.

As they descended the stairs the music student put out a hand to me in shy, if reluctant camaraderie.

'I believe you play the violin?' he offered as polite conversation.

'Yes, but, how did you know?'

'Well now it was me that told him.   Did you not say that you wanted to study music but your sister had other plans for you now?'

'I did...'   I had not mentioned what instrument I played, I was certain of that but I did not challenge him on that.   It must have been a lucky guess.

'There now!   You would not mind that Lorenzo knows that you share the love of the same thing then?'

'I am sure that I am nowhere near as competent,' I muttered, feeling desperately shy and wanting to get away.

'Perhaps I will hear you play some day,' said Lorenzo magnanimously.

'Oh no, I could never do that.   Besides my violin has gone into storage along with my sister's things while she is away.'

'Well now, Lorenzo was saying that he will be playing in a concert next month and perhaps you will join me there,' offered the inexorable Malachi.

'More a recital. String quartet,' the music student amended.

'I would like that very much,' I said as I took my leave of them with excuses about homework which I was desperate to get into.   I ran up the stairs to my room.   My hands were shaking as I put the key to the lock.   My only desperation lay in the direction of my escape.   I put the television on and watched the news with that kind of keen avidity that takes nothing in.

I did not see the music student again all that week and I was afraid of using the bathroom lest I should bump into him but as before there was little trace of his use there.   He must have cleaned up so well.

My thoughts bounced and waged upon themselves at the prospect of the concert. I had never attended a concert or recital before that was not a school performance and as I had advanced in music over the last several years at school I had been the performer and seldom the audience.

I was tremendously excited about the event but the thought of being once more in the presence of the music student also filled me with anxiety and inadequacy.   His image flittered like a moth to light about the edges of my thoughts.   I became increasingly restless and unsettled as the date approached.

I was no good with attractive men. I could feel them appraising me with a look of amazement that I could in any way be related to my sister.

As the days went by I looked out for the music student as carefully as I looked for Malachi, but only Agatha was in evidence. She sometimes stopped me in the passage and would politely ask how I was getting on at the college. There was something vaguely familiar about her face but I could not imagine what it was. She was always so heavily plastered in make-up it was hard to see any kind of recognition there. She would stare hard at me as if she knew something about me, something I had forgotten and only she had the key to unlock it from my memory.

She mysteriously asked me one day if I had heard from my sister. It was the first reference ever made about Peggy and I wondered how she even knew about her. Then I remembered that she had known my name when I first arrived. She had known that I was booked in to the secretarial college and I had come looking for accommodation nearby. Peggy must have known. Peggy must have contacted her.

I became alarmed when one day she asked about my mother.

'Has Peggy told you yet about your mother?' she said. Just like that! Straight after a remark about the weather. I was so taken aback I did not answer. What did she mean? What was it that Peggy had to tell me I wondered? Her eyes penetrated mine in vague silence.

There was something disconcerting about Agatha's eyes. Behind that mask of mascara and heavily plastered eye-liner were those snake-eyes that take in everything and leave out nothing in their appraisal of all they absorb, like the Medusa.

'We haven't heard from her in many years,' I answered with an astonishing honesty. I usually lied about her when people asked and told them I had letters from her every week.

'Ah, yes,' she said slowly. 'I see.'

I wanted to shout out at her. 'What is it you see, you old bat?' But had I done so I might lose my accommodation and I remember how hard it was to find. Besides which, I was far too timid to talk out like that. Rejoinders were the concession of my thoughts and never my speech.

I guess she was well meaning. She was trying to insinuate herself upon me for some reason, I could see that, but she lacked the charm and subtlety that Malachi had. If he had appeared to have known something about me, he would never have made a direct approach to question me and I would have been too afraid to ask him what or how he knew. I was still in need of obscurity.

The following day I saw Malachi coming in through the front door.

'Hello,' I called out.

'Well now,' he said warmly, giving me his wonderful smile. 'There is a sight that will bring pleasure to any man and where would you be going right now?'

'I was thinking of taking a walk to the park,' I said.

'Would you have any objection to an old man joining you?' he asked. I told him I would be delighted with his company and we walked out together to the street. He chatted away as he had done before and I found myself once again captivated by him. The days of loneliness were swept away to insignificance. I hardly noticed the park as we talked and I involved myself in conversation. I told him about the books I was reading and he listened intently, waiting for my questions and opinions without offering any of his own but his rapt attention. It was as if his listening became a liberating release of my own thoughts.

On the way back he invited me to have coffee with him at a small bistro on the corner of our road.

There was a feeling of warm familiarity as we walked on down the road. It was as if I had been asleep for so long and suddenly found my family once more. We chatted and laughed and talked about the concert. It would be Haydn's String Quartet in D minor. I knew it well.

We talked about the kind of music that pleased us and laughed about the pop music that belched up from the basement flat from time to time. I was with an old friend. One who did not spring personal questions about my family and life or remind me of painful ones.

I was, at once, more aware of an expanding universe where things came together in a remarkable and comprehensible way. Answers were simple and clear but those inaccessible questions remained, still strangely murky where restive memories had been lost in dormant synapses.

'You have such wonderful hair,' he said looking at the long plait down my back. 'Now why is it that you always have it tied away like that? Will you not let it loose that I can see it?'

I smiled as I untied the rubber band that kept the plait intact and shook out my plaited hair. There was a rush of pleasure from within that anyone could find me or my hair appealing.

'No one has ever remarked on my hair before,' I said.

'I always thought it was ugly. Only my mother when I was little...' I began, and then stopped as a suppressed memory of her moved from shade to substance in my mind. Somehow an image of her brushing my hair before a mirror rose up into my thinking. I had not thought of it before.

'It's like a flame,' he said. 'A brilliant fire, see how it catches the light.'

'That is exactly what she used to say,' I said as if remembering had woken something inside me.

'Who was that now?' he asked. Was he trying to make me say something about her?

'My mother,' I said slowly.

'Ah.' he said.

There was something about Malachi.   It is hard to explain. When I was with him I found myself talking and laughing as I had never done before in my life.   I came alive.   As for his contribution to the conversation, well there was little more than a whimsical smile and warm Irish encouragement.   He seemed to listen carefully to everything I had to say, as if it concerned him; smiling here and there or offering some comment, making me feel clever and witty. No one had made me feel like that before. He was the father, the grandparent and all the family that I had lacked rolled into one loveable and appreciative audience. Malachi oozed a kind of generosity that made you feel good about yourself. He was like a reminiscence of something past which I was unable to name distinctly or conceive.

He seemed to have sensed that I had been lonely and he arranged that we should meet more often at the coffee-bar. So our meetings became something of an occasion, nearly every day before the concert that I now began to look forward to with quiet eagerness.

There was never a mention about the music student, despite my longing to know more about him and my curiosity that he was never in evidence.   Instead, I unburdened myself about the tedious days at the college and my life with my sister. I said very little about Father or his many female friends or his indomitable wife Eleanor. Step mother. And Malachi never asked.

When the day of the concert arrived I was quite jittery about what to wear.   I had begun to wear my hair loose to please Malachi and gone to a hair-dresser to have the edges trimmed and turned to soft waves in small emulation of my sister. I even drew out some of her old discarded makeup to enhance my eyes and lipstick to give me colour.

I chose a long floral skirt and a plain cotton blouse with a ruffled collar from a Laura Ashley's shop that was about to go into liquidation. Of course by the 1990's the Welsh fashion designer's clothes were beginning to be seen as outdated but they were perfect for me, they reminded me of someone I had known when I was little and Laura Ashley was hitting the market with the rush of a tropical rain storm. I guess it gave an old fashioned and demure eccentricity to the modern extreme world of Biba and hot pants then. The clothes suited my personality.

I was ready far too early and went to knock on Agatha's door to ask if Malachi was there. She looked confused for a moment when she saw me. Then she seemed to mutter to herself, 'oh do be still and go away, oh no, not now...' It was a strange kind of soliloquy that passed between her and some other invisible source behind her.

'Would you like me to come back later?' I asked timidly.

'No, no. You look so much like... I was startled. You are even wearing the same...' her voice tailed off.

'Is Malachi in?' I asked feeling very disturbed by her strange behaviour, suggesting – what? I was uncertain what to do.

'I will wait for him at the cafe,' I said. 'We are going to a concert this evening. I don't know if you knew.'

Dear God, I thought, what if they were a couple and she might resent my seeing so much of him. I felt myself blushing as I ran off out of the front door before she was able to answer me.

I hung about outside for some time feeling foolish and fretful. Was the whole evening one in suspense only? I took myself off towards the cafe. One of the students from the basement flat passed me and did a double take as he turned to stare at me.

'Hello' he called.

I gave a guttural mutter in reply and hurried on when I saw him hesitate ready to stop and talk. I couldn't talk just then. I was feeling far too confused and out of sorts.

I found myself ordering a coffee I did not want and sat near the window so I could see Malachi coming. I seemed to be there for ever as I watched the time devour the minutes to when we were supposed to meet and then exceed the time. Half an hour past the start of the concert and I was about to get up and walk away when I saw Malachi walking very fast towards me.

'Come along,' he said, 'no time to waste.' Together we speed-walked to the bus-stop, caught a bus and sat silently staring ahead – just four stops to go and there we were.

We crept into the back of the hall. The music was already up to the second movement, that slow bit which allows background sounds to filter through. A few shush-mutters warned us as we took seats closest to us.

If this was an amateur performance it was outstanding I thought. There was no way that this was a music student we had come to listen to.   I was barely able to enjoy the music as my mind agonised over the excruciating circumstances of my being there, out of time and out of place and I wondered with amazed curiosity why Agatha had referred to this man as "Student".

The "Music Student" was looking magnificent in black.   His hair had fallen about his head like a mop out of water and it sort of romanticised his image even more.   There were two men, both the violinists, and two women.   A rather plump one with a very firm hair set was the violist and a tall rather beautiful one with long black hair was the cellist. I noted on the programme that she was Anna Maria Alberini.   My stomach turned for the second time that evening. Whilst she shared my first name, Lorenzo Alberini shared her second.

The rest of the programme was wasted on me while I chided my wild expectation.   It was an exquisite performance, unlike anything I had ever heard but the music was assailed by agonised thoughts of my inadequacy and unjustified, covet assumptions.   I was in the wrong place, wrong time, wrong situation.   How stupid I was, how inadequate and plain and vain and, and...

There was a short interval when many left their seats in search of a glass of wine or coffee.   Malachi was very quiet that evening. We sat silently observing the awkward movements of a conspicuous audience.

The second half of the concert was something Baroque which I don't remember now.   One of the violins was replaced by a piano which was interesting, if unusual.   I can only say that a sense of relief swept over me when it was over and we could disappear once more into the cover of our own private spaces.

We were out in the street when I saw Lorenzo coming towards us.   There was something open and elegant about the way he walked, as if he was exercising some command over the ground he was walking on. Yet there was also a shy, reserved feel about him, evident in the way he kept his eyes ahead as if to avoid contact.

I met his gaze as if by accident.   He greeted us with a slow smile, then gave me a more lingering look which made me wonder what I had lodged in my hair or if there was some smudge on my face.

We talked politely about the music and the programme and commented on its excellence. Well, I let Malachi do all that. He was so good at it.

'I must go,' apologised Lorenzo, 'the others are waiting for me.'

He directed a brief flash of a smile at me and turned into the night.

Something melted in me with that smile, even with the knowledge that he was married to the lovely Anna Maria.   It would explain why he seldom used his room. It must be a pied-a-Terre for when he was in that part of town.

My mind lapsed into a bunch of tangled thinking.

I could not ask Malachi. It would not be right and what would he think?

I suddenly became aware that Malachi was chatting away once more in his old friendly way and I had not taken in a single word he had said.

'What's that?' I asked.

'That,' he said laughing, 'Is a good sign that you and Lorenzo share an interest.'

I had no idea what he meant by it and lacked the temerity to ask.

Chapter 8

I discovered that it was a large Jamaican lady who occupied the attic flat on the floor above me. She would tramp around that flat sometimes in the night with what seemed like ten-ton boots and to accompany her movements, she sang a good deal. Not loud but softly moaned hymns that she was practising for Sunday church.

She was frequently going out. I could hear her groaning as she climbed the steps back up to her flat. She also seemed to have several visitors who came and went during the day. I wondered why she could not have been given rooms closer to the ground floor that she would not need to climb so much.

'Hellooo my darlink,' she would say when our paths crossed. It gave me a strange feeling to be greeted with such familiarity by someone I did not know. I was unused to any terms of endearment and it made me recoil back into that shell I slipped into so easily.

The first couple of greetings from her I muttered a nonsensical grunt as a response, feeling myself go bright red. Then after a time I managed a reciprocal "hello" without endearment attached.

One Sunday morning as she was returning from church and I was coming in from a long walk in the park that was a good mile stretch away, our paths met.

'Where you bin goin' this lovely monin'?' she asked in her cheery voice, all jollied up from singing in the church I should imagine.

'Just been walking,' I said, rather hoping that the conversation would end there. But Lillibet Archibald had other plans for me. She appeared to know my name, but that was no surprise in this house where everyone seemed to have foreknowledge of me.

'You are Anna,' she said putting out a hand to me. 'I am Miz. Archibald; Lillibet to my friends. You can call me Lillibet,' she offered.

'Thank you,' I said trying to move away but she was rather large and had blocked my way.

'Why you don come up and have tea wid me?' she enquired.

'Well, er...' I hesitated trying to think something up that I would be busy doing.

'I'm rather busy right now.'

'No, you not. You jus come in from a walk. If you have time for walkin' you have time for talkin'.'

'I'm not much good at talking.' I insisted.

'Oh yes. I see you with that ole Malachi talkin' away and now you have time. I see you waitin' to find him an talk some more. He ain't around today. I see that.'

'You do?'

'Yes I do, and I have eyes to see plenty here. Come girl. You carry them parcels up the stair for ole Lillibet and I give you tea.'

With that she dumped two heavy carrier bags of shopping at my feet which I was obliged to bend down, pick up and follow her panting body up the flights of stairs; all the while searching for some excuse to deposit the bags politely and leave before she could persuade me further.

Lillibet fiddled around for some minutes looking for keys and then opened the door without them. She marched inside chuckling to herself that the keys were only for show that she had to make the pretence of locking her door or those pesky students from below would get wise and ransack her flat.

The flat looked pretty well ransacked already. The heavy orange/gold dreylon curtains were half drawn allowing a half light to enter, outlining her old, rather worn furniture. Items of clothing were scattered about here and there, along with an accumulation of bright cushions, stuffed toys and other sundry items.

She cast off her shoes by kicking them from her feet into a corner of the room, then fell heavily into an arm chair. It was one of a pair on either side of a gas fire in which a lurid red light lit translucent coals of varying shades, imitating some exotic rare stone. She was in the chair arranged closest to her television set. Next to her was a substantial side-table filled with objects of regular use: a remote control, several pairs of earrings, a packet of boiled sweets, cotton buds, a couple of unwashed coffee mugs with more beneath, along with the scrunched tissues. This was Lillibet's chair.

'Now, you go in the kitchen honey-chile and put that kettle on for old Lillibet and then we can have some tea, now you hear?'

It was a directive not to be refused. The kitchen was as untidy as her living room but with more light that came in through a grime-smeared window. Dead and dried-out pot plants lined the window-sill and beneath that was a sink full of unwashed plates.

I was not too certain where to begin. However, Lillibet did a good job of instructing me from her arm-chair in the next room, where I would find things and what to do with them. I was trapped.

There was a light tap at her front door and someone came in.

Damn and blast, I thought, it sounds like Agatha has come to join her.

I took my time washing plates and setting out tea things and generally trying to tidy the mess but it seemed her guest was there to stay. Finally I took two mugs of tea through on a small, rusted tin tray with the idea of passing off my tea to Agatha and excusing myself.

It was not Agatha. This woman was unkempt, dishevelled and aggressive looking. She had a mass of fuzz-curled hair that covered most of her face and blue tinted glasses that concealed her eyes. Her mouth was a gash of blood-red lipstick through which she snarled contemptuously.

'What's this?' she said looking in my direction.

'Now there Constantine you be polite to my friend. This is Anna from downstairs.'

'What you letting in trash here for? You tell her to clear off or I will.' Her voice was coarse with a strong accent, heaven knows where from, not English nor anywhere I had heard before.

'I tole you, you keep that bad mouth of yours shut or you go.'

Lillibet sounded out her ultimatum from an experience of authority.

'I will just leave the tea things here and perhaps see you another time,' I said backing for the door.

'Now just you take your seat young lady an Miss Constantine will take hers or go out.'

I obeyed against my better judgement but then I had spent a life of compliant, hushed obedience. It was second nature to me to follow an order. I offered the second mug of tea to the old harpie which she took ungraciously while Lillibet insisted I make another cup for myself but I was adamant that I did not wish to.

Miss Constantine was not to be dissuaded from her battle front and continued to berate modern youth, untrustworthy tenants at Number 63 and especially any woman with red hair. She had always had it on good authority that red hair was a sign of duplicity and all red-heads were tarts.

I was used to being taunted for my red hair and easily switched off.

I sat on the edge of one of the large armchairs while the two ladies swapped opinions about the prevailing shifts in the capricious world about them.

I had time to look around without being observed while doing so. I was fascinated by the many colourful prints of Eastern Gods around the walls. They danced with multiple limbs displayed at irregular angles or sat clasping snakes. There were several replicas of Buddha from fat and laughing to lithe and meditative. Not to be outdone, there was a large picture of Christ with a bleeding heart attached to his chest and looking pretty sad about it. Then, to validate this Christian recognition, a garish crucifix of a dying Christ, grotesquely impaled, took centre stage on the mantel.

I was remembering something about God not wanting any other god before him when Lillibet looked up at me and said, 'It was also written in my kingdom there are many rooms...'

I shot her a backward glance.   Was she reading my mind or was she just taking a lucky guess at what I was thinking?

'You can't expect her to understand what you are saying Lillie. She is pure heathen; you can see that at a glance.'

It was the point at which I felt enough was enough and excused myself before either could say another word.   As I retreated down the stairs I could hear Lillibet berating her other guest all the way.

'What you go say dat for? She such a nice gel with no big ideas about herself or nothin.'

Where on earth was Malachi?   If only he would turn up again.

I needed some comfort that afternoon.

Only the very next day when I was coming back from college, I found him outside on the pavement talking to one of the young students.   They were laughing and I felt a pang of envy that he had not found me to talk to.

'Anna Catherine,' he addressed me in my old name and as always, I was taken aback.

'You come here and meet Jason. Jason here is a student of law. Anna Catherine is a musician,' he told Jason.

'Really?' said Jason with interest.

'Oh no,' I responded hastily. 'I played the violin at school but I was not good enough to make a career of it. No, I'm afraid I am just doing a boring old secretarial course,' I said, feeling a deep blush creep up from my shoulders.

'Well you can't go wrong with that.   Whatever you decide to do later, secretarial skills will come in useful.'

'That is what my sister says,' I responded.

'There you are now,' settled Malachi.

The law student was short and rather round.   His hair was prematurely receding, signifying the later model that would sit behind a desk looking important.   But he had an interesting face which looked kindly at me. He emanated that kind of buoyancy that minimises all else into a cap-full of trivia that is easily resolved and he alone would be able to unlock the sense of it all.   When he was emphasising a point he would rock onto the ball of his feet, like a wave that rises to greet the shore. The movement compounded his enthusiasm and lent conviction to what he was saying. I imagined him in court impressing a jury by the single use of his stance.

It felt good to be in sparkling company.   For once I was not inclined to move off but remained there while the subject of music and starting to play again was mulled over. Malachi suggested that we all went to our usual haunt, namely, the corner coffee bar and it was met with great enthusiasm by both the law student and myself.

We found seats out on the pavement.   The law student informed us that we were his guests and asked what we wanted. I was flustered but Malachi told him that I only ever drank Cappuccino.

'Excellent choice,' said the student, 'shall I say Cappuccino all round?'

'Now then,' said Malachi with his jaunty air, 'Only a few weeks ago, Anna Catherine would have refused to come here if there had been someone she had not met.   There has been a great breakthrough in these past few weeks while she is gaining her independence.'

'Is that so?' the law student asked.   'We have all wondered about you and how silent you were. I feel rather privileged that I am the one to know you first.'

The thought of getting to know the other students left me in a state of confusion but once more Malachi came to my rescue.

'Give her time.   This little butterfly will choose her own moment to emerge.   She has been limited to her sister only, since she was five, it will take time.'

How on earth did he know that? I had not told him that. While I frowned over the last statement the conversation returned to music and composers.   When we agreed to favour Mozart the exchange went on to his early genius and then progressed to other genius and gifted children and from there, how a child's mind can be controlled.

'"Give me the child until he is seven," said Francis Xavier, "and I will give you the man,"' quoted the student.

'That was the Jesuit motto implying that the best opportunity to indoctrinate a person into a life time of religious dogma is when he is very young.' I said.   'I remember it from school ... somewhere.' I stopped, considered what I had said and recoiled into myself, regretting my input with a blush, wishing I had remained silent. How affected I must sound!

The law-student picked up the topic and continued with it without comment. Talk became topical and political, drawing in all the more aggressive features of recent news and how the young had been affected.

'It is reported that terrorists are methodically and intentionally targeting vulnerable young people and children; radicalizing, indoctrinating and grooming them to carry out acts of terror.'

Oh God, there I go again – I agonized. I was making absurd attempts at conversation and sounding so pretentious, so pompous, as if I could not help myself from being so.   I was so unaccustomed to conversation. I was not used to this.   I would open my mouth and out came those over structured, out of place statements. Remembering something I had read that had stayed in my mind, adopted from somewhere that led nowhere and sounded like cheap catch phrases.

'That's what they say about street-gang culture,' continued the law-student with such effortlessness at conversation, making my futile statements less raw and untried. I envied his fluency at communicating his thoughts. Words slipped off the edge of his tongue with the ease of autumn leaves floating from the trees.

He had a lot to add about genetics, environment and that nature/ nurture stuff and about the unique quality of each and every human to make his own decisions.

'Free will and all that?' offered Malachi.

'Yes of course it is all about free will. If we choose to become indoctrinated, to follow blindly, then that choice binds us... makes us what we are. And that choice in itself proves the premise.'

'And what about those first seven years? Might they not affect the life thereafter?' Malachi suggested.

'We can all recall those images of experience, those rhetorical little homilies thrown at us that shaped us, made us or unmade us but they are not everything that we are. Those first seven years are indeed vital but they are only pro tem.'

'What if they are not, what if they have really cast the dye of how we are?'

'We are what we choose to make of ourselves. Most of us can help ourselves to avoid falling prey to negative guidance or quickly overcome a disturbed childhood and if we do fall, we don't just say there; we can't. Getting up is what we do. Figuring which pitfall to avoid next time.'

'You are wrong. A disturbed childhood is like a disabling wound that takes years to heal. Sure, some heal faster than others and we all have to "pick ourselves up" as you put it but the scars are still there, they never heal. There is no way to rid the scars,' said Malachi.

'You would make a good counsel for defence,' the law student laughed after a silent moment to deliberate on what had been said.

Malachi looked in my direction, it was as if he was waiting for me to ask something and I took the cue as if unconsciously directed to do so.

'What then of the young child that has been indoctrinated so well that great chunks of his memory have been eradicated?' I asked.

'What in particular do you believe has been eradicated from your memory?' the law student enquired intuitively, as if he was already in convocation with the litigant.

'I am not sure,' I said, hesitant about being the complainant when I had no idea about what it was that had beleaguered my mind for so long. I was even surprised that I had used the word indoctrinated. Where in my mind did that come from? No one had indoctrinated me, yet I said it and regretted saying it. It must have just been a continuation of what was said before.

'Well, indoctrination is the wrong word,' I added hastily.

'I want to remember my mother. I want to remember the last time I saw her, and I can't. I am told that she left us and went away with someone. I remember being told that it was a bad thing but I can't even recall what that is. She used to write to us and bit by bit the letters stopped and no one talked about them or why they had stopped. Now it seems that people I have never met before seem to know more about her than I do.'

'Do you believe this forgotten memory has anything to do with your current shyness?'

'No, well, not particularly. We led such sedentary lives, my sister and me. We had lost touch with family, grandparents and all that and our father simply had no time for us. My sister is not shy. Quite the contrary. She is not at all like me.'

I stopped talking and looked over at Malachi. What was it that had made me open up and talk? He had said so very little, yet with the confidence of his presence I had begun to join in with the conversation with this other stranger and open up with things I had hardly dared think about. It was a curious reflex of circumstance and setting. I suddenly became very self-conscious. All the attention was directed at me and I was feeling excruciatingly uncomfortable about it all.

'Perhaps,' said Malachi, 'your sister was feeling just as bewildered as you about it all. Perhaps she had been directed to be silent about it because the experience had been just as painful for her.'

'Yes,' I said slowly.

I looked down at my hands. My fingers wrapped around each other in a reflection of the confusion that had arisen in my mind.

'I have to say that I don't wish to talk about it anymore - please.'

The law-student stood up tactfully and said he had so much work to catch up with he felt it time he left us.

He bowed rather formally towards me and said he hoped he would see more of me now that we had met.

'Perhaps you might be tempted some time to come and join us fellow students for a drink one evening?'

'Thank you,' I said

'Before you add a "but" to that,' he intuited, 'let's just leave it at that and hope you will think about it,' he added kindly.

We laughed.

After he had gone I told Malachi about my meeting with Lillibet Archibald and the impossible Miss Constantine. He made no comment about either but listened intently.

'It's all a process,' he said. 'We are all confounded by life and we are all trying to make our way. Just as you will soon be ready to remember what it is you have forgotten and then you can start to put your life together. Why not take young Jason's suggestion about taking violin lessons again? You can take an advance course and perhaps someday you will be playing with Lorenzo and his sister Anna Marie.'

His sister! I jumped conspicuously. All at once nothing else mattered for now.

'I never see him,' I said. 'Does he live there all the time?'

'He comes and goes. That is the way.'

'Surely he is not still student?' I asked.

'You will have to ask him all these things yourself,' replied Malachi with a gentle smile of knowing about his face.

'He uses his room sometimes when he is practising for a concert. Ask him. He will be there in a few days or so.'

Asking any more would be seen as prying and being over interested. I wouldn't allow myself that. I would wait and hope to cross his path when he was there.

Chapter 9

I had an email from Peggy saying that she would be in London on business around the end of the month. I looked forward to seeing her and at the same time I felt apprehensive. There was a new me emerging and it might not meet with her approval.

I had started to ask about Mother. I had talked about Mother to strangers and all that was strictly forbidden. Father had ordered it so. She had said so often enough. Anyway, I felt less scrupled about it in that I had not seen him in the seven months since I had been living in London, so what did it matter?

I met Peggy at the hotel where she was staying just off Hyde Park Avenue. This was the life that Peggy had ordered for herself. It was how she fashioned things for herself, that grandeur, the exclusiveness and expensive. Her job, I thought, must be paying her well. This was all part of the longed for stability and independence she had always talked of.

She was looking prettier than I had ever seen her.

She was different now. Not so anxious all the time. She had lost that haunted look, as if she had misplaced something and had no idea how to replace it. She was gradually shedding herself of the past.

She told me that she had had a letter from Eleanor complaining about Father's recent behaviour and wanted advice.

'He is up to his old tricks again,' I said with little sympathy for the stepmother that had alienated us even further from the father who was already distant.

'Poor Daddy, none of them have ever understood him,' Peggy said.

She had that kind of unconditional love for him that excused anything that he did. She had always been like that. She would defend his absences, his forgetfulness at paying us our monthly income till we had several times lost electricity for days till he had paid the account. We had been threatened with eviction so many times that we learnt to hide when the agent came round. Often when we ran out of money for food Peggy had been forced to go and see him at his office, only to be told he had gone out on some business lunch and his secretary would fund us temporarily. If I had felt angry I was never allowed to express it for Peggy was always ready with her next excuse, her next explanation.

Though, I had to admit to myself, that since he had opened a bank account for me to pay my allowance for rent and college fees, the money was there each month, regular as clock-work.

'Just remember, Anna,' she would say. 'He has been a good father to us under the circumstances.'

Of course "circumstances" implied the "Mother" word I was forbidden to use.

Chapter 10

I tentatively broached my suggestion to Peggy shortly after she had arrived.

'The students in the basement flat have invited me to a party there this weekend.'

I knew how much she loved parties, any parties - and I had so little to talk to her about while she was around.

'I told them you would be with me and they said I must ask you to come along. What do you think?'

'You - going to a party! Well, there's a first. Of course I'd love to. I am going to be frightfully busy most of the time but always time for a party. First Anna, you must do something about your dreadful hair and I have told you before, you must wear mascara on those horrible lashes of yours. White eye-lashes are not becoming!'

I had not mentioned anything about the other more colourful residents at No. 63, least of all dear Malachi. Peggy would have been far too scathing and Malachi had become special to me. If she had suggested some reason not to talk with him it would have caused so much stress.

She got a taxi to me in the late afternoon. I had no idea what time she would arrive. A loud bang on my door was all there was to announce her and there she was, submerged beneath a mountain of parcels from a shopping spree on the way.

'For my baby-sister,' she announced enthusiastically removing things out of bags with recommendations on how and when to wear them.

'My God Anna, who was the drag-queen that came to the door? I thought I had come a bit late for the fancy dress party tonight.'

'It won't be fancy dress and you are probably referring to the landlady Agatha. She is not a drag-queen. Quite nice really, sort of harmless with no personality to speak of. I don't have much to do with her except pay the rent each month.'

'Thank God for that. She was really quite scary. I thought she was a young girl at first till I saw her face and saw that she must be at least sixty if a day. What are the students like in the flat below?'

'I have only met one. His name is Jason and he is studying law. You will have something in common. He's actually very nice.'

'Is this a new interest in your life?'

'No, no – not at all. I have only recently met him. We chatted, and last week he asked if I would like to come to this party. I wouldn't have accepted if you had not been coming.'

'Oh really Anna! You must learn to grow up and do things on your own now.

'There is someone else who lives here who may come. Well he uses a room here to practise his violin. He is someone who...'

I stopped not quite certain what to say about him.

'He is both strange and wonderful Pegs. I can't explain. He is very tall and dark and kind of mysterious. Well, I am hoping he will be there.'

She stopped and looked at me a while, studying my face as if probing my thoughts, but she said nothing. I caught the smallest glimpse of a sardonic smile. In it a story hung behind this moment, a secret history that only she knew and wished to exclude everyone else from. Though I might have taken a hundred guesses as to what it was I knew that being aware of it might spell danger, as I saw the calculation behind her eyes. Then she picked up her hairbrush, ready to perform some kind of revolution to my hair.

'Before we go out tonight I am going to give you some tips on your make-up, find you something gorgeous to wear and I need to trim the end of that long mane of yours. Got any shampoo or do I have to go out and get some?'

It was an evening of primping and fussing. Those were always the best parts of going out. The rest was downhill after that.

The noise that was coming up from the basement was already in full swing long before we left to join it.

Peggy's hair had been given some expensive attention at one of London's best salons the day before. She had swept it up into soft curls at the top of her head. Her ears dangled long silver things that sparked as she moved her head. There was always something exotic and superior about my sister. What she wore and where it was bought from were matters of great importance to her and it showed in the finished product.

I guess it was that evening that I saw Peggy for the first time as she really was. I had accepted her life of many partners, her glamorous fantasies and her needing to be noticed as sophistication. Out of the blue it struck me that being admired and wanted was of vital importance to her.

Oh yes, Peggy had her needs, constant and urgent needs, much like the ones father had, in a way, but there was something more that she showed that night. It was as if she was trying to discover something within herself. I would even have gone as far as to say she wanted to show me that something.

Peggy had always dressed in expensive clothes and laced herself with expensive perfumes. She had surrounded herself with flippant friends and acquaintances; those shadowy, showy people;

ghosts hiding between their shallow appearances with their temporary tinsel trappings.

Despite the camouflage Peggy was not like that, not inside. It was as if she was hiding something of herself and this was the only way she knew how.

I could not help but admire her.

I watched in wonder as she removed a very chic looking trouser suite from a Harrod's bag. It was off white and the soft silk blouse underneath was a kind of oyster-shell pink. This was her view of dressing down.

The finishing touch came with her shoes, the start and end of her lovely body. Shoes were her absolute and supreme necessity for adding height, glamour and supremacy over all others. An expensive pair of Jimmie Choo's impossibly high heels stretched her long legs to a towering height of cat-walk perfection.

Of course she would stand-out in a room full of penniless students.

That was what Peggy was about.

It was what Peggy wanted most of all.

I insisted on wearing jeans but she won the battle over a long floral shirt which I had to agree suited me. She did what she could with my thick red hair, left to drape over as much of me as it could conceal. The heavy mascara treatment made me look like someone else. Agatha did cross my mind!

The student flat was surprisingly large. One big central room served as kitchen/living room and whatever other use it might perform, off which, three bedrooms branched.

The music was loud but conversation fell to a hush as we stepped into an over-crammed room-full of people.

The law-student hailed me from across the crowd and fought his way through. He made a pretence of not noticing Peggy at first but his eyes would not allow themselves diverted from her for long.

As everyone's heads turned in Peggy's direction, I slithered in her wake.

'Anna, what a lovely surprise that you have come, you are looking so beautiful. I was half expecting you not to turn up.' He gushing and flattered like a long lost comrade in arms. Then followed that familiar surprise that this was my "sister?"

He could not take his eyes off her.

He found us drinks and dragged people over to meet us. Which, with my sister, was more of a stave off than a drag to. She was soon in the mesh of things.

I slunk over to a less congested corner and purveyed the scene at a distance, disinclined to join in.

I feel claustrophobic in tightly packed spaces. I evaporate into a state of non-entity. I had only accepted Jason's invitation because Peggy would be with me and I knew it would please her; besides, what else could I do with her?

We had never had much to say to one another.   We were two sisters thrown together from a tacit necessity thrust upon us.   A disparity of age and interests was not all that separated us. Our roles cast from necessity made Peggy the more than competent leader and me the submissive devotee and there the union remained.

Drawn together as we were, in an unvoiced conspiracy, those dark corners were inviolable.   They left an uninfringeable tension between us.   Yet I believe we truly loved and respected one another. An invitation to a party full of admirers was something I could only delight in offering to her.   Perhaps all I could ever offer her.

Content as I was to be away from strangers and crowds, Peggy needed outside stimulation. She loved parties, clothes and social chatter. I had little or no interest in any of those things.   And there she was, centre stage of a throng of much younger neophytes ready to swoon over her and absorb her every nuance, her every word. I had been there so many times before; dragged to noisy, tedious parties, watching my beautiful sister being engulfed by adoring admirers.

Jason's other two flat-mates came up to introduce themselves to me.   There was Eric, an accountant in training and Jodi an actress training at a drama school nearby.

Jodi was small, with very short hair which spiked about her head giving her a kind of urchin look, appealing and comical. Two over-large, soft, doe-eyes peeked out from those strands that were allowed to fall around her forehead.

'I'm Jodi,' she said. 'I have seen you come and go some days. Sorry I didn't come up to you before but you always looked like you didn't want to be disturbed.'

'I'm Anna,' I responded.

'Yes, Jason told us. I think he was rather taken with you. Pleased as punch you came tonight.'

'I think a lot more pleased that I brought my sister,' I said looking towards them.

'Oh I don't know, my vote goes to you any day,' she said kindly but I hadn't wanted a compensatory vote and I felt myself blush.

'Ah here's Eric! Eric this is Anna.'

'Yes, I know,' said Eric.   'We have this sort of silent greeting thing,' he grinned.

Eric was tall, languid and sallow. Our paths had crossed a few times over the past several months but I had never felt inclined to respond to what looked like could be a lurching approach. It was clear he would make up for lost time that evening.

'I noted you don't have a drink in your hands. Here, I brought you this.'

'One of Eric's lethal cocktails,' warned Jodi.

'I'm afraid I don't really drink,' I confessed but confessions of that sort don't quite wash at parties. I had learnt that much. I took the drink, thanked him and sipped it obligingly. Should I say, I doused my lips and felt them anaesthetize instantly.

I was longing to slip away. Peggy was still talking to Jason.

Over Jodi's shoulder I saw Lillibet squeezing herself into the room with Miss Constantine right behind her looking like sour grapes. Jodi turned to see who I was looking at.

'Oh, here are the upper tenants. We had to invite them because of the noise.' She explained almost apologetically to me.

'Shall I go and greet them?' offered Eric.

'No need, they seem to be settling in quite happily without any assistance.'

Lillibet was laughing in her usual ear-splitting raucous roars which even managed to surpass the deafened the buzz of a room-full of loud talking.

'Can I meet your sister?' Eric was asking.

'Why don't you just go up to her and introduce yourself, she will be more than pleased,' I said with relief that he need not stand there and watch me drink his lethal concoction, which after a second sip had scoured the inside of my mouth and burned its passage to my stomach.

He and Jodi soon gave up on me and moved off in the direction of Peggy, at which point I was able to put my glass down.

I was sliding towards the door when I saw the "Music Student" standing in a doorway. His elegance and posture stood out among the young group of students. He was looking in the direction of my sister. A catch of despair trapped itself in my throat. Now he would be lost entirely to me. I saw her threading her way towards him. Of course she would. I noticed that he had not moved.

I slowly inched my way to the exit door, suffocated and panicked. I had to get away now. Miss Constantine was suddenly before me her scratchy voice extended in a sour greeting.

'What's your problem? Not leaving? Got your lovely sister with you, I see.'

She was clasping a drink in a patterned glass advertising Scotch Whiskey . 'What on earth have you done to your hair? Badly cut.'

How on earth did she manage to ferret out all my flaws and feelings of inadequacy? It seemed to be a knack with her at which she was highly intuitive.

'Just the ends cut, that's all.' I hated myself at once for rising to the bait and sounding petulant and defensive. Blast, why did I always have to react?

'It looks like it's been hacked by garden sears and that top does not go with your red hair. You should know by this age that red heads are limited to the colours they choose.'

Behind her, squeezing her way through the tight pack of human mass came Lillibet. She was ablaze in a dazzling caftan with a matching head scarf tied up to a kind of turban on her head. She was revelling in the mad scuffle.

All the while I was slowly manoeuvring myself like a chip on a game board. Pass one body and then another, nearly there.

'Where you think you goin honey chile? My you look be-oo-ti-ful to-night!' she said staggering syllables for effect.

'No I don't,' I said impatiently. 'My hair is wrong and my shirt doesn't match my hair.'

Miss Constantine was wearing a confident smirk which annoyed me even further. I had given in to her and satisfied her vitriolic sarcasm. Lillibet gave her a sour look. 'That someting you said huh? She just like to say these things honey. You look good and Lillibet knows when someone look good.'

Lillibet noticed that I had no glass in my hand and immediately offered me hers.

'You got no drink honey chile. Here, you will love this.' She held the drink to my mouth. A cherry was caught on its rim and it smelled strange. The sip was elbowed from behind her to become a gulp which fizzed up my mouth and spilled itself down to my chin.

'Now you take this here while I get another,' she said with the enthusiasm of one of Christ's disciples feeding the multitude.

The drink hit my brain as fast as the overspill had reached my chin and it soothed my nerves in an instant. At the same time another student caught my attention by asking some inane question.

Looking across the room, I saw that Peggy was in deep conversation with my Music Student. I took another long drink from the glass. It seemed all at once that nothing really mattered much anymore.

Who cares? I did not care. Who was he anyway, still a student in his thirties no doubt. Who needs people like that? Not me.

By the time Lillibet had rejoined me my glass was empty which made her roar with laughter.

'That Miss Constantine she can drive anyone to drink.'

She offered the second drink, this time in a mug, and took my empty glass to refill it.

There was no room for dancing but students were gyrating on the spot to the music and one took my hand and attempted to turn me about.

I looked up again towards Peggy and at that moment the music student turned towards me and raised a hand in greeting. My hands were now busy. One held the mug Lillibet had given me; the other was clasped by the student. He looked back at Peggy and moved his back towards me.

The music changed and so did the student. Jason had found me and was saying something but sound had become incoherent and I smiled and then he was hugging me.

The patterns were repeated with all the revolving people and the sweet drink and the warm feeling it was giving me. Soon the room too revolved – noise – movement - lack of air – garbled conversation. My legs were becoming weaker and soon ceased to hold me upright.

I could hear Malachi's voice say, 'Help her. Clear a way.'

I came to, outside, at the basement steps. The night air swept over me like a cold compress to a fevered head and a sea of faces leered over me.

My sister's voice: 'She's not used to alcohol. Anyone give her alcohol?'

I sat up feeling violently ill. I need to get to the bathroom. Now. The front door was opened above and I was shown into a first floor cloakroom. Must be Agatha's apartment. I just made it to the toilet basin where I was sick, over and over.

Peggy was with me but Malachi's voice was somewhere, offering a glass of water.

'Malachi,' I said.

At that point I was vaguely aware of being taken upstairs to my room where I lay down.

Peggy left me there.

'Best to sleep it off,' she said and left me to a nightmare of throbbing sounds from below and a thundering head and a room whose walls swivelled round me at great speed. Voices came and went: Malachi's, Lillibet's and once or twice I imagined the Music Student's quiet voice.

I slept.

I woke up in full daylight. My door was open and Peggy was walking in and out. I went to the basin and splashed my face, my mouth felt bitter and my hair had stuck to my neck.

I saw Peggy across the landing coming out of the Music Student's room and a black darkness descended upon me.

'You're up,' she said, coming towards me.   'I need to get going, so busy today.'

'You stayed the night here?' I asked.

'Yes, Lorenzo asked me to stay.'

'Oh,' I said weakly. 'And you like him?'

'Not bad, very nice looking but a bit dull for me.'

'Oh,' I said.

Finding him dull had not stopped her from sleeping with him and now he would be smitten with her as all the men in her life were.

I only saw her once again; very briefly. It was at the airport before she flew off, with promises to get together again - some time - and so pleased I had found my feet at last.

Speaking With Strangers

Chapter 11

There are those ensuing, solitary, aftermath days after an event when the mind goes into reverse gear replicating those sallow and embarrassing moments with shame. How badly had I behaved? What could the Music Student have thought of me? I was so palely insignificant next to my sister whom he had clearly favoured.

Where had Malachi disappeared to? There was no sign of him, only Agatha upon the stairs each day, wearing something new and garish. I could hear her talking behind her door as usual. Voices, only voices and no one to see.

One by one each day I passed one of the students who asked after me and I crawled with shame. Eric believed it was his drink that had toppled me and was full of apologies.

'I came to find you but you were dancing with someone and you seemed quite alright really. Next thing I heard you had passed out. Now, how about I make it up to you?'

'Make what up to me?' I asked, feeling distinctly uneasy about what seemed to be another invitation.

'I feel responsible for you becoming so sick,' he answered. 'What about a coffee up the road?'

'I really don't think that's necessary. I am fine and I have so much work to catch up with. Thank you so much Eric but I am in such a hurry.'

'Come on, where is the hurry?'

'The hurry is with me,' came Malachi's voice from almost nowhere. 'I told her that I would be here at this time and asked if she would kindly be ready for me,' he lied.

'Oh Malachi,' I almost cried. 'Oh, you have come,' I said.

'Well, another time then,' said Eric as he moved on down the basement stairs.

Malachi chatted away as we moved in no particular direction away from No 63. Moving away had a reciprocal effect of releasing the tensions from what had been.

The conversation had not yet converged upon the focus of the party but out of the blue he said, 'That sister of yours has a lot on her mind.'

'Yes,' I answered. 'A new job, new country, new people but she manages all those changes far better than I could.'

'No, I do not mean those kinds of things. I mean the hidden secrets she holds all to herself. They are eating at her and she tries to cover them up.'

'It's about our Mother,' I said. 'Mother left us quite suddenly and we are not allowed to talk about her.'

'Who will not allow it?'

'Father. I think it is Father. She says he won't allow it. He has never said anything to me. They do a lot of talking together and I am never included. I never have been. It is as if they are protecting me. Silly really. I have accepted that she does not want to have anything more to do with us. It hurt when I was little. It hurt a lot but I put it out of my mind.'

'What exactly did you put out of your mind Anna?'

'The fact that Mother left us for another woman - Father said that.'

'And do you remember the last time you saw her?' he continued to quiz me.

'It's no use you're asking me Malachi. I can't remember. I simply can't remember. Every time I have thought about her I struggle to remember. I tried to speak to Peggy about it and she became so cross that talking and thinking just made me so unhappy I stopped thinking when we stopped talking. I think because it was easier that way. And now I simply can't remember. And believe me, I have tried. Just recently, I have tried and tried. Somehow you reminded me of her. I started thinking again when I met you. I can't explain how, but I have.'

'Perhaps the memories will start to come back soon,' he suggested. 'Anna, you must start to play your violin again.'

'Well, I would love nothing more. I would start right away but I don't have it with me. I wanted to ask Father for it but he has just been so busy and Peggy said it was not a good idea. I have to put all that behind me. It makes getting on with life easier, she said. It has gone to his house somewhere to be stored with other things Peggy and I left behind.'

We walked and talked for hours it seemed before we turned and came back to No.63. The party with all the foibles attached were behind me and no longer counted.

Chapter 12

I had a phone call from Father, quite unexpectedly, to tell me he had my violin and was bringing it to me the next day. I was amazed. I had intended to ask him to find it for me but the thought of asking for something from him had made me delay. I thought it must have been Peggy who had told him that I wanted it. Though I had not mentioned it to her at all, she had always been so disparaging about my practising. 'Dear Peggy', I thought.

I was ready waiting at the window for him when his car drew up. Strange, mixed feelings converged upon me, seeing him there, out of context with my new life.

A young woman sat in the car with him as he got out. She stared ahead as if she would remain invisible till he hurried back.

He was apart from her yet yielding to that which attracted her to him, like a male cat always on the prowl. That was Father, driven by an unquenchable appetite for pursuit.

I slunk back behind the door of the house so that he would not know I had seen them together and waited for him to knock. I waited a moment for him to think I was getting to the door from an unseen place then opened it.

He was distracted, outside himself, shifting, wanting to move on.

'Hello Daddy, this is so kind of you.'

'Annie, good to see you. I hear you were wanting this?' he said, giving me a peck on my cheek and handing over the tattered old violin case along with a box-full of my music.

'Oh yes, yes, thank you so much. I thought I would get over needing it, well, nowhere to practise. Oh, how did you know?'

'I had this phone call. Well your sister also mentioned once that you would want it at some time but she thought it might distract you from what you were doing. I thought it was a good idea. They said you had talent at school and that you should have continued with it.'

'Oh, I don't think so really. I was just not good enough to make a career of it. Peggy told you I wanted it did she? Well, that is so thoughtful of her. I thought she found the violin a waste of time.'

He had that furtive look of urgency he always had with us. I knew it so well. He was not to be trapped or held on to. Not one to banter with argument at the best of times. He stood there at the door, shifting tautly about as he ran through a list of all the urgent calls he had to make that week with a brief agenda of his social duties. It was as if he were rehearsing a calling of the minutes of his next monthly meeting at work.

'Can't stop I'm afraid. I have to get going. Trouble with Eleanor these days, frightfully jealous, seems to think I have another woman round every corner.'

'Oh dear,' I said. 'Whatever gave her that idea?'

He had only enough time to place the box of music onto the steps and hand me the old violin case. I took it gratefully and smiled as he turned with a brief wave and was gone.

Even if there was somewhere to take him to talk, it would have been a waste of time. He would always have somewhere else to go to – business of course!

It was a relief to see him go.

Back in my room, I removed my beloved violin from its case. It was just as I had lovingly last placed it. The resin box was broken in its last rough transit and bits of resin had scattered about the inside of the case. The soft piece of cloth I had laid over the violin had crumpled to one side and dust had somehow crept in and covered the shine of the amber wood.

I gently removed it from its box, released the bow from the lid and held it beneath my chin. I cast the bow across the strings and played one cord. It was badly out of tune. The strings had become slack in their silent, fallow state. It took some time to tune.

I had only played a few chords when there was a sharp rap at the door.

Of course, it was Agatha: the guardian of protocol. She stood there, garish, grotesque underneath her pan face, a dead thing with no real passion beneath, I thought.

I knew she was there to stop me playing and I was sorely vexed by her principles.

'I think I told you, I will not have music practising in these rooms,' she said, playing to rigid rules she had set like a school teacher demanding obedience.

'You must ask Lorenzo when he comes tomorrow. He will let you practise there.' She added her recommendation almost apologetically. It was as if the rule she had set had been for a reason. Perhaps the sound of a violin in particular might be uncomfortable to her. After all there were other sounds of music that penetrated beyond the confines of the basement flat and Lillibet's attic apartment and they had never been stopped.

Damn and blast, I thought. I might have known. And how different would it be if the Music Student let me practise there? He was just across the hall. I would have to hire a practise room somewhere and Father had not offered an allowance for that.

The thought that the Music Student would be there the next day took the edge of disappointment and irritation that now I had my violin, I could not use it. I polished its wood and cleaned the bow and then the old tattered case.   Then I went through the music, quietly humming the pieces from the sheets of music.

The warm glow of an old and comforting friend had been returned to me and it filled my evening.   I hardly noticed the dusk come up over the windowsill till it had crept into the corners and turned the day to dark, until only a small speck of sun peeked from below the horizon.

Chapter 13

The end of the year with the course exams was looming. Nothing too difficult: Bookkeeping, elementary office routines, typing, short-hand and all those necessary evils for working in an office. Basic, boring and basic.

I got back to my room, threw down my books and once again opened my violin case, just to hold the violin under my chin and feel that accustomed sense of calling upon that warmth of habitual familiarity

There was a gentle knock at the door. My heart leapt with surprise to see the Music Student looking tall and handsome and so utterly unavailable to me.

He greeted me quietly and I smiled back shyly, wondering quite how to regard him now that he had had a liaison with my sister.

'I see you have your violin,' he said, looking at it in my hand. 'May I?'

I handed it over to him and he drew the bow across the strings, creating that flawless note that only masters of the instrument can do.

'What about Agatha?' I said. 'She told me not to play in here.'

'She won't disturb us now,' he answered. 'Reverend Gregory is in and talking to Elizabeth upstairs.'

'Reverend Gregory?' I repeated.

'I take it you have not met him yet?'

'No, I guess he lives nearby?'

'I suppose you could say that. He seldom comes away from Elizabeth's flat. She has been an adherent of his for many years now. Or it could be vice versa. He tries to lead her away from her Eastern beliefs but was fighting a losing battle.'

'I see,' I said, but did not.

By referring to "Elizabeth", he must mean Lillibet, but further translation of his meaning was lost to me. I was not too certain why some "Reverend's" visit with her would silence Agatha's complaining, but I did not question him. He was looking through my music whilst I was piecing together information in my mind which made little sense.

'Come with me.' He gestured towards the door to his room whilst handing me back my violin. Then taking up several sheets of music he had selected, he left the room to go across the passage to his own.

His room was not at all as I expected. It was much larger than mine. All the walls were lined with sound-proofing. He had several book cases filled with books and music scores with a metronome placed in central position ready to pace obedient time. There were a couple of plain chairs and a table, one small wardrobe and one very small narrow bed. Peggy could only have slept here on her own. The offer of his room must have been so that she did not have to leave me in the night if I needed her. I felt foolish and touched at the same time.

I smiled to myself.

He closed the door behind us, placed a piece of my music on a music stand and asked if I would play it for him.

I placed the violin under my chin, lifted the bow and drew it across the strings to test the tuning once more.

Then I started to play.

He had chosen Claude Debussy's 'Clair De Lune', transposed from piano, for which it was written, to violin. I knew it well. I had played it for a music exam and could play it now by memory.

I finished the piece and put down the violin to look up at the music student who was standing at the window, looking down at the floor, his hand on his chin.

'That was what I expected from you.' he said. 'I had this feeling about you when we first met. You should have taken this up. You have wasted a year on that course you have been doing.'

He seemed almost annoyed with me. I was uncertain how to respond. I fell silent and looked towards the door.

'No, don't think of going,' he said almost sternly. 'You have a lot to catch up with. There is a lot of work to be done with your fingering, the bow and how you
are holding the instrument. You have been badly taught. Now, I will start with you at once.'

There followed a music lesson unlike any I had had before. His approach to music was one fixated almost fanatically in what he was doing. It seemed that everything I had learnt, from holding the bow to where the violin was placed beneath my chin was incorrect. He made me hear the sounds each note was making and differentiate between sound and pure sound so everything I played sounded quite different.

He managed to bring out from my old instrument sounds that I did not think were possible.

Who was it that said the violin was "scraping horsehair over cat guts to evoke the most expressive feeling."?

We had been thus preoccupied for over three hours when there was a knock at the door. He opened it. His sombre, dark sister stood there looking pensive and anxious. They spoke in hushed whispers at the door and he said he must go.

He folded the music he had with him, put his own violin into its case and ushered me out.

I was feeling a little dazed by it all. He closed the door to his room and simply said, 'Practise these pieces till you have them perfect. Here, take this key, I have another. Please use my room any time you wish to come in and practise. I will see you again.'

His sister had already descended the stairs as he locked his room and without any further communication or farewell he was gone, down the stairs and after her, as if in a hurry to catch her up.

It had all happened so quickly from his first appearance, through the music lesson to the end. There was no mention of times or dates or how. He had not even introduced me to the lovely Anna Maria, nor had she even cast a single glance in my direction. They might well have been a couple leaving behind a servant who had been left with instructions for domestic work for the week ahead.

I was at a complete loss to bring the situation to a conclusive whole. It had been such a strange meeting. There had been little conversation but for discussing the music, its interpretation and the handling of my violin. It was as if I had ordered the lesson and he had come obediently to give it. But there had been no such arrangement that I knew of and we had not discussed his fee or how much I was to pay for his room where I could practise.

Someone must have ordered the lesson. They must have told him I now had my violin with me.

Father did not know him. Therefore, it must be, I thought, that my sister had kept in touch with him.

I was feeling distinctly uncomfortable about it. At the same time I felt a wonderful release of energy flowing through me.

Once again I was in contact with my music.

I longed to speak with Malachi and ask him, but Malachi was not in evidence for days.

Speaking With Strangers

Chapter 14

I knew so little about the Music "Student", but I knew enough by now to realize that he could hardly be described as "Student" any longer. He was clearly a professional musician and an outstanding teacher.

Where was he living when he was not occupying his room? Why did he still keep the room on if he had somewhere else to live? Somewhere, no doubt without the restriction of disturbing the landlady?

What was it that had upset his sister that day? Why did he come to give me that unordered lesson and spend so much time with me?

Recurring questions eclipsed my every thought. They pursued me to college each morning and swamped my concentration.

When I got back from college each day I was drawn as by a magnet to the music room where I could instantly loose myself in music. I could hardly call practice what I did for pure pleasure.

I would enter the room cautiously; knocking first to make sure that he was not there. I looked around at the shelves of books and the piles of music which the whole room was comprised of as if to absorb the essence of the man to whom it all belonged.

There appeared to be a good many books on psychology; large, thick volumes with journals of unintelligible jargon on the same subject. Perhaps a study interest at some time, I wondered?

Next to a pile of Haydn's sheet music was a long leather covered box with a flute inside. I noted that there were volumes of music for flute and remembered that application to a music academy required a second instrument. This must have been his.

I played for hours on end, uninterrupted, till the pangs of hunger reminded me that I had passed the time to eat. Time simply moved beyond a measurement when I was playing.

For four glorious days I came home excited at the prospect of such wonderful involvement and soon lost myself, not in solving the voices of the composers but it trying to perpetuate them. I had been playing for about an hour that evening when a violent knocking on the door silenced me. I opened it to find a strange looking man standing there.

He was bent over at the shoulders which dwarfed his already short stature. A clerical black bib with the white choker collar identified him as the "Reverend Gregory" that Lorenzo had referred to.

There was little saintly cordiality from behind those eyes but a fierce kind of antagonism, like a blast of cold air from an open door in midwinter. It seemed he had at sometimes had a stroke which had anaesthetised the muscles of his face and twisted his left eye downward. His eyes glared from that strange contortion to his face.

It occurred to me, at first that he might have been some relative of Malachi's for there was a vague similarity there. I could see some distant parallel but not quite place how, for he could also be described as a complete antithesis in every other way. His voice, his bearing and his eyes were all different. These eyes were cold and hard and he had an unnervingly peevish drone to his voice.

'What are you doing in Lorenzo's studio?' he asked. His voice was harsh and blunt, his whole stance menacing and hostile. It whipped my senses into that hollow blackness that shreds the soul, slicing my wits to a trembling idiocy. The stark and senseless unexpectedness of the man lost my voice to answers.

'I, er. He, er,' I stuttered, clutching my violin still in my hand with its bow tucked under an arm.

'Come on spit it out! You what? Why are you holding his violin? You have absolutely no right to be here.' He was working himself up into an unreasonable fury and becoming louder and more aggressive with each word, encouraged by my ambushed docility.

'It's my own violin.' I attempted to explain but he was having none of it. He was ready to stake his claim at apprehending an unworthy victim.

'Liar, thief, vandal!' he shouted, backing me into the room. Raising the stick he carried for his own balance he brought it down hard upon my right shoulder. I was far too stunned to notice pain just then. Utter terror had paralysed me. I was pinned to a bookcase while his wild and flailing arms hit out, grabbing, punching and pinching, tearing the buttons loose from my blouse.

'The Lord will punish you, break you with iron bars...' he yelled.

I began to shriek out a feeble 'help' when all of a sudden, behind him, as if appearing from nowhere was Lillibet, brandishing a large wooden spoon she must have grabbed as the nearest weapon she could find on her way down to my assistance. She brought it down hard upon the assumed "Reverend's" arm. He cowed instantly, withdrawing his gloved hand with a wild yell.

'Now you git on back up those stairs,' Lillibet shouted.

He seemed to crumple. He was holding his head in his hands and moaning softly to himself, 'Oh my head, my head,' Then his voice altered and he made a perfect impression of Agatha's voice. 'Not here, not here, out at once...' said her voice. Then the voice changed and became Miss Constantine's. 'Slut, red-head slut.'

All the while Lillibet had the man in a vice-like grasp and she was dragging him up the stairs. Just before he was about to disappear from sight another voice came through.

'Anna Catherine, Anna my darling, look after yourself.' And the door closed upon him.

'Mummy,' I called out. 'Mummy, is that you?'

I felt foolish and weepy. It was her voice. Was I also going mad?

Speaking With Strangers

Chapter 15

Memories un-refreshed, become like distant echoes of a forgotten dream, till rekindled by some spark of recognition of something. Even then, they are blurred like the sepia-print of old photographs that become the shadows of a memory.

As several years have separated me from that time, I find it difficult to recall the details of that time, that day. It was the pure unexpected shock of the drama within it that lingers. I remember going back into the room, putting away the sheets of music I had been playing and folded up the music stand. My hands were trembling so hard I kept dropping everything in my desperate haste to get away.

Once back in my own room I locked my door and stood there, staring into space. What was all that about? How, how did it happen? Why did I think that was Mother's voice. I had forgotten her. I had forgotten how she sounded but he had managed to imitate her so well. How, how, how?

It was some cruel trick to wound me in some way.

The pattern of my life had been to withdraw myself from all those confrontations that meeting people implied. This experience was like an affirmation of all the dangers of encounters with strangers. The attack had been so unexpected and so direct it brought back that aggression that our father showed to Mother and their bitter arguments.

Childhood shared with my sister was one of compliance. We did not fight. I was always too submissive to argue and Peggy was always so convincingly right. It was easier to hide away and avoid people and her too at times when she got angry. It had worked before and would be sustained with certainty now.

My right shoulder and arm began to throb where I had been struck. The distorted mirror reflected black bruising that crept from my shoulder to my neck, a souvenir and effect of the terrifying episode. I went to bed early that night taking pain and nightmare into restless sleep. I woke the next day feeling stiff and uncomfortable, wondering how I would manage the day ahead with work to do.

There was no one to talk to about it. There was no one I wished to talk to about it.

I skipped college that day. I could not face a day of people around me, besides it was too hot to consider wearing a scarf to hide a bruised neck from inquisitive minds. We were in the midst of end of year exams which soothed the ache for something I would rather be doing. I struggled to apply myself with diligence to the trivia I considered before me.

When I heard a knock at my door I chose not to answer till it persisted louder with my name.

'Anna, it is Lorenzo. I have come to see how you are. May I come in please?' Seeing him standing there at my door gave less pleasure than I had that first time. I was now feeling distinctly wary of surprise visits with no clarification. It was all too much like my childhood with Peggy.

'Hello Anna,' he said. 'May I come in?'

He noticed my hesitation as he stood there. I saw him look at my neck and bruised arm.

'I am so sorry,' he said. 'I did not know that he had caused such harm to you.'

It had occurred to me that if Lillibet had not come when she did I dared not think what might have happened. I wanted to say that I thought the man was obviously insane and dangerous and should not be allowed out of a mental institution, but I could not. Something told me that there was a connection somewhere with them and the old man was being protected precisely from that.

'It's fine,' I said quickly. 'Really fine.'

He seemed relieved to let things go at that. Somehow the "mishap", for want of a better word, had made him less formal than before, shy even. It was as if he was struggling within himself to say something but could not. He was embarrassed about my injury but also keen to avoid too much mention of it.

'I'm not much good at saying things,' he began. 'I realize that my first lesson must have struck you as...' He stopped, not knowing how to go on.

'It was wonderful,' I said rather quickly. 'I learnt more from you in that lesson than I have ever been taught.'

'You see Malachi told me you could do with encouraging - to get you back to your music. He said you were a natural musician.'

'How would Malachi know? He has never heard me play.'

'You will find that Malachi knows most things,' he said softly. 'And he was right.'

'Where is he? I have looked out for him every day for this past week and I've not seen him. Where does he sleep?'

'On the first floor.'

'With Agatha?' I asked rather surprised.

'Well, yes of course, Gregory, Constantine and others generally emerge from there or even Elizabeth's flat from time to time but she usually keeps them all in check. Gregory can get very out of hand and it was unfortunate that he slipped past her. He thought he was going to see me. It's a long story. I just can't explain it right now.' He stopped, walked over to the window and stared down as if a great weight had dragged him down into a depth he was unable to escape from.

'Without my music, I think I would go crazy some times,' he said.

'I know.' I said.

He turned and looked at me. There was at that moment an exchange of some unspoken reminiscence which each in our own way had a silent connection to.

'Would you like another music lesson?' he asked.

'I can't pay you,' I said. 'As soon as my exams are over, I hope to get a job and I can pay then.'

'Please, don't think of paying for lessons. You have a lot of talent. It has gone unnoticed and unappreciated for too long. It took several phone calls from Malachi to persuade your father to bring your violin. He would be disappointed to see all his efforts go to waste.'

'Malachi did that for me? I thought... Is he going to pay for my lessons?'

'No. I am offering you my time because I owe so much to Malachi.'

He stopped, went to the door and opened it, then turning back to me he added, 'Besides I find you interesting, gratifying to teach, you absorb so well what I am showing you. Are you coming?'

He held the door open while I snatched up my violin and bow and followed.

'Agatha has gone shopping,' he said as I looked around cautiously.

The lesson lasted far less time than the one before. My shoulder and arm ached too much. He said nothing but seemed to understand, watching and listening quietly this time.

'Good,' he said. 'Really good. Learn these.' He pointed to pages of Bach's violin concerto in G minor. 'You need to know all the composers well. Mozart may be a favourite of yours but you can recognize the absolute beauty in these also. For me, I find the Russian composers have that raging passion of the soul that I feel here.' He touched his heart with his hand. It was hard to imagine him with raging passions. I had not seen that side of him, more Liszt or Brahms perhaps but it is surprising how wrong one can be on initial impressions.

He paged through books of music scores, pulling out pieces for me to learn. I thought perhaps Tchaikovsky's romantic music or Prokofiev's symphonies but he was putting out the neoclassical stuff of Stravinsky and Sasha Argov the Israeli composer. He said he had a great preference for the Russian-Jewish composers. No doubt a preference come from family connections. An essential to learn was Joseph Yulyvich Achron's Hebrew Melody for Violin and Korsakov's Flight of the Bumblebee which he said would be good for my technique.

'You will need to know many more than those obvious and popular pieces you have learnt when you audition for an academy.'

'I have made no plans to audition,' I said.

He stopped what he was doing and looked up at me. 'Malachi said...' He paused, silent for a while, then said, 'Let Malachi tell you himself.'

It made as little sense to me as everything I had experienced and seen since coming to live at 63 Macdonald Road and I chose not to pursue it.

'I will be busy all this week but perhaps the following Saturday evening. Will that Saturday evening do? If you have some engagement on, I can come on Sunday?'

'Any Saturday evening will be fine, in fact any evening at all - if that suits you,' I said. 'All my college exams will be over by this Friday so I can devote so much more time to playing. But, I have to admit, I am now worried about disturbing anyone if I practise in your music room before that?'

'Perhaps pay Elizabeth a visit first to make sure the coast is clear.'

'Elizabeth? "Lillibet" she called herself, how will she know?'

'She will know,' he said, then wishing me goodbye he left.

I began to see him in a different light. He had become less awesome and more human, more amenable and much more likeable. I was beginning to think of him more as "Lorenzo" and less as the "Music Student/Teacher". Still, I knew so little about him, as I did Malachi, Agatha and all the rest.

Chapter 16

I had my qualms about seeing Lillibet before using the music room. My last sight of the crazy old man was of him being dragged off there. It was the fear of being interrupted by him and the desperate need to get back to my music that persuaded me that it was a wise thing to do.

'Well, you don say! Look whose here to visit ole Lillibet. Come on in gel and we have some tea.'

'Lorenzo told me to see you first before I go to his room to practise,' I said hastily, deciding on "up-front" rather than dithering vacillation.

'Is that coz you are worried about that ole devil The Reverend. You don worry about that boy, he goin do you no harm. Not while ole Lillibet here.'

'He didn't seem like a boy to me,' I answered. 'He seemed more like a deranged old man.'

She rattled with laughter as she went ahead to the kitchen where I could hear her filling the kettle. Perhaps she was lonely and could do with a little company. It would be unreasonable of me not to spend at least a few minutes with her. I followed her there and saw with surprise that the room had been all cleaned up, dishes put away and the windows so clear they shone.

'It's looking nice in here,' I applauded.

'That Agatha, she come in here some days and she clean and tidy up for ole Lillibet. She don like a mess, Agatha.'

'She is not too fond of noise either,' I added. 'Which is why Lorenzo has offered me his soundproof room to practise in.'

'Well, we all have our ways. Good and bad ways. It's the getting round them ways you must learn. Agatha, she is no dumb fairy. She has a good heart and she means well. She just had one damn bad luck life.'

Circumventing her inner knowledge she went on in her general theme about everyone she knew.

Lillibet liked to talk.

While she put out mugs of tea we lightly discussed the negative aspects of man-kind that were a simple ellipse of something better beneath. I found talking to Lillibet was rather like opening a can that had no description on its cover to discover something rather extraordinary inside. She had a wealth of understanding of everyone in the house. She seemed to know the students in the basement flat like old friends yet they had not mentioned much about knowing her.

I had enjoyed my tea with her. No interruptions from any of the rather weird flat-mate companions made the time so much more enjoyable. She assured me that Agatha was busy baking that afternoon and we would have no interruptions. Small consolation to me as Agatha was the least of my worries.

'What about Malachi?' I asked. 'I miss him. I have not seen him for days now.'

'Malachi come and go,' she offered. 'He has many places he go to visit but that ole Malachi, he very interested in how you goin on wid your violin.'

'How does he know, if he is seldom here?'

'He know. Like your Mummy she know also.'

'How do you know about my mother? We haven't seen or heard from her in years. She has just cut us out. My sister Peggy won't even allow me to talk about her.'

'That cos Peggy she has too much pain inside about what happen to your Mama an her own goddam mix-up.'

'My mother just walked out and left us,' I said as a kind of endorsement of our reciprocal neglect.

'You gon forgot it all. When you ready you remember it all and then you come to Lillibet and she tell you more. Now it time you go practise, I hear that ole Miss Constantine gittin up a storm to come and sound off that bad ole chest of hers.'

How she could hear Miss Constantine's approach was beyond me, but the threat of the nasty old dragon's verbal abuse was enough to leave without further argument.

At the door she handed me a small jar of rather sinister looking ointment.

'For that damn bad bruise you hidin' there under your scarf. Help with pain too,' she recommended.

How on earth did she know? Even more remarkable – it worked!

Chapter 17

With my wonderful renewed involvement in music again, time was absorbed into a shrinking of days. College finished and I did as the other students did. I went round the employment agencies to look for a job.

My first job was as a receptionist at a dentist.

There were few secretarial skills needed and the duties were simple enough: phone calls taking appointments, hearing complaints, filing and the odd bit of typing. It filled the gap of time before I could play the violin again and provided me with an income to stay where I was.

Peggy kept in contact. We exchanged those obligatory pleasantries with one another, commenting on the observable about changes in our day to day lives without entering the deeper aspects of points of view with sense and sensation.

Father rang from time to time telling me that he was going out of the country on business or away on holiday somewhere exotic and hoped I was doing well. He never asked about my music or how I was feeling; but then, those were topics that had been avoided by us all since Mother left us.

Those forbidden thoughts of her returned and filled my mind in the middle of the night when I could not sleep. Life had become so different, so curtailed and partial. I was now without rudder and oar to take me to some destination aiming me in the direction of what to do and where to go and what not to think.

Somehow getting a job and being independent had none of the merits that my sister had found. There was none of that sense of fulfilment she had talked of. At night I thought about her often and began to wonder what Lillibet meant about my forgetting. I could only remember crying inconsolably after Mother had flown away. That was all. I began to wonder why I thought of her in terms of "flying away". Some small senseless childish image had wedged somewhere in my psyche of Mother leaping off a cliff or a ledge somewhere and flew away somewhere beyond our reach. I dismissed the thoughts as childish fantasy. It was how a child would imagine her journey to another country.

My life had been woven from forgotten memories and held together by the magic of music. Having an instrument to play had torn me away from the isolation that was our life. Where Peggy liked to go out and be with friends, I liked to be on my own with music at my fingertips. First the piano and then the violin which took over and enveloped my whole life, a salve to all those niggling little queries and doubts.

I looked forward to Sunday evenings. It was the day that Lorenzo had set for my music lesson.

The enigma of Lorenzo and his sister remained as tightly closed as an oyster in its shell and I was confident that some pearl was trapped inside. There was something fixed and unvarying about his outer shell, always formal, polite and focussed upon the music lesson with no distractions beyond. It was as if he was performing the duty of giving lessons as a function born of a part he was playing to some unseen adjudicator perhaps a sort of penance.

He had lapsed back into his original formal attention to the music lesson and there was never another mention of what had happened. I could say that his lack of geniality and ease made attention to the music more concentrated which was easier to cope with. Being fixated on the performance of playing became the obliteration of the chaos I was feeling inside.

I don't believe he noticed much about me but being the object of musical instruction. My music technique was consummate but I played with a lot less feeling than I did when I played alone. It was only then that I opened out to the music and let my soul melt into the sounds and what they conveyed.

There was something majestic and awe inspiring about Lorenzo. He was so beautiful, so elegant. His hands were long with fingers that knotted at the joints and moved and contoured with such smooth grace over the strings. He became my sole object of admiration. I began to worship him as one does a beautiful, inanimate work of art. I was pleased that Peggy had not taken him as her lover as that quintessential model of perfection would have been lost.

If he had been soft and kind like Malachi my emotions would have turned me inside out. It was as if he did all in his power to make sure that would not happen. I regarded him rather with respect and reliance and he in turn made sense of my life now. He offered that stability that I had lost when Peggy was no longer there to take control.

But it was Malachi who was the basis of my life. The fact that he would just turn up when I needed him most gave me a sense of security I had never known.

Those questions that begin to churn about asking for meaning were part of my whole thinking now. Confusions that had pursued me since early childhood now stood relentlessly before me as megaliths of stubborn stone. Not only was I living in darkness regarding my parents but that concept of soul and life became blanketed by statements like "the great unknown". This was where

God lived and where souls kept their secreted magnitude. It was a place that I needed to embrace and understand fully so that I could become free.

There were those rare and vibrant moments of awareness when I was listening to or playing some piece of music that moved me. I cannot express nor duplicate how those sensations left me. I can only recall a strong sense of excitement and knowledge that flashes in single vivid moments of being vital and alive. When it passes it goes so completely that rational thinking cannot keep up, and the pace and the content is lost in that indeterminate state in which dreams evaporate.

With music, I felt sometimes as if I had seen through a window into other realities that are inexplicably a part of my own life. But in a corporal world, I was trapped somewhere in that state of not knowing, blind ignorance and a need for revelation of the truth. That ultimate question "who am I" was constant. How could it be answered when I lived among strangers whom I could not fathom and those only two members of my family would not talk?

Malachi's unexplained and sudden appearances as if from nowhere but always on cue gave him the aura of a kind of Angel and it was a time for me when credence in such things was easy. He exuded a kind of secret answer to all the questions, yet spoke of none. His way was to encourage me to think and to talk and explore possibilities with my own reasoning.

It felt as if he was always there, visible or invisible, always a constant presence in my heart ready to help when I needed help most. Sometimes several weeks would elapse and there was no sign of him then suddenly he would appear.

I had not seen Malachi for quite some time after the incident in the music room with the mad "Reverend" and my talk with Lorenzo. I was feeling a little doubtful of his interest in my music when so much time had passed and he was not even aware of the continued lessons I had been having with Lorenzo.

Then out of the blue, he appeared one day.

'Going out for a walk?' His voice came from the hall as I was going out.

My heart leapt.

'Malachi where have you sprung from?'

'Nowhere and everywhere,' he answered with his wide mystical smile.

We walked in silence for a while until those cogs of perpetual motion in my mind itched to ask questions.

'Lorenzo said my music lessons were your idea. A sort of obligation to you.'

'Lorenzo gives you lessons because he wants to.'

'It doesn't seem that way Malachi. He is so set, so driven - and the object of his visit is to instruct, to teach as if he is teaching as a kind of penance and sometimes I feel uncomfortable about it. It feels that he is so unhappy about where he is and what he is doing. I want to pay for those lessons.'

'Then pay for them.'

'I have no idea how much to pay. I am also worried that I will offend him. He is so hard to talk to, to ask anything but questions about music.'

'That is Lorenzo's way. He has always been like that since he was a boy but underneath his mind is as full and active as yours.'

'I find that hard to believe. - You know Malachi I can hardly sleep these days for thinking. It is not that I am searching for someone to talk to. I am used to silence. I mean I am used to not talking or having anyone to talk to but this silence of Lorenzo's I find confusing. There seems to be some kind of world conspiracy - not to talk to Anna about anything. My sister and my father were the same. They seemed to get into huddles with one another, talking and I was locked out. They did not discuss things with me. Peggy seemed almost determined that I should know nothing. She kept a kind of cold silence about secret things that she felt I should not know. But she could talk about trivia, you know, things that did not matter. Oh God, could she go on about nothing. You know, parties, the men she had met, her conquests and her discarded lovers and how upset they had been. It made me all the more silent.'

'Silence is the prompt of the mind,' he answered. 'It is important because it is the mind's source. Silence is the foundation of those stages of inner growth when we begin to release the material plane and become more acquainted with the region where spiritual activity commands its own laws.'

'Sounds like an advocacy for being a nun or a priest.' I said, thinking of those pious missions with in their eccentric sobriety.

'Of course there are those who wish to withdraw entirely from the world in search of spirituality. But being reserved and shut off from the world does not bring you necessarily into a spiritual state, instead it can create all kinds of mistaken assumptions. You need to start by believing in yourself.'

He paused, looked at me with his muted smile as if waiting for me to say I understood.

'I am not sure I know much about myself or what to believe about myself. I am always afraid of what people think of me, so I hide from them.'

'We seldom see ourselves as others see us.'

'Is it important that we should? I mean, I really have no wish to see what people may think of me. It would terrify me into permanent exclusion of life.'

'No, not always, for each person plants his own personal impression that comes from his own inadequacy into his opinion. We all have our opinions, just as you have them. It makes little difference to the person you are privately assessing. The question is, how will we be remembered? Man is usually given the stamp of approval or disapproval by the last thing he did. It is like that when you get old. It is not how you were but how you have become.'

'What if you can't do anything to change how people think of you even is if it is entirely wrong?'

'It does not matter. God and His saints and angels know and that is enough.'

'I know nothing about my family. I know nothing about where my mother is.'

There was no way of admitting, even to myself, that my thinking was the diverse and miscellaneous chaos that was my mind but I selected that which was the most troubling to me.

'You know Malachi I have this fixation about my Mother.'

'The mother who has made no contact for years?'

'Yes, well, no one can answer the questions about her. Why did she fly away as she did?'

'Fly away?'

'Yes, Father told us she had flown off to meet her girlfriend.'

'And you saw this flying act; this flying away?'

'Yes, that's what is so strange. I have this picture of her in my mind, flying – not in an aeroplane but in the air. Then I remember crying.'

'Is that so? Now do you not think this is a child's concept of imagining how she left?'

'Yes, of course it is. But Malachi it is so real in my mind, so vivid. I used to ask my sister about it but she would not answer. She got upset.'

I stopped. I could not go on for a while. What was in my mind had become like some tremendous overspill of emotion mixed with confusion.

'Malachi,' I said. 'Malachi, I think something happened to Mother - and I have no idea how to find out what it is.'

'What about your grandparents now? They will now.'

'I have no idea how to find them. Father would not let us see them after Mother left.'

'Well you must surely share a surname you can look up?'

'Father's parent's died before I was born. I remember Mother's parents but I cannot remember her surname.'

'Leave it to me.' Malachi said. 'I will find them for you and get them to contact you.'

'How will you do that?'

'Malachi can do anything,' he said with the inspiration of a smile.

-

Chapter 18

My job was a methodical exercise in coping with the mundane. No one willingly motivates a visit to the dentist without painful cause and reluctant purpose. It is a necessity undergone under duress leaving behind an atmosphere of imposed bravado. Patients slithered in to the waiting room; some made small talk to the receptionists others looked furtively about. Few were made to feel comfortable by the head receptionist Jennifer, a woman in her late forties who had been working for the dentists for many years and prized her position as a mark of personal importance.

I was taken under the wing by Jennifer. While the familiarity of first name terms might appear to close the gap of her senior position as receptionist, the intimacy stopped there.

Jennifer had the notion that most people she came across would at some stage let her down and did not like her. She consequently disliked everyone and showed it with an offhand attitude which gave little confidence to patients visiting the dentist. It was an impression she clung to and it, in turn, clung viciously to her, replicating all those negatives that are inherent in her fellowman who never fail to oblige with expectations.

Jennifer was a good mirror for my own feelings of inadequacy. I saw myself reflected there and began to observe my own emotional responses with censure.

The necessity to work involves all those other necessary obligations of personal exchanges and learning something new. It was often like walking in the shifting sands of a bog, no knowing which areas would drag me down into a depth and loose me in the mire; then times of boredom from repetition, and times of simply not knowing how to act or react to moods and circumstance, exposing all those vulnerable areas.

My sister would have ridiculed my reactions and Malachi would tell me that I was learning something about myself.

I got through the day by thinking of its end when I could loose myself once more into a world of music where I felt safe.

The very act of going into the music room, placing the pieces I wanted to play on the stand and taking my violin from its case was pleasure in itself. Each composer revealed that something which was built-in to his soul and each piece of music told a story which I could perpetuate with my own emotions. For those glorious hours of playing, I was lost in another world. I could escape from my thoughts.

Lorenzo came dutifully each Sunday. There was a brief greeting followed by a discussion of what he would hear first. He would stand at a distance, near the window and would rap on the window sill when he wished to make a point, give advice or correct a mistake. The lessons seldom went much beyond two hours when he would stare at his wrist watch and say with quiet authority, 'that will be enough.'

I don't even remember my music teacher at school, Miss Abraham, being quite so formal. She would always say something gracious and pleasant. Trivial perhaps, but just enough to imply her commitment to my efforts, none the less a sign of recognition: 'that's nice dear', or 'my you have been practising', or 'how do your parents feel about how you are progressing?' I would always make something up that would sound suitable about what parents may or may not think about the progress of their child.

The subject of Lorenzo's teaching fees still rattled me. I was as uncertain now to broach the subject as I would have been to ask some personal question about him or his sister. And the likelihood of that was next to zero though my thoughts probed every possibility. So the situation lay in a state of temporary suspension and the months passed thus.

It was the custom each month to pay my rent to Agatha at her door. She requested the exact amount of cash in an envelope with my name and the date upon it. She never invited me in but on the first day of every month, which was when she expected the rent, she was ready nearby to answer my knock. She would come to the door in her usual sombre stance to take my envelope, examine the money inside and promptly hand me a receipt.

On many occasions she would appear to have someone with her as I could hear conversation, mostly argument going on when I knocked. It would stop at once or subside to a whisper, then came a shuffle of feet before she came to the door.

I noticed on these occasions that she always wore gloves. In fact, thinking back, she had always worn gloves. A strange convention, but then Agatha herself was strange.

I would sometimes pass one of the students from the basement coming up on the same mission of rent and we would chat. We had reached that level of informality where we exchanged observances of the weather, the pressure of forthcoming exams and problems with finding the right jobs.

From time to time I would get an invitation to one of their party evenings. I never went of course and was only grateful that their music would drown out any sounds that might creep out from the music room.

One particular end of the month rent-day fell on a Sunday. It was one of those quiet Sundays when even the air stops still to take cognisance of the sobriety of that day.

I saw Jason walking back towards the landing. He greeted me with his usual affable friendliness.

'She's not in, I have been knocking for a while,' he said. 'I should come back later.'

'Perhaps because the first of this month is a Sunday,' I responded. 'Do you think she might have gone to church?'

'No, absolutely not,' Jason answered. 'In the three years I have been here she has never been to church. She is a confirmed atheist I believe. That is the job of old pastor Gregory. He is a fanatic. I gather you have come a cropper with him?'

'Yes,' I said, surprised at the efficiency of word passed around this house about what goes on.

We chatted briefly. He asked about my music lessons and how I was progressing. Then he turned and went back down the stairs. So the students must know about the lessons too!

It was curious that Agatha had not responded to her tenants coming to pay rent. It was most unusual. I decided I would attempt to knock. I thought I heard movement from inside. After a few moments I heard a key being put to the door and slowly the door opened.

Out of the obscurity of the room behind her, Agatha stood, looking dishevelled and out of sorts. Her usually neat appearance was in disarray. Her hair was crumpled and her make-up smudged. She seemed to stagger on her feet like an unset jelly. She did not appear to recognize me. She stared as if I were someone she might have known somewhere in a distant past and recollection was slow to dawn.

'Come in,' she said. 'A fearful headache. Quite dreadful.' Her voice was slurred and different.

'I am so sorry,' I said. 'I should not have disturbed you. It's the rent money. You know - the first of the month as you asked.'

'Rent!' she repeated as she stood there, uncertain and shaky. She smoothed back her hair from her face and I noticed that for the first time she was not wearing gloves. The fingers of her right hand were twisted and bent as if at some time they had been horribly crushed. I looked away. Her hands were a private thing she had kept to herself. I had witnessed what she had gone to so much trouble to conceal.

While she tottered unsteadily on her feet, trying to regain a lost composure, my eyes at once immersed themselves in the curious interior of the room.

It was a large drawing room whose windows faced the front of the house. At one distant time it might have been described as elegant but its drift with time had fragmented it into a crumbling mass of deterioration. A strong, musty, stale smell, redolent of decay, clung to it like decrepit age, where black mould grew from the exposed wall from which curls of wallpaper had come away.

Agatha groaned, took some shuffling steps backward to an arm chair which buckled the back of her legs forcing her to sit down heavily upon it.

She still appeared semi-comatose.

I hesitated.

I should go, but curiosity got the better of me and I continued to glance around.

I found myself standing on an ancient carpet, worn and patched in parts, its pattern of swirling colour, now string shreds of weft and warp.

The room was darkened by those heavy damask curtains the Victorians loved to use to shut out the day. Its fabric had begun to flake into tattered strands where it had been handled. Too fragile to draw any more, they were held back with fraying tassels which drooped like a blown rose whose petals have become caprice to the wind.

An eye-catching, modern screen television, placed on an elaborately carved console table looked out of place where a terrible clutter of antiquity was heaped in timeless preservation. To add to the dark of it all, heavy Baroque bookcases lined two walls. Its books were bound in leather of faded greens and russet reds and stamped in diminished gold.

A reader, someone who loved books had lived here.

A glass cabinet with arrangements of china figures and delicate porcelain was carefully displayed like a miniature stage-set. They were those incongruously clothed shepherds and shepherdesses of swaggering, posed figures in reclining attitudes of days gone by.

This had been the home of a collector.

From the ornamental mantel-piece to every table top and shelf was a collection of the decorative and garish from some rococo Eastern European connection.

Someone had put all this together and everything had been left in perpetuity of preservation, gathering dust and memories. And someone else was holding on, unable to release it all. Even the portraits on the walls stared down in defiance from their guilt frames, their compelling eyes forbidding outsiders. They were all of flowered, laced and jewelled ladies and dandy men: bead-eyed, white-wigged and sculptured hair bearing ornament and flowers.

Their faces had lost the edge on glamour; now cracked and darkened by age and ingrained dust.

Who had shared this preserved mausoleum with its loneliness kept neat and tidy, despite decay?

I was still staring in wrapped absorption when Agatha snapped back to life with a jolt and asked me what I was doing in her living room – uninvited!

'I came to bring the rent money,' I said defensively. 'You let me in.'

'Oh,' she said, recoiling from her attitude. 'Well, thank you, I have not yet made out your receipt. I will do it later and bring it to you.'

She walked briskly back to the door which she opened and let me out without another word; my mind tightly involved in all the details of what I had seen and Agatha's strange manner.

Later that day when Lorenzo came to give me the violin lesson, he seemed even more withdrawn and on edge than usual, as if precipitating a question from me that he was reluctant to give. It was as if he sensed that overspill of curiosity in my mind. How I longed to speak with him, reassure him and discover what it was that so troubled him, for clearly he was trying to cover something that he found deeply disturbing.

I played, he listened. It was a piece from Debussy's "Des pas sur la neige". He played the same piece and his voice seemed to reach through to me as mapping a pattern of sundry thoughts to music. It touched my soul and silenced those racing thoughts. When he had finished we both sat, silent a while, looking into a space before us, as if our souls had linked and communicated something special. It had nothing to do with the mundane or arcane or the distortion of secrets kept unanswered, for the whole world was there within us.

Then he got up and said, 'Next Sunday?' and left.

Chapter 19

Christmas was approaching along with that bitter cold that accompanies it. Winter had supplanted autumn, shaking off the mottled leaves from those old labelled and tamed trees in the park. It had set its mark upon every living thing and those that could avoid it ventured out with caution.

Since Peggy left I hated the thought of Christmas. The last one was a sharp reminder of my single and solitary status. There were cards from her and Father of course, but no offer to go and stay or share a holiday with either of them.

This year was promising to be a replica of the last.

The three basement students had already gone home for the holidays, like swallows leaving for the winter and the house was hollow and quiet since they had gone. Even Lorenzo had gone away somewhere with his sister. He had not embellished the point and I had not asked. I simply resigned myself to a lonely time.

I decided that I would buy presents for those of us left behind at Number Sixty Three and the thought of that preparation gave me a warm feeling of belonging there. I bought a long brightly knitted scarf for Agatha, a warm shawl for Lillibet and then I wondered about Miss Constantine, she was always so unpleasant on the occasions that our paths crossed but I did not want to exclude her so I bought chocolates for her, perhaps they might sweeten her. I had only once seen the aggressive Reverend Gregory and had no idea where he slept or even if he lived there, he was definitely going to be excluded.

I thought long and hard about what to get Malachi. What would Malachi want? Perhaps nothing, but I remembered that he wore old worn knitted mittens when he was out, actually most of time. I did not remember him not having them, so I bought him new ones.

I decided that for Lorenzo I would put a small tree in his music room and decorate it with little glass balls. Despite that he had given no indication as to when he was coming back. I imagined the tree would stay there, never seen, till it had to be taken out. Nevertheless I bought the tree and decorated it, then stood back to see how pretty it was, feeling that mellow goodwill you get before Christmas but saddened that it would only be me who saw it.

I thought back of the Christmases that Peggy and I shared and how excited we became when Father dropped in with a fresh tree for us each year. The old box of decorations was hauled out and never lost its evocative significance. Each year I would say something about Mother perhaps coming back to see us as it was

Christmas, each time Peggy would stop what she was doing and glower at me, telling me I had spoilt it all by my reminder.

I thought of Mother now with the tree looking pretty and the silver baubles catching the pastel-muted light from the window. It had been years since Father had read her last letter to us and I wondered about her and where she was and what she was doing now. I felt somehow that she was near me, watching over me and a glow of warmth put fresh hope and purpose to my day.

I invited Lillibet to come down and inspect the tree.

She was delighted with it. Clapping her hands in delight she asked me to do a similar tree for her. She walked about the music room, inspecting the books and the music. She remarked how this large room had always been a music room, empty but for books and a waste of good space that she could well do with.

'Sometime I hear you playin' when I go by quiet. That Agatha, she don' say noting' about noise no more. I catch her listening too, jes outside the door. And she say noting.'

She put her hand up and felt the soundproofed walls, giving them a rub. 'See... this stuff is good, you has to stand right outside to hear.'

She opened the door and stood for a moment, wanting to say something. Then she held her head to one side and gave me a long look.

'You are good, girl, you damn good.'

I smiled at her. That was praise I valued most and I thought how lucky I was to have her on my side in a world that was so full of obstacles.

Our silent moment together was interrupted by a long hard ring to the front of the door.

'Postman?' I suggested.

'That goddam postman sure like to make a noise this time o year,' she commented as the bell rang again noisily. This time the postman kept his hand on the bell with a persistence that would wake the devil.

'Where that Agatha, she don't answer that door?'

'I'll go down and see,' I offered. The bell continued to ring with impatient shrill blasts.

I opened the door and there, looking like thunder stood my stepmother.

'Eleanor!' I exclaimed. 'What are you doing here? I thought you and Father had gone away.'

'Your Father has gone.' She spat out the words.

'He has gone with some little tart he has found and he has left me.'

'Oh dear, poor Eleanor,' I commiserated as well I could without even the smallest real compassion beneath the words.

'Would you like to come in?'

She had already walked in, pushing herself past me into the hall-passage.

'Have you seen him?' she asked almost threatening, as if I had him hidden somewhere.

'Well, of course not, why should he come here?   He never comes to see me and I am never invited to your home, so how would I know where he is or what he is doing?' I replied, incensed with long pent up resentment.

'Of course we invite you; all the time.   It is you who refuse to come.' She replied with unconstrained rectitude.

'Well the invitations have never reached me,' I answered, unconvinced of her authenticity.

'It seems I am not the only one that has been lied to all these years,' she said, mellowing her tone.

'What exactly do you mean?' I asked.

'Your Father always told me that you and your sister did not approve of me and wanted nothing to do with me.   I tried.   I really tried.   That day I brought you here, he told me to be brusque with you, to drop you and go before you became offensive.'

'I don't believe you,' I snapped at her.   'You are lying because he has hurt you.   Anyway Father never stayed long with any woman. We knew that you wouldn't last.'

The inexorable words tumbled out of me like a lanced poison released from a deep wound.   It was all the suppressed censure that had built up over the years of anguish and hurting over our silent abandonment.

'My dear girl you are so wrong about...'   She stopped, changing gear in mid-sentence, took a deep breath.   Then there followed a thought of altered impact which she muttered touchily as a kind of parting shot.

'It is little wonder your poor mother committed suicide.'

She spoke without recrimination or reproach but with what sounded like sincere feeling, or was I missing an ulterior motive for the consequences of my reaction?

I was stunned.   Suicide? Never!

'She did not commit suicide,' I struck back at her passionately. 'She is still alive, he said so - he said so.   She will simply not contact us.'

'I am so sorry Anna.   I am truly sorry.   You have clearly not been told.   Perhaps I had better go.'

Eleanor's aim was as transparent as clear glass. I could see that she was speaking for affect, provoking me into a position of compliance but I was too naive to challenge her effectively without losing ground.

'No. No you can't go. I have wanted to know for years about Mummy. You must tell me.'

'Come back with me then,' she said gently as if luring me into some kind of trap.

'I can't. I, I have to practise my violin.'

'No you don't,' came Agatha's voice from behind me. I was suddenly made aware of her standing there.

'It is high time you were told the truth,' she was saying; but it was all too much for me to take in. Anyway, how did Agatha know about Mother?

Lillibet had already fetched a coat and my handbag from my room and she was standing there holding them out to me.

'I go now and lock the door for music room and yours, an Lillibet look after everyting. You go now girl. Go do some talkin and come back tomorrow.'

'No, I mean yes, I will come back with you Eleanor but I must come back this evening if that is alright with you - please.'

I felt myself shaking as I put on my coat and followed my stepmother out of the front door.

I had wanted answers for so long, but not like this. Not these answers. Yet I knew at heart they were the truth that had been evaded all through my growing up and I wanted to know why.

It took an hour and a half precisely to get to the village where she lived. She drove in silence all the way, concentrating, perhaps scheming, how she would approach the subject of my Mother. And all the time I felt that sense of something underhand and ulterior about all this.

I was surprised by the house. It was not what I had expected. It was not in the heart of the country as we had been told but set in the centre of a small village, in the built up area of Surrey, fast becoming a conurbation of London. The house was certainly large but a look of recent neglect about it had spilled to the garden which was resonant of a seaside hotel out of season, with no seasons to follow.

Father would not have liked that. Father liked perfection. Perhaps he was the cause of this neglect.

When we got inside she took my coat and invited me into a warm kitchen where a large red Aga radiated its excess heat. She put the kettle on and we sat at a heavy, bleach-scrubbed table on perfectly contoured bentwood chairs.

'How long has Father been gone?' I asked rather clumsily.

We hadn't talked till now. She had spent most of the time crying while she drove.

I sat stony faced without saying a word to her.

This was such a different Eleanor. I was finding it difficult coming to terms with her and the situation for that matter.

She made a great blast into a giant tissue and wiped her red eyes.

'Two days ago. I thought he might come back. You see I had found out about this other woman months ago and I have nagged him about her. I realize now that I overdid it. I think it drove him away.'

'No,' I answered slowly. 'I don't think so, he would have left anyway. I think you can congratulate yourself that you have lasted longer than any of the others he has had.'

'Why would you girls not come and live with us?' she asked almost petulantly.

'We were told you would not have us, you were not used to children, you did not like them and you were dreadfully jealous.'

Eleanor began to wail again. 'Not true, not true. I was simply aghast at the amount of money he sent to you both each month and I said so. "How can they possibly spend that kind of money, what are they doing with it?" I said to him.'

'It was only a few hundred pounds each month Eleanor and that had to cover everything.'

'My God! Another lie! How could I have been so duped? Have I got "fool" stamped across my forehead? It was my money, my money he took to give to you.'

'I am sorry Eleanor I don't know what to say. But I have come here to learn about what you said about my mother.'

'Wait here,' she said. 'I found some papers and things only last night.' She left the room and I heard her rummaging in boxes in the next room. She brought back with her an old shoe-box that had been wrapped in brown paper.

'He had kept them hidden. I was looking for evidence you see, about this wretched woman. Here, take this,' she said thrusting the package at me and went to find herself a tissue box.

'They were the reason I came to find you today. They are all about your mother. I think you should see them.'

She placed the tattered old box before me and went to pour water from the kettle over tea bags in delicately pretty china mugs.

All Mother's photographs that had been removed after she had "left" were put together and neatly piled against them were press cuttings.

'Mummy,' I whispered to myself as I stared back at the old memories of her. There were pictures of her with Peggy and me at different times of our infancy and they were happy. One was with our Grandparents at a Christmas party. I was sitting in a high-chair, Peggy next to me with a paper hat on her head looking sweetly at the camera. Mummy was holding a glass of wine up to the photographer. She looked so happy. We all did.

I took the photographs out one by one and held them. Some were in an old tattered envelope with an address on the back I vaguely remembered: Granny's house.

I silently determined to find them again.

I opened the first newspaper clipping.

'Woman Throws Herself from Balcony in front of Her Children and Husband.' There was a picture of a mangled, unidentifiable body lying on the side of a pavement somewhere. The skirt had hitched up indelicately around her panties and the legs lay at distorted angles from one another. A patch of dark blood had etched itself into a pattern around where her head lay twisted grotesquely to one side.

It was someone and no one.

It was my Mother.

Eleanor found it easy to cry. I could not. I was shocked. Horrified. My whole life had been a lie, an equivocation. There was no certainty, only ambiguity with the people I had once trusted completely.

I had always attempted in my childish way to resolve my confusions by becoming an idealist, a wishful thinker, never imagining a darker side to those I loved and trusted. Peggy too had fallen for this trap in showing a strong streak of denial about anything "negative". I suppose it was easier to believe that Mother was somewhere safe writing those short, trivial letters to us, composed by Father.

I remembered how anxious Peggy had become when any questions were asked that would mean she would have to face a memory she chose to forget.

Of course children take sides. They assign all the anxiety-provoking truths to a "bad" parent labelling the other as always "good". And Father had been so good at painting Mother as wicked, what was that he called her? – "Lesbian"? Why? We had no idea what it had meant but it sounded bad enough to go away and leave us on our own while she was away somewhere. These days the word had taken on trivial irrelevance of such little consequence that the accusation made no sense.

What do they term this denial category of behaviour: "a child's coping mechanism.?" The good parent / bad parent solution is then transferred to that cosmic battle between God and Satan. I read that somewhere and even now I don't quite fully comprehend it.

There are those moments when the revelation of a truth strikes like a bolt of lightning, revealing a whole new world of reality. It was this moment that became a turning point in my life.

Those issues that once I had skirted around now took on a significance of greater magnitude. The frailty and brevity of life, its meaning and cosmic significance and the impact of imposed ethics and ideals, they all began to swamp my brain and body as if they had always been there and I had not really looked at them properly before.

They say the truth will set you free.

I began to remember, and I was not free. I was drawn in by the heavy chains of responsibility for knowing the truth.

The story in the paper said she had jumped. I saw her fly. She had not jumped. One of us pushed her. I dare not think who it was.

Eleanor was still crying. She sat at the kitchen table with her nose buried in a piece of kitchen-towel and kept mumbling about how good she had been to Father and how he had abused her generosity and now that she had begun to age she was no longer attractive.

She had certainly grown more matronly since the first time we saw her with Father. She was vivacious then, arrogant and vivacious, and so full of confidence. Her hair was that manufactured colour of corn that had been styled in swathes of well managed curl about a flawless face and her clothes were always immaculate.

She had been outwardly aware only of herself and the impact she was having on our father. If she had truly been happy to embrace his children into her life there was no visible sign of it.

He had brought her to the house one day. It was a day when Francis was away visiting her family, somewhere in the Cotswolds I seem to remember.

She had walked about the house commenting on how drab it all looked and what she was planning to do with a new house she had in mind. We took as little interest in her then, as she did in us. She was simply another of Father's many girl-friends.

I guess most children regard their parent's whims as an occupational hazard that children go through. Father's unswerving whim was that constant need, I came to accept, that all men had for change and variety. One accepts those things of recurring habit in parents as the norm and we had always accepted Father, just as he was – a compulsive profligate. After all he loved us. Had he not fought for us and won?

And there Eleanor was; several years later, several pounds heavier and older and all her hopes and ambitions with this man she had married had come to this devastating moment of solitary exclusion from his life.

'Men are like that,' I offered feebly. Well, that was what Peggy would say.

'Oh no, no they are not,' sobbed the inconsolable Eleanor. 'I left a wonderful husband to go to your wretched Father.'

'More fool you,' I could not help myself saying.

'Yes, you are right.' She submitted to defeat. 'I have been a perfect idiot.'

There was something about the house that I was beginning to find insufferable. It had gripped me like a tight choker about my neck that I was unable to shed. I had a desperate need for fresh air, for release from all those entanglements. Her state of self-pity was exhausting to say the least.

I needed to get out, to go. After all she had accomplished what she had set out to do by presenting me with visible proof of my Mother's horrible death and making Father appear somehow culpable. How much more did she know I wondered? Had she secreted all that information herself for just such a moment as this? He surely would have destroyed old memories, not kept them.

I guessed she had been keeping them secreted for years, for just such a time she had guessed would happen sooner or later. I mean, the woman was no fool.

'Eleanor, the time is getting late. It will be dark soon. I must get back. I have so much to do.'

'No,' she shrieked. 'No, you can't leave me. I won't let you. I have just found you.'

A nauseating thought.

'You have not just found me Eleanor you have known for a long time where I live. You could have come and found me any time you liked. Now, I must go.'

'So this is how you repay me for telling you the truth about you mother. I should have known. You are just like him. My God, you come here, take those ghastly little pictures and now you want to go. I had a feeling you would not stay once you had seen them. I told myself that ages ago.'

'Hardly ages Eleanor, you told me you only found them last night.'

How long, I wondered, had she ferreted away those stolen pictures and all those press cuttings? Of course she kept them for just such an occasion as this. Were they her insurance that he would not leave her?

I was clearly part of some strategy she had to either black-mail him or to punish him for leaving her. She had taken me there quite deliberately to show me the evidence in order to break open a hornet's nest for him. It was obvious she had been fully aware for some time about Father's ruse to keep Mother's horrific death from us. Or was it an "us"? Had Peggy been part of this conspiracy of silence also?

I guess there had always been that nascent certainty that a plague of dangerously incriminating truth lay heaped beneath a posy of invention. Why does one go to such lengths to avoid painful truths when truth is the quest from which the meaning of life springs?

A part of me wished to look no further but now those gnarled and garbled images grew to a pervasive cancer in my mind. I needed answers. All that subterfuge had shaped me into a withdrawn and shrinking image of self-loathing.

Eleanor had gone to phone Father. He must have answered for I could hear her raving about my being there and what I was about to do.

'How will you shut her up now?' she was saying. 'There will be no more money from me to pay her off as I did to your other brat?'

Warning signs were telling me to go and go fast. What she meant by what she was saying and what it was all about, was at that moment beyond my care. I had reached my saturation point for further information.

I took the box of pictures and slid out of a back kitchen door. It was cold out there. I slipped on my coat and walked briskly to a side gate.

Steam from my nose rose into the late afternoon gloom as I ran towards the High Street we had passed through earlier.

Two women were standing at a bus stop chatting. It must mean that a bus would be coming along soon so I waited with them, shifting my feet on the icy pavement. At a distance I saw Eleanor's car stopping at a junction and I swore under my breath. I leapt behind a garden hedge as she drove fast into the road I was waiting in. She shot past and at that moment a bus came from an opposite direction. It did not matter where it was going. I could get off where ever I could find a railway station going to London.

Anywhere, that was away from that wretched house.

Chapter 20

I got back to the nearest tube station to home at 6.30 p.m. It was dark and rush-hour was still disgorging its overload of human freight in and out of stations. People with vacant-eyed focus moved in cycles of direction getting to destinations that would once more identify them as more than fractions of a mass.

I felt apart from them all. An isolation, an island of dissimilarity, though I was yet just another human being getting home. 'Home'; what a comforting sound for a place of strangers whom I had nothing in common with but small conversation.

At the exit of the station I saw someone I recognised standing waiting for someone. He held up a gloved hand and smiled.

'Malachi,' I called in warm surprise. 'What are you doing here?'

'I have come to meet you,' he said, quite simply.

'How on earth did you know I would be here?'

'That foolish Agatha should never have sent you away with that woman. It was not the way to find out.' he said.

'She told you then?'

'I know you had to find out in your own time, but going there was a mistake. Some people when they are hurt want to hurt back at anything or anyone they can find as a target. It makes them dangerous.'

'I could have told you that.' I answered.

'But you did not know it before today,' he said taking my arm and walking with me.

'There is a good pub on our way,' he said. 'I think you could do with a drink.'

The pub was full of strangers looking as if they had all come from another world into that dark cavern entrenched with the musty aroma of old beer kegs and stale tobacco where smoke hung like heavy clouds from the ceiling. For those smoking it was some kind of balm and for those who did not, it clung unsolicited to hair and clothes and mustered around the throat and stung the eyes.

Malachi did not notice, this was a place he was at home in. He bought us sandwiches and what he called "Porter" an import from Ireland no doubt. It was certainly new to me and its taste indifferent to me.

We found a corner to sit and I found myself talking as I never had before; disgorging all those anxieties, suspicions and dread of what I had remembered about my Mother. It was a strange release, a liberating catharsis of all I had bottled up in my life.

We went through the photographs and laughed and I was happy. Perhaps happier than I had realized, for a weight had been lifted.

Such a short time ago this astonishing old man had been a stranger. He had mysteriously stepped into my life as if from nowhere. In some extraordinary way he had released something in me that had burdened my soul and even with the terrible knowledge at my fingertips I felt free and calm, inexplicably so, or was it just his presence there, calming, reassuring, fundamental.

It had gone eleven o'clock by the time we left.

Outside, the cold night air drew me back to that dark world I lived in.

Malachi had said good-night and disappeared into the night at the door. He was living elsewhere I guessed and not with Agatha. Getting back to my room once more, the gravity of everything hit me. I was alone again.

I toyed with playing the violin but the house was so deathly quiet even the sound-proofing might filter sound in that space of quiet.

I woke later in the night from one of those multifarious dreams that make no sense when you wake. My mother and my father and my sister were all jumbled in a scenario that defied reason. I put on the light and lay there propped in bed looking out into the room that encased me. As I gazed beyond that haze of semi thought, scattered objects took form and life. A pile of clothes thrown across a chair, a handbag, its zip opened and the odd items inside spilled to one side, a plastic shopping bag, a heap of paper, a violin case perched against the wall: they all took on strange images, faces, heads, trapped somewhere between where consciousness links with the subconscious.

What if no one was who they said they were and we were all inventions of some greater mind that played havoc with reality?

I lay there, tense and alert; trapped by imagination and the overspill of recent information and event. Then, as dawn crept its light above the window-ledge, I slept.

Chapter 21

Christmas came and went, almost unnoticed that year. I ate turkey with Lillibet and Agatha in Lillibet's flat which we all helped to cook and to wash up afterwards. Lillibet did most all of the talking.

Agatha was her usual sullen self, saying little and hardly daring to express an opinion or to smile less she crack her heavy pancake shell she hid behind. It was an intense kind of connection that I had not expected.

Everyone else seemed to have vanished and I did not ask. I accepted it as it was. And they too did not ask about my stepmother.

Bizarre you might say, but that was how it was.

I spent that interim holiday time between Christmas and New Year in the music room playing for several hours each day, trying to perfect all the flaws in my technique that my music teacher had pointed out.

Just before New Year, even Agatha was gone, leaving only Lillibet and myself alone in the house. There was no sign of Malachi and I guessed he too was away, perhaps to Ireland to visit family. He didn't say.

The evenings were long and bleak after I had exhausted myself with practice.

I went to sit with Lillibet and listen to her chatter. Somehow the comfort of strangers was reassuring to my sense of wellbeing.

There was still no mention about my family and I volunteered none. It was a subject that had been closed so long that it had burrowed profound grooves into my life from which I continued to recoil.

Instead, I was about to learn all about Lillibet.

Lillibet was born somewhere in the West Indies. She was not too sure where, she had never gone back after she left. She had no memory of either parents, only that she was told her father was from Jamaica and her mother from Martinique. She had learnt to speak a style of English mixed with a style of French which was spoken in those parts. A patois known only to themselves.

She had been rejected by her family when she was born for she had been born with a harelip. She was taken care of by an old aunt, of no particular blood relationship, she called "Grandmother", who had loved and cared for her.

Lillibet had learnt early in her life to make fun of herself. She described with amused detail, how her teeth had grown at odd angles and how she had to be fed soft foods because of the shape of her mouth.

Her grandmother would feed her boiled green bananas cooked in an old iron pot balanced over an open fire.

'We was poor, girl, I mean poor. We like beggars. No spoons or forks to eat fancy, we eat from calabash with fingers, like this,' she demonstrated, laughing in her boisterous good-humoured manner.

Lillibet regarded all of life a hilarious joke, fashioned just to tease the unwary and amuse her.

'Only food I knew till I was ten was mashed plantain and salt fish. Then missionaries find me one day, I be hiding in the sugar cane. Those kids in the village liked to chase me and torment me. They call these names: zombie, mojo, orenda, witch, devil, snake-girl and they throw stones at me. They don't understand how it is to be me. I was pretty scared of folks then. I fight back but they too many. Then one day this white boss man come by on his horse, he see the children chasing sometin and he come after them. 'What that hiding in my cane fo' he shouts and I am still like them rats cornered.'

'I'm not surprised and I can't think why they should call you those names.'

'Well girl, that another story. Anyway the white-boss he drag me out by my feet and I am a hollerin and shoutin fit to call that obeah into business. "Why," he says, "It that little kid with the hare-lip I heard about." He take me up onto his horse while I scratchin and screamin and we go to the mission hospital. There he do a lot of talkin to this one and that one and they get Grandma and she come and tell me they are going to take care of me and that strange mouth of mine. Well, I never got to see that ole mouth before, we had no mirrors but when they show me in this big mirror in the hospital I cry till I am sick. I - am – ugly, fit to bust. They keep me and grandma there a few days, talking mostly about what they goin to do with me. They talk a lot about God and Jesus and halleluiah and they mend my crooked mouth. When I come out that hospital my mouth all bandage and much pain they tell me, 'you stay here girl and learn ways of Jesus.' Months and months I stay there and when my mouth heals up and my teeth put right it is like some strange magic because no kid will hurt me no more. Oh they still call me names. You see, Grandma, she is obeah.'

'What's that?' I asked.

'Like you know, black-magic, voodoo, witch-doctor. You look frightened girl. Why that? You know Lillibet your friend and don't harm you.'

'No, I suppose it's like you said about the village children. If you don't understand something, well it's a bit overwhelming when you hear about it first hand. I have no intention of throwing stones at you though.' I said, trying to make a joke of my insecurity or how I should react to her information.

It seemed that Grandma was some kind of spiritualist/clairvoyant. The locals would come and consult her about some relative that had died and Grandma could give them the low-down as to how the relative was faring on the other side and offer any messages that needed passing on.

Grandma had taken on the tiny infant Lillibet, who had been cast out at birth by her parents, with the hope of making a future apprentice - kind of witch of her. I imagine she was chosen simply because her life was cheap and no one else wanted her. And Lillibet was confident that she had more than surpassed Grandma's expectations in that direction.

She talked about her life at the mission school and the kindness of the man who had discovered her hiding in the sugar-cane.

He had taken her under his wing, so to speak, and found her a good pupil, willing to learn.

Lillibet was never reunited with her own family. They had abandoned her when she was tiny and really felt that her survival and cure was attributable only to the old sorceress who by now had a good grip on her soul. "Bad magic" they called it because that was what the church had told them it was.

'Bad things are only that intention to be bad, knowing what you do is wrong, even trying to pretend it not bad. But when intention is good, how can it be called bad tings?' she asked no one in particular.

'How did you happen to come to England?' I asked.

'After Grandmammy she died, the old man told me one day that he was going back to England to his house there and he ask if I like to go with him, maybe do some cooking and cleaning for him when he is there. I say yes, I heard tell of this place England and it sound good. I go and I stay. This house you see, it belong to old man. He was a good man. He goes away long times and he comes back, always comes back here and he brings with him those that need help. Lillibet she know these tings and she set by and she help also.'

'I thought the house belonged to Agatha,' I said.

'Agatha, she one of many the house belong to. That, pretty bad story. I tell you one day. It enough now you just learn about your Mama and tings that need settlin in.'

The "settling in" of unwanted information was something I was reluctant to pursue just then. The empty house, Lorenzo away somewhere, the sense of unknown and uncertainty of the continuity of my life in security was more than I could cope with.

Chapter 22

I woke one morning to see soft flakes of snow float down past my window. Outside a web of white had coated every house and tree and pavements were thick with a grey-white sludge. People battled through in high boots and coats pulled tight, carrying shopping bags with small rations for the opacity of the weather.

I felt marooned standing there looking out from my observation tower.

There is that stressed urgency to break away when one is cut off from an easy access out. But right then, there were few options: the shops to get emergency supplies for Lillibet or a frozen sea of snow in the park which would be full of children throwing snow balls and making snow men.

My mind began a labyrinth journey of all recent events. I began to wonder where Eleanor was now or Father for that matter. There was an ominous silence after the storm of confrontation. Funny, I thought, that she did not pursue me further or try to coax me back that day or since. She seemed to have just given up the chase.

I had not heard from Peggy for quite a while, she said she was going away over the Christmas period with friends. Of course I would hear nothing from Father, especially since he would know by now that I knew the truth, well, as much as Eleanor had surmised.

I would not allow myself to reflect upon the significance of my mother's death. Grief and pain had long since been spent and effectively removed from my sensitivity. Mother was that dream I once had whose shadow had been disconnected from reality, but I was still left with that old curiosity.

I was ready to look again at the photographs and find that address that was printed on the envelope there. There was no name or telephone number that went with the address. My mother's maiden name had been so effectively erased from my memory by a deliberate incommunicado that I was unable to even remember a single letter or syllable of the name.

I stared long and hard at the name of the house and the address as if it would come alive for me. There was a small trace of recognition that seemed familiar but I was not certain. I could have asked Peggy if she would remember if it was our grandparent's address but she would have stalled me. I knew that with certainty.

The yearning to belong somewhere that my mother had been, kept my plans hushed.

I was so undecided and uncertain what to do that I took the box up to Lillibet's flat with me, hoping she would offer some advice.

Her door was open. Voices were coming from the kitchen. I called out but there was no reply. She was talking with Agatha.

Agatha must be back from where ever she was visiting. I called out once more. The conversation sounded intense and Agatha's voice was agitated. I was about to turn round and go back out when Agatha looked up and saw me standing there. She looked startled but Lillibet called after me to come on in and join them for tea.

I noticed at once that despite Agatha's brightly veneered face, the make-up was unable to disguise a blue-black bruise on her swollen left cheek and eye which was severely blood-shot and almost closed up. She was as usual wearing her white silk gloves, at least one camouflage properly accomplished.

It was difficult not to mention the evident injury but it remained unvoiced lest it embarrass her.

In trying to disregard the damaged eye, I forgot my own inner conflict and spoke with a defiant bravado about the pictures.

They both poured over the pictures, glancing up at each other as if to exchange some secret knowledge they had and I was beginning to feel distinctly uncomfortable.

'I wondered if the address on the back of this envelope was my grandparents,' I began. 'I'm not sure if they would like to meet with me, that is, if it is their address and if, of course, they are still there.'

'Of course it is,' said Agatha almost impatiently. 'They will be expecting you.'

'How could you possibly know that?' I asked, not a little irritated, remembering the bad advice to go at once with my deranged stepmother.

'It is always a good thing to find out the truth,' she answered defiantly.

It brought to mind my curiosity about her black-eye but thought that that sordid truth was a "good thing" I could do well without knowing.

Chapter 23

Over sleep and time there is a forgetting. Way beneath the layers of fresh experience, residual memories remain dormant, emerging sometimes in a dream unembellished by words. Then one day some small cue evokes reminiscence.

My thoughts had been fed by imagination, distorting fact and nullifying the actual tangible truth. I needed clarity. I needed to find answers.

I was determined to go to the address on the envelope and find my grandparents.

The very first day I had off work, I took a train and a couple of buses out of town to the small village of Selborne in Hampshire. It was a long journey for an unknown destination and an unknown reception if it was the right one.

I got off the bus in the middle of the village and walked. The house was part of a group of old houses on the edge of a wooded common, where the gentle ridges of downland lead to Chawton. I remembered from somewhere that this was where Jane Austin had lived. The very address in itself offered something faded and romantic that I longed for.

The house was set back from the road behind a tall privet hedge. A narrow, pebbled entrance centred round a circle flower bed. The garden was in its winter-worn phase of emptiness. Bare flower beds were raked and ready for spring flowering and bare branched shrubs were scattered at intervals of barrenness.

My heart quickened as I approached the front door. I felt that somewhere in a distant dream I had been here before, played here and been happy here.

I stopped, uncertain what to do.

Should I simply ask who lived here to try and recognise a name?

Would they announce themselves right away?

Should I say outright that I was looking for family but family whose name I could not remember? How odd would that sound? My courage waned. I turned; my nerves suddenly defeated.

I was ready to walk back down the drive when a woman poked a head out of a window and asked if I was lost.

'Yes, I am,' I replied. 'I was looking for people who lived here once, but I am not sure if they are still here.'

'Who would that be?'

'My grandparents, but I don't remember the surname.'

The woman opened the front door and came out cautiously, inclining her head towards me.

'My God, you look just like her. Father, it's one of Felicity's girls. I'm sure of it. The youngest, had that red hair, remember?' she called to someone over her shoulder. 'You must be - are you Anna Catherine?'

'Yes,' I said, 'Yes, I am.'

'Do you remember who I am?' she asked.

'I think I do. I kind of recognise you. I have forgotten so much. That's why I am here. I want to remember,' I heard myself saying in a weak voice.

'I am your Aunt Sophie, your mother's sister. You were about three or four when I last saw you,' she said, looking hard at me as if to discover more about my motives for coming unannounced and with so futile a reason.

'You must come in out of this cold and see your Grandparents, perhaps you will remember them,' she suggested.

My entire memory seemed misplaced, wiped out even. After all, they came from a time for me, when sentences and words summarizing impressions and images had not yet been properly formed by verbal description. Now I was trying to put language to those concepts.

It was difficult to estimate Sophie's age. I could only describe her on this first impression as round. It was that kind of "plumpness" that irons out wrinkles for age definition.

She was round in every aspect. She smiled through round pink cheeks set in a round head, set upon a round body, hugged closely by a thick, navy, polar-neck sweater with navy trousers that seemed glued to her large legs. Her hair was like Mother's, but there the similarity ended. Like most large people she was charming and cheerful.

We entered a draft-excluding anti-room where I was freed of my coat and damp shoes before proceeding to a room whose temperature was stiflingly tropical and stuffy. Two large reclining chairs were occupied by an elderly couple whose faces touched that edge of distant, unspoken memory.

Sophie kept up a chatter about my Mother, their childhood and how everyone had lost touch, and the pity of it.

I was now to expect the delight of grandparents.

I did not, however, find a single trace of delight in either of the two who sat, unmoved and unmoving, watching and mute.

'Mummy, Daddy,' Sophie announced, addressing the pair as if childhood was only a small breath away.

'Look who is here, it's Anna Catherine; Felicity's youngest.'

Neither said a word.   The revelation of who I was fell on deaf ears.

The old man rose from his chair and walked unsteadily towards me as if to scrutinise more closely the evidence that had been presented. He was still tall, though bent from age. His white hair fell in an untidy mop about his ears and his steel grey eyes peered at me through thick lenses.

'Got my hair,' he observed.   Then with a slow and deliberate appraisal of me he said: 'Why now?   Why have you come only now?'

'I have only recently found your address. I thought Mummy was still alive... I have only just heard that...'

'Stuff and nonsense,' he bellowed back. 'It was your choice to stay away from us. You all caused her suicide.'

'I was four when she went away from us,' I said. 'No one told me. Father said she had left us for, for ...' I could not bring myself to complete the sentence, so much was blurred memory, so much was piecing together what I had been told.

I was at once, incensed, offended and emotional.

It was as if the intervening time had been hanging suspended by a duration of speculation and release. There was, in that moment, an intense consciousness of something. It was as if some unseen presence that I could neither touch nor feel but I knew with certainty was there, was prompting me. I felt strangely liberated.

Something snapped inside me.   I knew I must not run, as I would have done previously. I must stand my ground and answer for myself, regardless of rebuke.

'We never talked, Peggy and me.   We never spoke about her. Peggy would not allow it.'

'What about that Father of yours?'

'He was never around.   Peggy and I have lived alone together most of our lives. Our Stepmother did not like children'.

'Ha, serves you right, little beggars. That farcical custody battle. They said you both wanted to stay with him. He took you away from her. No one fought to go back.
My God, she was devastated!' he interrupted.

'That's enough! Quite enough Gerald; who knows what those children have been told, who knows the truth, the whole truth of what happened?'

'Yes Daddy, you have said enough, you can see she has no idea what you are talking about,' fat Sophie shouted back.

An electrified suspense deferred the next onslaught as each one gathered momentum for amassed thought.

I did not to wait for further attack to explain myself.

'I only recently came into possession of a box of photographs of Mother and some rather horrible press-cuttings. Up until then I was led to believe she was still alive and not wanting to see us for some reason of her own. Your address was on an old envelope with Christmas photos inside.   There was no name, and I did not remember one. I wanted to find you to know what happened... Well,' I paused, while they stared back at me, absorbing disbelievingly what I had said.

'It was nice meeting you.   About time I left. I see that I am not welcome. I see that my father at least did not lie in telling us you wanted nothing to do with us. The lie that my Mother was still alive I imagine was to protect us from her suicide.'

My throat had grown a knot that demanded tears for its release. I would not cry in front of the old monster.   Not if I could help it.   I made for the front door, grabbed at shoes and coat and let myself out as hastily as I could.

It was the old woman, my Grandmother, who came after me.

'Please, please don't go Anna Catherine. I have prayed for the day I would see you girls once more.'

She was standing in the cold, holding the door open while I struggled with shoes and coat. I looked up and saw the glisten of tears in her eyes.

She was small and frail.   Her thin, silver hair wore that commissioned perm of her age but she was still pretty beneath the waning of time.   She was not dressed for outdoor cold and I saw her shiver.

'Come back, come into the kitchen, your Grandfather will not follow us there. You see we were told so many things by witnesses who professed to have seen what happened.   You can't believe it all, but you can't help being affected by what you hear.'

I turned back inside, but this time I did not remove my damp boots or my coat lest I found a need for further quick exit.

Aunt Sophie was standing behind her, putting a shawl round her old, bent shoulders.   She gave me a warm smile and led the way to the kitchen where a large old kitchen range was burning mildewed smelling anthracite.

She filled a kettle while my Grandmother found me a seat at a round kitchen table. Things here were neatly arranged for the ease of ordered living. A starched, blue-checked cloth prepared the table for cups and saucers to be laid upon it at a moment's notice and this was one of those moments.   I was less prepared and wishing desperately that I had not come.

'I'm not much good with people,' I began. 'Peggy and I – well, we have lived alone for so long, I don't know quite how to react when someone is cross like that. I just don't remember what it was we did wrong. We never talked about it you see. Well, Peggy would not allow me to talk about it. I did ask. I was always asking when Mother would write to us again. It made her angry you see.'

'What about Julian? Did he ever tell you anything?' Aunt Sophie asked while she was arranging tea for us on the table.

'He told us that Mother had gone off to be with some woman.' I began.

'More, the other way round,' interrupted Sophie.

'He told us that since Mother had become Lesbian she would have no time for us.' I persisted in that track, more to see what reaction the truth of it might bring.

'We had no idea what the word or implication of it meant. We thought it was some kind of illness.'

No one spoke, nor contradicted. I took a deep breath and continued. 'Father would read us letters from her from time to time. We were not allowed to keep the
letters for ourselves or even read them. He read them to us; nothing very informative, just that she was working abroad and had no time to visit us, that sort of thing. There were no terms of endearment which you would expect from her, just factual letters. Then they stopped by the time I was about eight. When I asked him if she was going to write any more, or if he had an address for her, he told me she had moved and no one knew where she was. Why should I not believe him?'

'But surely, you saw her die,' my aunt interjected.

'I must have done. That is what the papers reported. I have forgotten. Only now, I have vague recollections of what happened. For years I have had these terrible nightmares. Sometimes she is fly, you know, actually flying in the air with her arms out in the wind. Sometimes I dream she is lying on a pavement with blood all round her. Peggy said it was just a bad dream. I think Peggy wanted to believe that as much as I suppose I did.'

I looked up at the old woman as if to find an immediate answer there.

'Is that why Grandfather is so cross?'

'Yes, but there is much more to it than that. But why did you not phone us, come and see us?' Grandmother asked.

'I had only just turned five when Mother left – died I suppose – at that age you do and believe what those in authority tell you to do. Peggy once asked if we could see you. It made Father angry. He told us that you were interfering and would take us away from him.'

'How could you believe that, you must have both known we loved you?'

'I don't know, there was so much confusion at that time. I have no idea what was going on with him then. I remember we moved around quite a lot at first till we found a place with one of his girl-friends who minded us for him while he was away working.'

'But his work did not take him away,' answered Sophie.

'I don't know. I don't know. I am finding it all so hard to come to terms with. All the lies. All the secrecy. Peggy has always been around for me. Protecting me, reassuring me and if it was fine by Peggy, it was fine by me. She has gone to Canada to work now. She hardly ever comes back even to visit. If she is here on business I wouldn't know. She has cut herself off like he did. Like Mother did.'

I took a breath that hiccupped in my chest as a volume of pain and uncertainty welled like a flood bank in me. I had not come to be interrogated and the pressure was building up.

A voice from the door said, 'Witnesses told us that one of you children pushed her. What do you say to that?'

'Go away Gerald, can't you see she is upset? She was not quite five when it happened, how will she remember?'

'I remember what happened when I was five. Sent to boarding school. I remember every blasted moment of it.'

'You remember it because you have talked about it repeatedly over the years, refreshing your memory of it each time it was repeated.'

'I want to know which of the little blighters pushed her.'

'Go away Gerald. We will know in good time but perhaps not now. The most important thing to know is why.'

'She wasted her life on that blighter,' the old man persisted. 'I said so at the time, no one would listen. She should have gone on with her music. She gave up a brilliant career just to marry him.'

'I have her violin,' I said. 'She had begun to teach me before she...'

'And you expect us to believe you forgot the rest of it.' He glowered back.

'I don't expect you to do anything. I wanted to know more about her. I want to remember and yet I am also afraid of remembering. It was a dark time. That is all I know. You seem to have all the answers. You seem to know much more than I do. My mind is a blank of that time but it has done something terrible to all of us and especially to my sister. I, I just feel it inside me.'

No one spoke. I was shaking with the passion of speaking out, of reaching for the darkness. I was unused to giving long speeches. For the first time in my life I had confronted someone about that time. Perhaps the old man's anger had provoked a resentment I did not know was there.

My grandmother got up, ushered the old man out and came back in.

'Seeing you has brought back a terribly sad time for us,' she said. 'Forgive him. He just doesn't know himself sometimes. Ever since that time...'

'Where are you living now?' my Aunt interrupted. 'Perhaps we can come and see you when Daddy has calmed down a bit.'

'I am living in a part of Notting Hill in London. Number sixty three MacDonald Road,' I added.

Both Aunt and Grandmother stopped and stared at one another.

'That was where she went when she was...'

'There must be some mistake,' I said at once. 'The people who live there see no one and they have been there for many years.'

'There was some old Jamaican woman. I think she called her something like "Lilly". She was a clairvoyant and told fortunes. Felicity heard about her from a friend. She was desperately unhappy at the time and she went to see her.'

'Oh my God, no wonder they knew so much about me. But how would they know...?'

My mind went into a whirl of speculation. The information that my Mother had had connections with the house I was living in and the people in it caught me off guard. It exposed those carefully restrained tears that had been building up since I had arrived. Now they broke their bank and flowed in a wild release of everything I had bottled up in years.

'I need to go,' I sobbed. 'I need...'

I stood up and went towards the door as the old man returned with more to add to what he had not said before. They had deduced an entirely prescribed scenario from past hearsay and the prefiguring of random witnesses and held us responsible with the result.

Grandmother was busy admonishing the old man and everyone was talking at once. I needed to get out, become free, to release myself from all the confusion. I had overturned a hornet's nest and was suddenly suffused with an overpowering sensation of panic.

The over-warm kitchen, faces staring, confronting and accusing, an angry family needing explanations, when I had come to them for one. It was in that momentary flash of anguish that my nightmare surfaced before me. Darkness eclipsed the room like a gloomy shadow as grief and despair exploded like a hand-grenade in my chest.

I had started out that day so positive that I was getting somewhere with all my blurred past and origins. Now that composure had vaporized into thin air. A fluttering of distant thoughts reached through to me. Kaleidoscope shapes and images and voices crossed and exchanged before me. I felt the raw longing to reach back and touch the past and change it.

I tried to sort out the voices and scenes as they flitted through my mind like paper caught up in wind, elusively moving away as I tried to snatch at it. Voices came as if from a tunnelled distance summoning me to look. Like a mirage they stayed for a moment then they were gone. I saw my Mother. She was standing, pressed up to the ledge where Father had pushed her. Her face was white with an expression of pain and fear. I saw my sister next to her. She was in a state of visible conflict. I heard my father's voice, insistent, sneering, goading. What I heard were words, mere words that come and go in a child's mind. They came to me as meaningless phrases meant for adults only to understand

My sister's voice: 'Don't fall Mummy. Please don't fall.'

Father's voice: 'Let her go if that is what she wants. Go on Peggy love, give your Mother a hand at what she wants. See how she wants to fly over the edge. Don't you dear?'

Mummy's voice: 'Give me back my children. I want my babies. I can't live without them Julian, please.'

We are screaming, Peggy is holding on to Mummy's hand. Mummy is balancing on the window ledge where Father has pushed her.

Father: 'Jump, because you can't have them. Just one push Peggy and your mother will be happy and think how happy we will be together Peggy love. Let her go Pegs and she can't interfere with us any more, then you can have everything I promised you.'

Peggy stops screaming, she looks back at Father. There is something between them. I have seen it before. She lets go of Mummy's hand and she calls me to come closer. As I rush toward Mummy Peggy shoots her leg out before my feet. Her action is so slight, so quick you would not notice if you were not looking out for it. I tumble forward, grasping at Mummy to break my fall go and push her off balance. All at once everyone is shouting, screaming, crying.

'Watch her fly girls, watch her fly.'

We are now both shrieking hysterically. Peggy realizes what she has done and she has become quite crazed. She did not mean it, she keeps saying.

I snapped back to the over-warmed room again, feeling hot and confused. My face scorched with uncontrollable sobs. I tried to explain what my mind had remembered and as I spoke it all felt so unreal. I omitted to tell them that I had been tripped deliberately nor did I give the words of conversation that had been etched there in my mind. I simply told them Mother had been so sick all morning with terrible stomach cramps and she had been standing at the window when I tripped and fell, overbalancing her.

'It was all my fault. I pushed her. I didn't mean to.'

Now my grandmother is holding me tight.

'It was not your fault Anna. Not your fault. Your mother was such an unhappy girl towards the end. She did not know what she was doing.'

'But she did not want to jump. She was feeling very sick that morning, she said she didn't know what was wrong with her and she was only trying to get his attention, just as Eleanor and Francis did in their own way.'

'It was what the fortune-teller told her,' Aunt Sophie said.

'What? What was that?' I asked.

'She said that Felicity would lose her children unless she did something to get them back. She told her that she was in terrible danger.'

I groaned inside. Was that all that precipitated so much.

Aunt Sophie offered to drive me back but I declined the offer. I said that I needed the journey back on my own, to think. I needed to space all those jagged edges in line to make sense of it all.

The buses were slow and the wait for the bus changes was long. The icy pavements bit into the soles of my boots and I felt that raw cold enter every fibre of my body.

I had been cut adrift from this family and now I had reunited with them but it was not the reunion that I had hoped for. I could not feel that sense of "bonding" that is expected of family ties, or so I had thought.

Father and Peggy had shared that intimate kind of filial link. I did not belong to their secret code. They always talked alone, excluding me. I was the baby the other side of the closed doors. People don't talk in front of babies.

I learned piece by piece that baby was my role: a separate thing. I was unconnected by age and who I was. I was fed information as it was required and I accepted it as bona fide.

We had lived an unnatural life, carefully steered beyond the eye of Social Services: unobserved, unnoticed and unwanted; never drawing attention to ourselves. It was a life above suspicion of fault yet always touching on the boundaries of dysfunction. A breeding ground for defect.

No one could condemn our surroundings nor our lack of supervision, for someone was always calling. The callers were Peggy's older friends.

Peggy always passed as a lot older than her age by the way she dressed and made herself up and by the people she mixed with. She got into pubs and drank alcohol, unquestioned, long before she was legally allowed to. She even managed to drive a car, illegally of course, way before she qualified for it.

Father left an old car left with us. He taught her to drive out on a farm tack nearby when she was thirteen.

'If you are careful enough,' he said, 'no one will check you out.'

They would be gone for hours while I stayed home playing the piano.

The time was never measured. We simply did our own thing and got lost there. That was how it seemed anyway. I was always happy to be left alone to play uninterrupted.

Now I was just beginning to surmise things and surmising so often becomes lost in a warren of blind paths.

I stamped my feet to keep them from freezing solid.

Frozen air wrapped around me like a shroud for my dead past, offering no comfort. My frosted breath steamed out shades of old ghosts that swirled about my head. Easy to get lost in hallucination.

Early winter darkness came down like the wings of a bat and settled into the afternoon, clawing its way into my already darkened mind. I stared out of a lit bus into black oblivion outside and my sad reflection looked back.

I was tired. So tired.

I got back to accustomed ground, not wanting to be seen by anyone, not even Malachi. This was something I had to face alone.

I slipped the key into my door and turned on a light. The comfort of familiar surroundings relaxed me but that sting of loneliness that had burrowed so deep into my life prickled the air and tainted the empty spaces.

Chapter 24

Why do we put such emotional store by blood ties, genetic links and all that goes with it? We seek out those similarities that bind us: grandma's hair – father's eyes - a sibling's crooked teeth as if they matter. Scientists base premises upon things of substance, but they are merely substance without shadow.

Filial responses to biological stuff are all about identification. The desire for a lineage of perfection is something to feed an ego upon. But those connections are upended when minds don't meet and hearts beat different tempos.

It is assumed that the child of a thief is expected to become a thief as the child of a mathematician is expected to become a mathematician and the child of a musician must be musical. But what if we come from a source which is light years apart from each other? What if we are individuals linked by some other distant past and our blood ties are merely incidental?

Of course family matter - up to a point, but there is that generation divide that makes us different people anyway.

As I came to know my grandparents from trying to establish lost roots I realized that, what separated us was not just propinquity but the experiencing of time together. Even my Aunt sat before layers of dividing events which were another life, her life and a life without my knowledge or her knowledge of mine. We were in essence, strangers; so that when she talked to me it was with the forced intimacy of known family ties and not genuine camaraderie.

The grandparents came from that wartime era with its own nomenclature of speech and address and customary respect for rank and order.

Grandfather's claim to glory lay in the war as a fighter pilot. His fears had been spent on old battles and his shame lay in that he had survived when friends and comrades had perished.

As we speak of pixels, air bands, broadband, microchips, satellite navigation systems, they spoke of ration books and shortages, the pitch of overhead aeroplanes and bombed sites. Grandfather could talk at length about his experiences and knowledge of Lancasters, Wellingtons, Halifaxes, Messerschmits and Spitfires. Grandmother spoke mostly about her children and wartime scarcities for them.

As my generation would rush through a day of snacked breakfast and lunch and TV dinners, they divided their day with punctually ordered repast from early morning tea, breakfast, elevenses, lunch, afternoon tea, drink time to supper or dinner. Together they lived as if time had merely slipped its course and it was their duty to uphold old values and put them back on track.

I had never expected a great connection with them. Or perhaps I did, if I am honest. I don't know what I expected really. But our relationship had been tainted by an ugly past and it would never reach the warmth of the real strangers at No. 63 MacDonald Road.

It was at most, an uncomfortable liaison with little joy but a necessary link to help me understand a time that I had been forced to forget and needed so desperately to reawaken for some deep inner reason that I had not yet come to know.

I locked myself away after that first confrontational visit.

My emotions remained raw and new. I even avoided Lillibet. I had no inclination to reopen the nightmares.

I went to the music room and locked myself in there for hours at an end, playing with an intensity that drove me on relentlessly, almost challengingly aggressive. If the mad Reverend should call again unannounced I would be ready for him. I would fight back. I did not care.

My next music lesson was anticipated with a mixture of apprehension and anxiety. I had done little else but practise since my teacher had been away, but I longed for his appearance with a kind of hunger.

He was late. I stopped in the middle of the piece I was playing when I heard the door open. He looked pale and tired. A couple of deep bruises on his face suggested some battle he had been in over his festive or not so festive season.

'Hello Lorenzo,' I said quietly. 'I missed you.'

'Anna,' he returned. 'You did?' He seemed momentarily off guard, confused by this admission. It was as if I had overstepped the mark of familiarity as pupil. However, my courage had been nurtured by recent family confrontations and I continued.

'Did you have a nice Christmas with your family?'

'In parts, yes. What did you do?'

'I spent most of Christmas with Lillibet. Agatha too on Christmas day, then she went away for New Year. Then a few days ago I met my grandparents.'

'Your Grandparents?'

His short responses were suffixed with an element of doubt.

'Yes,' I continued, not to be forestalled by his brevity of conversation, not now.

'I last saw them when I was four. I needed to know something about my mother. It seems she has been dead all this time and I have been led to believe she was alive and just avoiding us.'

'Parents are that uncontrolled lottery element in life, without which we would not have life and whose influence can make or break us.'

He did not look at me while he spoke, unpacking sheets of music and laying them down on the table. It was as if he was speaking words he had read somewhere, they were detached and distant, as if he did not really want to go there. That was something I understood.

The music he brought with him was something he bought over Christmas, he said. He would like me to play it with him.

Was it a gift, I wondered? If so, it was not given as such, but I was touched at his thought and his choice. It was Tchaikovsky's violin concerto in D minor op. 35. It is a beautiful piece of music. I knew it reasonably well but I had never played it. He thought it a good test for sight reading.

Lorenzo played the music through first.

There was that inexpressible core about his playing that stirred my very being while listening to him. It was as if some part of his soul lay in that piece of music - as if he was ridding himself of some deep and inexplicable pain that the composer had experienced and wrote of himself.

I felt those overwhelming tears burn shadows to my eyes and sear my soul. Lorenzo was as unable to express himself to me, as I was to him but his playing tore me apart with its beauty. When he came to the end he saw that I was crying and we both stayed silent for a while, enclosed in our own individual worlds that blended in essence but did not touch.

I staggered through the piece, far too restrained and emotionally caught up to repeat anywhere close, the performance I had just listened to. I stopped half way to excuse myself.

'No, no, keep playing,' he said almost sternly. 'You have a gift Anna and you need only to practise to get all the music you can into your mind and your heart. You need now also to start on a second instrument. They will need that when you go for an audition.'

'I am not good enough,' I began. 'I play because I want to. The violin I play with is not even mine. It belongs, it belonged to my mother, you see...'

'I am beginning to see many things Anna and one is that you must go on. You can even apply for a scholarship. I have the contacts. I can see you practise but there is so much more work to be done.'

So the music lessons continued, along with discussions over which second instrument I should commence with. I had played Mother's piano till it was taken away but I had not progressed beyond grade III so I felt justified in trying another instrument altogether.

I noticed that Lorenzo played the flute and we thought to begin with that. I had to first save up to buy one and my salary was not large. I would not dream of asking Father to help. Since I had started work his allowance had ended and so had all contact since my visit to Eleanor.

I wished that I could have spoken to him, just once, to ask what had gone wrong and why he had felt it necessary to lie about Mother's death. I supposed it was something private between them which I would never know. I could only stab at guesses as time went on.

Of course Mother had not really wanted to jump off that ledge and perhaps it was only out of the heat of the moment that Father had driven her there. Knowing him now, I think he was the one who really wanted to escape - the one who was seeking to escape everyone. And so all those skeletons remained undisclosed their cupboard.

A funny term that: "skeletons in cupboards" with so varied an implication. That was something I was yet to find out.

Chapter 25

I became used to the presence of someone always hanging about the landing when I got home, as if lying in wait for me. Sometimes in the hall or sometimes just outside the front door. If it wasn't Agatha, it was Miss Constantine ready with her sarcasm and bad language, sometimes it was someone I had not seen before but did not wish to become acquainted with and on some occasions it was old Gregory, lurking furtively about as if not wanting to be seen.

I had become accustomed to him now, as he was with me.

Sadly it was seldom Malachi. We would go out when we met for a stroll or coffee and we would talk.

I longed to speak with him. Yet often I was rent in two by his talk-energy. I would question and was enthralled by his answers and later when I re-examined what he had said I was tantalized by his narrative. I could be caught up in an explosion of speculation to be dropped back to earth bewildered and empty and uncertain still as to where reality lay.

Then there was dear old Lillibet. I was always pleased to see her.

She stopped me crossing the stairs one afternoon. I think she had been lying in wait for me.

'Why you not come an visit your ole Lillibet no more?'

I was flustered. I did not know how to answer her. I was simply not ready for confrontations or cross examinations and I knew there was so much unsaid about her knowledge about my Mother. In a way, I simply did not want to know. Perhaps it was because I was still not ready to know.

'I have just been so busy lately,' I said.

'Too busy to eat I see. You gettin real thin girl. Now you come up and have someting with Lillibet when you take your break. Lillibet cook you someting good you hear.'

In recognition of her kindnesses to me I thanked her and half-heartedly agreed a time, then promptly regretted my weakness as soon as she had moved on.

At the appointed time, I distractedly looked at my watch and put down my violin. This would have to be quick.

I would tell her, 'this will have to be quick Lillibet, I have still four hours of practise to do.'

I heard her singing happily in the kitchen when I got there. She was making some Jamaican curry that she told me no one could equal. She gave me spoons and forks to take through to the table that shared dining/living room space.

I must have bypassed him when I came in. He was sitting in a chair in semi-darkness. I had not seen him. Then from the corner of my eye the semblance of a shadow etched itself into my line of vision and became substance.

His clerical collar was twisted and his jacket looked unwashed and crumpled as if broken by the hardships of life. He looked past me, not noticing my presence, or disregarding it.

My first instinct was alarm, then on reflection I was filled with irritation that I had not been forewarned.

'Lillibet,' I called out. 'You have a guest. You did not say.'

She came into the room carrying a large earthenware pot which she set onto the table with a noisy thud.

'Oh that ole Gregory. He won't do you no harm. He take his pills now. Lillibet see to that.'

Indeed 'ole Gregory' was looking like someone on heroin with ADHD, not a flicker of aggression about him, but I noticed with alarm that his eye was wearing the same purple badge of a good fight that Agatha had. Same eye too, I mused. I dare not ask if they had been in combat with one another but all the same it must have been one good fight!

I wanted to leave but it would have been seen as churlish. I decided to avoid all eye contact, (sounding the pun) as one would a dangerous dog that only the owners loved.

The meal was eaten in silence by the old cleric and with enthusiastic chatter from our hostess. Subject matter never counted for much with Lillibet, she talked about everything and nothing but she did not mention my family or ask if I had been successful in finding my grandparents.

Suddenly, out of the unremitting chatter, Gregory looked up at me and said, 'I hear you play sometimes.' His voice had taken on a different, placid timbre. His face was kind and tender yet more intense. It was as if he had become someone else.

His interruption silenced Lillibet, who looked at her guest, waiting for more to be added to his speech but it had come to a halt and he continued to stare ahead.

'I hope I do not make too much sound beyond the walls and disturb you.'

'No, I stand right outside the door and listen. I played once before my hand was injured. You are good, very good.'

'Like her Mama,' Lillibet added.

For a moment I did not know how to respond. I just stared at her. I had the urge to ask her to tell me more. I was ready to hear more but not in front of this awesome man whose manner changed with the wind. I was on tenterhooks with him there, remembering the last time and the evidence of recent battle upon his face.

At last, I felt I could not hold the question any longer. I turned to Lillibet and said, 'I have heard that you have met my Mother.'

'I know your Mama well,' she answered referring to the present.

'You can't "know" her Lillibet, she is dead. I know it now.'

This was some kind of cue for the old cleric to begin another character transformation. He stood up on arthritic legs, expanded himself to the size of someone put out to battle and hurled forth his sermon. His harsh voice returned along with the roughness of his expression

'A sorcerer and a false prophet.' He stormed.

'Now you just sit back on down. No more of that you hear,' Lillibet retaliated but the old man was determined not to be quelled. The old harsh voice he had before took on the resonating sonorous tone of an old style pulpit lecture; 'Watch out for false prophets they come to you in sheep's clothing, but inwardly they are ravening wolves.'

'Now you know Lillibet's no ole sheep and you in't no one can quote from that book; besides they be that bit 'bout that Pharaoh who summoned his sorcerers and magicians.'

Dear God, I thought, here it goes again. I should have known sanity would not prevail.

There was madness in the old man's eyes.

What title had he been given - "Reverend"?

There was little reverence in the fixed and beaded eye as he continued with quavering voice in full gale-force: 'Ye shall know them by their fruits. Do men gather grapes of thorns, or figs of thistles...'

Banter continued between them like dialogue from a badly written farce, with much rehearsal between them. It was as if he were acting out the role of a distant past when preaching the fear of God was a cleric's directive to keep his flock compliant to the "word"; with the quotations and incantations of a charismatic evangelist.

'Enough!' commanded his hostess at last. 'Now you git out ole Gregory and we be havin Mr. Peaceful back agin.'

There was a kind of established rapport between them that was time evolved where Lillibet's authority and command had the greater influence. I could see that there was a great fondness she had for him, much as she had shown to Agatha and the cantankerous old Miss Constantine. For the moment she yelled out, he sat down and became cowed, a separate and essentially different person. He bore a deadly resignation about him as if he were isolated from all surrounding life, not muttering a single further word. He looked at no one. Now and then he gave a scornful laugh of contempt to show that he had no wish for contact from the world around him.

'Now, that right. Don't know which one you is right now but you stay this way you hear, or you go back downstairs.'

I could not presume to know the intimate workings of either minds or meaning, or guess what this was all about but I was reluctant just then to remain any longer.

I made my excuses about practising and left.

The music room was like an oasis in a world of confusion. Its devised encasement of sound, turned outside movement into a hush.

As always, I was left with the aftertaste of bewilderment about the strange and complicated people whose house I shared and once more I cast myself into the abstract depths of music.

Chapter 26

Having opened the door into family life I was soon absorbed into its every implication. I revisited there when things calmed down but no one mentioned Mother any more. It took time and observation to learn the family's preferences and weaknesses, their individual expressions of taste, likes and dislikes and opinions. Opinions of course, counted for a lot. Grandmother expressed hers often with cool but decided forcefulness. My Aunt's opinions were thrown out in frank, outspoken candour. Grandfather's opinions were delivered with intense passion and I was soon to learn that he had opinions about everything.

I wondered where my Mother had fitted in. I had never got to know her. I could only glean that little bit of opinion from her family to realize that she was one of those throw-backs that, not following family tendencies towards a more academic leaning, had been the family musician and was thus seen as an oddity.

I was still clinging to a past which involved the security and the protection of my sister and I was still a stranger to those people called family. I wanted to write to Peggy and tell her that I had met them but Peggy was distancing herself ever more widely and her email contacts had become mere shortened phrases of where she was going and the people she had met.

Her new life had swallowed her up and amputated her past. My own messages to her were as brief. How could I explain the eccentricities and oddities of the people I was – if only vaguely – in touch with? How could I tell her that our Stepmother had revealed the truth that she and Father had so cleverly contrived to hide from me? How could I tell her that I had met the grandparents who had condemned us both for our mother's death?

After the emotionally turbulent first meeting I had with them, I had decided emphatically that associations with relatives was something strictly relegated to the past and had no place in my already complex existence. It was Aunt Sophie's cheerful overriding persistence that made me succumb to a meeting with her; after all, she had shown the most kindness to me.

We had agreed to meet somewhere on mutual territory in London. It was a meeting, contrived to bridge that eclectic disparity of soul and mind and distance for the sake of family ties that are meant to bind

There are a million well-known places to meet up in London. Aunt Sophie picked the obvious one, Trafalgar Square: open, busy, noisy and anonymously full of diverse and assorted lacklustre and jaded life.

There is a kind of frantic feeling about meeting someone you don't know well in a crowded place where worlds meet worlds. This famous landmark never slept. Nelson on his plinth, guarded by four great lions amid splashing fountains stands sentinel to eternally moving pedestrians. Red busses and black taxis impatiently vie for space on an overcrowded road which snakes from blind alleys and crosses and is crossed by others, to be held up for anxious moments by traffic lights. There is a constant cacophony of noise and pressure to keep moving on to somewhere else more important. Aggression and irritation of the locals spill over with fixed stares at the foreigners who want to be dazzled and identify with the famous and the feral atmosphere.

At best I like to feel anonymous in uncluttered and less defining spaces. I did not look forward to the venue or the meeting. I felt confused, anonymous and out of sorts, unsure if I would be identified and rather hoping I would not. Even the pigeons had that frantic look about them expectantly waiting to be fed as they strutted about in random circuits, then flying off in unison, circling the air, waiting to swoop down once more where food might be offered.

There was a tap on my shoulder and my aunt was standing there, wrapped in a large brown coat with fake fur framing her plump red cheeks.

'Anna Catherine,' she cried out as if I had just been found in dense woods. Well, it might well have been a dense wood that she should find me there: more like the proverbial needle in a haystack.

She embraced me warmly and flourished a hand around the scene before her; 'Wonderful, isn't it?'

What could I say: never wonderful - awesome perhaps? I could only nod and wonder where and what next. Infinite choices: portrait gallery, interesting shops, St Martins National Gallery, busy roads, museums or perhaps choice of coffee shops spilling customers onto cold pavements, queues of people standing waiting to be seated.

What about the park......?

I had heard about the famous St James' park but had never been there.

On a cold day late in January when pavements are hard with invisible ice and a wind blows round every tree and building, gathering momentum to swirl and catch every piece of flesh, entering any chink in the armour of clothing, nothing too much is over exciting. Cold-silenced ducks finding shelter on frozen banks come to life for any scraps of food that people bring them. They are the focus of attraction and the point of conversation.

We found somewhere to go and sit and order hot coffee, a far better choice than overfull cafes and pubs redolent of stale beer and cigarettes. Though I think Aunt Sophie would have preferred a pub, she gracefully succumbed to the expression on my face.

I have always felt intimidated by London pubs with their medieval gothic gloom and the masses that gather there, morphing into emulated murkiness with sycophantic tourists marvelling at the sustained antiquity. But not for me, that cramped and crowded claustrophobia with the world crammed up, chest to heaving chest.

'I thought it better that I saw you without your grandparents. They are still hurting from the loss of their child and you are sensitive about the mother you have lost and never known.'

It was an insightful and tactful start I guess, a show of empathy for all concerned. Though I felt the excuse for the lost child was carrying it a bit far after thirteen or so years. Then, they could never know how things really were with Peggy and me, and I would never really know how they had all suffered over the years.

'It sounds like you and your sister have not had it easy either,' she was saying.

'We had each other,' I said simply. 'But I have always wondered...' I stopped, not knowing how to go on. How do you describe emotions that you have not come to grips with or understood fully yourself? How could I explain the pain of my sister's silence and my father's absences and avoidances? How could she answer the thousand questions that no one would willingly speak to me about?

I had learned silence and acceptance. It was my music that had helped to do that. The more I needed understanding, the more I had drawn 'myself into a world of music. And that in itself was hard to explain.

I would have liked to talk to her about Mother and her music. I knew that she was a musician. I remember her playing. I even remember when she went out some nights to play in concerts. That is all. My time with her had been blanked from my memory. No one talked about it and Father hated the subject. But it was clear from the start that Aunt Sophie was someone who did not deal in complex issues and any contact I might have with her would only ever be nonessential stuff.

'All those made up letters from her. Father read them to us. I can't understand why people need to make things up.'

I spoke more as a soliloquy broken free from my thinking, than a communication. It came across as a platitude awkwardly delivered. I did not intend it to lead to any deeper discussion.

'People do all sorts of strange things when they are confused inside,' she replied quietly, as if to herself. I guessed she spoke from of her own beleaguered past and I felt myself warm towards her.

'We were close as children, your mother and me.   We had two older brothers you see...'

'I didn't know that.'   I said, surprised that the family was even larger than I thought.

'Yes.   Oscar was the eldest.   He died when he was sixteen.   It was one of those freak accidents.   He was with Stuart, next one down in age.   Stuart was fourteen at the time.   They were playing with one of those toy cross-bows, but this one was a little more adult than a toy.   Stuart was holding it and Oscar was at the target, a round disc they had tied to a tree.   Stuart aimed just as Oscar bent forward to adjust the disc and the arrow was loosed.   It punctured his lung.

Just an unlucky freak accident.

We lived way out in the country then, Daddy had inherited a farm in Wales, on the border of Herefordshire.'   She tailed off a narrative that had been told before, perhaps many times and each time caused that deep and stirring pain for the repetition of it.

'Daddy went mad.   He blamed Stuart.   He never allowed Stuart to forget it.   Well, he sold the farm shortly afterwards and we came to live where we are now.

Daddy was an accountant before the war.   When he came back he joined his father on the family farm and made an attempt at farming.   He was never much good at it and after the accident he went back to what he knew best.   He never refers to that time.   All his recollections come from his war days as if there were nothing in between.'

'What happened to Stuart?' I asked.

'Stuart emmigrated to Australia.   Funny thing really; he and Felicity were the most alike, always the closest.   He played the violin.   It might be why Felicity started, but she became far better than Stuart.'

She stopped and stared into her empty coffee cup as if to find a remaining spark of her sister in there.

'Stuart became a school teacher.   He is married and has four sons.   One of them has taken up music – pop stuff.   He has a pop-band of his own and doing well out there.   They have even done some recordings.'

There was something sad about Sophie.   It was as if all the chickens had left the nest and she had been left behind to mind the old parents and she was now looking back on all she had lost for no fault of her own.

I had emerged out of dark memories to haunt them and they simply did not know what to do with me.   She was trying so hard to incorporate me somewhere but did not know quite where to slot me in.

'Do you think I have done the wrong thing? I mean, coming to find you all?' I asked.

'Of course not, whatever would give you that idea?' She was determined to be tactful.

'Well Grandfather was certainly not pleased to see me and Father told us many times that Mother's family wanted nothing to do with us.'

'Daddy was shocked. You suddenly appeared on the doorstep and you look so like her. Apart from hair colour,' she giggled. 'She was Daddy's favourite. She was going through a difficult time with your father. She would come to stay with you girls and she was always in a state about something. She and Daddy talked. When she died he became ill. I stayed home to take care of them both. Don't know if I shouldn't have gone far away myself. It was my work that kept me at home.'

'Where do you work?' I asked, puzzled that there could be anywhere close enough to find work.

'Animals,' she said. 'I work with animals, a sort of animal rescue. We take in strays and horses that have been treated badly, you know, sort of general animal home.'

Sophie, with her friend Ben, had bought a piece of land next door to her parents with an old barn they managed to convert. They called it "The Hovel". Sophie was able to see to her parents and care for their menagerie of rescued animals.

'I could have invited you back to The Hovel but thought it best we met elsewhere first. You know, so much explaining to do first and my life-style is very rough and ready, not like Mummy's home which has been kept in pristine condition all her life.'

Not having experienced her "rough and ready" I could make no judgement. I could only wonder why she had chosen the heart of London to meet me as it could only be an extreme opposite of what sounded like her "life-style". But of course, she knew nothing about me and the choice of venue was her way of trying to find an equal footing with me.

As it was, we had little in common with a generation gap and our separate and different lives but Aunt Sophie made up for it by talking of her childhood with Mother. Even there, it seemed, were two very different people.

Like me, Mother was a solitary child. She was the taunted and bullied child who spent her play-time at school in the music rooms, practising. Father was the first boy-friend in her life. They had met while she was a student of music. He was already working. What he was doing then was not known. Mother had simply accepted whatever he told her. His parents had apparently already died when they got married.   Not much was ever discovered about his background.

After they were married the family never saw much of him. Mother would visit her family alone with us children.   He was, as we had grown to concede, always away on business.

'He suited Felicity in so many ways.   She had her music and her girls and he had his work.   No one ever seemed to get to the bottom of what he was doing but it took him away a lot and she came home with you little girls.   It was the last couple of years before she died that things changed.   He became very secretive and difficult and would be gone for days on end.   When she came home she was depressed.   Something must have happened between them but she never disclosed what it was.   She seldom spoke about what was troubling her, not to me anyway.   I wondered if she had met someone else but as I said, she never confided in me.   I discovered that she was seeing an old fortune-teller where you live but there was little else I knew about it.'

'She is still there,' I said.

'Who do you mean?'

'The old fortune-teller.   She has an entire floor to herself and seems to run the place, but I have seen no sign of fortune-telling yet.   Not that I have noticed. I keep meaning to ask but things sort of get in the way.'

We sat silent for a while, wrapped in our separate thoughts.

It was time to wonder outside again.   A waitress was vigorously cleaning our emptied table in an attempt to rid us from it. We found a cold bench under the drooping tendrils of a leafless willow and sat watching a pair of Muscovy ducks with their red spotted heads swim out to an island where others of their group were settled into sheltered undergrowth.

A shiver passed through me.   It was as if we had unearthed old bones whose souls had not gone to rest.   The ducks shelter evoked in me all those shadowy spaces where we go to hide away old memories.   There was something unspecified and mysterious about this meeting with a newly fledged aunt, not even known to me such a short time before.   Now we were linked by a past that had little to do with me, yet had become my life.

I began to think of my own newly acquired shelter at Number Sixty Three.   It was an interim belonging but it was all I had and my music was there.   All at once I wanted to be there.

Chapter 27

As the cold of January turned towards an even icier February I welcomed ever more my retreats into the music room. I would rush there from work always hoping not to be spotted on the way, sliding past doorways like a fox to its lair.

Lorenzo never altered from his unequivocal focus on my music. He presided over each lesson with a dedicated air of attention. It was as if neither of us had another life beyond that room or a single emotional reaction to anything other than the music and its interpretation.

The metronome ticked and I followed its instructive beat; often, more than a little stoically possessed. Attending to melody and phrasing were paramount. My mind never deviated from form. That is, while he was there and the lesson ensued. Afterwards I would think back on his every nuance, his every expression and how he was looking. I would go to bed feeling warmed and fulfilled somehow as if another dimension of life was opening up before me.

I would try to imagine simply being with him, hearing him tell me that he loved me. I told myself it was only time before he would declare wild and passionate love to me.

Of course I had fallen in love with him. I think I had loved him the very first time I saw him on the stairs with Malachi. I was certain that somehow Malachi had arranged our meeting for that very purpose.

The bruises on his face had turned a sallow yellow making him look even more winter-drawn and ashen than ever. It seemed as if the sadness he carried with him was painted in numbers by those streaks of sombre, fading colour.

I had come across a second-hand clarinet from a music shop. I could not find a second-hand flute that I could afford. While Lorenzo could instruct me on the dynamics of the flute we both worked at finding the notes and cords of the clarinet.

Finding how to play the clarinet diluted his intensity for a while and he allowed himself to laugh at errors. I suggested that I could take lessons from someone in his orchestra. I assumed that he played in an orchestra. He had never up to then disclosed what he did or where he went.

Accustomed to being kept in the dark about most things, I was content to invent my own conclusions. Asking if he had taught other instruments besides the violin was the first attempt I made to try and reach what he did.

For a moment he looked uneasy as if his anonymity was something he preferred. 'No,' he said. 'I will take it away with me and see what I can learn. It may need fresh reeds and I have no idea if it is sound yet.'

The lessons became much longer and some Sunday nights I never got to bed till past midnight. There was still no mention of fees and it all felt too uncomfortable to ask about them. He would tell me when it was necessary.

I felt a silent kind of intimacy with him, unexpressed, unexplored and so out of bounds yet it was a dream place where I had begun to spin so many thoughts. It seemed that life would never allow me to be more than an outsider of everyone's life. I was the intruder looking in.

Even Peggy now had her life entirely apart from me and I could never be part of it. Her joys and sorrows would only ever be hers and not mine to share. Even if I heard about them and lent a sympathetic ear, they would always be something apart from me. My new-found family could only ever be strangers as much as those that shared that house with me. Time and experiences had created for them a pattern to live by and react to and I was no part of it but a small cue from an old ache they could not forget.

Deep down, I longed for a sense of belonging and recognition. I had been the outsider for so long, looking in, anonymous, even to myself. Only my music allowed me to belong somewhere sacred within.

While Lorenzo had become that pinnacle of all my dreams, anticipations and emotions, he too lived a life outside and beyond that which I could reach or touch.

Disappointment was something always at the tip of every expectation. It seemed to be thrust at me by some invisible force waiting to see me fall; as if I was unused to it and must learn it. But I had long since learnt to live within myself and not become affected by the least that life could offer. I was determined to fight on till I got to the truth of life. And when I had found it out – what then?

There had to be more, more than this. Composers knew it and wrote it into their music. Answers came in sound rather than words and with it I felt a recognition of everything that was happening inside my head. It welled up like a fountain head and filled me with light to go by.

Chapter 28

January makes its appearance soon after Christmas by offering a tidy new year with fresh hope. It brushes away the mess of mandatory celebration, propelling us towards resolution and determination. Then, when it has reached its end and the cold has settled into extremes, changes happen, by circumstance more than planning and the new year with its new number has become as commonplace as the year before and February is regarded with impatience.

By the end of February two of the students had moved out of the basement flat. Jodi had left to play a small part in a new television series somewhere in Scotland. She felt she had been launched and was free to fly. Eric had moved into a flat in Islington with someone he had met. That left Jason the law student who was not too keen on sharing with unknown students anymore and he invited me to take on one of the bedrooms in the basement flat.

I liked the idea. My room was small with no real cooking facilities and exposed to the open landing where either, Agatha, Constantine or Gregory would always be lurking.

Besides their intrusive presence, Lillibet and the strangers who occasionally came to visit her crossed the same landing at all hours of the day and evening. I guessed Lillibet's guests may have been clients come to have their fortunes told. I never asked.

The rent was unchanged. Jason insisted upon paying the major share. He had progressed beyond the articled clerk stage at his law firm. It was within reasonable travelling distance of the flat, which suited him and he had no need to move himself. As he was earning a great deal more as a legal fledgling than I was as a dental receptionist I was happy to accept.

I felt a little sentimental about my old room, wondering if it would soon be occupied but I noted with satisfaction that no card went up in the window of Agatha's front room on the fist floor offering a room to let.

The basement furnishings were pretty basic. A couple of hard backed chairs, a solid rough dining table which served also as a kitchen table and two well-worn sofas which had been truly romped upon by a mass of students over the years no doubt. The walls were filled with wonderful photographs taken by Jason, an amateur but excellent photographer. They were mostly random and abstract shots of people in everyday postures making pertinent and poignant statements of life. They showed a deeper side of Jason that I had not given credit for before then.

From the very start my relationship with Jason was easy and uncomplicated. Arrangements with all domestic schedules were happily agreed upon light heartedly with little fuss. We would take turns to do the cooking and cleaning of the flat which had received minimal attention in the past. I soon learnt that Jason's "turns" became less evident as time went on but it did not matter to me. It was an activity that suited me. It allowed me to take silent possession of those domestic chores I had always done before. Peggy was never too keen on doing those menial things in life that create some kind of order out of the chaos she preferred to live in.

I chose a room furthest from the door to the landing which could be shut away so that I could even practise there some days when Jason was out. I equated the room with my own identity with my few possessions and pictures and curtains I found in a charity shop in the high street.

The feeling of expansion and companionship relieved the cold edge of isolation. Jason was good company when he had time to spend with me. As he was becoming more involved with his studies, he would withdraw early into his room with his books emerging only to share the odd meal.

I was happy and more than content with the change.

While our arrangement suited us, it had a strange sliding effect on all those above the stairs. Miss Constantine took the trouble to shout abuse about my morality from the top of the stairs when she saw me, while the inexorable Reverent Gregory lay in wait out in the street as I was about to turn down into the basement steps. He would erupt out of shadowed stealth with his preaching. He loved words and phrases like "lewdness", "shamelessness" and "the evils of fornication when living with a young man". He would wrap them round his tongue and spit them; delivering an exhortation of his own hidden guilt I imagine.

I wondered if Jodi had received similar warnings.

I learned to ignore him; just pretend he was not there; embarrassing though, when people passed by and stared. He was obviously insane.

Even Agatha seemed to want to have something to say. She would look up at me when our paths crossed with that silent inner reserve she had. When I went to her door to pay my share of the flat rent she looked at me quizzically and asked if I knew what I was doing moving in with a man and what would my father have to say about it.

'Really Agatha!' I said. 'I have had such a nasty reaction from all of you. I like the space downstairs, my room was cramped. My friendship with Jason is not what you think. I would have thought you would know that.   You seem to be privy to so much information about me. Besides, what I do is private.'

The muscles of her face visibly relaxed with my reply.   It was as if my answer satisfied her curiosity.   I could not imagine why they had all taken such interest in what they had assumed as a sordid liaison with Jason.

Chapter 29

I had a free afternoon one Wednesday due to several last minute cancellations. Jennifer the receptionist "organizer" told me in her usual curt tone that I could leave early.

It was like a day off school.

I decided to use the time to call on Lillibet. I had not seen her in several days. When I reached the top of the stairs I saw that her door was slightly ajar. I called out but she did not answer.

I wondered if she might have a visitor but it was unusually quiet. I could not hear anyone talking.

I called again but there was still no reply. Then I went inside.

Her living room was in more than its usual state of disarray. A pungent smell of incense curled its way to my nostrils. Incense was Lillibet's answer to every malady, physical and mental.

I stood there wondering what to do.

A shuffling sound came from her bedroom. Lillibet was sitting on the side of her bed, half in, half out. An oversized fluffy gown shrugged itself about her shoulders, swaddling a long purple nightdress. Her hair stood in messed strands about her head where hollow eyes looked back at me from deep wells of darkness.

Something had happened to her and she clearly needed help. For a few stunned minutes I remained rooted to the spot, unsure what I should do.

'Are you sick Lillibet?' - An absurd thing to ask someone looking half death, with unfocussed eyes in an ashen face.

She groaned as she turned towards me.

'Been sick,' she explained. 'Very sick - that damn rum maybe. Lot of pain and sick.'

'Have you been drinking Lillibet?' I asked, though I had never known her to drink in excess.

'I gettin old,' she said. 'That what - I gettin old. Not watchin out over tings I should be watchin. Can't fight this no more.'

'I am going to make you some tea,' I said. 'And by the look of you - something to eat.'

I helped her back into her bed and pulled up her covers. Something was wrong, very wrong. I could only sense it. She needed help.

I found the kitchen in a terrible state. It took a good hour to clean it up after I had made tea and taken some toast to her.

Miss Constantine suddenly appeared at the door as I was clearing the mess in the living room. She started with her abuse.

Whilst Miss Constantine's abuse was part of the territory that went with her and I was no longer offended by her, I was not in the right frame of mind for it just then. I turned on her.

'Oh for heaven's sake Miss Constantine can you do nothing but slander and use foul language, can't you see that Lillibet is ill, very ill. She needs help. Go and fetch Agatha. Ask her to come up here and give me a hand. You are as useful as a cracked bucket in a flood.'

She just stood there, eyes blinking, shocked at my outburst. She seemed to crumble into herself. She lowered her head and shook herself like a dog ridding itself of water. When she looked up again she had come to rapid and unexpected attention. She seemed to transform right before my eyes. Had I not been so preoccupied I would have been startled at the change in her.

'Here,' she said, 'give me that cloth.' A new voice emerged from her as she straightened herself up to an "Agatha" deportment. As she took the cloth from me I noticed the twisted fingers of her right hand. What had happened to them all? They all seemed to bear the same scarring.

I could have sworn that Agatha was there, but for the hair and the clothing. She busied herself cleaning and clearing Lillibet's rooms, silently and discreetly just as Agatha would do.

I looked in on Lillibet.

She was sleeping.

I returned to the kitchen to see what would be needed. Most of the food in her fridge was rotten. I made a list and got ready to go out.

Miss Constantine was sweeping up the mess of old tissues, sweet papers and food debris in the bedroom when I put my head round the door to say I was going shopping.

'Yes, no hurry. I am here now;' came Agatha's voice mimicked to perfection.

I hesitated at the door.

Remarkable - I thought.

I turned to go back down the stairs, hoping the dreaded Gregory was not there to intercept with fresh passages of biblical homilies.

The coast was clear.

It was a good fifteen minute walk to the nearest supermarket at the end of Williams road that ran parallel to MacDonald. I bought as much as I could carry back. It was mostly those immediate necessities, adding fruit to the list and what would make a good soup.

On the way back I thought I caught a glimpse of Lorenzo's sister Anna Maria across the road. She was with someone. They were talking as her companion turned. I imagined it was Malachi but they had already turned into a side street and were gone.

My shopping bags were heavy and I needed to get them back before my arms dropped off. I kept going.

The house appeared empty of intrusive occupants.

Miss Constantine was gone - nowhere in sight.

I peeped in at Lillibet. She was still asleep. I unloaded the shopping and began to peel onions and chop vegetables for a soup. I was soon lost in a world of preparation and organizing my flittering thoughts. Cause and consequence moved in a progression of assumption and all kinds of mental invention as I cooked and fussed about the kitchen.

I heard Lillibet shifting about in the bedroom. She was looking a bit calmer, her face damp with sweat from her sleep. I brought a wet cloth from the bathroom and washed her face.

'You a kind girl,' she said. 'Like your mama.'

'Lillibet, what's all this about my Mama. We both know now that she is dead. She has been dead for years.'

'That right,' she said, turning in the bed to reach for the water I had brought her. I helped her to drink, then she fell back into the pumped cushions and I covered her up.

'I will be bringing you some soup to eat soon,' I said.

I was busy in the kitchen when I heard voices at the door. Malachi was there with Lorenzo and Anna Maria.

They had brought a doctor with them.

I thought I had seen Malachi across the road. Miss Constantine must have wised up for once and gone to fetch him.

They were talking in the next room. 'Arsenic poisoning' I heard and began to pay more attention.

The doctor was talking about poisoning and Anna Maria was crying. I caught only snatches of what was being said.

She was saying something about the situation becoming dangerous once more and if it did who would be responsible.

Lorenzo's voice was quieter, placating and calming.

As they came to the door I heard the doctor say; 'Well at least you have had someone take care of her.'

'That my little friend Anna. She always look after her Lillibet. She's in kitchen now fixin sometin for me.'

Lorenzo put his head around the door.

'Anna,' he said. 'I believe you found her in this state.'

'Will she be alright?' I asked.

'We will all be alright with you around,' he smiled at me.

My heart did a leap. It was as close to approval that I had ever had from him. He had never commented on my playing even when I was sure I was playing exceptionally well. But for this small care, he had acknowledged me.

His sister joined him in the kitchen. He introduced her as "Maria".

Maria was a female version of her brother. That is, in looks only. She spoke with a much more dramatic tone, giving lyrical weight to certain words while using her hands to clarify what she wanted to say.

'This is a terrible business,' she said. 'I don't know how this happened. Lilly is so careful these days.'

She thanked me profusely for all the trouble I had taken over her "Lilly", as if Lillibet belonged solely to her.

'No trouble,' I said. 'I will keep an eye on her every day now.'

'Thank you,' she said. 'My father won't bother you anymore. I really pray he won't.' Before she could say any more Lorenzo was calling her urgently to go.

Then he was gone. They were all gone, leaving behind a rebounding significance of what had been said. I could not imagine who their father was, that he might become a bother to me.

This had to be someone I had not met yet.

Another riddle added itself to a list of perplexing mysteries.

I sat with Lillibet for the rest of the afternoon. After she had eaten some soup and drunk a lot more water prescribed by her doctor she was looking a lot better. She said the cramps in her stomach were lessening and she was feeling a lot stronger.

Later that evening Maria came to sit with her. She was looking less fraught and less talkative. Lorenzo must have silenced her. There was no further mention of her father who might have caused the trouble.

Lillibet was pleased to see her and they soon became engaged in conversation about the family which was outside my orbit so I said goodnight to them both. They both entreated me to stay but I said I needed to practise.

On the way down I stopped outside Agatha's apartment. I heard voices and weeping. I knocked but there was no reply and when I tried the door it was locked. I was also alarmed to see a small bolt had been unobtrusively fitted at the very bottom on the outside of the door. Surely not, and by whom? There must be another answer or way out for her.

I would not, could not, interfere or intrude again on anyone that day.

I went to play my violin.

Maybe, only maybe, Lorenzo might call in.

I called in on Lillibet each morning before work and when I got back in the evening. She was feeling much better and ready to resume her life of laughter and light.

Whatever had poisoned her was never mentioned and I never asked.

.

Chapter 30

I had given little thought to the family I had so recently found. The purpose in finding them was to reawaken the memory of my mother. Somehow I must have been aware all along what had happened but I had craved affirmation and perhaps support.

Now they were there and I was here and nothing had really changed.

My aunt was keen that we should keep in touch. She phoned me quite regularly to see how I was and I guess I was warmed by her interest.

She did not mention my grandparents or if by any chance they wished to see me again. When she invited me one week-end to visit her in her own "rough and ready" home I went with diverse feelings. Was it another rehearsal before I saw my grandparents again or was she genuinely interested in seeing me, for myself, I wondered?

I knew, the moment I saw her "rough and ready" that I was dealing with someone who did not exaggerate.

Aunt Sophie's "Friend", Ben, was a man old enough to be her father.

Ben was not a man who dressed on ceremony. He was wearing a pair of old jeans that has seen better days and most likely had lasted a tad longer by being kept away from a washing machine. They were tied in the middle with binder-twine keeping a frayed, crushed shirt in place.

He came forward smiling, putting out a hand that had become a toughened tool over many years of hard labouring jobs. It was a wide and pleasant smile, exposing a row of age-browned teeth set in a face as weather-worn as his patched corduroy jacket.

He told me I looked like my aunt. I had no doubt it was said as a compliment but I struggled to know which part of me resembled her.

It was a cold day with a threat of snow in the air. We were all wrapped up against the day without removing outer clothing even when inside. To add to the tension of cold we all spoke in polite terms of feigned composure, wanting favourable reception and wanting to indicate it.

The afternoon passed pleasantly enough with Sophie and Ben working hard at trying to incorporate me into the family mould, showing me all their most prized and valued inventions created from natural materials, and there were plenty to be seen, particularly in the large kitchen, which took up a good three quarters of the entire barn.

'Ben did the conversion all on his own,' my Aunt boasted, describing him as an artist. She was clearly proud of all their Robinson Crusoe achievements, flourishing a hand at this or that, explaining the difficulty in finding the correct woods and metals to develop the articles that no one else has ever had the imagination to accomplish. A bit like modern conceptual art that has become a subjective inner expression that means something only to its creator; it's jumbled image neither pleasing nor displeasing, but simply the manufacture of the turmoil of subject matter in a psychotic imploding kind of expressionism.

What Ben may have put into the conversion in skill, he had lacked in taste or visual artistic concept. This was a conversion for convenience rather than comfort.

The now converted barn at one time had been part of her parent's garden. The land had been extended to include another several acres of adjoining pasture where several scraggly old ponies and four flea-bitten donkeys grazed, ranging in girth from skeletal to round as my aunt. They had those desperate, mean looking eyes where a cruel past was reflected. Anyone who came too close was challenged by a retaliating nip.

My Aunt's nature was to feed. It grieved her that anything thin should be seen on her property and she assured me more than once that in time they would all have gained weight. I had no reason to doubt her.

After the fostered equine family, I was given a tour of the rescue kennels full of pleading dogs, imploring all visitors to take them home.

The animals belonging to the house had fast learnt the laws of first come, first served and each took precedence over seating according to the laws of primary interest. I found a seat at the kitchen table on an old crate clear of a prior occupant and there I had a well-thumbed photograph album inescapably put before me.

They were all those self-conscious records of significant occasions when cameras were at hand to capture a treasured moment. I looked with benighted interest while Sophie sketched identities and arbitrary meaningless histories of the unfamiliar. They were of course, pictures of family I had never met and would never be likely to meet; pictures taken on those family-shared significant occasions. There was no immediate consciousness of belonging to them. I was the observer from outside, looking at a slide show of some other family to which I had inadvertently become linked. I could only look on with an outsider's interest where envy sat in pockets of self-pity. I had spent a childhood dreaming about family that had happened without me.

There were so few memorable occasions in our childhood and practically nothing recorded as far as I could remember - not counting the Christmases we had when Francis was in our lives. While Sophie itemized the unmemorable pictures of family members, my mind absent-mindedly followed the course of those happy times with Frances. There was a special Christmas when she was with us. I think Father was there for part of the time. She had bought a tree and helped us to decorate it. Somewhere, now in a storage-box, were a few pictures taken by her of Peggy and me in front that tree and I remembered being very happy.

Father never took pictures. Cameras were never prerequisite as there was never a thought or necessity to record anything. Photographs were things other people had. These pictures made me aware how distanced we were from one another.

A roar of laughter between Aunt Sophie and Ben brought my attention back. They had found a picture of my mother with me sitting on her lap. All at once, it was too much. I did not want to look at any more. The overwhelming sense of loss caught me unawares, stifling me.

I made an excuse to go to the bathroom.

The bathroom was beyond the kitchen, a strategy of plumbing. It provided a ceramic basin, used mostly to wash dog bowls in, an old rusted bath whose taps were in need of fresh washers and a toilet with a long chain with the flush above, most likely rescued from some ancient dump-site.

It was a curative purge on self-pity; a bit like taking smelling salts in days of old when one had the vapours. The shock to the system soon regained a state of equilibrium. My mind went into a ninety degree re-adjustment spin.

If I had been used to bathrooms as places to go to get clean, this was one that rearranged that concept. I was sufficiently mind-blown by the primitive plumbing with its grime encrusted toilet and bath, but the sight of the unwashed laundry strewn about the floor, waiting for attention that seemed permanently delayed, brain-washed me from any regrets of the past. Surely my Mother was not part of this kind of life-style?

Peggy would not like being here.

I returned to the kitchen feeling a little dazed.

My Aunt now occupied the milk crate. One very grimy chair was vacant but I eyed it half-heartedly. Dogs of all description occupied everything else worth sitting on, even the cushions thrown on the floor for them; while a variety of cats watched from higher vantage points.

'These are the lucky ones,' Aunt said, imagining my search for a clean chair was a look of sympathy that the dogs had nothing better to sit on. 'The rest have to be kept in kennels outside till someone can claim them.'

I had to repeatedly assure her that I was unable to rescue a single one of them because of where I lived.

From an old gas cooker that looked like it had seen better days, Aunt had produced more cakes than one could shake a stick to, besides the biscuits and odd looking sweets which she had assumed all young people hankered for.

While the kettle took time to boil she showed me their small sitting room, which led off from the kitchen. An old piano occupied most of the room space. 'Do you play Aunt?' I asked.

'Oh no, not really. Well, not any more. I keep that to remind me that I should keep it up but I never have time. What about you? You mentioned that you had taken up the violin. How is that?'

'Good,' I answered. 'Peggy and Father never thought I was good enough to take it up after school but I plod on. I love it.'

I lifted the lid of the piano exposing the old worn ivories gone dull yellow with age: some missing and some cracked. I played a cord or two but it was badly out of tune.

Aunt stopped and came over. 'Well, if your violin is not up to scratch, the piano sounds good enough to me.'

'No, I have left it too long for that.' I said.

Just then I heard voices at the front door. Ben was greeting someone. I heard the sound of feet stamping wet and mud from boots.

'Ah, Mummy! Good. I am so pleased you decided to come. She is here you know, just as I said she would come.'

My Grandmother came in from the cold. She must have trudged across the muddy field from her own house. The distance between the houses was perhaps a mere forty or fifty steps away, yet a whole new universe of difference existed between them.

On one side of the fence was a life-time of organized and precise domesticity to this very different, gypsy existence side. I wondered about all that accountability of heritability, genetic influence and the pre and post natal environments that are talked about.

Grandmother was busy removing her coat and woolly scarf when I came through to see her.

She was smiling expectantly. There was a different look about her from the last time we had met.

'Hello Grandmother,' I said shyly, uncertain if I could address her so.

'Anna Catherine,' she beamed. 'I thought we had quite put you off coming back when you were last here.'

'Not at all,' I answered. 'I don't think Aunt Sophie would allow me to be put off.'

'She plays the piano Mummy. She has so taken after Felicity.'

'Can we hear you play?' my Grandmother asked.

'Oh I haven't played the piano for years,' I said, 'I have quite forgotten how.'

'Perhaps you can start again,' Grandmother offered.

'I play the violin now,' I said.

'Ah, the shame of that and we have no violins any more, your Grandfather got rid of his soon after...' She stopped mid-sentence as if to avoid bringing back a subject that was now anathema to us all.

'I still have Mother's old one. I play with that,' I said before another memory should spoil the afternoon.

'She can bring it with her next time she comes,' my Aunt said with a supportive tone that however I played would be agreeably acceptable to them. The very fact that a member of the family had learned the rudiments of a musical instrument would benefit the genetic perfection to which they liked to believe they belonged.

Sophie's energetic chatter pivoted on the instant to any subject as it reached her brain; from her sister, to her brother, then, how a Springer spaniel had howled when they played. Laughter all round with anecdotes from Grandmother.

From there the conversation tailed into all her animals and music, thankfully, was lost in the thread of things.

Music had always been a private thing, apart from playing with music teachers. I had been made to play at school concerts and been torn me apart with nerves. Audiences did not enter my enjoyment of music.

Though it was a happier afternoon I remained awkward and out of place. It was as if I was looking into a doll's house of images that belonged to me but I could not minimise myself to be part of.

I could not help that inner feeling of betrayal to my father and my sister that I had gone beyond their wishes. All the same, I had this need to belong there, even if there was little or no parallel to bind us. Our new-found relationship was a bond that expected nothing more than the blood tie that linked otherwise total strangers. They were a comfort and at the same time, a convolution of confused emotions, buried and unearthed. They had led lives whose customs and etiquette revolved around those sedentary and unchanging conditions that shaped their world. The thought of an advancing or altering future would terrify them, as I was soon to learn.

When it was time to leave I felt a sense of relief in disengaging myself from the tension within, yet, somewhere, I felt a jolt of separation that this might not be repeated.

Aunt Sophie willingly drove me back into the thickening dark of late afternoon. Headlights of passing cars blazed towards us, blinding and illuminating like the questions that pounded in my thoughts as I debated all the issues of the interminable reasons for my being there.

I lay awake that night, the inside of my head illuminated with the clarity of sleeplessness and new thought.

I felt comforted in the shielding retreat of my new room where landmarks of recognition stood sentinel to my sanctuary and safekeeping. The few familiar things I had brought down from my small room above were those habitual, identifiable things that bind a mind with custom and security: poster-pictures, childish ornaments I had kept and resting near the wardrobe, the battered case of my violin, comfort of my soul.

I am safe here, I told myself, safe from strangers withholding truths and impossible emotions.

In reality, I was stranded in isolation to surrounding life. I had a firm and deadly resignation to my singularity. Once more on my own, I tried to sift realities from those subversive parts that people conceal about themselves. Out there was a world full of strangers with all their own uncertainties and I felt no part of any.

Those questions that had followed me from childhood, surfaced now and stood severely before me like whispers on the wind. I was still trapped somewhere in that state of not knowing. I was haunted by secrets that I was not sure I wanted to know. But, like a small match-light in the darkness, tiny revelations of the truth were creeping through.

Chapter 31

It was Sunday morning. The winter was drawing back its spiked cold, suggesting a fresh start with that luxurious feeling of spring in the air.

While I had seemingly lost all contact with my sister, I had regained a family gone astray.

Lorenzo would be there in the evening. He had spoken of concerts and interviews with prospective music schools.

A wonderful sense of anticipation filled the day.

I had started to feel less shy of playing with Jason as an audience. He was as full of praise as Lorenzo was silent. I think Jason had found in me something unique that he had not encountered in other females that he had known. He said he enjoyed my silence and he loved to listen to me play. He even enjoyed my battle with Lorenzo's flute and the clarinet that I was slowly coming to grips with. In fact, what ever I did was met with boisterous commendations from my flat-mate.

I longed for even the smallest similar reception from my teacher as I longed for Sundays.

This was Sunday, my special day of the week and I knew the whole day would stretch to long hours before he came. I had no inclination to fill the time with any other company. So, from early in the morning, I went to the music room to practise. Practise, as in rehearse or prepare is an imprecise term to apply to the joy of simply playing for pleasure.

Music to me was like a language, its words were the chimneys of the soul that released the smoke from the fires that raged within. It was something abstract, something physical and exciting. Playing was not practise, more a question of becoming engaged in interpretation of something surreal, intangible, non-figurative and caught beneath the sheaths of sound I felt the presence of my music teacher becoming more and more alive.

What I did not allow myself to realize, was that in reality he was so far removed from my fantasy that he had become this unreal thing associated with the abstract quality of the music.

I never imagined for a moment that he might lead a life of suffering and complexity far more confusing than my own.

By the middle of the afternoon, the clear morning that had greeted the day had become overshadowed by dark threatening clouds. Then the rain came. It came in soft petals to start; giving way to heavy drifts that pummelled the windows and invaded sound.

After a brief break for lunch I spent the afternoon playing my violin, defying the intrusive sounds from outside.

As the appointed hour of my lesson approached, I played more hesitantly and perhaps conspicuously, hoping he would be impressed by how much I had learnt of the music we had gone through.

I came to the end of the piece I was playing to realize it had not been interrupted half way through as I expected.

He was late.

He was never late.

I looked out from the dry side of the window onto the wet world outside.

It was dark now.

Street lights and house lamps lit up those patches of gardens and pathways visible by the borrowed light. The rain began now to beat down hard and relentlessly, with a determination to punish every single thing left exposed beneath its wrath. The earth submitted, giving its broken soil and debris to the rush of water, driving it towards the flooding gutters on the road.

Slowly the downpour subsided to a drizzle and the window pane wept small tears in its leaving.

It was a rain that lent irritation to my impatience.

I paced the floor.

I started another piece. This time I put the clock before me to see how long since the time I had expected him. Two hours went by.

I stopped.

I put on the kettle I now kept in the music room and made a mug of tea. I could not drink it, nor could I play anymore. Three hours had gone by.

I left the door of the music room slightly ajar and went down the stairs to the flat. Jason was reading under a spot-light lamp. He looked up.

'Lesson over?' he asked.

'No. He didn't turn up.'

'Did he phone to say why?'

Suddenly I did not want to explain any more. Jason was offering coffee or a glass of wine. I was far too restless. I excused myself, went back up to the music room which was still empty and I closed and locked it. Then I went upstairs to see Lillibet.

Of course, I thought, her door is closed and no sign of lights beneath the door, she is asleep.

I walked back down the stairs and halted on the landing to Agatha's rooms. I tried once more to suppose where Miss Constantine slept, where the Reverend Gregory slept and Malachi.

I was sure by then that Malachi must live elsewhere. He was the least evident of them all. He only seemed to appear at times of crises. It was always as if he had been called.

I must have been standing there for some time before I felt the eerie sensation of being watched. I turned round very slowly as if expecting to see someone standing behind me but there was no one there. A cold chill went down my spine as if some supernatural thing, some dark mystical portent of gloom was lurking in those shadows of non-answers. My curiosity eternally unquenched.

I studied the door to Agatha's rooms. The outer bolt was unfastened. I heard faint movements inside and tried to measure the spaces and distances of each sound. It was past midnight yet I was certain someone was awake: Agatha, Miss Constantine, Reverent Gregory or even Malachi perhaps? Should I attempt to go in? Should I just go back down the stairs and wait for morning answers?

It was very quiet. The earth was at rest after the heavy rain. While the road outside was empty of passing cars, the house slept in the ensuing silence.

I tried the door to Agatha's apartment. It was unlocked. I crept in silently, placing each step without making a sound. The living room with its outdated and tired ornament was empty of any living thing. A single table lamp burned, lending a showy glow to the room. A room beyond was lit. The door was open.

As I looked into the starkness of that bedroom, I saw upon its single bed a man whose face was not in range of my focus. On the chair next to the bed, Lorenzo sat, holding the old man's extended hand in his. The old man was talking in whispered tones. I could not hear what was being said but Lorenzo patted or stroked the hand in response.

None of the others from the house were evident; tucked up in other rooms no doubt.

I was suddenly aware of something disturbing, even threatening in the space about me. It seemed to creep beyond that violet end of the visible spectrum, where those flashing images or movements vanish as you turn your gaze upon them. I was assailed by flashes of images, echoes of desperate panicked voices, a shattering blast; then, a crypt-like terrifying silence.

There was something about this room.

I felt suffocated and desperate to get out.

Quietly, slowly I stepped backwards to the entrance door and closed it softly behind me.

The lights were on in the basement flat. Jason was still sitting there reading.

I knew he was waiting up for me.

It was so late, past one by now.

'Come on old thing,' Jason said kindly. 'A drink is called for.'

He got up to pour me a glass of wine. I saw that he had been drinking all evening. There was an empty bottle by the bin and he was pouring from a second, almost empty bottle as he opened another.

I sat at the kitchen table, feeling numb and confused. There had to be a way through these eternal tangles, a logical route I hadn't thought to follow before. Thoughts and images drifted through my mind. My body was tied into knots of tension. How was I going to break through all these endless walls of conspiratorial silence?

'Jason,' I said. 'Have you ever felt so out in the dark that no one, nothing made sense anymore?'

'All the time, old thing, all the time.'

'Lorenzo was not there to give me a lesson this evening,' I said.

'Anna, don't you realize now that you are way beyond his classes. You need more from someone outside of here. You play just like him. No, that's not true - you are better, much better. I have stood outside the practice room some Sundays and heard you both.'

'No, that is not true. Lorenzo is a great master. What you thought was me, was Lorenzo...'

'What is it about the man!'

Jason was unsteady on his feet. His face was flushed from the wine and it had made him excitable.

'Both you and your sister after him! I mean it is laughable.'

'What do you mean, me and my sister? Peggy is not here. She can't be...'

'Remember that night of our Christmas party here when you brought her? Well she was practically throwing herself at the man after you had collapsed and been taken off to bed'

'You don't know Peggy, not like I do. Peggy is just like that. It's just her way. She likes to be noticed. If she thinks someone is not taking enough interest in her she pursues them. My Father is the same...'

Once I had started to talk I found I could not stop. I had never talked so much to anyone. I began to talk about our childhood, the loneliness, feelings of inadequacy, loss of our mother and the inherent guilt that impressed itself upon me. I talked of Mother's family that I had recently discovered and the revelations of truths that were only now dawning upon me. I talked about my music, its solace, its escapism into another world.

Jason listened.

I explained about how Lorenzo had brought me back to life with his teaching, how he had inspired me, driven me to go on.

Jason got up to make coffee for us.

I told him about Lillibet and the encounters with the strange characters who seemed to appear at all times of the day and evening from Agatha's rooms.   I told him that I longed to ask questions.

Jason did not speak or comment.

I wanted to know how Lorenzo was connected to them all.   I wanted to know how Lillibet knew so much about my mother.   I wanted to know why all of them had a deformed right hand.

'They used to occupy this flat.' Jason said, breaking his silence.

'Who?' I asked.

Surprised by his interruption I came to a halt in my long flow. It was as if I had simply been talking to myself and I was suddenly aware that I had an audience.

'Lorenzo and Maria.'

'How do you know?'

'Jodi was the first one living here.   She had your room to start. She talked of rows and screaming in the night and then, all at once as it were, they moved out and the flat was offered to her. She was relieved to get out of the main part of the house.   She said it was creepy.   She advertised for other students to share with her and Eric and I replied.'

I heard the sound of the front door above open and close.   I peeped through the curtain.   A faint opalescent light of early morning had cast grey shadows to a fading night.

The tall dark figure of Lorenzo departed into the penumbral gloom of early morning.

'Jason, I have kept you up all night. It's morning almost.   I am so sorry, you have work starting soon.'

I did not mention seeing Lorenzo or my beating heart as I saw him go.

'You also have work in a couple of hours, you will be tired.'

'I simply hate my job,' I said. 'I want to look out for something more inspiring that will pay more.'

'There is a job going at work, training opportunity for a legal secretary. Would you be interested?'

'Oh yes. Anything with a bit more brain energy to it'

'I will bring the details back this evening.'

He was standing up and stretching.

'Thank you for listening Jason. I feel I have bored you and wasted a whole evening.' I leaned forward and gave him a kiss on his cheek.   Jason turned towards me and pulled me to him.

Kissing turned from the innocent to an unexpected wild eruption of passion. I wrenched myself away.

'No, not like this Jason. I am afraid I have given you the wrong... Oh God, Oh Jason. I am so sorry.'

'No.' he said. 'I am sorry. I am such a fool. I thought...'

He abruptly left the room and closed his bedroom door. I heard him go to take a shower. I washed briefly at the kitchen sink and left before he came out.

Chapter 32

Dilemmas in life never come singly. They come compacted like mangled steel in a press with other issues often of equal intensity and one thing compounds the other. Picasso shaped thoughts ran riot in my brain and even those sluggish body parts were refusing to coordinate with intention.

I was dreadfully tired all morning. People were repeating themselves to me and all the time a stark sense of floundering, like a fish out of water, jumbled my emotions. My skin prickled as if something intangible was about to happen. It was there in the air I was breathing in. I felt it under my skin, recognising it as something with meaning as if my brain had become alert to something that goes far beyond understanding.

I called off sick and left work early.

As I fumbled with keys to the basement I caught sight of someone watching me from the window above. Then the front door opened and Maria was standing there.

'I have been waiting for you,' she said.

'You would have had a long wait. I don't usually come back this early.'

'Yes, I know Lilly told me but she said you would be back earlier today.'

'Oh God,' I groaned; 'another of her psychic predictions huh!'

'It's my brother. You need to see something. Can you come?'

'Of course,' I said, alive now with curiosity. I relocked the door and followed her back onto the street outside.

'What has happened Maria?'

'You will see, you will see,' she kept repeating with an irritating insolence to her voice.

'Is this about your father?' I asked feeling exasperated. I felt more entitled now to ask after all these conundrums thrown at me out of the dark and never having the courage to ask before.

'Don't tell me you don't know. Not by now you don't know. Lorenzo does not want you to know. No one can be that simple,' she said irritably.

Maria had that almost shrewish nature of someone sure of themselves. It was a kind of confidence and pride that beautiful people so often have, using the authority of their superior looks to ride roughshod over anyone they felt inferior. She spoke fast and with emphasis with that London twang: a touch of cockney and a touch of class and beneath the sounds were the stresses and cadences of just the remotest Italian intonation.

On the few occasions I had seen her, there had always been a kind of desperation to her manner as if she had been perched above a volcano about to erupt.

'Well; take it that I am that stupid.' I said, feeling offended but too tired to cope with it. My emotions by now were raw-edged and breathing came with a pounding pulse of exhaustion reaching every nerve of my body.

'You will soon see when we get there.   You want to see something?   You want to open your eyes and see? Lorenzo he says you don't see. Lilly says you don't see.   They all say you are the best.   The best – pah – what do they know about the best? They don't understand music.   Lorenzo and me we went to college of music, we studied music.   We know what is best.   Lorenzo he says you need to learn.   I guess you not even ready for music school.'

All the time we are walking, fast, she talks with breathless explosions of sentence upon sentence. As if she is laying volleys of gun-fire at a target she has not quite come to set her sights on properly.   But each sentence strikes home to me like the taunting pinpricks from a Lilliputian on a bound up Gulliver.

We passed several side streets before turning down a lane of mews houses, mirrored by a similar row facing outward into the next street.

Large, extravagant, Victorian planters filled with sprouting spring bloom glamorised the still cobbled road outside.   There was the flavour of, perhaps pretentious, affluence about the place.

We turned up to one of the houses in the very centre of the row. The front door was left slightly open and a large Italian looking woman was standing there, framed in light upon dark. She had the same mane of thick dark hair Lorenzo and Maria had but hers was streaked with grey.   Her olive skin stretched over plump limbs and face.   Above her large mouth a faint moustache line spoiled a once beautiful face, now age and care worn.

It seemed she had been waiting there.   She and Maria broke into conversation as soon as she saw us.   They spoke fast, as Italians do.   Then, turning to English Maria introduced me.   It was her mother.

The mother gave me a small smile and said; 'Ah Anna the musician Lorenzo is so proud of.'

'Is he here?' I asked, thrilled to be the object of his pride.

Before I was answered, we had stepped into the small compact living room.   It was alive with an assortment of ferns and plants in tubs and baskets all round the room whose lavish furniture was a cacophony of other colour.

Just off this room was a bedroom with its door wide open. There were bedclothes strewn about the floor. From a mound of pillows I saw at once the ashen face of Lorenzo.

He was asleep. His face was bandaged and blood had seeped through, suggesting a wound to his left cheek. Even in his sleep he had that troubled look about him that he bore most of the time, unless he was listening to or playing music.

It was a large bed. It took up most of the room space. Lorenzo was lying on his back, still fully clothed from the night. Only his shoes were tossed at the foot of the bed.

Next to him lying sprawled beneath the bed clothes lay the tousled form of a woman, fast asleep.

It was the middle of the morning and they were reposed as if it were midnight. I knew he had been up all the night. I had seen him so. But this woman? Why? Why was I being shown?

The shock of seeing him there, the woman next to him, the overwhelming tiredness, the tension of waiting, the suspense of life itself took a toll on my senses.

All the time Maria was talking. Telling me to look. To open my eyes to what was happening around me. Look and see something... what?

'...she says she is jet-lagged She needs a place to sleep. She needs Lorenzo. She has so many needs - and my poor brother. He has so many problems. What can he do? She has him tied up into small knots...'

The woman in the bed came to, raised her head, and stared.

I stared back.

'Annie, what the hell are you doing here?' demanded my sister, sitting up in the bed without even a blush to cover her.

'Lorenzo and I...' she began.

I did not want to know. I turned and ran from the room.

'Wait!' Maria was calling. 'You've seen nothing yet – wait...'

What more was there to see? What more was there to know?

I was running blindly down the street, my shoulder bag hitting at my back like a prod pushing me onward. I came to Number Sixty Three but I could not go in. I needed space, time to think - I needed ... I needed...

I walked on briskly to the park. It was full of people.

People belched out of every pathway, talking in pairs, some in rowdy groups. There were mothers with small children, pushing prams, people with dogs, old ladies feeding breadcrumbs to the ducks.

I came to the edge of the pond and stared into the brown reflective water. Single white feathers of the birds that lived there floated on top of the water like small canoes waiting for passengers.

All outside sound had stifled to nothing. I was at once, outside myself, and yet deeply aware within. I was breathing in another reality. A spark of brilliance had lit up my brain and I saw things so clearly around me. Flowers and plants had taken on that kind of twilight luminescence and seemed more alive than I had ever noticed before.

The sun had passed the centre stage of sky and was edging back slowly down to earth. I had been standing there for hours it seemed. Just staring.

It was then that I felt my Mother standing close by.

Then I saw her.

She was out in the centre of the pond. I saw her standing on that island of contrived bush and plant. She was smiling at me.

'We are so alike Anna Catherine. All this confusion people bring into our lives. All there is left is the music.' I heard her say it. I know I did.

'Mummy,' I called out to her.

I threw down my bag and stepped into the icy water ready to wade out to her. She was fading. She was stretching out her hands to me. I am so sorry.

'Mummy – wait – wait for me,' I shouted for her to hear me. I was waist deep in the water. 'Mummy!'

In the distance I heard the sound of shouting – calling. The water suddenly got deep, very deep. The mud beneath my feet was sucking me down. I sank into the water as it rose up over my head. I looked up and saw the sun there through the filtered ripples in the murky water. It filled my throat and gurgled down into my lungs. Then nothing.

It seemed I had woken. I heard their voices.

'Do you know this woman?'

'Yes, yes it's alright I know her.'

'Malachi,' I said in my mind. 'Is that you?'

Hands were dragging me away from the bank. Two wet figures leaned over me while I choked up muddy water and felt my lungs explode with rasping violent coughing. An arm pushed me around and beat my back. It was Malachi's hands that held me up. His right hand took my muddied hand and held it. The fingers were twisted and gnarled; at some time they had been badly crushed and broken. Then I saw no more.

Chapter 33

I woke up feeling dazed and confused.

There were those swishing sounds of hospital movement. I was wearing an uncomfortable shift that was open at the back. My skin felt dry. Particles of dry mud clung to parts of me still unwashed by who ever had cleaned me up while I was unconscious.

I sat up and put my legs over the side of the bed and the room seemed to sway about me. A nurse rushed towards me from nowhere, telling me that I should not get up yet. Not till the psychologist had seen me. Faces from other beds had turned towards me, staring.

'I am alright,' I assured the nurse. 'Really I am. What am I doing here?'

'Wait,' she said, 'I will get someone who will come and talk to you.'

'I really don't wish to talk,' I answered. 'I just need a shower. My hair feels dreadful and I feel so uncomfortable, so...'

I felt myself fall backwards into the bed and the nurse busied herself tucking me back inside, folding down the sheets into the mattress as if to trap me there. I was given an injection and I felt myself drift back into the floating sleep I had just emerged from.

Someone had found my shoulder bag. They had seen the address book I kept with me. Under F were of course 'family' in large capitals. Naturally for them the people to contact, but for me a disaster under the circumstances.

My grandmother and aunt were with me when I came round from the drowsy, morphine induced sleep. They had been waiting in a corridor for that very event. Those all-consuming limp sweet smiles of concern were sprinkled upon me like sugar to sour fruit. All I wanted to do was get up, get dressed and go home.

Home was not an option.

I had to go through a performance of questions. Had I been taking drugs? What had happened? Was I depressed?

No doubt my grandmother and aunt had filled in the gaps for those concerned with the details of my mother's suicide. So it was decided categorically that I had intended to kill myself.

I have no idea how those subliminal levels of the subconscious work or how my brain had driven me that afternoon. Shock following extreme disappointment with no sleep was the real truth, but I could tell no one.

It appeared that I had slept for hours before waking up the first time. The second sleep was added for hospital convenience. I remembered no more after hearing Malachi's voice. Nature's way of healing a tired brain I guess.

Being bombarded by other people's speculation of my intent and having to speak about it, put a solemn slant on the day's progress. How could I describe something I could not understand myself? If I had said a psychic vision was my reason for going into the water, it would have compounded their conviction that I was on drugs or alcohol or better still, psychotically delusional.

I was not left alone for a moment and the desire to leave and get home became uncomfortably fixated. I had barely time to sort out my innermost thoughts and reflections upon the day before.

I decided to succumb to the situation. I was, after all, feeling much calmer after sleeping for so long and decided at last to make a confession that I had had a lot to drink at a party the night before and I did not know what I was doing. I stuck to the story like gum to a carpet and it worked.

The qualification for bed-space eliminated my necessity to remain there. They released me with a bag of mud soaked clothes and a warning.

My aunt had gone back to the flat and brought fresh clothing for me with a determination to take me home with her. She had organized everything, from informing my work that I would not be able to return for "health reasons" to somehow contacting Father who sent money to compensate for his absence saying that perhaps I needed a few months off work to sort out what I wanted to do. It was just what I needed and I accepted gratefully.

For two solid days I took the over-kind fussing of my aunt and grandmother. Grandfather even appeared a few times to greet me amicably. It seemed he had mellowed towards me. Perhaps their belief in an attempt at suicide was an acceptable passage back to his heart!

I took long walks along mud caked country lanes, accompanied by a dozen eager dogs and tried to ease the confusion of my brain.

I needed to assess my music: whether I was good enough to continue with a career in music or to give up and use it only as a hobby. Maria's words that Lorenzo thought I was not up to standard for music school hit deeply and profoundly.

When Peggy had told me I was not good enough to pursue a career in music I had always thought somewhere, somehow I would. Now it seemed everything had changed – overnight.

How could I have been so foolish? I had filled my head with dreams that had come to nothing. Something would always happen to drown out hopes of anything substantial in my life. I realized how stupid I had been to entertain the idea that somebody like Lorenzo could form an attachment to me or even find me tolerable. Of course he had never praised my efforts to play better each time he came to give me a lesson. I could never be any better than I was.

I thought of the story of Eve, when she had eaten the apple and saw at once that she was naked and ashamed. She had been blind before she bit the apple. I had bitten into a bitter apple and the lights were on, and I was feeling dreadfully humiliated.

I wondered at those inviolable urges we are subject to in our small life that expose all those fragile vulnerabilities and hit one like unstoppable sneezes: the embarrassing impulse tears, inescapable laughter, inexorable anger, unguarded irritability and that compulsive physical attraction - in my case, inevitably to the wrong person.

I figured that all this time my sister must have been paying for the lessons and it was how she must have been paying for them that hurt, so I thought.

But then again, I was making all sorts of assumptions from that place of ignorance from which I seemed permanently kept - in the dark.

I got back to the flat in the afternoon. Jason had left an awful mess of empty bottles and unwashed dishes. He must have been drinking a considerable amount.

I felt a pang of guilt about Jason. He had been kind and had wasted an entire evening, night even, waiting for me and then listening to me and my unstoppable self-pity.

I spent what was left of the day cleaning up the mess and preparing something for his supper, to make amends.

I could not bear the thought of retuning to the music room and for once I did not take solace in my music but cleaned and cleared with enough passion to wear out all I touched.

It was late when I heard Jason put his key into the lock and come in. He gave me a wonderful smile to see me back and said he would have tidied up if he had known I would be back so soon.

'Oh yes?' I teased and the tension about his face eased.

'I am so sorry,' he began.

'No, Jason you have nothing to be sorry about. I am the one to apologise. I kept you up all night and then spurned you. Jason, I don't know what to say except that I have been such a fool for so long.'

'What happened to you?' he asked. 'I thought it was me that had driven you to some desperate act. Your Aunt came here asking about clothes, she said you had tried to drown yourself. I thought it was all because of me.'

'No. Nothing like that. I was dreadfully tired that morning. Like you I went to work without sleeping and just decided to knock off for the afternoon, come back here and sleep. I was feeling emotionally drained.'

'I knew that. I should never have tried to kiss you then. I too was tired and also came back early. I would have seen you here and apologised. But you did not come back did you?'

'No. Maria was here waiting for me. She said she had something to show me. I went back to their home with her and she led me to a bedroom where Lorenzo...'

I could not finish my sentence.

'What? Was Lorenzo with your sister?'

'How did you know?'

'She came here later. She said that you had seen them in the same bed together. She told me that she had been pursuing Lorenzo for months. He did not want to know. She was pretty agitated about it. If you ask me, I'd say it's a bit of the pretty girl who always got what she wanted and suddenly it was not available. She accused him of being homosexual and that it was high time you went on to a music college and that he was holding you back for some perverse reason.'

'That is what Father said about Mummy,' I said almost to myself.

'What was that?' he asked.

'He told us Mummy had become a lesbian and that was why she had left us. Only she hadn't left at all. He had physically kicked her out one day. Strange! It is as if I am remembering it for the first time. He told us he had won custody of us. I think even that was a lie.'

'I guess we all have our ulterior motives for saying things in the heat of the moment.'

'Oh, Father never said it in the heat of the moment. He carried the story on to all hideous lengths that left us so confused. I will never know what really happened. It was their story. It was their experience that no one else can know. We can only stab at guesses as to how it was.'

'Yes it is strange how things turn out in the end,' Jason said. 'I thought you would never come back and here you are. It calls for a jolly good bottle of wine I was saving.'

'It doesn't look like much saving went on here while I was away,' I said, humour returning like a midsummer morning.

'You know something Jason? I will really enjoy sharing your wine with you this evening. I'm so pleased to be home.'

We laughed a lot over the meal, remembering funny things we could pull out of some random and capricious memory.

Those more sombre memories were filed away and forbidden expression that night.   It was as if we were both making a conscious effort to get on and forget indiscretions of a recent past and all those confessions that had been given too much weight.

The atmosphere which had been a little fragile to start became almost purposely careless, even perhaps suggestively amorous with the assistance of alcohol.   There was an exchange of glances, smiles and even a brush of hands but no more.   Then, after we had eaten and cleared away plates left to congeal for some time, Jason came into the kitchen with something held behind his back.

'Just one request,' he asked.

'Depends.'   I smiled.

'Some wild Irish music or pop played with abandonment tonight,' he said handing me my violin and bow.   'None of the clever classical stuff - right?'

I placed my violin lovingly beneath my chin and charged into any tune that I could think of that came to my head, dancing and wild.   Hope with its eternal recovery had returned.

Chapter 34

It was my aunt who arranged for me to have an audition with a music college. I was nervous about it.

I had not seen Lorenzo in a few weeks. He simply never returned to the Sunday evening lessons. I learned to hide my shattered disillusionment.

If he had been there I could have spoken to him, asked what was needed of me to continue with my music. Was I was good enough?

There was no sign whatsoever of the characters who lived in the house. Agatha's absence surprised me. Agatha was nearly always around at some time of the day or evening. I realized that something had happened, somewhere, somehow and Lorenzo was involved in some way.

It was several days before I returned to the music room to play. There was a haunted feel about the room as if tragedy had stuck it with a violent force and all that had been there in the past was gone.

I took my violin out and played several cords till Mozart echoed in my brain and I played beyond the hollow emotions the room had left behind.

When I came to the end of the piece I went upstairs to find Lillibet.

I could hear her voice from the bottom of the steps leading up to her. She was busy with someone. She had incense burning and she was pontificating in her old know-all drawl. I waited till the session was over and the delighted patron had passed me down the steps.

'Come on girl, Lillibet knows you are there. What you hangin' about there for?'

'Hello Lillibet,' I said. 'You seem to have been very busy lately.'

'It been a bad time for us all,' she said.

Part of me longed to ask about Lorenzo but my pride got in the way. I hated for anyone to know what I felt about him. If he was with my sister and I was stepping onto hallowed ground, I should be the last one to ask.

'Maria, she say she take you back home?'

'Yes, she kept telling me there was something I should know. Something you were all surprised that I did not know. Well now I know it and so what. If that is what Lorenzo and Peggy want - that kind of relationship, well so be it. If Lorenzo found my standard of music so inferior I really can't think why he continued to give me lessons. Anyway... anyway he has now stopped so we all know where we are. I really don't give a damn Lillibet, not a damn.'

'Lorenzo! Jah, Lorenzo he been very shake up these days. Now he is sick an that mad sister of yours she won't leave him be. Maria like a clucking hen over her brother. I say, "Maria you leave Anna be, she will know things in her own time."'

'Well, it's nothing to do with me.'

'You got all tings messed up in your head girl an it not for Lillibet to put right. You find out in your own way.'

'Where is everybody?' I said to change the subject. 'I have not seen Agatha for days or the others.'

'Agatha gone to family. All is quiet now. Better that way. Too much trouble here these days.'

I was longing to ask her why Lorenzo had suddenly stopped coming. Why that Sunday he was sitting on the side of the bed of yet another stranger from Agatha's flat? Why had he stayed there all night with the old man? How had he acquired the injured face? What had happened to him? Had she known about his affair with my sister all along? Why had I never been told?

Instead I gazed absently at a multi-limbed goddess with a blue body doing a strange dance while lotus blossoms fell from the sky.

'That is Guanyin,' Lillibet explained. 'She is goddess of Mercy, known by many
names.'

'Is she important to you Lillibet?' I asked.

'Pity, compassion, kindness to others, yes. Very important. Like forgiveness that the priests can give you for just saying what you did wrong, then wham just like that they say God forgive you.'

'Do you really believe that Lillibet?'

'They many tings I believe and many I have big doubt about. I believe what I see and what I hear.'

'Is Guanyin one of those things you believe in?' I asked.

'That picture belong to my master,' she said without answering me.

'Your master?'

'Man who bring me here, who fix my mouth. This is his house. He believe in many tings and he look for good in all.'

'I thought you said he was dead? Who does it all belong to now? I remember you once said you would tell me.'

'I say it belong to him because his spirit is still here.'

'What about my mother? Is she still around?' I asked, feeling foolish at the absurdity of the question and a part of me wanting it to be true.

'I knew your Mama. She came to see Lillibet and we became friends; also she was friends with Agatha. Agatha like her very much.   Always people with music seem to come here.   Your Mama she was very unhappy.   She say she married to a man who should not be married.   He no damn good as a father and he no damn good as a husband.   As short-time lover he is number one.'   Lillibet found this extremely amusing and had to break for a while until she got over her laughter.

'I tell your Mama, you gon leave that man afore he take everything from you. You know it a long story girl and it finish now. Here you are and Lillibet take care of you like your Mama asked.'

'Do you ever see her?   I mean, where is her spirit sort of thing?'

I had, by then, become accustomed to the idea that Lillibet's eccentricity was steeped in the occult but they were still fantasies to me.   It was all new ground for me and I was incapable of knowing how to approach them or name them.   Much of me repelled the very idea of spirits returning and speaking from the dead as it were. Yet a part of me was fascinated.   I tried not to dismiss those debatable subjects out of hand as utterly incredulous and I would still like to think that I keep an open mind, but there are so many dubious aspects of this kind of phenomenon. I could understand how the subject is so often dismissed with contempt by the masses.

'Not always. To see spirit – spirit must be there and willing to be seen. This is not someting you can make happen just cos you want it happen.   Sometimes you can call them to you but these days Lillibet afraid to do too much voodoo stuff.   It cause too much problem.'

'How is my Mother now?   Is she happy? Do you know?   Does she blame us for her death?'

'She done blame no one.   She is sad that she did tings the wrong way and lost.   Now she want you to get on with your violin.'

'I want to but I have become so downhearted since Lorenzo gave up on me.'

'Lorenzo, he not give up.   He has big problems.   You go see Lorenzo, you know where he live now.'

'What if my sister is there?   I don't want to get in their way and these days I just never know where she is. I don't even know if she is still working in Canada.'

'Your sister still working there.   She is just like her father.   They want, want, want all the time never satisfied then they throw away when they get what they want.'

'How do you know so much Lillibet?' I asked.

'Lillibet know and keep eyes and ears open all the time.   She not here now.   She is busy now over there in that cold place. When she want to come she just come.   Now Lorenzo.   Ah yes

Lorenzo, he is a big problem. You go see him, tell him Lillibet send you.'

'What about Maria? I get the feeling she does not like me. She was trying to tell me something but to be honest when I saw my sister in bed with Lorenzo – it was such a shock. I had not seen Peggy for so long. She has been silent. Peggy has always been my whole life. Why Peggy?'

'This world is full of why questions girl. Only you can figure it out.'

'But it seems you have all the answers to everything Lillibet.'

'No my child. I am as much in the dark as you are, being older gives you more experience not always wisdom.'

'I seem to know so little. Everyone around me seems to know so much. I was feeling so safe and had hope with my music.   I had no need of outside knowing. But now the importance of my music has gone and I have this desperate urge to know things.'

'We are all in the same dark place trying to find our way out.'

'Then why do people come to you to get answers from you if you are not all knowing?'

'What they want to know they already know.   I just tell them what's on their mind.'

'Why do you say you talk to those people who are dead?'

'To be dead is to be without a body.   It is only another reality. One without the physical senses.'

This was as mind shifting as the many differing bible interpretations every Christian sect imposes upon its parishioners. When I was still at school I had attended a variety of churches in search of meaning. None had ever made any sense to me, as if coherence and reason had lost substance.

I always felt intimidated by those fanatical invocations that people with obsessive beliefs in something start up as soon as they feel threatened by another belief system which they instantly imagine as darkness. I abandoned church going for that very reason.

I was clutching at straws trying to find myself and, I guess, a mystic answer, obscure as it was, was as good as anything right then.

'You go now to find Lorenzo.   He home now.   Later he going out - go now.'

She walked me to her door and stood there as I walked down the stairs. She was smiling encouragement.   Lillibet was always smiling.

Chapter 35

I convinced myself that it was no more than Lillibet's firm persuasion and assurance that persuaded me to go right away. Deep down I longed to rush back and find out what I had lost, or thought I had lost. Was it that which she had intuited?

I walked with purpose in my stride. Of course, I should find out why Lorenzo had simply not turned up to that music lesson, no explanations or excuses. A sense of indignation and effrontery fuelled my motives. He owed that to me at least.

I came to the mews and walked up the front steps to the house that I had last run from and hit the polished bronze to the white painted wood clearly and loudly three times. Then I stood back with a sudden impulse to run.

My impudence evaporated in that one instant. It was replaced with apprehension and cowardly regret at my foolish boldness as soon as the door opened.

An older man looking ashen and pale stood there. He was a cross between Agatha without her make-up and Reverend Gregory without his clerical bib.

'Yes?' he inquired.

My jaw dropped. He was holding the side of the door with his right hand, the mangled and twisted hand. It was precisely at that point that the truth that I had been so blind to, for the first time began to come together like pieces of a very simple puzzle. Why had I not seen before, put two and two plainly together, why? What had made me so blind?

'Lorenzo.' I mumbled. 'I came to find Lorenzo.'

'My God, you have taken your time to come round,' came Maria's voice from behind him.

Maria was looking startlingly beautiful in a green silk top that flowed down over a pair of old jeans. Her lovely long black hair hung loose about her shoulders.

'Lillibet sent me,' I heard myself saying. I squirmed at my cowardice, shifting accountability to someone else.

'Lorenzo,' she shouted over her shoulder.

Lorenzo did not appear but her mother did.

There was the sound of movement in a room beyond.

'Lorenzo,' the mother joined in, 'come see who has come to visit you.'

A back door audibly opened and closed. Who ever had been there was going out.

'I came about my music lessons,' I said weakly, realizing Lorenzo did not want to be seen by me and was making his escape while he could. 'I owe him so much money for the lessons,' I continued sounding ineffectual and without conviction.

'No, no,' said the man with yet another voice unlike either Agatha or the Reverend. I turned and stared at him.

How did he do it? All those voices, those characters? My voice within shouted out to my soul. - No, no, not Malachi also, please don't let Malachi be one of them.

'If he gives lessons at all he does so because that is Lorenzo...'

'I, I think I need to be going,' I stammered. It was obvious by now that Lorenzo had escaped me. Maria was already marching off to the back of the house, vainly calling to her brother.

Lorenzo had gone. Perhaps down street that ran parallel to the back of the property. He did not want to be found. The mother was talking fast in a flurry of Italian words spoken in irritation.

I had made a terrible mistake.

I took my leave without any word of farewell, going too fast to hear the calls to stay, wait a minute. It was all too much.

What a fool I had been. What a complete and utter idiot.

Chapter 36

I thought a few days away with my aunt would be sufficient brain-washing to recover from my ordeal with the snub; to say nothing of the rude awakening from crass stupidity at not recognizing the fact that I had been talking to the same person all that time.

I needed time to think about all those personalities I had become involved with. What had it all been about?

Auditions for the music academy were due in a few days. I made the mistake of thinking I could practise and go from there.

It all took time to sink in as the reality dawned lingeringly in pockets of awareness.

I couldn't bear the through of Malachi appearing as if from nowhere to be charming and trying to explain it all, as yet another part of the entire charade to deceive. Malachi: who was Agatha and Miss Constantine (ridiculous name), Reverend Gregory and now some other unknown.

For once, explanations and answers were the last thing I wanted. Even the thought of seeing Lillibet with her insinuated replies was something I needed to avoid. I needed to rid myself first of my unawareness, my lack of common sense.

I telephoned my aunt to ask if I could come there later that evening. I did not explain why but just that I wished to prepare for the audition and needed somewhere quiet.

I wanted to explain first to my flat-mate about going away and ask about paying my rent till I got back and could decide where else I was going to live.

Jason was comfortingly as ignorant and amazed as I was of the deceptions. He said he had no idea, never had, and never thought to question.

'Eric once had the idea that Agatha was a transvestite,' he said. 'We talked about it and the others thought there was something so strange about her that we could not begin to fathom.'

'Transvestite?' I asked. 'No, I don't think so. She was very real about her femininity. I never felt she was playing a role. She was never awkward or uncomfortable in her clothing. I remember years ago, when I was at school; Peggy had a male friend who dressed in female clothing. It was quite shocking at first. He came to the cottage with other male friends, as a male. Then one day he pitched up in these rather odd female clothes, wearing make-up. Peggy chatted as if there was nothing wrong. Peggy was like that. She accepted everything as a matter of form. Nothing every phased her.'

'Except Lorenzo - from what you say.'

'I have no idea what has gone on between them. I no longer care either,' I said nonchalantly, while the sharp pang within reminded me that I did.

Jason listened carefully about my reasons for getting away but was unsure that I was making the right decision.

'Don't you think you are running away at the wrong time?' he suggested. 'I mean, you are in shock and the man who has been teaching you has suddenly deserted you for no reason.'

'There is a reason,' I interrupted. 'The reason is Peggy. God only knows why she should influence him to stop teaching me.'

'Well, as I said before, you are way beyond what he can teach you now. To me you sound professional.'

'You are kind Jason, and a good friend but I know there is so much more I need to learn and I need to perfect my technique. Oh dear, it is all so baffling.'

Once more Jason came up to me and put his arms around me. This time when he kissed me, I did not pull away but stayed there, thinking of Lorenzo and wishing...

Was I doing something that Peggy and Father did to such perfection: wanting something that I could not have?

'Do the audition,' he said. 'Then come back here, don't move away. You need to face your fears Anna and you will need a friend to come home to from the music school. I hear they push their best pupils very hard!'

He smiled at me in that encouraging way that I imagined he would be with a client come for legal advice.

'I will see how it all goes,' I said. 'I may not get in of course, they have hundreds of applicants every year and only take a few and I am not as good as you would like to think.'

'They would be insane not to take you,' he said.

Chapter 37

Each day I died a thousand deaths. Every thought splintered my mind with hope on one side and dread that I would be rejected as not good enough on the other. I could wallow in the depths of insignificance and inadequacy and moments later I could come alive again with a hope that somewhere, some-impossible-where, things were going to be wonderful with a life of only music ahead. I could be stirred into life by a piece of music that touched my heart and evoked a restoration to my soul. Then I would stop at a disruptive thought and start again and make each new starting point a recollection of how I used to be, in a barren life that made no promises and gave no answers.

I had grown with the idea that my sister was all there was and that things would fall apart when she was not there. That had not happened. Instead, I had learned to move on and find myself and my own strengths. I still missed her from time to time. I longed for her also to be part of the caring family once more and for her to come in out of the cold of searching for something that was lost and could not be found where she was looking. I knew, deep down, that my sister was deeply troubled, but why and how had not yet become known to me.

My grandparents, Aunt Sophie and Ben had all been there to greet me when I arrived. The feeling of warmth and acceptance was a balm to the aches of the recent past. Practising before the audition was seldom without an adulating audience. While I felt uncomfortable playing to at least one of them most of the time, I knew that I must get used to an audience.

Grandfather said I played like my mother. My aunt said I was far better and my grandmother cried every time I played, which was disconcerting to say the least and it all left me feeling self-conscious and awkward.

The auditions were held at the Music Academy. There seemed to be a hall full of distressed and insecure students waiting, some alone, some with a member of family there to give courage.

Though I had worked hard for many hours each day, when the time came to play I felt at ease. It suddenly did not matter if I got in or not. I knew that my new found family would want it but at that moment it did not matter anymore to me. Jason had assured me that there were always jobs coming up where he worked and I could slowly learn the mechanics of a legal secretary. Something, he said, of great value. Music would always be important to me. It was my escape from life where I could hide for a while, expressing some great longing or passion of a brilliant composer. It would always be there for me. I needed no audience to live in that world and acceptance meant a public world of listeners and spectators, which I could do without.

I played a passage of Mendelssohn's violin concerto in E minor, opus 64. It was a piece that Lorenzo and I had played together several times and for a while it brought him to life for me. When I finished I looked up to see faces looking intently at me.

'How long did you say you have been playing?'

'Most of my life, when I have had the chance to play.'

'Who is your teacher?'

'Lorenzo Alberini.'

'Lorenzo teaches here part-time. He never mentioned he had such a pupil. Remarkable.'

I did not find it remarkable. I was used to Lorenzo's secretiveness. I had no idea that he was teaching elsewhere. I had, in fact, little idea of anything that Lorenzo did, in or out of his professional life.

'He is no longer teaching me,' I added.

The questions went on while I was putting away my violin. They conferred together and I ceased to be interested in their opinion. I told myself they did not matter. I had done my best. Or had I? I didn't care really.

I looked towards the door and at that moment I saw a tall dark figure disappear from behind the door. My heart skipped a beat. I knew at once it was Lorenzo. He had come to hear me audition. I took in little of what was being said to me after that. That they were praising my playing did not matter at all. The fact that he had cared enough to find out I was going to be there, that he had come to listen was everything to me.

Chapter 38

I knew that I could not live with the family. I had spent an entire childhood relatively alone. I could not begin now to be fussed over and never left alone for the remainder of my life. I could not even stay too long now the audition was over. I needed to get back to what I had accepted as "home".

My acceptance to the Academy was told to me the day of the audition but I told no one. I waited for the formal acceptance by post and began to plan my life around it.

Father offered to pay the fees, so did Grandfather and so did my Aunt. I agreed to borrow them from Father. I thought it right that he should at least help.

When Father met me for a talk he said something strange about Peggy not demanding such vast sums from him anymore. I told him I was not aware of Peggy ever receiving vast sums from him and he laughed. It was one of his short cynical laughs. It was a laugh I remembered that he reserved for Mother and the women he had discarded. I had no wish to pursue the matter.

I assumed that he had divorced Eleanor, as he was embarking on a new marriage. The young woman I had seen in the car with him I wondered? No, of course not, this was someone he had only met three months previously on a business trip.

I decided then and there that accepting financial help from him for college was a necessity to curb him and at the same moment I wondered if I was beginning to think like my sister.

It turned out later that I was offered a scholarship to commence a little later. I felt pleased to decline any further help from my father.

I was to find that a music college, when I started there, was a totally different matter from a secretarial college. I enjoyed every part of it. It all involved my favourite pastime.

Before the college started I began to return regularly to Lorenzo's music room to practise, always hoping that one day he might look in.

When I went back into the flat each evening Jason was always pleased to see me. We swapped stories of our very different career progress. I liked to think we had a friendship rather than call it a relationship. I found myself avoiding any intimacy with him. I had exposed too much of myself over the past weeks and I had no will to continue in that way before it became expected of me.

Jason had taken a series of photographs of me while I was playing my violin and attempting the flute. They printed out in quite exotic expressions of someone I did not recognize as myself; wonderful really. I thought him clever to contrive such ideals out of the ordinary.

They looked like a beautiful girl from a dream, with flame coloured hair, lost in a world of her own. He used them when he had exhibitions of his work. He asked if I minded. Of course not, why should I? No one would know me from them they were so cleverly taken and developed.

I went to call on Lillibet a few times each week. She was often busy with someone so I went away. Part of me was hoping that she would come up with some news about Lorenzo.

Neither of us mentioned him or my discovery about the strange and very different personalities that had stemmed from Agatha. The conundrum stuck like sticky jam to an unwashed face: wanting to know and wanting not to know.

The more I thought about it the more I avoided the issue.

Agatha had of course returned to her apartment as always. When I saw her talking to Lillibet I would disappear fast. I found I could not cope with the deception of the camouflage that altered her so utterly. If there was any sign of Miss Constantine I would slink away hastily before her contrived offensiveness was thrown at me as part of that ridiculous role she was playing.

When I did happen to bump into either character there was no sign of recognition that I now knew they were the same person. It felt like a kind of madness in which I was taking part. Surely, I thought, the old man, whose name I had yet to discover, had witnessed my comprehension of his varied disguises. It was as if he/she intended to continue with her/his charade. I was still, at that stage, uncertain of which true gender the original character was.

Of course I could have left and gone to live elsewhere to avoid my discomfort but they had all, Lillibet, Jason, Agatha etc become like a family to me, less as strangers in fact than Mother's family and closer to me than Father and Peggy had ever been.

I had enmeshed myself in that strange household and I was in some way, waiting for a revelation that would unite me with a reality that I was in need of.

I had not seen Malachi in months and felt sad that he was perhaps also avoiding
me. It was an appalling disclosure now to imagine him as a shared personality that did not in reality exist at all. Whatever element there was in that original character I could not understand how someone with Malachi's depths could share such genesis.

Chapter 39

As spring gave way to warmer and warmer days, heralding a hot summer, my life seemed as satisfactory as it ever could be. Months had gone by without any further contact from my music teacher and a weight dragged silently upon my heart. I saw him sometimes, at a distance, at college. He never saw me and I had that awful inclination of a stalker to find him, trace his whereabouts and spy on him, but I kept those dreadful dark emotions at bay and found it easier to avoid being where I knew he might be.

I turned my mind to concentrating hard on perfecting another instrument. It was an exercise in thought channelling. I was getting on reasonably well with my clarinet and even playing flute with certain flare. I seemed to please who ever taught me in whatever instrument I played but my violin was the old friend through whom I could bare my soul and any recommendations of praise mattered little, the music itself did more.

Back in the flat Jason was working hard. He was seldom back early those days. Then for weeks at a time he was there all the time, looking depressed and ill. He was not willing to talk about what was happening in his life. It was as if he had met someone who had turned him inside-out and the relationship was making him morose and aggressive towards me. He snapped at the slightest provocation and found fault with anything I did. It was like living with Peggy again.

He had been like a cat on a hot tin roof for weeks. Then he suddenly changed, became cheerful and light hearted. We even shared a bottle of wine. I guessed he must have had good news. He said that he was about to change jobs. He had applied for a job with a law firm with an international reputation and was waiting to see someone about it in a few days.

When I told him that my sister was working for an international firm of lawyers he began to search irritably for something in a kitchen drawer and grunted acknowledgement without paying any attention to what I was saying.

I put his edgy behaviour down to work stress and tried to keep out of the way as much as I could. A lack of attentive communication did not matter. Thereafter conversation came in ebbs and flows of the day's events. I learnt to take my cue from him when to speak and when to be silent. I was used to Peggy's moods which could last for weeks.

I went to college one morning expecting a long day before me but by midday it seemed the music teachers were holding some kind of conference and by the time I looked for a practise room they were all taken by students using the free time to practise. I went home instead, hoping that Agatha would not be around if I played my violin in the flat.

I unlocked the flat door and was surprised to hear voices. They were coming from Jason's bedroom. I called out to him to announce that I was there so as not to surprise him unduly if he was there with his new "clandestine" friend.

Jason came out of his bedroom looking bright red in the face as if he had been held upside-down in a furnace. He was not wearing his usual work clothing but had pulled on an old sweater in a hurry. It was so unlike Jason.

'Sorry Jason, I did not mean to disturb you. I came back early today, some kind of teaching conference. If you like I will go upstairs and practise in Lorenzo's room.'

Perhaps it was the word 'Lorenzo' that triggered a spontaneous reaction from the room beyond.

'Jason, here a minute!' The command from the next room was perfunctory, it was the voice of control and instantly recognisable. The door burst wide open and my sister stood there wearing little other than a large man's tee shirt that swamped her size zero body. Her hair was tousled but her make-up was intact, leaving her that clean clear beautiful look she always managed to retain.

'Peggy!' I gasped, startled, to say the least.

My mind took time to adjust and make sense of this astonishing appearance. I had guessed that Jason had a "secret" lover somewhere but not Peggy - surely, not Peggy. She was with Lorenzo, wasn't she? Of course she had come to see me. I hadn't seen her in months and Jason was kindly entertaining her till I got home.

'Peggy, how lovely to see you! What a huge surprise.' My dull slow grasp of circumstance engaged my brain in slow, shocked stages.

I had come from a childhood of constant companionship and close bonding with my older sister. I had, in the past year, become isolated far away from her with few visits and a dwindling communication between us. I had always thought that separating from her would be devastating but to the contrary, I had survived more than adequately without her and the disparity of time and distance had gone by without too much thought as time elapsed. I had barely noticed the several months since the Christmas party when she had met these people who were surely – strangers to her? How and when, I wondered had these familiarities become so fixed?

There was, however, still a lingering remnant of vulnerability without her and a trace of dependency, and the belief that anything she did was acceptable and I was the unworthy younger sister who had just not gotten the hang of things yet.

It was only later that I realized how her absence had made me stronger-minded, more determined and full of emergent courage. This unexpected return in such close intimacy with my flat-mate was shocking, but then there was so much of Father in her; that burning need for the clandestine, that frisson of the illicit. What on earth was she trying to achieve now? Why Jason, then again, why had it had to be Lorenzo and all so deviously programmed. Were they worth the prize? Were they worth risking our relationship for? Perhaps that was it. She was trying to prove something to me. As if there was anything that could be proven to me. Had she found out about my contact with Mother's family and this was her way of retaliation?

I was not going to react. I was not going to show that it mattered. If Jason was fool enough to fall for all this. If Lorenzo... My thoughts halted.

What of Lorenzo? Surely he was bigger than all this? This simulation of make-believe affection. How did they fall for it?

Those square shaped images bounced and challenged all my reserves. I did not know what to think. I turned to memories, revisiting our lives, much as has become the habit of my life these days. It was neither anger nor hurt that I felt at the deception but huge anxiety for this unrestrained sister. Wondering desperately at her motives.

I only knew that from that moment onwards, while I felt fragile beneath the skin I was at once determined to be strong and resilient outwardly.

'Why did you say you would be going into Lorenzo's room?' my sister demanded ignoring my mixed and feigned delight at seeing her.

'I have always used his room,' I continued, stunned at her impertinence at my answer and presumption that I should have discarded all connections with Lorenzo.

In that slow instance of mental computation, when surprise removes all appropriate response, I remembered that last shocking moment of our last brief encounter with each other. Only then did my mind turn back to the painful vision of her in bed with Lorenzo, an image I had been trying so hard to avoid thinking about. Only then, was I able to calmly respond to her without any trace of emotional outburst that would have come more naturally.

'I share the room with Lorenzo,' I said casually, choosing the present tense as a provocation to annoy her. I would not let her know that we had ceased all communication since she had put him too under her belt.

'My God, you amaze me!'

She threw the words at me, clipping each syllable with the razor-edged sharpness she used when I was much younger after I had done something horribly wrong.

'You have taken him from me haven't you? I wondered why he was avoiding me.'

Retaliation was what she wanted. I knew that silence would be the stronger weapon. I did not respond. I remained mute while my thoughts struck back with the force of demons at her while she snapped and accused idiotically, releasing a venom within that caught and poisoned the air.

At this point the silent Jason came to the rescue.

'Peggy she has not taken him from you as you say. Anna uses Lorenzo's music room to practise in. Lorenzo has dumped her as a pupil and she has had no contact from him in months.'

While Peggy's face relaxed, Jason's face tensed to a white starkness.

I hoped that Jason had begun a sensible computation of his own.

The only face with a look of serene satisfaction was my sister's.

'Well then. Nothing more to be said.'

She returned to her languid charm, flitting effortlessly from the compromised situation like a butterfly ready to settle on any privileged flower she demeaned herself of.

'Now that you are home why not make a pot of tea for Jason and me,' she purred with the equanimity of a contented cat that had killed the offending mouse.

'Of course,' I said, only too willing to escape embarrassment all round. We all needed breathing space to gather what composure the situation would allow.

I went to the kitchen area, such as it was, for it was also part of the living space, they retired back to the bedroom to whisper to one another in secret.

Secrecy: that was Peggy's marque. She liked to shield herself behind a smokescreen of secrecy. It gave her ascendancy over those who had been kept in the dark and it gave her the edge on any situation she wished to be in control of. I had always suspected that and now I knew it. I wondered how much Father had to do with the cover up of our Mother's death, or if she had orchestrated those letters and the ridiculous stories behind Mother's alleged abandonment. Or, were they just two of a kind? A case where genetics really does clone its offspring?

I didn't make a "pot" of tea. We didn't own a pot. I put tea bags into mugs, boiled the water and let the bags float on top. I knew it would drive her mad. Then I called out as nonchalantly as I could that tea was made and they could come for it.

More whispers.

Jason appeared first.

He had straightened his clothing and brushed his hair but he was still unable to look me in the face.

My sister, no doubt was working a lot harder on her appearance. That always took time. She remained in the bedroom a while longer.

'Well,' I began, disregarding the subterfuge which irritated me to the extreme.

'How long have you two been seeing each other? And for heaven's sake why the secrecy? I just wish you had warned me and been less covert about things. There would have been none of this embarrassing shock.'

'Peggy thought it would upset you,' began Jason.

'Avoiding upset has never had much to do with what Peggy has done in the past. I can't think why this should upset me.'

'You mean, um, you don't mind?' stammered Jason, for once lost for words when words were things Jason pulled out of the air with the aplomb of a Shakespearian actor.

'I take it that the law-firm you are transferring to is the same one as Peggy's?' I asked, ignoring the question of minding. Of course I minded. Peggy was playing games with him and it would ruin our friendship.

How long would this last? She was much older than him and he was simply not her sort, if Peggy had a "sort". Then again, neither was Lorenzo. She liked to pursue men till she had them worshiping her, safely in her grasp, after which they became a boring statistic. It was a kind of sport to her and anyone who had the vaguest feelings for me was always fair game.

'Well, yes, as a matter of fact Peggy has given me some extremely useful leads in that direction.'

'What about your plans for becoming a barrister?' I asked.

'Well, er,' he stopped as Peggy swept barefoot into the room. She was wearing a wonderful kind of floating envelope in extravagant swirls of brilliant blues and violet which drifted casually about her body. It clung here and there to her hips and breasts like an embrace, reaching just before her manicured, perfectly painted toe nails. Her hair was groomed and bright fresh lipstick emphasized her lovely mouth she puckered to give Jason an air-kiss, a reliable distance from his cheek, after which she superciliously took a mug in her hands, scooped out the offensive teabag with a long spoon and cast it with disgust into the sink.

Poor Jason, I thought. He was watching adoringly. He had no idea.

Once she had entered the room, conversation became stilted. She started to talk endearingly to me referring to me as her "dearest little sister".

'Daddy says you have taken up the old violin and found yourself in a music school. How typically persistent of my little sister,' she said, turning to Jason.

'She was always like that even when she was small. She would work her way at something like a little beaver. No fun, no laughter, just plain old bashing-away at something.'

'It was never something,' I began, 'it was always my music.'

'And remember the fuss you made when we had to leave that old piano of mother's behind when we moved into the cottage? I told Daddy you would get over it in time once your obsession had died down.'

I began to dislike her, for the first time in my life. I could see what she was trying to do. She wanted to be better than me. She was already better than me in every single way that could possibly be – except the music - and now she could only take over that part of my life that she felt she could manipulate.

She turned back to Jason. Maintaining the same elegance, she continued with a conversation they had been having in the bedroom, as if the interruption of her younger sister's appearance after a distance of several months' absence was a disturbance of minor importance.

While they chatted away about plans they were making I went into my room to pick up some sheet music and collect my clarinet. I felt loathe to even return to the room they were in. Unfortunately, as luck would have it, it divided my room from the only means of escape.

I felt suffocated by the whole situation.

Peggy was playing a game, a strange and disturbing game I did not understand. I wonder even now if she understood it either. Whatever her motives were they were lost somewhere in a deep subconscious swamp in which she had become lost. Why she was doing this, baffled me. She did not need someone like Jason (or Lorenzo for that matter) in her life. She was leading a fast moving life of travel and excitement. With her looks and grace she could catch any man she wanted from a much higher echelon of life. Someone much more suited to her in age, sophistication and wealth; the qualities she was really in search of.

Why Jason?

He was so out of her league.

Why was she playing him?

It was obvious that he did not matter a jot to her. I knew how would she turn him inside out and leave him and his career in tatters and there was nothing I could do or say to warn him without sounding petty or jealous.

A childhood with problems had bound us in some inextricable way, but it had that undercurrent disturbance that repelled also. A habit of secrecy had been nurtured where frozen images rose up from time to time not to be discussed, not to be reckoned with. Memories had become misrepresented by trying to cover up those images that had been too painful to remember and distortion upon distortion had made no sense in what was going on.

Peggy's strange actions came at a time when I was not ready to see objectively. I could only assess what had affected me. I realized only so much later that there were things my older sister had seen and heard and experienced which I would not even have been able to understand at that time. There were things that happened that she just wanted to forget and they were things I would never get to know or understand but somehow they had affected her in this strange way that gave her a craving for what she felt she was missing.

I realized it only much later. When it was too late - that Peggy was much more confused than I was.

While Jason was busy with all the terms of endearment under the sun, offering anything she might want, I slid out of my room, circumvented the open kitchen/living room and found myself outside the corridor's steps leading up to the front door.

As I got to the top step someone was waiting for me. His appearance startled me at first but that was quickly followed by a wonderful feeling of relief as I addressed him.

Chapter 40

'Hello Malachi,' I said.

The transformation was superb I had to admit.

His eyes were not the others' eyes.

His expression could only be his own.

In fact his every feature was uniquely Malachi.

How did he do it?

'You are on your way to practice,' he said in his soft-melting Irish voice - his own and not borrowed, I could feel it.   Was he the original and the others simply side shoots of his alter ego?

'Yes,' I said.   'I have missed you.   It has been so long.'

'Shall we go up together and put your things down.   We can talk there or we can go out for a walk,' he said.

'Go up to the music room,' I said, 'there can be no interruptions there.'

I unlocked the door with my own key, feeling the weight I was wearing on my shoulders lift as I walked in.

Someone had put roses in a glass jar near the window.   That single touch of life lifted my heart, together with seeing Malachi at a crucial moment in time, giving me once more, that comforting feeling of not being alone.

'The flowers?' I said.   'They are beautiful.'

'Lorenzo left them there for you,' he said.

'I thought...'

'Little Anna,' said Malachi, 'I have come to see you for the last time.   I will try to do some explaining.'

'What do you mean, the last time?   Every time I see you I think afterwards - that was probably the last time.'

'You know the saying,' he teased, 'the heart is willing but the flesh is weak.'

'The problem is, Malachi, whose flesh is it?   Yours, Agatha's, Miss Constantine's, The Reverend's and now I have met another, what are they – alter egos?'

'Yes, I know you have at last discovered the connections.'

'Connections!   They are all so different Malachi.   How do you do it?'

'I am not part of the others.   I come and go when I am needed.'

'Well, I will always need you.   The other personalities I can live without.   Perhaps Agatha I have grown fond of in her funny special way.'

'It is the personalities that I have come to explain to you.'

'An explanation a long time ago might have come in useful. It has all been such a shock,' I replied.

'Lorenzo and Maria have had to cope with them all their lives and they have been deeply affected by them, much as you and your sister have been with your own childhood.'

'Malachi you always seem to know so much, yet...'

'Jacob Alberini owned this house,' he interrupted as we took seats in preparation for our "talk".

'He was a great friend of mine. He was a philanthropist, a kind and gentle man, a humanitarian born of his own personal suffering as a Jew during the war. His family were all killed in concentration camps. Jacob survived.'

He paused a moment having thrown the poignant bait out for attention. Then he drew breath for what would be a long narrative.

'He had been living in London before the war. He went back to Italy to help his family and found himself trapped and interned. Jacob lived through terrible experiences which no one should have to suffer and he saw his survival as an extraordinary gift from God in which he was to help others.

After the war and a gradual return to health he realized that he had inherited all that his deceased family had left in investments around the world. Jacob was a wealthy man by rights but he spent the rest of his life giving everything away.

He travelled about seeing what he could do to help those in need of help.

He considered his greatest achievement was the rescue of a small boy. No one knew anything about the child, where or when he was found. The boy himself remembered nothing. The only detail the old man ever offered about the boy was that he was found with the remnants of a violin he was holding. He refused to let go of it, but his hand had been cruelly crushed and he was unable to play even if the violin had not been so badly broken.

Jacob managed to get through to the boy and gain his confidence. He called him Marcello after one of his brothers who had died in the camps.

This house was where he decided to live and where he brought the boy, gave him his name and told everyone that he was his child. The child could not talk at first, it babbled incoherent phrases. It was clear that he had suffered badly and was mentally very disturbed. There was not much treatment given to the mentally disturbed in those days except to hide them away in institutions.

Jacob lived for a time in Tahiti where he owned land which had been part of his family's investments before the war. He knew of an old woman in Tahiti with extraordinary powers. He had consulted her on many occasions and discovered that she had a deformed granddaughter with powers greater than hers. He found her one day and helped her with an operation she needed for a hare-lip and cleft-palate. He brought her back to see if she could manage the boy he had adopted. She did. She brought him back to life, she gave him a new identity and that identity multiplied as time went on. When the boy became troubled he would simply close his eyes and leave his body to go into a kind of trance state.

The Jamaican girl was the only person who managed to get through to him by just being there for him and speaking to him in a strange way that no one else could understand. It was as if she were reaching his soul.

By the time Marcello was in his twenties he seemed to have become healed of his past. He even managed to hold down a job working in a restaurant as a waiter. He had had little education but he had learnt enough to get by. School had been out of the question, he was afraid of people.

Jacob had many friends back in Italy who came from time to time to stay here with him. One was Eva, the daughter of an old school friend who was visiting London for the first time. When Jacob's son Marcello met Eva they fell in love and a few years after their marriage Eva gave birth to twins, a girl and a boy.

But the disturbance of something terrible that had lodged in Marcello's soul would never leave him. When his twins showed an inclination to learn music and their mother bought them violins, something turned in Marcello's mind that cast him back to a past that was so horrific that he was unable to face it. His way was to exit his body. Some would say, to take on another personality entirely, others would say that his body would be an empty vehicle for discarnate beings to trespass. The psychologists called it Multiple Personality Disorder. Later they termed it Dissociative Behaviour, as if by changing the term they were getting closer to an explanation.'

'And you Malachi, what would you call it?' I asked.

'What I say would make very little difference. You can't prove psychic incidence and I am not in the business of proving anything. People need time to see for themselves. That is something you have recently learned. Until you are ready to see, you will not see. People want replication to base proof upon and when they have it; they subscribe a new term to it that has mental implications.'

'I am not so sure I see, even now,' I said. 'I find it all so very disturbing. I don't understand this switching of male and female roles bit.'

'Male / Female: genders which alter with hormones and no more. When you sleep, you do not dream that you are female, or you are male, you are only who you are beneath all that.

Agatha was the first personality that came through. She had emerged when Marcello was still very young. Later she went out and bought female clothes and wigs and when she came home no one knew who it was. She had taken over so completely. She knew she lived here but she had no concept of Marcello what so ever. She hated to hear the children practise on their violins and insisted on sound-proofing the music room.

Eva reacted as you can imagine and after a time it was arranged by Jacob that they kept a separate house which he purchased for her and the children and Marcello - when he was Marcello. Agatha remained here, with Jacob. She closeted herself in her own world and confided in Jacob and Jacob recognized in her a sister that he had loved and lost in the camps.'

Malachi broke his narrative to walk about the room as if he were hesitating before he led me into another aspect of the story. The pause gave me time to ask.

'Is it true that Agatha knew my Mother, and perhaps she can still have contact with her? She once remarked that I looked like her.'

'Lillibet is good at divination and the art of fortune-telling. Your mother came to her, referred no doubt by a friend, when she was at a low ebb in her life, like many do, seeking some kind of answer from such people.

Agatha saw her there and there had been a kind of connection between them and they became friends.

They were two souls with a connection in time.'

'Are you talking about coincidence?' I asked, at a loss to understand terms like "souls with time-connections". Things now touched on a psychic, extrasensory dimension, a subject with a slow unravelling that never quite got to the bottom of facts per se. To me they were only ever hearsay arising from speculation. And, as he had already said, you can only see when you are ready to see. I was clearly not ready.

'Coincidence or "a twist of fate" is never as random as you may believe. As we are all connected, so do the events in our lives weave in an organized deliberate plan. You can no more split one life from another than you can separate rain from water. Strangers are old family you have yet to come to know, as the saying goes.'

'It does seem that I have been drawn here through a connection with my Mother,' I said as if to myself.

'Was my Mother ever aware of these personality changes?' I asked, wondering all the time about the absurdity of even asking.

'Some times when your mother visited, Agatha was there, sometimes when she visited Agatha was Marcello. These days Marcello only remains as Marcello for his family.'

My mind went back to the day I was looking for accommodation, how I was drawn here, how I had found that where ever I had been before had turned me down, how Agatha who was a stranger had been expecting me. It was a kind of visceral experience without conscious reasoning but it had seemed so right at the time.

Malachi resumed his narrative in a more reflective tone.

'You can understand how it must have been for poor Eva with the different personalities that were coming through her husband. It became more than she could cope with. That was when she moved out permanently to where they are now. Jacob had moved her mainly for the protection of the children. One minute Marcello was a loving husband and father, the next he was some strange woman or a priest or a beggar. Ah yes, you look surprised. You have not met the beggar yet. Well there are plenty of characters you have not met. Some are gentle but some are distinctly dangerous. They would attack Eva and children. Marcello would attack the boy who was a reminder of who he once was and might have become.

The worst part for the children was the shame and embarrassment it brought upon them as a family. They could bring no one home who would not become targeted by one or other of the 'alter egos' as you call them.

These days the body has become weakened by the many drugs it has been given and the unknown treatment it had in childhood and it cannot last much longer.'

Malachi stopped and looked into my face with a long and searching look as if to find in me a strength he hoped I had. The story had left me in a state of confused deliberation. Was it all a fabricated extension of this chameleon smokescreen or was he coming from a dimension beyond any scientific or psychological reasoning? Though an element of doubt invaded my reasoning, he had certainly caught my imagination and my trust.

'I feel the heart is not strong and after one of the violent characters has left it the body is wracked with pain and the headaches are getting worse. I feel right now a pain in my chest that stops me from breathing,' he said, leaning forward in his chair.

'I want you to be kind to Lorenzo, he loves you very much and you don't know it.'

'I certainly don't know it. I found him in bed with my sister for one thing. What was worse is that he simply stopped coming to teach me. There had been no warning or explanation of any kind. Then when Lillibet said to go and visit him, I went and he disappeared out through the back door as soon as he heard my voice.'

'Lorenzo is physically and verbally attacked frequently by his father coming in different disguises. He has been traumatised since childhood. Marcello instead of recovering from his childhood and learning to move on has re-affected his own children. Marcello knows this but is unable to stop the whole process.'

'What? Even with Lillibet's witchery? Surely she can cast a spell, or whatever it is she does.'

'Magic spells don't work like that, each step we take must be learned and felt and managed for its own value of learning. Life is not a matter of seeking answers, as you think; it is about learning which questions we should ask and without this understanding there can be no release.'

'I am battling to know who I am and here you are, seeming to know everyone though I am confused about who you are also.'

I heard myself rebelling childishly at the return of this personality exchange thing. Part of me did not want to understand.

'You are who you are because of those you choose to love and because of those who love you.'

He was becoming more and more obtuse and difficult to comprehend.

Indefinable, ambiguous, confounding issues were crowding my already confused brain. I tried to lead him back to something more tangible to understand. I wanted to trick him into a confession of fraud.

'You know so much about all these characters yet you say you are not part of them. I am sure that if I were to question each one, they would all say that they too are not part of the others.'

'It is hard to explain. In one way, we are all a part of each other and we all have actions that are reminiscent of a forgotten past that we have lived before.'

'Now you are suggesting the idea of reincarnation?'

'Why is that so hard to believe? The church would have you believe that you hang about in suspended animation till Judgement Day and that is accepted without a qualm.'

'I cannot answer that. Probably because I have never given it much thought. I have never even thought about the possibilities of a past life. I have enough trouble trying to figure out this one.'

There was a frustration about the conversation that provoked me towards mockery.

'What would you know about my past life Malachi?'

'It was connected with music. You have always been connected with music as your mother was before you. That is why you turn back to it so easily.'

'Easy enough to guess that but the geneticist would argue that I inherited a musical gene from my Mother.' I felt myself challenging him, perhaps even doubting him; yet curious about what he had to say.

'What about Peggy, I wonder what it is she was connected to, something glamorous no doubt.'

'I see a time of Medici subterfuge behind beauty, cunning, survival with poisoned rings.'

'That is horrible.   Now I know not to believe you,' I said indignantly.

'That, I am afraid, is the dilemma of truth. Every truth hangs in the balance of fantasy and intrinsic reality. It is up to each person to make that clear judgement for himself alone.   We are all adjudicators of life.'

'But then you say you are not of life, you simply borrowed the shell of an empty body from which you say you speak. What then about the time you spend in the ethereal sense of existence. What is that and what is it like?'

'Much as it is like for you right now in your body. Incorporeal beings are not burdened by the limits of the flesh but they are limited by the means to be in contact with those in the flesh. Death does not mean that you simply cease to exist, you make a transition of continuation, knowing that you are still in existence, but existence on another level.'

'It all sounds like some kind of illusion,' I said, speaking from the spiritual vacuum expanding within.

'We have to work our way out of the illusion in order to see our true being.'

It did not make sense to me.   Illusion implies nothing real, therefore call it deception for if illusion implies nothing is real then in fact the opposite is true.

My expectations of the psychic world have always far outweighed its revelations. I could never quite get satisfactorily to the bottom of the offered facts but then they never were "facts" per se, they were only ever hearsay, arising from speculation. Was this a personality from a collection of personalities impersonating a kind of angel offering truth in envelopes of personal wisdom or was he indisputable?

Malachi spoke in abstract terms of an evolving soul moving in cycles of evolution, of things that happened beyond my raw naiveté, but I was aware even in those adolescent gaps of my ignorance that I felt complete and cognisant of things I would come to understand more fully as I grew older. It was just like finding a lost key or a purse after frantic searching and then the sense of satisfied serenity and wholeness when discovering it, most often exactly where I had last placed it.

Being with Malachi was like that, even though I did not fully understand things at the time.

'There is a fragile balance between conscious and unconscious aspects of existence,' he was saying looking deeply into my eyes. His words were hypnotic and were evading me. My mind was slipping. I could not grasp what he was saying without wanting to tear it all wide open to reduce to ridicule.

'What about Jacob, does he use this empty vessel as you see it?' I asked, with the need to reopen the argument for clarification.

'No, he was in total sympathy with Marcello. Marcello, to him, was his son, his family, his world. Jacob was very weary when he left this world. He had no need to return to it. He had so many loved ones on that side and the desire to unite with them was strong.

I came because Marcello's children need protecting. I am not able to be here much longer and even Lillibet is becoming weaker since the poisoning. I would like to think I leave Lorenzo in your hands now.'

'If this is not a dream, or some concocted story to amuse me, then I take it that you are asking me to do something but I really don't know how or what to do. I cannot go on pursuing someone who runs from me.

Anyway, have you any idea how crazy all this sounds to me? I don't even understand my own life. How can I understand this, let alone know why Lorenzo sleeps with my sister and runs from me, when you try to tell me that he loves me. How is that possible?'

I stopped abruptly.

As I was speaking, I could see that Malachi was having trouble breathing. He had loosed the top button of his shirt and was sitting now, bent over and grasping his head as I had seen Agatha do on a few occasions before closing herself into her room

'Malachi,' I called softly to him. 'Malachi are you alright, here take this glass of water.'

He was too weak to answer. I managed to raise him up and lead him over to the narrow bed where he lay silent and in evident pain.

It seemed all at once, that what was once my friend had gone and in his place a dull impassive face looking back from a world of darkness and a life time of infinite loneliness.

The breathing became laboured with a peculiar nasal hissing in and out like a balloon being inflated by a pump. He started at me as if in recognition of something he had once known. His eyes swelled and filled with heavy ears that gradually, one by one rolled down over his sunken cheeks. Then a new voice came through him.

'You are lovely,' he whispered and took a deep breath of pain. 'There is something of her in you,' it said.

A tinge of disquiet twisted through my thoughts.

Who was this now?

Where was Malachi with all his wisdom?

'Please, go and call my son now, go, go at once,' the voice said, the eyes closed and the breath was clipped.

'Do you mean Lorenzo?' I asked, half serious and half playing into this macabre and ridiculous role.

'Yes, Lorenzo,' came the voice.

Then to try "its" patience I answered, 'You wait here Malachi.   I will go at once.'

Chapter 41

A strong wind had blown up the afternoon as if it would compete with the tempest in my mind. Sharp needles of rain exploded upon my face and swept my hair into a nest of fury about my head. I had no time to take a jacket with me but even an umbrella would have been impotent against the gusts.

I left the house and hurried to the mews cottages where once again I reluctantly struck the door with its defiantly bright-polished brass door-knock.

If the strange man were to come to the door I would know that this was all some silly prank of mimicry, but he did not. It was Maria who answered the door. I told her hastily and as briefly as possible what had happened and that the man had asked to speak to his son.

'Lorenzo is rehearsing with the orchestra right now; there is no way of interrupting them, not any more. Papa has ruined most of his chances like that. I will come with you.'

She snatched a jacket from behind the door and hurried along the street with me.

Neither of us spoke as we half ran, half walked the distance between the houses.

When we got to the music room Lillibet was there ahead of us. She was mopping the old man's brow and talking gently to him in her strange language.

'Papa?' called Maria, 'Is it you in there?'

The face was white and drained and in its state of infirmity it could only be a cadaver without personality.

'Did you bring my heart pills?'

'They are in your jacket Papa, where I always leave them. Now why don't you take them yourself, you know which pocket I always put them in.'

'Where is Lorenzo, where is my son?'

'Papa you know he can't be around for you to call on all the time, you know how busy he is.'

'I am dying Maria. Can you not see an old man die before you?'

'You have been dying for a long time Papa.'

'Yes, yes, it is so. I let go and then I find myself back over and over.'

'Angina, that what they call it. It leave him very weak after,' Lillibet said turning to me cheerfully, even behind eyes troubled with a pain buried deep down.

It was clear that she loved him and I wondered about her own personal life. She must have had one and not just been servant all her life to this neurosis allowed to fester.

He was sitting up.

He had obviously already taken one of his pills as the pain that had gripped him had subsided leaving him tired and weak. There was no sign of the Malachi character, everything about him had altered. Before me sat a man withered and bent from some ancient wound that would not mend; a repository of sins remembered and good deeds gone astray.

While barely intact of body, his mind slipped on and off track, there he was, crumpled in this shrivelled flesh sustained by a will and modern doctoring, ironically keeping his soul from flying to that unknown territory.

I wondered if much of this dramatic state was a means of attention seeking, but there was no doubt that his physical condition was as in much of a tangle as his psychological confusion.

Lillibet led him out to the landing and coaxed him to come up to her flat to eat something and talk. He followed like a lamb.

Maria and I stayed behind while she talked quietly about her father and the problems they had had over the years.

She told me how music had played a large part in their lives.

Marcello had been both wrapped up in music and destroyed by it. He had been a perfectionist and unless he could manage to produce perfect sounds he had grown desperate at himself and expected the perfection from his children with unblemished limbs.

'It is like he wants to die,' she said. 'He is always talking of "letting go" but I think he is actually frightened of dying. Instead he becomes someone else and his characters are so different and so disturbing.'

I thought of that famous speech of Hamlet's; "but for the dread of something after death, the undiscovered country from whose borne no traveller returns puzzles the will and makes us accept the things we have than fly to others we know not of..."

'I wonder which character he will adapt when he does finally let go,' I said.

There was a pause of silence as we crept into those hollow spaces that cling to the mind, filled with impressions of some sharp and pertinent episode that had shaped our thinking and affected our senses.

Then Maria broke the silence. 'Lillibet says your sister Peggy is here,' she said.

'Yes, downstairs with Jason.'

'Thank God, now she will leave Lorenzo alone. She is dangerous.'

I did not know what to say. I was so fogged up by the unplumbed state of affairs that to comment now about something I knew nothing about, would be to disclose what a fool I was.

Outside the wind raged at anything on the earth that could be moved. It battered at the window shooting tears of rain at fragile panes. Inside I felt cold. My shirt was sticking to me and I was made aware of my hair that still ruffled in matted clumps down my neck.

We were silent again.

Neither of us knew what to say next and the questions that separated us loomed as a dark gulf between us.

'Sorry if I brought you out when it was something ordinary,' I said.

'It is never ordinary where Father is concerned. Would you like to come back with me?' she asked politely.

'No, I will stay and practise, but thank you,' I answered.

'But you are wet through. Will you go down and change?'

'Perhaps, but it is no bother really, I will soon dry off.'

'She has taken over again. I know it. She did it to Lorenzo. She just took over. He was too soft to tell her he did not want her.'

'That's Peggy,' I squirmed with coupled loyalty and embarrassment for my sister. It was the way she was, she could not help it. It was her way of taking charge. Without that we would never have survived our childhood. I had so much to be grateful for. I found myself defending her once again.

'Can't you see she has adopted your friend Jason now because you loved him?'

'Oh no Maria, I have never loved Jason. Whatever gave you that idea? We are friends that is all. It suited us both to share the flat when the others left.'

It was becoming one of those girlie conversations that I have always avoided and I was wishing her to go. Maria was likeable enough and chatty but I was not in her league for that kind of female tête-à-tête. I never knew quite what to say next.

'Well don't ever let her know that or she will turn back to Lorenzo and we are only just regaining calm in the house, if you don't count Father.'

'Maria,' I stopped her. 'Why did he suddenly stop giving me violin lessons?' I asked bravely.

'I did not know he had. Lorenzo never tells me what he is doing. It was Father who told us that he had found this talented genius at the house. I don't even know how he discovered you. I know he spoke up for you at the college and arranged your interview and made sure you got in after the audition but if you had heard old

Harmshaw on the committee go on about you, I think it was already a foregone conclusion.'

She smiled encouragingly at me and I felt myself blush.   A warm glow filled me.

I may have been no closer to the truth as to why he simply never turned up again and avoided me but what she said filled me satisfactorily with pride and relief.

'I see he teaches there,' I said tentatively hoping for more information.

'Only part-time, he has too many other commitments. I am the one who teaches, but private lessons, you know.'

'All these books,' I waved my hand around the shelves. 'I thought at one time that he was a psychologist at the very least.'

'They mostly belonged to Jacob.   Jacob was our grandfather, well, sort of step-grandfather.   He was interested in Father's condition and tried to get to the bottom of it.   Lorenzo too, he started to study psychology for the same reason but I guess the music took precedence. No one really understands it. They give it names like Multiple-Personality Disorder and Dissociative Identity Disorder. What is it they say? Ah yes I remember all the wording, "personalities who manifest unexpectedly and at random, changing the character, the voice, the age where they lose time and reality..." They refer to the characters as "alters" and "fragments"... let me see, yes: "which are relatively limited psychic states that express only one feeling, hold one memory or carry out a limited task in the person's life..." and what-have-you.   They say that the condition stems from some childhood abuse, but in some of the case histories my brother and I read, the disorder started as early as the age of three.   What I don't understand is why many more people who have suffered great abuse don't all behave in this way.'

'Perhaps they react inwardly or in some other way,' I suggested.

Maria had ignored me, this was a subject that had confounded and confused her family and one in which she had taken a great interest.

She was going through titles on the shelves. She withdrew one, and finding a marker she read from it.

"'In complex multiples, the personalities are relatively full-bodied, complete states capable of a range of emotions and behaviours, the alters will have executive control and some substantial amount of time over the person's life... complex MPD with over fifteen alter personalities and complicated amnesia barriers are associated with 100% frequency of childhood physical, sexual and emotional abuse."'

She replaced the book and turned back into the room.

'Problem is,' she said, 'no one knows anything about Father's background, where he came from or what happened to him. We don't even know how old he is really. Old Jacob, our grandfather, never disclosed anything; about his life or anyone else. "The past is the past" he said.

I understand about the stress thing but what is also strange is that I have read there are people who have the disorder who have had no previous knowledge of stress, not real stress if you know what I mean.'

Maria had truly researched the problem. No doubt it had been the topic of family investigation and she was undoubtedly an authority on the subject of Multiple Personality Disorder.

She began quoting the books and accounts she had read and I felt myself getting colder and colder in my wet clothing. I was shivering uncontrollably when at last she took notice and insisted that I must go and get changed, despite my reluctance to go downstairs.

She told me that Lorenzo was playing a solo piece on flute at a concert on Sunday. It was that lovely Flute Concerto No. 2 in D by Mozart, a piece we had played together. Flute was his second instrument and he was good, she assured me. She suggested that I should accompany her. I began to find excuses but she called round the door on her way out.

'I will call for you at six on Sunday, be ready.' Then she was gone.

I crept back to the flat to find with enormous relief, that it was empty.

They had gone out.

I did not for a moment feel any sense of resentment nor certainly any envy. If it had been an amenably frank and unguarded affair I would have been pleased for them both but it was the clandestine covertness of it all that betrayed a sense of perfidy and purpose behind it and what the purpose was, left me feeling startled and vulnerable.

I towelled my hair and pulled on something warm and dry, all the while feeling a glow of expectation before me, despite my sister's Machiavellian scheming.

The confusions of Malachi's metamorphosis clung like bindweed about my mind but for now I would refuse to analyse the situation or condition. Lorenzo and Maria had done all that and come up with fewer answers.

I decided to phone my aunt and ask if I could stay with them for a couple of nights. Peggy was sure to be gone soon. She never stayed anywhere long.

Chapter 42

It is a strange association by custom that we unhesitatingly open our hearts and minds to family with less formality than we do strangers. One is bound to them from the importance we give to blood ties. That they are after all, the wellspring of our life's source, somehow means they have to matter.

Those incidental strangers one meets on the way are no less intimate, offering as many pitfalls or crutches or joy. It is the familiarity which arises out of shared experiences that binds us or casts us adrift.

Looking back, I recognise that I felt no desperate and immediate bond of love for the family. There had been too much time that had divided our knowledge and familiarity with one another. It was a kinship arising from a darkness of too many recriminations that needed time to mend. I had clung to them because they were family; like a rat to floating jetsam that would otherwise drown.

Getting to know my Aunt Sophie was a lesson in forbearance and understanding. If she had not been a relative I would never have spent the time trying to assimilate her many peculiarities.

She seldom sat still. It was as if she was following some unseen orders that propelled her into every unnecessary action. She and Ben eulogised the virtues of ecology with all its conservationism, acquiring other people's rubbish for which they found uses of equal uselessness. Their home was full of home-made furniture reconstructed from some obsolete item they had discovered on an old dump site. "Organic" was a by-word for unhygienic vegetables grown on sewage waste without pesticides to remove vermin and sharing insects. It was a wonderful excuse for not having to bother too hard about a crop which nature alone cared for.

"Drop out or cop out" were terms that could be slandered against them by those who had less reverence for family respect. I wondered how Peggy would have found her and how long she could have stayed there without irritation.

But there was the light side of Aunt Sophie, when she laughed. For she saw life only as a means of enjoyment and that was acquired by laughing mostly at herself, somehow turning a rock-hard self-interest into self-derision. She had opinions about most things and as far as I was concerned, a major opinion lay in the fact that I was making a huge mistake in not living with her and Ben, taking music simply as a past-time, after the real job of caring for animals!

Getting away often became an exhausting battle of wits.

The grandparent's house was something different, equally symbolic of the owner's identity. Their house had seen no alteration, no lick of paint or any other kind of uplift or adornment in as many years as their children had grown and moved away and had families and homes of their own. There was the same tiredness about the place as there was with its occupants.

There was no doubt that Grandfather was ill and declining rapidly into a sub-world of his own. He would emerge to make a comment, give a command or demand something, mostly for attention.

They had come from that generation that took for granted that men held the reins in all matters with the supreme role of control in marriage. The man did all the thinking and the woman gave up a mental life for one of grateful domestic servitude.

Grandmother had few opinions of her own that she trusted in, other than a remote and diffident affection she held for her children and grandchildren. Her home was filled with faded snapshots placed with care into square frames of differing dimension. They littered every shelf and table space rendering them useless for any other purpose. No one had noticed how the insubstantial print had faded with time and no amount of glass polishing that divided them from the corruptive air, made much difference to their waning.

To me they were strangers, encapsulated there in their smiling response to the photographer. Family I had never met and perhaps never likely to meet.

I was one of them and nothing to them, other than Mother's younger daughter Anna, no more.

Nothing but her terrible death would identify me with a time best forgotten.

My mother smiled at me from a dozen poses: as a small child to a lovely bride (Father's picture had been removed) and some with my sister and me there with her.

One picture of my mother came to my attention because of the gold charm bracelet she was wearing. My aunt explained that she had been given the bracelet when she turned sixteen. Aunt was given a similar one also. She had long since lost hers. 'Perhaps under a bale of hay or at a party' she laughed carelessly.

Mother had treasured hers. The bracelets had come with only a few charms and she had added to hers over the years, whenever she could. It became a heavy ornament of masses of charms she had acquired here and there as gifts or she had saved to buy them.

I knew that bracelet. I knew it well, and the memory of it silenced me.

My sister had claimed it and wore it all the time.

Grandmother was reluctant to be reminded of Mother. She would respond with the same "I don't remember" to any questions I asked.

Perhaps she accepted Mother's suicide as a failing in herself. I would never know. It was as if she had disengaged herself from life. Those old faded sepia prints of her showed that there was once a sparkle in her eyes and a posture that offered up an expectation of something vibrant and good that she was hoping for in her future life. It was that expectation that came with the fabled myth of happy ever after, "marriage will resolve all" nonsense. For, life's enchantment had withered when she had ceased early on to think for herself and not to complain about the drudgery that went with the commitment.

She expressed herself only in the joy of children and gave herself to the obedient attention of their demands. As the children left home she learnt to channel all her remaining energy into her husband's demanding and persistent needs, excluding all her own.

It was as if life had trampled upon her, not noticing her, expecting her to be there and fulfil her role.

Their house resembled that same pernicious decay of Agatha's flat, where the soul of Jacob had embedded itself for an eternity of diminished joy; a brief joy of youth and hope that was always remembered and would not return. Age creeps up unnoticed. Faded curtains whose cloth is worn, like the carpets whose stains are overlooked, are the remaining imprints of all the years gone by so soon .

Sleep became the unbidden occupation of the day and lent restlessness to the nights. Neglect and forgetting was the legacy of all those years of devotion. Even my Aunt, the remaining child at home, was neglectful of her. Most of her attention, when not spent with her animals was spent on Grandfather and his eternal demands.

They had a woman who came in once a day to clean, make beds, cook and go home. She was the most vibrant part of living matter in that house.

I stayed mostly at Aunt's house when I went to visit. They lived at a faster rate of crumbling disorder, as life was still an action and not a dying ember there.

On this occasion I stayed with the grandparents. I can't remember why I had been given that option at that time.

They observed me with quiet ambivalence and curious pleasure, watching to see what part of Mother there was in me and what part of my father might corrupt her better part.

I played all three of my musical instruments for them. They expressed such joy at my playing but concentration I could see lasted no longer than half an hour at the most, then minds turned in upon themselves and began to shut out the outside world of exhausted concentration.

I lay awake at night, listening in those waking hours between midnight and dawn to the plaintive cry of foxes on their prowl for what rabbits the local farmers had omitted to shoot. They were a starving breed now, of no further interest to man. Now that he was forbidden his pleasure in hunting them they were vermin, a nuisance - but magnificent none the less in their midnight stealth, furtive, watchful, sad.

All the time I was there I thought only of returning to my own home, the music-room and knowing someone was always there in some form or other.

I had to get up early to get the train to my first music lesson so I stayed up late practising in the guest room, distilling my thoughts into a soul of sound. At the same time I was guiltily aware that my playing was causing a disturbance.

Suggestions were put that I stayed on there, or lived with my aunt in her disorder. The thought of it curdled with an inner foreboding at the prospect and a reserved but courteous supplication to be excused for a rapid flow of reasons.

I never mentioned Peggy.

Chapter 43

When I returned to Number 63 on Sunday morning I found the flat still empty. There was no sign of either Jason or Peggy. It was tidier than usual which was surprising as they both regarded housework as a waste of time.

I had not been in for long when Agatha came through the door and explained in a fractious tone that she had spent all of the day before cleaning up after them. She had clearly smartened up since that time, as her hair was immaculate and her make up as dense as a heavy fog on a dark night, revealed nothing of the tired and ailing flesh beneath.

I thanked her and asked if she had any idea where they had gone or how long they would be away.

'Lillibet tells me they have gone out of the country but that Jason will return in a few days and without that...'

'Thank you,' I said cutting short the acidic tone with which she was about to describe my sister and really not wanting to know how Lillibet knew. Reality itself was hard enough to come to grips with rather than a speculation on the illusory.

Agatha finally departed after I told her that I had been invited out to a concert with Maria and Lorenzo that evening and I had a lot to do before getting ready for it. She had wanted to know details about the programme and which of the twins, if not both, would be playing.

It was with mixed feelings that I looked forward to the evening. All my qualms around Lorenzo had built up to a crescendo of complex emotion. I could not get to grips with my feelings about him, let alone comprehend why I felt as I did about him. After all, had he not succumbed to Peggy as most men had in the end? I had thought him higher than that and now I began to see him as less special.

I had lived all my childhood with the complex concealments that were a part of Peggy's make up. The mysterious subject of multiple personalities behind Lorenzo's extraordinary father should have been of little consequence. But the emergence of those strangers who erupted from him like an epidemic, were disturbingly real, individual and separate from each other. They worried me. If they were some kind of psychological reaction from a genetic flaw, they were remarkably cleverly done. If they were drug induced they were never out of character but constant to their individuality. My mind would spin from one possibility to another and never arrived at the same conclusion.

All the same, I busied myself with preparation that evening, making myself as perfect as I could and I could not deny an ulterior motive though it made me blush to know it.

Maria was late in calling for me and I was about to give up on her when I heard a car pull up outside. I grabbed at my jacket and went out.

Maria's mother was driving the large family Mercedes and to my utter amazement, the metamorphosed father sat in the front with her, looking for all the world an unadulterated picture of pure integrity and sincerity. He was perfectly cleaned up from the dense pancake of the morning. How on earth did he do it?

So this was to be a family affair and one in which the chameleon was hopefully in control over who was in command of the body.

I thought how interesting and entertaining the circumstances would be to an outsider, but to me, it was a nightmare and I realized for the first time how painful a predicament it was for the family.

Maria had already climbed out of the car to come to greet me. She smiled a look of relief to see me there.

'I am so pleased you are coming,' she said. 'Mama and I thought if you were with us there would be less chance of... well... you know what I mean?'

I nodded vaguely hoping that I knew what she meant.

'It will be the first concert he has attended in years and he wanted so badly to come. Mama said that your presence would be stabilizing.'

'I hope so Maria,' I said, then got into the car greeting her parents with a mind ready to spill over into which ever direction it would lead me.

I learned that evening that Mama Alberini had been dramatic soprano at some illustrious opera house in Europe at one time and now retained a place in choral music from time to time. When we got to the concert-hall it seemed everyone knew the family, even Marcello. Though how he was regarded was kept well veiled and thankfully he appeared to be very much in control all evening.

The whole programme was outstanding, starting with Rossini's wonderful William Tell overture. Lorenzo was just visible at the back of the violins but he made his debut in the next half with his flute solo in Debussy's Syrinx.

The Syrinx is full of magic given its name in reference to the myth of the amorous pursuit by Pan of the beautiful nymph Syrinx. The story goes that Syrinx does not return Pan's love but hides in the marshes. When Pan cuts the reeds to make his pipes he kills his love. I wondered at the resemblance of my own haphazard emotions or was my inadequacy playing me for worthless fool again?

The music formed white shadows, like sketches in the air. It was both fragile and strong, moving and affecting like a long and sacred prayer and I was swept away with admiration at how soulfully Lorenzo expressed the music, as if imparting his soul to some silent listener.

Drinks in the foyer at interval, we kept our seats, shifting nervously at the thought of Marcello becoming disturbed.

Maria had a boyfriend who played percussion. She whispered his identity and smiled. I paid little attention as my thoughts were riotously elsewhere. No sign of Lorenzo and no mention of him either. I waited in suspense of not-knowing and not daring to ask. It was a relief when the orchestra took up their positions for the second half of the programme.

It was over and I felt I had woken from a wonderful dream. People filed out afterwards into the night air like a release from prayer where an intensity of moment hung suspended in the music still lying softly on the air. In that moment of ambivalent anticipation of how the evening would progress, a small dread crept in to those darker aspects of my mind where all the 'what ifs' bubbled to the surface. Nothing was inevitable, as nothing was clear.

Overshadowing buildings framed that vaulted space between interlacing stars and illuminated earth and out of that lighted darkness a slow faith in something immense began to dawn on me. It came with a certainty associated with everything that could be seen and heard from the reminiscent echoes of the music.

I silently prayed that I could cope with this new and complex family and find strength where I could release all my irrational fears of rejection without showing that it mattered.

Maria disappeared to find her brother while I went with her parents to find the car. The city throbbed with the sound of traffic. Square-box, black taxis wove in between impatient cars and large red busses, making up time for hurried fares. Heaving crowds of nameless faces, come from every corner of the globe. They walked unsmiling along pavements lined with illuminated shops filled with glamour on artificially posed plastic figures.

Mrs Alberini kept up a constant chatter as she walked in strides of knowing direction. Her husband followed in whispers of silence. His health appeared restored but for grunts of absent humour amid the crowded streets.

I began to feel a sense of impending drama. It was that same vague intangible something that moved about in cycles of complex thought. What if he should have a transformation slip out here on the way to the car?   Who would it be this time and how would they react?

As we reached the spot where the car had been parked Maria came running up to us out of breath.

'I am staying here,' she announced. 'They are going to Louigi's for a drink. Anna will you join us?'

I opened my mouth to decline.   A room full of strangers with Lorenzo trying to avoid me was more than I needed right then but before I had said a word the father growled something in a language I did not understand.

'Basta, basta Papa, you promised that you would try this one evening to remain whole.'

Then a whole new voice spoke in a clipped tone: 'Wait, just wait and see how you will like this!'

'Oh my God,' Maria called out, 'not even for one day, one day - can he be trusted.   Mamma you said he was going to be alright.   I thought he had taken his pills.'

This was the scene the family had been enduring for all of Maria and Lorenzo's life, just as Malachi said.   It put my own family problems into small perspective.   Here was a situation that could not be walked away from but had to be endured and coped with.

'Maria,' I said with an imposed calm to my own voice, 'you go back to the party they are expecting you.   Let me return with your parents.'

'Agatha.' I called out.

I had no idea who these new entities were that had scratched the surface of a strange reality but I knew Agatha well.   She was strong and determined, if I could call her out now she could help.

The hosting body crumpled from the stern posture to one bent over and Agatha's voice came through.

'I can't be seen like this,' Agatha's voice said, in her dependable high-tone voice.

'Agatha we need you right now, please help us.' I said.

The two remaining Alberinis were momentarily silenced by our dialogue.

Agatha's voice: 'What is it that I can do, they keep coming and going and I am losing control.'

'No, you must keep control right now, just wait for us to get home and we can have a coffee together with Lillibet.'

Mama Alberini began chanting away in agitated Italian and Maria had vanished as fast as she had come.

'Now, let's all get in the car together and go home,' I suggested. 'Mrs Alberini I am going to sit in the back with Agatha.'

The lady was still talking in her own language but the person in her husband's body was no longer answering her. We climbed into the back while the excitable Mama got into the driver's seat. Without ceasing to draw breath from one long harangue she started the engine while looking into the rear-view mirror at us.

The car moved forward with two violent jerks, then smoothed its way through the crowded car-park. Ahead of us we saw Lorenzo accompanied by Maria returning to us at a fast trot.

'Agatha' covered her face with her hand and looked downward so as not to be identified in disgusting men's clothing, and remained silent.

The twins came up to the car out of breath from running. They were talking to their mother in her language. I did not look at them but kept my gaze before me. Let them sort it all out, I thought. The situation was at least under control, or as much control as could get us all home without another scene.

Maria opened the door next to me.

'I am so sorry to do this to you Anna,' she said. 'I thought we had it all under control with the drugs he had been getting. Look, Lorenzo is coming back with you. I want to meet someone tonight. He is special. Ah, look, I will speak to you again tomorrow, right?'

Lorenzo took over the driving seat while his mother got out and became the passenger next to him.

'Hello Anna,' Lorenzo said turning to look at me.

'Hello,' I answered. 'Will you not also greet Agatha, she has been strong enough to come through to save the evening. She should be thanked.'

'Thank you Agatha,' Lorenzo answered awkwardly and he drove on, silently.

I sensed from the shuffling and breathing sounds that the body next to me was in pain. I felt in the pocket for the pills but instead I found a small canister of Glyceryl Trinitrate Spray. I had seen it when Lillibet had taken charge before.

'This is what you might need Agatha. Here, take this.'

The sufferer took the canister and sprayed it into his mouth, then fell back onto the seat, eyes shut, body tense with pendant pain till it gradually relaxed and breathed with more ease.

Agatha's voice was gone and the Alberini's had returned.

'They all go when the pain comes,' it said. 'None of them can take the pain.'

'Well, you can and that says more to me,' I answered. 'That is how you have become,' I said. 'The bearer of pain and coping with it. Kind of like life – isn't it?'

He sat silent and still, his head still bent as if attending to some great battle that raged within.

As the theatres emptied and the night revellers moved on to home or some further entertainment, the traffic became a fugue movement of repeated stops and starts with allegro dashes when the moving traffic became freed for brief interludes.

Lorenzo and his mother were silent in the front as the body next to me slowly unwound from its seizure. My hand was taken and kissed, then sleep overtook it finally as it slumped back into the seat.

At last we reached our destination.

Lorenzo and his mother gently coaxed the sleeping figure to sit upright. While they eased it out of the car, I disappeared into the night shadows to walk home.

This was now my turn to leave unannounced without explanation.

Would he care anyway?

As I walked back along quieter streets my thoughts assembled a computation of all the things that had moved so fast from one strange occurrence to another. I was so preoccupied in my thinking that I hardly noticed the tall dark figure coming up behind.

'Anna.'

'Lorenzo,' I said.

'You left before I could thank you for managing the situation just then.'

'Well' I sighed; 'I left in much the same way you did and I was never able to thank you for all the wonderful violin lessons.'

'Your sister told me not to return. That you were unhappy with the way I was teaching you.'

'I guess I spent a childhood believing everything my sister told me, why should I expect anyone else to be less gullible?'

'So it was not true then?'

'Truth, as Malachi said, is something you find out for yourself.'

We walked on without saying anything. Why was everything about these people so double edged? My whole existence appeared to be fractions of some other concealment, held together by a strip of flimsy cellophane stick. It was bad enough that my sister's duplicitous actions were confounding and painful to bear.

'Why', I kept asking myself. 'Why?'

Part of me felt relieved to know there were reasons behind Lorenzo's abandonment, even if they had come in such a designing way to harm me - and from my own sister. Part of me wanted to know more with those strains of how and why that tangle up these issues. I was suspicious of the tenuousness of this meeting and at the same time I was wildly aware of the strained and electric enchantment of being in his presence. It was at once an exquisite moment of fragile chance that I wanted to go on for ever and at the same time I was ready at a moment to run and hide from.

Clearly there were things on his mind that I had not been privy to. How long he had been in touch with my sister? How had he landed up in her bed? How had she been drawn to him? How had she approached him? – Lorenzo, who was so unapproachable.

The questions lay heavily on my mind but I was unable, nor entitled to ask them.

We reached the steps of Number 63 and stopped, uncertain what to say or what to do.

'The music was wonderful tonight,' I said.

'Yes, an inspired choice,' he replied.

'I had no idea you were so... the flute...your second instrument or your first?'

It sounded so futile. I knew it as soon as I said it; so denigrating to such obvious talent.

'Your tutors speak very highly of you,' he responded, dismissing my question.

Yes, he had found my flattery debatable.

'You are certainly beyond my teaching.'

Now he was trying to opt out of any future coaching. I caught my breath and lunged into the next rash statement.

'No, Lorenzo, that could never be and I miss you.' (Oh God, too forward) 'What I mean is, I miss the lessons with you.'

I stopped, took a breath and thought boldly to continue (damn it). 'More than you know.'

'Is Peggy staying with you still?' he asked with a slight nervous tinge to his voice.

'No, she has gone off somewhere with Jason I am told, but I gather you know more about her coming and going than I do.'

I spoke with an attempted lightness to my voice, trying desperately to keep the bitterness I felt at bay.

'Your sister's motives and movements are as obscure and random as all Father's multiples that come and go at a whim,' he answered, shifting uncomfortably about, wanting to say more.

'I am sorry to hear that she had come between you and Jason. It was unfair on you.'

I looked up at him, straining to see his eyes in the shadowed semi-darkness. They were dark pools whose expression was masked from me. Would I find there an answer to his unbearable indifference to how I could possibly feel?

His dark hair and clothing had merged with the night giving him an inaccessible, spectre-like appearance and I felt shame at my hopeless expectation of the impossible. It felt as if I was falling down, eternally down through the fibrous roots of complex emotion to that empty place where powerlessness resides.

A street lamp caught a reflected light in his eyes. I saw at once a deeply disturbed look that exposed a sensitivity I had not seen before.

'Her relationship with Jason does not affect me as perhaps it might affect you,' I said, trying to sound dismissively casual while wanting so badly not to show any sign of the resentment that pounded still in my breast.

'No?' he said. 'I am sorry. I was led to believe...'

'What Jason does, is nothing to do with me,' I interrupted. 'No, nor is it any of my business what you or Peggy do either for that matter. Jason was just a friend, no more.'

I shivered suddenly and turned to the door to fit my key into the lock.

'Thank you for the wonderful music tonight, unforgettable. I really don't want to spoil it all with reflections upon your relationship with my sister. That is yours and hers and the music is mine.'

I opened the door with trembling hands floundering in the moment like hapless wreckage swept along in a tsunami current of bruised emotions. I had no rights to outrage or expectations from this man. He was far beyond me and my small reach.

'May I come in?' he asked.

'Of course; would you like a coffee or something to eat?'

'I think Mother was hoping to offer you something there tonight but you left rather hurriedly.'

'I wasn't sure what to do. You were all so busy and I did not like to come in between your family arrangements. I should have thanked her. I will go back tomorrow and thank her. It was so nice of Maria to invite me this evening.'

I could hear myself floundering with stiff formality. I was slipping off the easy tracks that I had glided on so well up till then.

'Can you make coffee?' he suggested, now taking the lead.

'Wine,' I said, changing my mind. 'I have some wine here somewhere if Jason and Peggy have not finished it all.'

'Good idea,' said Lorenzo taking the bottle from me that I had pulled from a shelf. He opened it carefully and slowly. I selected two glasses, from the random student collection.

This was something new and disconcerting. There had never been this kind of fluency between us before that did not involve music. But where to begin? What to talk about with Peggy hanging in the air between us, and the evening's strangers whose voices had barked out in other languages, filling the mind with further mystery.

How would I begin a conversation that involved my sister and happenstance when my own mind shifted and froze at each turn like a mouse in a trap? Of course the conversation had to pivot around her. Of course, he initiated it.

'I saw something in your sister that reminded me of my Father. It was as if she were trying to hide something deep inside her that could only be performed by some wild and unaccountable action. It is as if an old battle they have not been able to resolve in their minds has become distorted, like a nightmare being re-enacted all the time, altering their sense of reality. She would say things. I believed her at first. She was convincing.'

I kept silent, sipping my wine as a numbing palliative against what I was going to hear. I knew I had to listen. Curiosity and resolution to whatever it was that was happening.

'She kept phoning after that first meeting with her. She appeared to have gathered information about me and she wanted to know all about you. I could not say anything to you; she had sworn me to secrecy. It was part of her enticement to listen to her. She had so many wild stories. I tried to continue with your lessons as well as I could in between your sister's contacts. Then she said she was coming to see me to tell me something. Father was being particularly difficult at the time, raving, wild and aggressive. He gets like that sometimes.'

He stopped, looked at me. He held his glass to the light as if to find in its transparency, some answer there to assist him.

I sat with my feet twisted at an awkward angle about the legs of a kitchen stool, in expression of my mind. I kept my eyes looking into my own glass, staring and awkward. What could I add to this information which was unnerving to me?

'There is part of him that has to act out the violence that was once done to him. It is hard to say what drives him, or to understand the personalities that come through him. We know nothing of his family background, nothing of his childhood. Old Jacob told us nothing. He believed that we were all constrained by our own privacy.'

He had broken the thread of what he was saying about my sister and turning the story to his father instead, carefully drawing my attention away for the while.

'Are you saying that the personalities are all part of his inner psyche?' I interrupted.

'I don't really know. They all appear to have no connection with each other. They all have their own opinions, their own knowledge and experiences which are not shared with each other. As each one comes through they are totally oblivious of the other's encounters.'

'What about old Lillibet? I thought she was a fund of psychic knowledge. Can't she give an explanation?'

'Yes, but her speculations are not acceptable in psychiatric medical terms. We are taught first to look at aberrant behaviour as attributed to some genetic weak link or a diminution or enlargement of the neo-cortex, or even to some irretrievable memory experience.

Jacob believed in a kind of throw-back to some long lost memory of another time beyond which reason could not explicate. We have all looked into the phenomena and read what we could about it. We only know that Father's condition is extremely rare. There is of course the question: what if no scientific yard stick could be found to measure this abnormality?'

'Are you suggesting that you also believe Marcello's body is inviting in discarnate souls?'

'Elizabeth – Lillibet,' he corrected, 'and Jacob believed it.'

'Could that mean that we could all be subject to these invasions?'

'No. It is a very rare condition, as I said, and no one I know of has come up with an adequate answer. Reading about cases, I have found that the psychic answer is seldom mentioned. And for the psychological answer, well, it does seem to occur mostly with people who have been seriously traumatized in childhood, yet not all traumatized children are prone to MPD or psychotic behaviour.'

'Thank heavens for that but that does seem to suggest a psychosomatic reason and not some mystic one.'

'There is evidence on both sides but it is hypothetical with nothing substantially scientific on either side.'

'How do you place Peggy in this category? Is this what you are leading me towards? I mean, we had a topsy-turvy childhood but by no means traumatic. Peggy only had to ask Father for something and it was there in no time at all. Of course there were times when he hadn't paid rent on time but Pegs would make a fuss, go and see him and all was sorted.'

'Perhaps she was hiding more from you than you have even yet discovered.'

'What could that possibly be? I have discovered all the details and suspicions of our mother's suicide, or perhaps accident, as the case seems to be, and only Mother would know that really.'

It was inevitable that the conversation would veer back to my sister. I had no taste for any further discussion. I wanted it to end. How often had I had these conversations with stricken cast-over lovers who wanted to get to the root of her insensitive indifference.

'Are you still her lover?' I asked brazenly, almost unexpectedly of myself.

'I was never her lover.' He answered instantly as if affronted.

'No?'

'Peggy was determined to seek me out to follow me. That first evening when we met she had asked so many questions. She wanted to know why I was giving you lessons, how you were. She wanted to know my motives, why I should bother with you when she believed you had no talent. I assured her that she was wrong, that you were quite exceptional. I knew it the very first time you played.'

'But she arranged for Father to bring my violin back to me'

'No, Malachi did that. Malachi knew all about you.'

'This all feels like Alice Through The Looking-Glass. There are so many confusions over all those personalities that come through your Father that beg credence. I can't catch up and now my sister with all these hidden motives. It is all too much.'

I got up from the stool and walked towards the night-black window where I felt a thousand invisible eyes could stare back at me. Lorenzo too moved from his bench and stood looking at me, determined to continue with his vindication.

'As a family we have spent a life time of involvement with the surreal and truly psychotic. I have to admit that your sister's emergence has been more than I could cope with over these past few months. That night, that terrible night she came here; she made an awful scene outside and one of Father's more aggressive alters had come through, he began to join in the fray. Lillibet came down and called Maria who came at once and managed to persuade your sister to go home with her. She was making the most hideous accusations and threats. It took all night to calm Father down.'

'Why did I not hear what was going on?'

'You were in the sound proofed music room playing the violin. When Maria asked you to come to the house she wanted you to take your sister away with you. She was hoping for a repeat performance of the behaviour, but Peggy was just too smart for that and she climbed naked into my bed, you know the rest.'

'Why did you stay away? Why did you not try to explain it to me?'

'Silence and keeping away was the only way I could be rid of her. She had to be certain first that there was no more connection between us. It was as if she was trying to reach you through me.'

I felt the wine seep into those veins that lead to soothing sedation. I had always taken for granted Peggy's often outrageous behaviour. It was part of her personality. I had never known how deviously manipulating it had been. She had lived with this much younger sister for so long who had simply complied with every command and every suggestion.

'Poor Peggy,' I said at last. 'Why... what do you think it is all about?'

'I don't know. I really don't know. Perhaps I have not really been interested enough to know. I only know that I wanted to be reunited with you again, differently this time. Now that she has latched onto someone else she thinks you are connected to she might leave me alone.'

I looked sideways at him. His head was bent and he held the glass with both hands, the wine untouched. He looked back at me and I smiled at him. There had been so much pain; so much assumption gone wrong for the sake of secrecy, that concealment had silenced truth.

'Tell me about Malachi? I really want to know. He is different from all the other personalities that come through. He said goodbye to me the last time I spoke with him. He said he would not be coming back that the body was becoming too weak for all the changes.'

'Yes, I suspect that is so. I haven't spoken with Malachi for some time. It is hard to confirm or deny his presence as something special. I think you have to make up your own mind what you believe about it.'

'I really want to understand it all.'

'Have you spoken with Lillibet?'

'Yes, I have and I am left even more confused than before. I mean she is as, as ...wacky as all of this...'

'Lillibet is a wise old woman. If you really listen to her you will begin to understand.'

'I am not sure I want to understand. They say that ignorance is bliss, `tis a folly to be wise.

I sometimes feel I want to escape this house and all that is part of it but something draws me here. It has somehow become more of a family home to me than I have ever known before.'

'I sincerely hope you do not leave,' he said as he stood up and placed his full glass upon the table, untouched. He sighed, and then turned to me.

'I will have to go now. Busy day tomorrow. May we meet at the college and talk more about music there?'

'Yes, that would be nice,' I said.

He hesitated at the door and I stretched forward to kiss his cheek. As I did so he put his arms around me and held me there in an unexpected embrace. I felt myself tremble in his arms and stood back, feeling confused and self-conscious. Lorenzo was not the kind of person who would hug someone he had only ever treated formally.

'I am sorry,' he said and slipped out into the dark night leaving me uncertain and wanting.

Sorry? Why sorry? Was it for the familiarity of the embrace or for his time spent in secret with my sister?

Part of me was ecstatic but another part doubted myself and my presumptions.

I found something to eat in the fridge, long past a sell-by date but I was immensely hungry all of a sudden. I wanted more and did not know what more could mean right then. I chose bed and thoughts to battle sleep with.

Speaking With Strangers

Chapter 44

I did not see Lorenzo at the college the next day as I had hoped. In fact I did not see him there the day after, or the day after that. I enquired about him and was told that he had been ill and all his pupils had been referred to another teacher.

In the interim Jason had returned to the flat, looking sheepish and tired. Neither of us felt like talking and he stayed away for long hours at work. Evidently he had not given in his notice and was still with the same firm. I dared not ask.

I went to visit Lillibet each evening, when she did not have a client with her. There was no sign of Agatha or any of the 'alters', known or unknown.

'Where are they all Lillibet?' I asked.

'I expec they are givin the ole man a rest,' she said laughing.

'Which one are you missin? Surely not that ole Miss crosspatch Constantine?' She found this immensely funny and sloshed her tea in her mug for laughing so hard.

'No, not her. I miss Agatha, and I miss Malachi so much.'

'That ole Malachi, he not comin back. He movin on but any message you want askin you just tell Lillibet she pass it on.'

'No,' I sighed. 'No message, it's just that I miss him. It is sad that I won't speak with him again.'

'You sure you not missin that Lorenzo?' she smiled quizzically at me.

'Whatever gave you that idea?' I said indignantly.

'Plenty,' she answered and said no more about it though I was dying to ask.

I could not get that last meeting with Lorenzo out of my mind. He stayed there like a deep ache. I went over and over our conversation trying to recapture moments of significance. Was I beginning to obsess over him like my sister? I hoped not.

Even now, trying to recapture those occasions with their turbulent emotions is difficult. But emotion sublimates over time, like old pain. That intensity of feeling that once stopped you in your tracks and made breathing strained and thought a deep concentration, becomes a wry smile of self-derision over time.

Memory does not come in whole set scenes but in isolated pockets of stark, severe flashes. An incidence will flash before you like a haunting moment in a film. It comes accompanied by a cue from one single thought object and then a picture builds around the thought as you try to conjure the scene of how it happened.

It was the photograph of my Mother wearing her gold charm bracelet that seemed to stick in my mind, for no particular reason. It had brought a whole new dimension to my thinking just then, as if it had been planted there. I remembered it well because it belonged to my sister. I had never thought to ask how she had acquired it. It simply became hers. She wore it all the time. I suppose it had become so natural to her that she was seldom without it. It was simply an extension of herself and her personality.

'Put that down!' She would command when I lifted it to sift through the quaint tiny gold models. 'They are not yours!'

I never questioned her. You never questioned Peggy. Asking about the charms made her so angry that I lost interest in the end. I failed to even notice them as part of her apparel.

Now, for the first time I began to wonder how she had acquired it or all of Mother's bits and pieces that I vaguely remembered. She had held on to them all and I had never been allowed near them. Did her strange behaviour go all that far back?

Lillibet cornered me to tell me that Lorenzo was very ill. I wasn't sure how to react. Certainly it was an explanation for his absence at the college.

I had written a note to Mrs. Alberini and Maria to thank them for the invitation to the concert but I felt I owed them more, perhaps an apology for walking off so rapidly that night.

Perhaps the real reason I went round to their house with the weak apology was that I wanted so badly to see Lorenzo. I could use the apology as an excuse.

The father came to the door, looking pale and agitated but he was pleased to see me.

Maria was out with her mother but Lorenzo was there, huddled in warm clothes on a warm day. He looked up as I came into the room and he smiled.

'Lillibet told me only today that you have been ill,' I said shyly.

'Must have been something I have eaten,' he said.

'Poisoned, more like, stomach cramps, vomiting, really serious stuff;' came his father's voice from the door.

'You mean, like Lillibet?' I asked.

Neither of them answered.

The horror of which personality had been responsible would never be questioned – naturally!

'When will you be back at the college? I missed not seeing you,' I dared myself to say.

'Perhaps tomorrow. The orchestra have been more put out but I am on the mend and ready to start again. Yes tomorrow,' he confirmed.

I took a chair next to him and we talked about the music and the instruments we were now conversant with. He did not talk again about his illness or how it came about.

Marcello stayed in the room scratching at his skin every now and then as if he had some kind of irritation.

'It's the chlorpromazine I have been taking,' he explained and went out to find something that would relieve him of the itch.

'He has recently had his medication changed since the concert,' Lorenzo explained. 'He is determined to try and sort out the invasions.'

'Well, at least he is accepting help.'

'He is on a powerful anti-psychotic tranquilizer that should block the receptors in the brain's dopamine channels. It is supposed to control bodily functions.'

'It sounds drastic. Can you have been poisoned by...'

'No,' he cut me short. 'No, I know the reasons and I am doing my best to control the situation. Lillibet's medication helps.' He said almost rudely as if to stop me from questioning him further.

We talked more about music scores and about the string quartet he wanted me to join. He thought I would do well to be playing with people of my standard. I had no idea what standard I had reached and told him so.

I could see that he was still very weak and tired. I left soon after saying I sincerely hoped that he would be at college the next day.

There was no parting kiss this time and no warm embrace. I left feeling rather bereft of something I had gained for so short a time and lost.

He was not back the next day but two days later. I saw him in a corridor. I felt my heart quicken as he walked towards me. He had another student with him. I knew him as Jacques, a senior student who had come to hear me play once. He was short, almost frail looking and wore thick lenses, through which he peered with frightening intensity. He greeted me before Lorenzo had time to introduce us.

'Yes of course you would know one another,' Lorenzo said, his eyes flickered in my direction a moment then attended to the matter in hand.

We were to be part of the string quartet he was putting together. We went to find the other members and discuss music.

Lorenzo admired the work of Antonin Dvorak the Czech composer. He felt we should start with one of the string quartets -

romantic music, he said. He was hoping our orchestra would move towards Dvorak's orchestral symphony No 9 in E minor where there is a solo flute passage in the first movement which he suggested I could play.

It was as if there had never been any kind of familiarity between us. I was merely his pupil and that was how I was seen and recognised. I had no occasion even to ask how he was feeling or how his father was faring on the new drugs.

It occurred to me that the concentration on Dvorak might mean there was a Czechoslovakian connection with Marcello (an Italian name but after all, only given by Jacob who found him).

All that term was fully engaged in rehearsals and practise and improving my technique with the clarinet and flute and many wonderful occasions for seeing my old music teacher, once more taking an interest in my playing.

Chapter 45

It took several weeks before Jason and I were able to hold a conversation without either of us making an excuse to rush off and do something else or to go somewhere that was far enough to avoid each other.

He was perched in front of the television one evening, not expecting me back from practise so soon I suspect. I decided that the distance between us had gone on long enough. I made coffee for us both and took it to him.

'Thanks,' he said, looking up at me and meeting my eyes more directly than he had in a long time. He was about to add, 'but no thank you' but thought the better of it and took the mug.

'Only one sugar,' I said. 'See, I haven't forgotten after all this time.' I went and sat near him and took the television controls from him. 'Not this rubbish,' I teased. 'What about a good soapie?'

He hated soaps with a passion. It was an old bantering tease of ours and he fell back into stride as if it was still natural to him.

'Don't you dare,' he sparked back.

'Good, this means you are ready to talk to me,' I said.

'Don't know what to say. Just made one damn awful fool of myself,' he muttered.

'If you hadn't been so secretive I could have warned you. I spent a childhood with her remember. What did she do? Ignore you, tell you it was over or just walk out one day when you were miles away from any recognisable landmark?'

'Pretty much all of those things,' he said meekly. 'I should have realized she was just too wonderful for me.'

'Jason; that is the first stupid thing I have ever heard you say.'

'Why do you think she started pursuing me?' he said. 'I mean I never gave her the slightest encouragement. She just came here one day saying she was looking for you and she sort of moved in on me.'

'Why did you not mention it to me.?'

'She told me not to. She said it would upset you. But come to think about it, she came at a time I realized later than she knew you would not be here. I don't understand any of it. I am afraid there is something seriously wrong with your sister.'

'You are not the first person to tell me that in the last year or so and I don't know what to do about it.'

'She told me the most impossible lies about you and I have to admit that I had begun to believe in them. Sorry, old thing, but she was so damn plausible.'

'Can you give me some idea of what the lies were about?' I asked tentatively.

'She said that you had caused your mother's death, that you wanted your father all to yourself. That you had planned to have her standing on a ledge so that when she went to rescue her mother, you tripped her, pushing her mother over to her death.'

'Oh my God, I, I don't know what to say. I was only just five when mother died and I was never close to my father. In fact he rather terrified me as a child. He had a way of looking at you. Only Peggy knew how to manage him, control him, for want of a better word. They would go off together whispering and talking for hours on end in his bedroom while I watched television or played at the piano. I stopped noticing them really. I was closer to Mummy but I came to forget her. I was not allowed to talk about her.'

I found myself talking out all my thoughts and memories but they were limited to my own experiences and how I saw things at the time. It suddenly came to me that there had been more behind those secrecies between my father and my sister and now my mind began a more adult approach to what might have been.

The "what ifs" loaded themselves onto my thoughts till they reached an insurmountable surfeit. I felt sick to my stomach. I did not want to dwell on the matter any longer.

Thoughts and reflections of sound and sense that were once customary occurrence now spoke another language. A weighted silence between us gathered momentum from childhood reflections. Then I asked:

'Did you go to her place in Canada?'

'Yes, she has a wonderful apartment in Montreal overlooking the St. Lawrence. It was quite something, but you would expect that of Peggy. There is no doubt that she is professionally very switched on. She took me to her place of work and I met a few of her colleagues but it became apparent right away that there were no openings for me and the whole system was not what I have been working towards. Besides which it was quite obvious that there was something going on between her and a senior partner in the business. They were drawn into his office with what looked like and sounded like a lover's tiff. It was embarrassing.

The following day she just took off.

They said she was in London on business when I phoned the office.

I was just left there, hanging on in her over-the-top apartment.

I came home with my tail between my legs and told them in the office that there had been a family bereavement which excused my recent behaviour and talk about leaving them. And here I am; an older and a wiser man etcetera.'

'Have you heard from her since?' I asked.

'No, not a word.   Somehow, one would have to be very foolish to expect to. I know she has been back in the area.   I saw her one day walking towards Rose Mews.'

'That is where Lorenzo lives,' I said feeling anxious.

'Yes, she was fixated on him somehow.   She used to ask so many questions about him and his relationship with you.   She wanted to know how often he came here.   What relationship there was between him and Lillibet upstairs and Agatha.   Oh yes, she knew about the personalities and had rubbed up against one or other at some time. I believe she had even consulted old Lillibet at some time.'

'How on earth did I never know she was here, snooping around?'

'I thought you said you knew her, she was after all your sister with whom you spent an isolated childhood: your words!'

'That is what makes her behaviour so odd.   I just can't understand what she is attempting to do.'

'In some way, she is invading your life without your knowing it. Easy enough to do, you are always locked into that music room.'

'I wonder why she has returned to Lorenzo.   Why has she not got bored with him also?   What can she possibly gain from pursuing him now?'

'I guess we all chase the love that eludes us, clinging desperately to the very thing we think we are going to lose, never recognizing that it is already lost.'

I measured the significance of what he had just said, drawing together its consequence, as if pulling in a fisherman's net. I think you might say it applied to me.

'How about I make supper tonight?' I offered.   'A consolation prize as in offering solace, but at least a peace offering of sorts. What do you say old friend?'

'I say we skip the home cooking and I take you out.'

He was up on his feet and pontificating in his old ready for court action way.

We had a happy evening out.   We caught a bus into the busy part of London life where restaurants of every country abound, spilling onto the pavements as they do abroad.   The food matched the price which was not cheap but Jason was keen to show that he had not been undone by the extravagances of a woman who liked only the best.   I told him that a MacDonalds would have suited me more but he clung to his last resort at finesse and flourish and I went along with it.

It was what he needed right then.

It was like old times.

We chatted about all the things that mattered in the world and what did not matter to us and we both expressed the thought that it would have been nice if Malachi had joined us.

I did not mention my last talk with Malachi. I wanted to have at least one evening with some semblance of normality about it, even if it had been founded on the bewilderingly anomalous.

We came back to the flat feeling lighter than we did before we left but beneath the undercurrent of lightness there was a strange feeling of being observed. A casualty of the secrecy that Peggy had left in her wake, besides all those disembodied souls that lurked around the place waiting for a turn in a pliable body.

I played some Mozart for him and when it came to an end I saw that he was moved by the music.

I must not let him fall in love with me. It would be unfair to him as I had no feelings that I could respond with.

I went to bed and took my thoughts with me.

Chapter 46

It was an evening in August. I was just about to enter the flat, back from college. Maria called up to me from the front door. I went up to her and she told me that her father had gone missing. They had come round to Number 63 and searched but there was no sign of him.

I asked if he was still on his medication.

'That is the problem. It was causing an irritating itch which did not go away and he stopped taking it. He has never disappeared like this before. His way of disappearing is to climb out and let some other personality take over.'

'Maybe that is exactly what has happened. Surely there must be days on end when he is somewhere else.'

'No, we keep an eye on him, or Lillibet does and she tells us.'

'Perhaps none of them enjoyed the itch too much,' I said.

'But he has stopped the medication, so no itch.' She sounded agitated. 'Mama is going out of her mind, I can tell you.'

'And Lorenzo, what does Lorenzo think?'

'Lorenzo, Lorenzo, he is so locked up in his own mind and his music I wonder if he thinks at all.'

'Oh, well,' I took time to let the small information sink in and asked, 'What about Lillibet, surely she has answers.'

'That is what is so strange, she too has vanished. She never goes away and she has been gone all day. We are waiting to see when and if she comes back.'

'She was here last evening,' I offered. 'I went to pay her the rent money. Now that Agatha is not there to receive it she takes it. She seemed fine when I left, we chatted a while then I went to practise for the evening and the light was still on upstairs when I went to bed.'

'What time was that?'

'I don't know, I suppose after midnight, could be later. I practise late every evening these days, I don't watch the time, I want to...'

'Where is your blasted sister?' she interrupted. 'Don't tell me she is still around even after she has been told to keep away.'

I tried to imagine the scene with Peggy being told anything or how being told to keep away had come about.

'I have no idea where my sister is at any given time these days. She has cut herself adrift from me. I just don't know what she is up to from one moment to the next.'

I found my responses becoming as agitated as those I was receiving. What could this disappearance possibly have to do with me? How would I know what Peggy was up to and how could I possibly monitor her movements when they were so surreptitiously performed so as to keep me in the dark deliberately.

'I am sorry,' she said at last, 'really sorry. It is just that you have become so involved in our lives and Lorenzo's feelings for you. I just thought you might know.'

'Maria, I will try to help but I don't know how or where to begin. The problems with my sister you have been having, well, I am so ashamed, but I just don't know what to say or think about it all. And....and, Lorenzo has no feelings for me. He is just interested in the music as you say.'

'Well I will be getting home. Perhaps he is there. I am just so tired, so tired of it all. I just want it all to go away. With Father's problem, no man will stick around. I am just so afraid Jacek will find out and he too will leave.'

'Jacek, the handsome man you pointed out to me?'

'Yes, he asks to come home and meet the family. His family are in Poland and he wants me to go over and meet them, and that is before he has even been home with me. What do I do? How do I explain all this to him?'

'Well, you can wait till Agatha is happily settled in her apartment and then ask him around. I can keep an eye out – perhaps visit Agatha and keep her occupied for an afternoon.'

'Huh, you don't know how unpredictable it all is and now he has been missing for two days and no word from Lilly. Something has happened, I know it. I know these things. Don't ask me how. I just know.'

'Maria, he will turn up. Just wait and see. Lillibet has not been gone for long. Look, I will phone you as soon as either turns up.'

She gave me a weak smile and embraced me to say goodbye and talked briefly about getting together again, then she walked away down the road.

I turned back down the basement stairs and opened the door to the flat. I put down my violin case and took off my jacket. I went to my room and gasped in surprise, stunned into rigid immobility.

'Agatha,' I said, too startled to say much else.

She was sitting on the only arm chair which occupied a corner near the window, its arms frayed from old use and time and its pattern lost with an overall muddle of colour and fading.

She was looking back at me from the chair, sitting upright with her usual taut, straight-jacketed unease. Her hair was brushed but was not in its accustomed pristine neatness and her make-up perhaps a little less eye-catching and there was an absence of lipstick, but it was unmistakably Agatha.

She did not speak.

'They are looking for you. Did you know?'

Still she remained silent and her silence was disconcerting.

'I am going to put the kettle on to make some tea. I know how you like it. Will you join me in the kitchen, or shall I bring it to you here?' I asked, calm and control in a voice that otherwise knotted in my throat.

She remained seated. I walked back to the next room to fill the kettle, startled and unsure what I should do next.

If I tried to phone Maria, I might disturb Agatha and send her off to hide somewhere else. I decided to stay a while with her and perhaps after talking to her calmly she would tell me what was bothering her.

The kettle boiled and I placed the two mugs on a tray to take to her. When I turned around she was behind me. The look on her face told me that she was more relaxed and ready to join me in the kitchen.

'Oh good, you are here,' I said lightly. 'I have missed you Agatha. You have not been around in months now and the house seems quite different without you.'

'Is that so?' she answered with a satisfied purr to her voice, or so I told myself. She seemed pleased now that a part of her had melted.

She raised her gloved hand and took the mug to her lips to taste the tea.

'Nice,' she said. 'I think that is what I needed. I don't know what happened to me. I found myself here last night, not here, I mean in my apartment. It seemed something had happened, I don't remember what it was. I just know that there was a strange feeling that something bad had happened. I dressed and went to find Lillibet and she was not there. I stayed in her room for some time till I heard you go out this morning then I came down here. Something has happened in here and I don't know what it is but I came to wait for you to ask you.'

She was still not focussing properly and she seemed really upset. There was a new kind of rigidness about her that I had not seen before.

'Maria was here, did you hear us talking?' I asked. 'She was worried that her father, Marcello, had disappeared. Would you know about that Agatha?'

'Marcello,' she repeated his name as if hearing it for the first time. 'Marcello carries sadness about with him. He is not here now. I don't feel him around. No. It is someone else, someone connected to you,' she said.

'Drink your tea, you will feel better after. Maybe something to eat, yes?'

I made some toast and buttered it. She ate carefully, the way Agatha always ate. I could see she was hungry. She had probably not eaten for quite a while.

'Jason will be home soon,' I said, thinking gratefully that he would sort this problem out for me. It was Friday. He was always back early on a Friday. We had taken to having supper together on a Friday night.

It was his turn to cook. Something he did well with an extravagant flare and expensive ingredients and no doubt a good bottle of wine.

'I did not see him go out this morning,' Agatha said, now sounding much clearer and less disturbed.

'You must have just missed him. I went up to practise early yesterday evening and left him talking of getting an early night as he had to be up for an important meeting at work today. He was certainly snoring hard when I came in much later.'

'Snoring?' she said. 'Are you sure he was snoring? Or was he gasping for his last breath?'

'Agatha, what a strange thing to say,' I said, taken aback.

'It is just that something is beginning to come back to me,' she said. 'I just can't remember what it is or how it is that I know it. Why don't you check his room?'

I was already charging head-long into Jason's room, my heart beating fast as I tripped into every obstacle on my way.

Jason's always tidy room was a mess of clothing tossed everywhere, books lay in heaps of open pages where they had fallen and chairs lay over turned. I gasped as I looked at his tousled bed and scattered pillows.

He lay there, spread-eagled and fully clothed. His hands were paralysed in a final position, clutching skewed bed sheets as if to lift himself from his desperation.

I could see at once that he was dead.

His eyes stared out from a frozen glaze. His mouth was a hideous cavern from which a swollen tongue crept out to one side.

'Oh my God, Jason, Jason,' I shrieked. Agatha was standing at my side, her face a blank of white aridity.

'Just as I thought,' she said quietly.

I ran to collect my phone to dial 999 and scream description of the sight that was before me to a voice asking carefully which emergency service I needed.

It was irritatingly telling me not to leave the scene, to make sure the person I was describing was not still alive and asked if I had given any resuscitation.

Time ticked with the monotony of a metronome that changes beat with the smallest flick and my heart changed pace with every noise that came from outside.

They were there in a comparatively short time but it seemed to me to be an age as I looked around Jason's room to see what might have happened.

'How, how', I shrieked at him as he lay there, rigid and unresponding.

Sirens announced an ambulance and police cars. I rushed out to show them where to come.

When I turned around I noticed that Agatha was gone.

I led a troop of uniformed men and women treading purposefully through our private basement flat to Jason's room where he lay in a frozen pause to be examined, stared at and speculated over.

It was hard to imagine that a mere whisper ago it had been a place that Jason and I shared; was now was public thoroughfare to strangers and professionals doing their job. And Jason was their target and their focus. Only it was not Jason any more. It was just a hideous corpse eternized as a depiction of his final moments in agony and without dignity.

'When did you find him? How long is it since you last saw him alive? What is your relationship? Why did you not notice him earlier? Who else lives here? Who else has contact with the deceased?'

He is not Jason any more, he is the deceased.

The shock had made me shake quite violently.

They were going through his things and through the flat. They wanted to know where I slept. One of them had noticed the two mugs and the kettle that was still warm. Who, where, when...

Then I saw Lorenzo and Maria arrive and they were being held back at the door. Agatha must have gone to tell them what had happened. More questions, more answers.

I was so cold.

Someone was opening my violin case and going through its contents. What for, I wanted to shout, why.

Please, I kept saying please but I could not find anything to ask. They started to talk of next of kin and informing the relatives. A picture of Jason's adoring parents rose up before me and the horror became intensified.

'I think she has been asked enough questions. You can see she is in shock.' Lorenzo's voice was followed by assent but a reminder not to go too far as material witness and first at the scene of the crime etc.

'You can't stay with us tonight,' Maria said. 'Much better you come back with us at least tonight so the police can do their job.'

A stretcher on wheels was being pushed along the kitchen floor towards Jason's room and a black body-bag lay on top. I could not bear to look any more. I just wanted to go, to leave it all behind.

They would not let me take anything but a few items of clothing with me. I had to leave everything, my violin, my clarinet and my flute left in their cases, to be looked at prodded and opened carelessly, negligently, by those doing their job.

The police cars and ambulance had stirred up local curiosity and a crowd had gathered outside. As we walked out, there was a buzz of speculation as eyes turned towards us.

Lorenzo had brought their car and we got in as quickly as we could.

A sigh of relief burst from me as we left the incriminating scene behind.

Maria and I got out silently outside their house while Lorenzo drove on to park the car.

The mother was waiting at the door to greet us. She was looking shaken and for once here was a drama that had not evoked a torrent of foreign words. I wondered what Agatha had told them.

When Lorenzo came in I repeated the whole saga again for them all to hear. This time I included the things that Agatha had said.

'Did you mention what Agatha said to the police?' Mrs. Alberini asked quietly.

'They wanted to know who had drunk tea with me. They saw the empty cups. I merely told them that the landlady had come to get her rent and joined me in a mug of tea.'

'Weren't they suspicious that you drank tea with Jason lying dead in the next room?' Maria asked.

'I don't know. I just know that something told me not to explain about Agatha. I was shocked. I told them I simply went into Jason's room and found him. I told them I could not remember why I wanted to go in. I just did.'

'They will think it all odd,' Maria said.

'It is odd. It's absolutely mad. I can't think what has happened. And where is Agatha now?'

'Agatha left shortly after you discovered the body. Father is back,' said Lorenzo.

'You see. You see why I could not mention Agatha right then. What if, what if Jason has been deliberately murdered? They would arrest her right away.'

'Of course he was murdered. No reason why they should not arrest you. It's only your word, young trollop.' It was Miss Constantine's voice from behind me. I turned and saw her expression and character written there on Marcello's face, his body otherwise stood before me in everything that he was.

'It was only your word,' she spat out at me, like a hissing cat. Then she doubled up holding her head.

'Oh my head, my aching head.' Marcello's voice returned.

'Basta, basta Marcello,' said his wife. She rose instantly from her chair and led him out of the room.

He looked dishevelled and tired but there was no trace of Miss Constantine's expression or Agatha or any trace of her make-up about him. He was saying things in their language. His voice was agitated and she was soothing him.

'Oh my God! What am I doing here?' I cried out. 'This is all so mad, so crazy and now so dangerous. At a time like this I just can't take the insanity of these changes of character.'

'Come,' said Lorenzo leading me back to a chair. 'Come and sit. You are in shock. Here, take this brandy. It will calm you then we can talk about all of this. I think you did the right thing not to mention Agatha's conversation. They would not have understood.'

I took the glass and gulped the fiery drink which burned its way down my throat but the anaesthetic was instant and I felt myself warmed. Lorenzo sat beside me and took my hand.

'Where ever Lillibet is will soon come to light and she will know what has happened. Can you bear to wait?'

'How do you know that she too is not lying dead somewhere?' I asked. My misery had at last overwhelmed that bank of involuntarily tears of grief and shock. I could not stop crying.

Suddenly everyone was suspect and everyone had a motive.

That anyone should suspect me was beyond thinking about.

Lorenzo put his arm around my shoulder and held me. Under any other circumstance I would have melted under his touch, but the irony of the paradox became a conflict of discomfort and guilt. Poor Jason who would have loved to put arms around me if I had let him, was dead. I would never have allowed it to happen because I was longing for Lorenzo and now I wished that it was Jason with me, back, alive and I had another chance to tell him how important he was.

Unspoken words of culpability lay heavily on my mind. First Lillibet's poisoning, then Lorenzo's illness that had lasted for days also, leaving them both so weak and now poor Jason who had not survived whatever it was that he had been given.

Of course it was still unclear how Jason had died. The forensic detectives had arrived at the scene very promptly and whispered their instructions so that the body was removed rather quickly. I assumed a quick post-mortem would give results faster than speculation. I heard them say there was no visible sign of injury to the body, it must have been poisoning.

But why? Why would anyone want to harm Jason? Of course my conviction lay with one of the 'alters' gone mad.

Marcello had been put back on the irksome drugs. He returned to the living room later, twitching, sullen and silent. I could not bear to look at him.

They had to do something now. The man was dangerous. Who would he kill next?

Later that evening Lorenzo went back to Number 63 to see if Lillibet had returned. A yellow cordon had been placed around the railings in front of the house and he was told no one could enter without police notice. He told them that the property belonged to his family and that he occupied the music room where he wished to go. He was accompanied inside. Once inside he realized that if he went up to Lillibet's flat they too would go there to search it.

Unable to do any more, he waited outside to see if any lights might come on in the top floor.

It was late when he returned to say there was still no sign of Lillibet and our anxiety intensified.

It was obvious that Lillibet was the linchpin of the family. They consulted her over everything and it was her voice they relied upon. Maria explained that it had always been thus since she was a small child.

I learned that Lillibet had had a more than intimate relationship with her benefactor Jacob. It seemed that they had not only shared a bedroom, they shared confidences and decisions and the upbringing and care of the foundling Marcello. No one doubted for a moment that her disappearance was for a good cause and it was only a matter of time before it was resolved.

If, of course, I debated with myself, she were to be accused of being instrumental in any way over Jason's death, her defence that she too had been poisoned would be dismissed because (along with Lorenzo's poisoning) neither had ever been reported. I reasoned that she might have disappeared because she knew in fact, that she could be incriminated.

I never doubted that one of the personalities had been instrumental in Jason's death. Agatha had known so much and yet she was convincingly surprised to see Jason dead. What would the police make of it? What would the police make of all the personalities? This was a condition known to be extremely rare, they would simply classify Marcello as insane and everyone would be punished. I could not bear the thought that Malachi who lurked somewhere in that psyche would be incriminated also.

The question as to how the guilty 'alter' had achieved his or her act of poisoning was difficult to imagine. Of course it had to be stopped.   The family appeared to have no control over these changes or what to do next.   They all believed that Lillibet would have the answer but I had doubts and vast confusions.

Bed was a last resort of the evening. I was given the small guest room, made tidy and fresh for me by Mrs. Alberini and Maria who spoke comfortingly to me. Lorenzo went out once more into the night to try and catch a glimpse of any sign of life at number 63.

I was woken in the night from a deep sleep, hearing someone in my room. I woke, startled to find myself in the strange room.   The rush of reawakened sadness hit me once again, then concern.

Someone was in my room.   I saw the shape of his body standing there in a long grey dressing gown.

I sat up and called out, 'who is it?'

Malachi's voice came through.

'Don't take fright little Anna, I just came to say you must go home to your Grandparents and Aunt tomorrow.'   Then the lights were turned on and Lorenzo had come in.

'Father, what are you doing in here?'

A very startled Marcello blinked his eyes: 'Don't have a clue.'

'Then come back to bed Papa.'

His mother had come in to see what was happening and a burst of irate Italian curses spouted from her again.

I hardly slept for the rest of the night.   Thoughts raced in tornadoes of blurred images behind my eye lids as I drifted in and out of a half sleep of conspicuous danger.   There was an inevitability of something about to happen.   One had only to wait. There was nothing else to be done but wait.

Why had Malachi come back to warn me?

I wanted to tell Maria or Lorenzo but what if I was being warned about one of them?

I was unable to make any arrangements or discuss intentions as to where I might or might not go.   The police were at the door very early with a more pressing decision as to where I was to go.

'We would like you to come down to the station to help us with our enquiries,' left little room for choice.   It was to the point and intimidating.

Lorenzo offered to come with me but was told that it would not be necessary just yet.

Chapter 47

The questioning began all over again.

It was a small square room, bare but for a table with hard chairs either side and on one wall a window with opaque glass. Someone was watching from the other side, certainly. Like you see in police investigations on television.

The same questions from the night before were asked by a different inspector, more imposing, more solemn and more serious. This time they had gathered more information. I was asked about my relationship with my sister. Was I jealous of her? Was I angry about her affair with Jason? Was I angry that she had stopped a relationship between me and my music coach that she had considered unhealthy? What had I to say about my mother's death and my part in it?

I was stunned and pained. Where had all this come from? I asked if they had spoken to her and I was not given a direct answer but asked why I should want to know.

Then I was left there to think. I was left for what seemed an eternity. Then a police woman came in. She was plain clothed and spoke with less intensity. She asked if I would like to have a solicitor present. Why would I need one? It was advisable. I asked if I could telephone my father and ask for help from him.

'Daddy something awful, no, utterly dreadful, has happened.'

He listened and I heard him clear his throat. Someone was asking him questions in the background. The current partner, wanting to know.

'I will see what I can do,' he said and put the phone down without one word of commiseration or empathy.

I was left in abandoned isolation a while longer.

The same woman came in and put a book before me. I read the title: "The effects of poisons on the nervous system." Then I looked up and saw her watching me intensely.

'What do you have to say about that?'

'Well, nothing. I am not sure what you are expecting me to say. Are you trying to tell me that Jason was poisoned?'

'What gave you the idea that he had been poisoned?'

'I, I don't know. He looked so dreadful when I found him. His tongue was... He looked as if he had been in terrible pain.'

'A person can die in many ways looking like that without poison.'

'Well, why did you show me that book?'

'Because we found the book in your bedroom.'

'No, I don't believe it. Someone must have put it there.'

The conversation went on and on with varying degrees of pressure that I must confess to what I had done, till finally, I had my rights read to me along with my conviction.

'This is not happening to me. It can't be happening.'

I was taken to a cell and left there, my pulse flexing beneath my skin. The walls closed in on me and the pure terror of the situation hit with the force of a violent blow to the solar plexus. Why had they incriminated me? What for?

I sat in my solitary space with nothing to see but a graffiti scratched wall before me and a space of panicked thought. I listened to the hubbub of movement through the reinforced door and heard a range of voices laced with authority. Through the darkness of the hours, I prayed silently for someone to come and help, hoping upon hope that my father would come.

I did not notice day turn to night or night become day again, it was all one long torture. Food came in, was left without a word and the stark abandonment continued. Then I was told to come to the interviewing room, my solicitor had arrived.

He was waiting for me, a Dickensian sketch of a man, waiting for sombre news.

He introduced himself as Alain Hooke and shook my hand.

He was old, or so he seemed to me then, perhaps in his fifties. A plain grey oversized suit hung from a stooped and frail back. Its colour had the effect of turning his sallow complexion even more pallid than it need be. Tufts of downy grey hair sprouted from the more fecund spots of a mottled scalp. Heavy spectacles came to beneath a bush of eyebrow and below, hawk eyes watched my every move.

He was economical with his use of words and asked only a few questions.

He said he had applied for bail and I would be out as soon as the bail order had come through. They had no concrete evidence other than what my own sister had given them and the book of poisons found in my room was devoid of fingerprints which opened a new direction of speculation.

The implications of my sister's "evidence" filled me with alarm and distrust. My sister? What could she have said? The lawyer was unable to say right away but he was 'looking into it.'

'Who sent for you?'

'Mr. Alberini. I have worked for the family in the past and I am cognisant of their problems.'

He said no more but the words signified a confidence of justice at last. He would be able to set the records straight and put the right person to task. The whole complexity of MPD was more far reaching in its destruction than I had first imagined.

Chapter 48

I learned that although it was Mr. Lorenzo Alberini who had posted bail, it was Father there to greet me as I came out.

I started to cry as soon as I saw him. It was the familiarity of his face, the recognition of the only parent I had really known in my life. His anticipated appearances had always come from a craving for his presence, the dominant figure of security. He had always been venerated as parent and protector, even if he had never really been either. Protection and authority had always come from my sister.

He led me to his car.

'Where do you want to be taken?'

'I suppose back to my flat, or can I come to your house, just for a while. I need to regain my balance somehow. I am still so stunned by everything.'

'I have to tell you before you come that I have married again. My wife will be there and she has not met you yet.'

'Your wife? Then I take it you and Eleanor got divorced?'

'Eleanor died. It happened about a year ago now.'

'Oh my God! I am so sorry. I went there you know. She came to fetch me, she was so upset.'

'Yes, I know. She told me.'

There was no mention of the box of photographs or finding Mother's family. I was too shocked at the thought of Eleanor's death.

'How did she die? I mean, it must have been so sudden. She did not seem to be ill. Upset certainly, but not ill.'

'Poison,' he answered. 'It seems that she drank poison.'

'I don't believe it, Eleanor was not the suicidal type.'

Then the impact of improbability struck me. It was an immense coincidence. All these poisonings!

Malachi had known where I had been, he had been waiting for me that night when I got back from my stepmother. He was there to sooth and comfort me. Surely he had not followed me, found out where she was and poisoned her. It just seemed so implausible so improbable, yet the thoughts of all those poisoned people around me. Lillibet had known so much about my mother and her family. No, can't be Lillibet I reasoned, she was still suffering from the effects of poisoning. Why was the lawyer, and all the Alberini family for that matter, so keen that I did not disclose Agatha's last conversation before I found Jason's body? She seemed to know that it was there. Miss Constantine was ready to see me punished for the crime and someone had deliberately left a book on poisons in my room.

Had Lorenzo sent his lawyer to keep me silent, had he paid my bail from guilt? What was it they were trying to do?

My thoughts rattled around my head as we drove. We hardly mentioned the reasons for my incarceration.

I was still too dazed about Eleanor's death to think of a new wife.

Conversation with my Father was as if we were strangers talking about the weather and touching on my musical career with vague interest. There was even bare mention of his contact with Peggy.

We drove east and found a destination on the outskirts of Lewisham, close to the park which rose up ahead of us.

So this was Father's new home. It was of little interest to me now as it would have been when I was much younger and longed to know where he was and where he was living when he was not with us.

The house looked much like all the houses on that street, built no doubt by a developer to satisfy an expanding Edwardian population. I am not too au fait with dates of houses. Double storey, sash windowed and red brick gave its identity to the same architect to all the houses that dated the street, excluding the modern clean white drainpipes snaking up the sides. The only varying distinctions between the houses were the gardens. This one was devoid of shrub, tree, hedge or any vegetation for that. A white graveyard-gravel neatened the front. The back garden was fenced out of sight.

As soon as we had arrived I wished that I had asked him to leave me back at my flat. I could have phoned Aunt Sophie and asked if I could go there. That had been my original intention.

The front door was neatly painted anaemic white. A Hessian "Welcome" mat suggested feet were thoroughly cleaned before entering.

As was compulsory by the front door, everything inside was white, from carpeting to ceiling; a modern trend to make any other colour vibrantly highlighted. That came in the form of a small Pekinese, bounding towards us, with a bright blue beribboned tuft over his eyes.

'A good idea if you don't mention where I collected you from, or all these recent problems – Jerry is not used to this sort of thing,' he whispered to me.

I wished again that I had not come and I wished to avoid Jerry like the plague. The "sort-of-thing" I had been tainted with hung like a bad smell in the air. It stuck to my hair and to my clothes; the same ones that I had been wearing since...

I remembered with an acute heart flinching throb.

Jerry was about my age. She was wearing tight lycra pants with a loose top that came to her knees. Her hair was a transparent blond and was swept up to the top of her head in a pony-tail.

'Pleased to meet you,' she said, offering me a damp, limp hand and smiled through her rosy-pink lipstick and heavy mascara which brought the last memory of Agatha suddenly to my bruised mind.

'Didn't know he had kids till last week and your sister turned up.'

'Oh yes? You have met Peggy then?'

'Every so pretty she is. You are the one plays the piano hey?'

'Well, violin really.'

'We have a piano here, Julian bought it for me, didn't you Jule? - when we got married. I said I might like to learn.'

The piano was Mother's. It had been polished up and looked strange with all the white furniture. I recognized some of Eleanor's things there too. A couple of the paintings I had seen in her house and in the kitchen, her uncomfortable kitchen furniture, painted white now with cushioned seats and pretty bows.

Jerry was different. So different from Eleanor that I found her a comfort of empty minded ease and idle chatter. I found myself liking her. She was a diversion from the horror of the past few days and the fact that I could not talk about it now was a distraction if not an obstruction from wanting to move on.

At the back of my mind the rattle of sickening thought bounced me from reality to role-play, a performance of will because Father had orchestrated it so. My impulsive appearance was presented as my desire to meet his new wife.

She brought out all the wedding photographs. It had been one of those girly weddings with a dress that would have propped up Nelson's column in time of earthquake. Jerry was exceedingly proud of it and out of sorts to think that her husband's daughters could have been there to see her outshine the two of them. It would have been no hard feat with the younger one but the older one would have been impossible. No one outshone my sister, she would have seen to it.

There was neither the smallest spark of jealousy from the guileless Jerry nor the tiniest hint of self-consciousness. If she had known about Peggy and me we would have been invited. If she said it once, she said it a dozen times.

Father left us to our girly interests and disappeared into his study. It was hard to pull away.

By evening, they both drove me back to my lodgings after a late, diet conscious salad lunch. They left me outside with a flurry of assurances and appeals from my enthusiastic stepmother to keep in touch.

Chapter 49

I saw with relief that the condemning yellow police tape had gone but the curtains on the first floor were still drawn to shut out life beyond them.

I longed for the solace of Lillibet to be there.

I let myself into the basement flat and saw the disruption left behind by a team of experts looking for clues. Jason's bedroom door had been left open.

It was as if he was hiding there from me and it had all been some hideous mistake. I had dreamt it all.

When I put my head round the door I saw the mess of bedding still heaped there and I gulped back the sob that had resided so long in my throat. His walls still carried pictures of the girl playing her violin; a sickening reminder of her culpability in his death.

My room had been thoroughly gone through. Every drawer opened and left like that with vestiges of finger-print dust coating as many surfaces as there were. On my bed lay my open violin case. My violin lay to one side where someone had gone out of their way to cause it as much damage as possible. Someone had carelessly unwound the turning pegs in the peg box and scratched the scroll while doing so. Both the D and the A string were gone and the G and E lay sprung to one side. The bridge was snapped in two and I noticed that something had been forced into the F-holes. The chin rest had been loosened and fell to the floor as I lifted the violin up. Then I heard something loose slide around inside its hollow. With careful turning and probing I managed to shake it free.

It was a small plastic bag with white powder inside. My stomach turned as I held it before me. It could only be one thing. Incriminating evidence placed there. But why had the police not found it themselves? Why had they taken so much trouble to destroy the violin to no affect? It seemed obvious that they had been looking for just such evidence and I had it now in my hands.

My dilemma was: if I took it to the police right now, how was I going to convince them that I had found it? If I took it to Lorenzo and Maria, would they not simply hide it hoping that their father would not be suspect? I needed to talk to Lillibet.

I carefully put all the pieces of the violin back into the case. It was then that I noticed the bow was missing. I found it finally, under my bed. The ribbon of horsehair had been pulled out of the frog at one end and the adjusting screw had been taken off completely and was nowhere to be found.

Why would the police find it necessary to destroy the bow I wondered? I placed it back into its position in the case, carefully folding what I could of it neatly around the bow and I thanked my lucky stars that I had left my other instruments behind at the college.

Then I went up the stairs to see if Lillibet was there.

Agatha's apartment was locked and so was the music room. I had left the key down in the basement, so I carried on up the stairs to Lillibet's flat. Her door was open. Well, not open. It was unlocked, just as she always left it. Nothing had been touched there but there was no sign of her. I went into each room and looked in cupboards, under beds, and behind chairs where anyone might be lying in hiding or...

I dared not think.

I noticed a photograph next to her bed that caught my attention. It was Lillibet as a much younger person and she was standing with a picture of an older man with his arm around her shoulder. I recognised him as Jacob. The Alberini's had several pictures of him in their house.

There was a visible and touching attachment between them. You could see it in the picture. It shone through their eyes and in their smiles. I thought of how she had devoted her entire life to him and his problem, arrogate son. She was protecting him now and I wondered how.

On my way out I reached to open the door and saw a stain of blood on the handle.

I was loathe to stay a night on my own in the house.

I rang Aunt Sophie. She volunteered to come and fetch me at once and I accepted. I went to pack some things into a bag, taking my violin with me like an injured animal that needed rescue and sanctuary. I could not leave it where it had been so damaged.

The whole house exuded a palpable sense of fear mingled with sadness and horror. Every corner and every space in the house pulsated with a dark, unshakable force as the evening shadows crept up like a stalking lion, waiting to find me out and pounce with violent suddenness sending me back to prison.

I closed all the doors I had opened and locked the basement flat up.

I decided to go out and wait outside. I could not bear the thought one moment longer of being alone inside with all those ghosts, tenanted and new.

I walked to the end of the road where I could watch the direction from which I knew Aunt Sophie would be coming.

I stood behind a lamp post, as if its small concealment might give me shelter and there I watched and waited.

After several minutes I noticed a police car draw up and park on the road opposite Number 63, as if to conceal its arrival. A short, stout man in plain clothes walked up the steps to the front door. He must have had keys, for he let himself in and disappeared into the darkness of the unlit hall beyond. He had gone to search for something I thought and clutched at my violin, safely in my keep. I was certain that the sachet of white powder that had been placed there was what they had been told to expect.

Just then I saw my aunt's car coming towards me and I hailed it.

Speaking With Strangers

Speaking With Strangers

Chapter 50

Lengthening shadows cast by the last of the sun, morphed the colours in Aunt's garden to a luminescent glow.   There was a sense of disquiet in the obscurity of evening gloom.   It leaned upon the end of an exhausting and emotional day.

Ben came out to greet us.

As I stepped out of the car I was struck by the profound impression of unspoken words that tensed between us.   The evident absence of the usual bonhomie that I had always received before was replaced with curt, almost formal greetings.   There was something else, too, something I just could not put a finger to, a kind of veiled evidence they seemed to have that had incriminated me before I had arrived.

I began to question my reasons for coming: consolation, commiseration, empathy?   There was certainly none of that here.   Perhaps I had ostensibly come because of the imagined Malachi's voice that night at the Alberini's house telling me to come here.   Now, I felt that by coming I was colluding to a pact I had not yet become wise to, whose rules I did not know.

I had walked into a kind of trap.

They already knew all about Jason's death and my arrest.   I did not ask how they had found out.

Aunt was uncharacteristically quiet. She was like that when we met.   She had solemnly asked how I was and how things were going with the police investigation.   I told her that I was totally mystified about everything and that I was reluctant to stay in the flat. I mentioned that Father had come to collect me after my bail had been posted but I did not say who had paid the bail money.   It was as if I was being guided in what to say and what to omit.

There was, all the time we spoke, a prevailing awareness that she had already condemned me in her mind and something, or someone had influenced her.

I helped her to peel potatoes for the evening meal and asked about Grandmother.

'She has a guest staying tonight.'   She answered almost too quickly; as if to silence me and keep me from her.

There was scarcely any chat between us over supper.

Ben talked almost too enthusiastically about two more dogs that they had taken into their care. It was a painful and forced charade like a badly written play acted by players who had forgotten their lines. Suspicions, gelled upon the edges of thought dragging upon my negative self-esteem till I wanted to run and hide, somewhere, anywhere.

When they had eaten they got up to go and see to the dogs and put out evening hay for rescue donkeys that had arrived recently.

I offered to wash up the dishes and Aunt accepted gratefully.

It was when I was stacking plates onto a low shelf that I saw something shine on the floor near the sink. I bent down to pick it up. It was the tailpiece of my damaged bow. I studied it carefully. It must be a mistake. It was small enough not to notice if it had been dropped. I opened my violin case and fitted it back onto the bow.

Someone in this house had removed it. Someone here had deliberately damaged my violin and pushed the white powder into the F-holes at the front. But why?

I decided to hide my things and my violin. I took them outside with me and found an old wood pile behind the house with a corrugated roof covering. I slid my things behind some logs and then walked in the direction of Grandmother's house.

There was a window at the back which had no curtain. Sooner or later their guest would pass the window.

I was prepared to wait all night if necessary, to see who it was.

She was wearing a demure pale blue top with a loosely fitting skirt, her hair was swept into a chignon at the back and she looked to all the world like a dear person caring for the elderly grandparents.

I saw Aunt Sophie and Ben go in through the kitchen door and they all disappeared from sight.

What on earth could they be saying?

All at once I saw the treachery of my sister's life, how she could manipulate and control through her secrecy.

I stood there in the garden, a mind blown wide open, stunned and appalled. I had not been prepared for this. This was not how things should be happening. This was supposed to be the workings of one of those disturbed "alters" - not my sister, never my sister.

How on earth was I going to manage this unexpected situation? It seemed way beyond my control. I could see it all now, how clever she had been. If one of the family died of poisoning in the next few days, it would be known that I had visited and if I suddenly departed without warning it would be seen as an act of deliberate scheming.

I decided to return to Aunt's house and wait.

I left my violin hidden and took back my clothes and waited.

Half an hour later Ben came in first dropping off some empty sacks in the outer room. He was followed shortly after by my aunt.

I thought of every way I could get round the situation. I had to beat Peggy at her own game.

I chatted about Father's new wife and then told them that Peggy had written to me to tell me how she met her and how well they got on. I felt I must pretend that Peggy and I were in constant contact.

'Peggy also said she wanted to come and visit you Aunt. I explained where you lived and she said she would phone soon. I do think it a good idea that we all got together. She said she wished to come here to see you with me.'

I could hear myself, babbling implausibly and I could not shut myself up as I walked myself further and further into a tangle of lies.

Aunt Sophie scratched at the edge of her eye then checked her finger for a phantom irritant without lending a word to what I had said, then she asked Ben to hand her a cloth to polish her saddle that had already been done quite recently.

A warm current shot through to my brain as awkward disquiet swept over me.

I knew that whatever Peggy had told them, she had sworn them to secrecy. That was Peggy's way. I could not deviate too far from what she might have said to them or they would know for certain that I was lying. I had to touch on the truth, somewhere, somehow, presupposing what she had said to them. Of course it would involve Jason. The papers had already printed the story of Jason's death.

I remembered the police questioning me about my rivalry with my sister over Jason and suspect that they too had been fed the same story. Aunt would now believe that I was angry with Jason for leaving me for my pretty sister. I had to think of something better but I could not. I rambled on about Peggy's friendship with Jason and how pleased he was to be joining her firm soon, and how grateful I was to her for helping an old friend. I found myself rambling on and on over trivial nonsense, knowing all the time I talked that I had gone on too far. But I kept telling myself that I had to face the situation square on.

I said: 'Well, I am off to say goodnight to Granny. I am sure she won't mind being disturbed just for a moment.'

'Don't go,' demanded my Aunt so harshly I was taken aback.

'Why ever not?' I said meekly.

'Your sister is there and I don't think she wants to see you.'

'Oh, how lovely.' I said. 'Of course she wants to see me; she said so on the phone only this morning when Father collected me.'

Lying was easy, sounding convincing was a lot harder.

'She is upset about her boyfriend,' my Aunt replied.

'Which one?' I asked innocently. 'Lorenzo or Jason or her boss she says she has been in love with for some time?'

'Well, let's leave it till tomorrow,' Aunt said, suddenly looking drawn and tired. 'I don't think I can take much more of this.'

She got up and went to her bedroom and Ben followed her. I could hear them arguing in hushed tones that rose and fell like an incoming tide.

I knew with certainty that before the night was through Peggy would do something. She knew that I was there and before long, with the wonderful use of mobile phones, I was certain that Aunt Sophie had contacted her to say I would be going round in the morning. Peggy would want to make all her secrets look plausible. And if Peggy wanted something, she wanted it right away. Patience was not one of her virtues.

I knew she would not wait till morning.

Sure enough, within half an hour Peggy was at the kitchen door calling out 'Coooie...' in her charmed voice.

I got to the door before Aunt did. I was already waiting. Aunt would think that Peggy would do as she had advised and wait till morning.

No. I knew more about my sister than she did.

There she was, looking beautiful and tearful.

'Peggy,' I called out happily. 'How nice that you came as you said you would.'

She looked startled. This was a new Anna, born of independence and growing up fast. It was all very bizarre. Meeting in the very place she had sworn to me all through childhood, was a nest of vipers who wanted nothing to do with us. Despite the fact that Father was party to the lie and certainly its instigator she had been thorough in its effect.

For once, Peggy was at a loss for words.

She blew her pretty nose noisily and spoke as if through tears, strangling her lips into a fragile smile.

'Annie, you are out I see.'

'Isn't it wonderful, I expect you have been told? They have found the poisoner,' I said.

'No, I did not know,' she said. 'They have surely made a mistake.'

'Why? How would you know that they had made a mistake? They would never have allowed me out of prison if they had not discovered something.'

'Well, have they found the hidden poison?' she said, looking intently at me. She was so transparent. My clever sister with all her plans laid out so carefully only to declare them all in one slip of the tongue.

It was the first time I had witnessed a crack in her usually cast-iron self-assurance. It was from that time on that the worn-out limitations of my world began to shift. Nothing was as I had assumed it to have been and that knowledge turned my thinking to pure concern. I saw her as she was for the first time, behind her beautiful face. Her forehead pleated above her brow then smoothed to soft innocence.

I thought of all the personalities that had emerged from Marcello and marvelled at the duality that lies hidden in man. How long had she been watching me in that house without me knowing? How long had she lurked in shadow, ferreting, finding out, burrowing and why?

'Oh, you mean a small flat packet of it. Why yes. They did find it and you will never guess where.'

Aunt Sophie was looking from one to the other of us not knowing which direction to cast her gaze.

'Where?'

'It was deposited by Lillibet at the police station. She seemed to know all about it.'

'Who is Lillibet?'

'Of course you remember her. You went there to have your fortune read. I think about nine months ago now. She was very ill shortly after your visit but I expect you heard about that also.'

I had already put Lillibet's poisoning down to her and presumed in that moment the explanation for their meeting, for there could be no other. I watched the flicker of recognition go past those tiny nerves in the eye that betray deception.

Mother had consulted Lillibet when Peggy must have been old enough to find out. At some time she must have weighed things up as I had.

'I never went near her.' She was beginning to flounder like a netted fish. 'I don't even know what the hell you are talking about.'

'Well, if you girls are going to argue, I will go into the kitchen to make tea and we can sit and talk sensibly,' said Aunt disappearing rapidly out of the room. When she was out of sight Peggy hissed at me.

'What the hell are you playing at?'

'The same game you have played all your life Pegs. I have watched and learned and finally come to the truth.'

'You would not know truth if it hit you square in the eye.'

'Well, funny you put it that way, because that is exactly how it came to me. I couldn't believe it at first but asking why would be fruitless right now.'

She shifted uncomfortably towards the table in the dining area of the room. Remnants of supper's crumbs lay un-swept. She shuddered.

Reiterated conversations and images flickered rapidly across her eyes in a never ending stream. Something deep had disturbed her. A secret, a disturbing secret, and she had become the very embodiment of concealment and all that was underhand.

What had made her like this? Why had she become this monster? I had never seen this side. I had never known it existed. I had only ever seen perfection.

Our lost childhood had become like one of those Russian dolls that you peel back to find a mystery but are faced with the same face, again and again, shrinking to a small nothing.

She turned back towards me, ready to put up a fight.

'I take it you brought your precious violin to charm the family with?' The corners of each sharp word spoken precisely and slowly, impacted with covert insinuation.

'As a matter of fact, yes I did. The police were a bit rough on it but I expect it will mend. I just shoved all the bits back in its case and brought it with me.'

She had a smile on her face like a cat that has just discovered the mouse's escape hatch.

Aunt brought in the tea and poured it out. Only Aunt and Ben had sugar with their tea. I noticed Peggy take charge of the sugar bowl, but unless she had learnt some sleight of hand there was no way she could contaminate it.

She sweetly ladled the sugar in the mugs and stirred it vigorously. The gold bangle clashed each charm like a peel of bells.

At that moment I knew how she did it. I remembered that Malachi had talked of her time as a medieval poisoner, with poisoned rings. The charm bracelet had lots of little pots with lids that could be lifted up.

Before anyone had taken a cup, I stood up clumsily, pretended to trip and knocked the entire tray and table over. Two mugs smashed on the rough slate floor, the others lay empty on their sides.

I may have been horribly wrong. I may have misjudged her. I could not take the chance.

Peggy shrieked. She began to berate me and my stupidity till Aunt Sophie intervened.

I bent at once to pick up the shattered mugs and spoons, placing them on the fallen tray. In my haste to retrieve the mugs I sliced my hand rather severely on a severed edge.

'It's not important,' Aunt said. 'Here, old Jock will help us out. Come on old boy,' she called to an old Alsatian curled up on one of the chairs. 'Here you are come and have some spilled tea,' she invited.

'No. No Aunt!'

I grabbed at an old tea towel and began mopping up the liquid as fast as I could with Jock looking quizzically at me over my shoulder, wondering why he had been deprived of a perfect opportunity to help out.

Peggy was sobbing inconsolably at the table.

A part of me wanted to rush to her and comfort her, another part was thinking of the terrible image that remained photographed to my inner optic nerves of Jason's body lying frozen in those last moments of agony.

What ever could it be that had made her do what she had done? Surely, nothing could be bad enough.

Old Ben, with his life coarsened manner calmed the evening by opening a bottle of old brandy he had stored somewhere in a cupboard.

'This will do you all a bit of good.' he announced finding an assortment of glasses and filling them for each of us.

I took the saturated tea-towel to the kitchen to wring it out. The cut in my hand was bleeding ferociously. I went back hastily to mop some more of the spilled tea but old Jock was there before me licking at the sticky remains.

I groaned and sat down, feeling depleted. I pressed the damp cloth to my deep cut in an attempt to stem its bleeding.

I could not explain what might happen to the dog. What if my assumption had been wrong? I would have incriminated myself even more. I pushed the dog aside and returned to my cleaning which annoyed my Aunt and amused my sister who had swallowed her brandy in one gulp and reached for the bottle to fill her glass once more.

The brandy had reached its target. Peggy had become her old self, remembering old stories of our child-hood and Father's many girlfriends. She was actually being very amusing.

Aunt had subsided into a dream of attention and distraction and non-action. Ben was watching.

I sat there with the cloth pressed tightly to my cut, praying quietly that my suspicions were wrong.

The old dog scratched at the door to be let out. Ben got up to open the door. Then Peggy excused herself and said good-night.

It was after she had left the room that the nausea hit me. My stomach had begun to knot. I ran my mind through what I could have eaten that no one else seemed to be affected by but attention had been drawn to the sound of the dog's retching outside the kitchen door.

Aunt opened the door to see what it was all about. The dog was foaming at the mouth and seemed very distressed. She tried to lure him inside but he was distressed and aggressive by then.

'What is it old boy?' she asked.

Ben answered her. 'He drank the tea that had been spilt.'

He turned towards me with a steel glint of hatred in his eyes. 'You tried to stop him. You knew the tea was poisoned. What was it? Wrong person going to be poisoned? Guilty conscience hit you at last?'

'We need to get him to the vet,' Aunt was shouting. 'For God's sake Ben, lock her up somewhere. We can call the police on the way, tell them the sugar has arsenic in it and they can collect her at the same time. We need to get this dog to the vet sharp.'

Ben grabbed at my arm, dragged me over to the lock-up larder and I heard the key turn. Then I heard them close the kitchen door and the car start and drive off in a tearing hurry.

Once more I was incarcerated in a small dark space, feeling desperate, vulnerable and utterly helpless.

I had said too much. I had shot myself in the foot and now I had confirmed all the secrets that Peggy had planted surreptitiously in their minds.

Chapter 51

Trapped, panicked, doomed helplessness and nausea absorbed me all at once in a sticky web, as if waiting for the onslaught of a hungry spider ready to devour me. All I could do was succumb to iniquitous fate.

I thought of the tea I had mopped from the floor and its likelihood of containing that white powder. I had held on to the damp cloth after wringing it out, tightening my grip to it to stem the flow of blood on my cut. The poison must have somehow entered my blood stream. I had not thought of that possibility. I found a switch to the larder light. I examined my hands. There was a distinct redness around the wound and my hand was beginning to swell with the poison.

I felt panic grip me in the chest.

Soon the pain in my stomach had overtaken my anxiety. I was violently sick on the floor but there was little I could do about it. Poor dog, I thought, he would be far worse, he had been licking up what he could. How much had he ingested? It had worked so fast.

Poor Jason.

I began to shake uncontrollably. There was a noise in my head. I did not hear the bolt on the outside of the door slide open. I only saw her standing there. Large, smiling, black and so welcome.

'Lillibet! Where the hell did you come from?'

'Never you mind girl. I been waitin for this to happen. I needed to be round to pull you out. Now you come on out to yor ole Lillibet at once. I take you home an fix you up. You not so bad. You done eat none of that stuff, just touch it.'

'No, more than that, look – I cut my hand.' I put out my swollen arm and she grunted, moving fast to the door, dragging me behind her.

A car was waiting outside. Lorenzo sat silently behind the wheel with the engine running. I wondered only fleetingly how they knew where to come and when to come but the pain in my gut overtook all other speculation.

As the car reached the main road we passed several police cars driving in the direction from which we had come.

'Just in time, I think you could say.' Lorenzo spoke quietly with a slight edge to his voice. 'No use going back to No 63. They will go straight there when they find you gone.' He drove with grim determination, overtaking cars when he could. I sat in the back with Lillibet, a blanket drawn about my shoulders and a frantic shiver down my spine.   Every nerve in my body was locked into a tight spasm of frenzy.

I stared out of the car window mentally tracing the outlines of London's architectural movements while matching my breathing to the sharp spasms of pain.   I urged my whirling thoughts to straighten and willed myself not to be sick again by concentrating on the rush and stop movement of the car.   It was all I could do to stop shaking violently.

I felt unreal. I was like a character taken from the scene of a badly made film and spliced to one where the pace and context were better known.

It was as if Lillibet had been raised from the dead and Lorenzo had come out of a dream, like a knight on a white charger, ready to rescue me; their joint presence was surreal.   I felt I would soon wake up and find that horror still lurked, ready for facing.   Lillibet was talking softly and kindly all the while, reassuring me that I would soon be sorted out, she knew how.

Strange how it is, I thought, how kindness after battling with chaos, prompts those unwarranted tears.

Chapter 52

My mind is blurred to what happened next.

I know that Lillibet made me take a hot bath infused with herbs and smells from strange bottles that she always seemed to have with her. She even submerged my head in the water, rubbing at my face and hair. She said the poison must be drawn out. Then she gave me a disgusting tasting infusion to drink. I was fiercely thirsty and drank with less resistance to its taste. I continued to be sick for what seemed hours of exhaustion.

I lay back too tired to move.

Sounds, colours and shapes merged while a never ending stream of wild images moved in slow flashes across my tired brain, drifting through those dense layers of sleep. I woke from time to time to find dark night surrounding me in a series of nightmare drifts.

I seemed to be ill for days with Lillibet constantly at my side, talking to me incessantly it seemed. She slept in a bed next to mine and woke when I woke and poured that concoction down my throat at every occasion she could.

As I slowly drifted back to some kind of responsiveness I could look more discerningly at my surroundings.

The room I was in was strange to me. I imagined I had been taken to the Alberini's home but there was nothing here that I could familiarize my mind with. The curtains were orange with pink pineapples printed at various angles. The carpet was a royal blue and had been witness to a few spilled meals. On the wall opposite the bed was a picture of Christ on the cross, head bent low, with a brilliant sunset like a splash of scrambled eggs behind him. On the adjacent wall were various posed pictures of the Queen with that stringent smile she offers out to her humble public.

I tried to sit up and reach for the glass of water on the pine table next to me. From the doorway, a small figure that had been lurking there leapt forward and took the glass to me. At first glance I wondered if it was some kind of sprite or hobgoblin that Lillibet used as a familiar in her sorcery. I focussed on the small black face and it smiled the prettiest, gleaming, white-toothed smile back at me.

'You feeling better Miss?'

'Yes thank you,' I said taking the glass and drinking thirstily.

'Cousin Lilly say you been very sick Miss.'

'I guess I have,' my voice croaked back, still raw from prolonged vomiting.

'Cousin Lilly say you be right as rain in no time and then you can play with me.'

'You want me to play with you?'

'The brothers don't bother with me. They say they too old to play with little girl silly stuff. I go fetch Miranda now she want to see you Miss.' And so saying she turned about and walked out, her pink track suit bulging over exposed nappy pants.

I could hear Lillibet's voice booming from another room of hushed whispers.

'What you been doing in there Lyla? You come on out at once.'

'Miss wants to play with Miranda;' came the quick response.

Lillibet was standing at the door with half a dozen other black faces framed at varying heights at the door.

'Bout time you was up,' Lillibet boomed. 'You done enough talkin when you sleepin, that for shore.'

It appeared that we were staying at the house of some of her relatives in South East London somewhere or other. There seemed to be so many of them and all occupying the inadequate space of small rooms.

So this was where Lillibet had come when she had vanished. The Alberini's must have known where she had come. So that was why none of them showed too much concern about her disappearance!

I was surrounded by a sea of faces and introduced all round. There was Cousin Paulina from back home and her husband John (local) and then there was Cousin Melissa their eldest and a respectable school teacher already, Cousin John Junior doing his A levels, also respectably done, Cousin Leroy, doing nothing particularly respectable but exploiting his mother's hospitality by disappearing from time to time, Cousin Emanuel working hard at respectability; then after a considerable gap of about seven years came little Cousin Lyla with her doll Miranda who voiced all that the family wished to say, with the aid of its ventriloquist owner.

From the moment I had woken I found myself surrounded by one or other of the family. Endless chat filled any silences that might inadvertently occur.

I soon learnt that a delicate body and a peripatetic mind have little resistance against constant buzz and other attention absorbing commotion.

Little Lyla waited in the wings for any absence of family to allow Miranda to express all the anxieties the family had been feeling. Apart from the wide mouth movement, the tiny raconteur was a contender for a certain future on the stage of ventriloquism.

'Lyla's Mummy says she lucky you not dead or Cousin Lilly got lot of splaining to do to policemen.'

'Is that so!'

'Yes and she say...'

'Lyla you come on out here girl. That enough talkin.'

'I not talking Cousin Lillie, it Miranda talking.'

 Lillibet appeared at the door with a mug of tea in her hand and a large smile on her wonderful face. "I tink to-day we go on back home Anna. What you tink?"

 'Anything you say Lillibet. I am feeling much better and would like to get back to my music.'   I suddenly remembered where I had last placed my violin and went cold.   Not only had it been rather badly damaged, but by now, with the heavy rain I could see outside, I could imagine it becoming soaked.   The case was old and battered and certainly not rain-proof.

 'You tinking of dis?' she said and from behind her back she produced the violin case looking a lot better than I had ever known it.   Inside was Mother's violin, perfect and not a scratch on it.

 'That Lorenzo took hold of that.'

 'How did you know?' I asked rather flabbergasted at all the magic she seemed to turn out.

 'I been watchin a long time now. I bin keepin an eye on that sister of yours. She in no fit state to be round people right now.'

 'Is it safe to go back now?' I asked tentatively.

 'Yes. It's safe.'

 'How, Lillibet?   What has happened since...?'

 'Your sister is in a bad way. I tell you when you get home. O.K. now?'

Chapter 53

Perfect pitch is said to be shared by some humans, along with bats, wolves, gerbils and birds for whom it facilitates identification of mates or meals. In humans it is described as an "autosomal dominant genetic trait" and comparatively rare. It is the ability to reproduce a tone without any reference to an external standard. In other words you can hear a sound and identify the corresponding note in music.

I have always known that I was lucky enough to have inherited this ability.

If, in life, perfect pitch is the ability to know someone well, to identify all their imperfections and their vices from the inside to the outside, then I have no ability in this direction what so ever. I was even alarmed at my unreasonable and primitive reactions, with the immediate instinct of wanting vengeance, exoneration and recognition of my own imagined flawlessness.

In life we use the word "justice" to disguise vengeance. We use castigation and punishment as the penalty for upsetting the system. We seldom look to the causes. I was guilty of wanting what I saw as justifiable punishment for my sister. A sister I had loved all my life and regarded as perfection.

I looked no further than the evil acts she had committed, asking myself over and over what it is that makes someone carry out a deliberate act of evil, with purpose and self-justification.

In Christian terms our propensity for evil is excused as the hereditary stain of Adam's sin, and sin, according to Catholicism, can be exonerated by the mere confession of it.

I tore hungrily into all those judicious philosophies and religions on the subject of evil. Evil, that belongs elsewhere, never close; never with someone you have loved so much and trusted. But trust for me had somehow lost its currency and faith no longer had conviction.

They say that character is formed in childhood and our inherent disposition is moulded by a genetic blueprint. The question is; are we sinful by nature or do we simply not understand what a sin is? After all, every generation alters what it perceives as wrong and what is right. We only know what the law of Karma, (spoken in Christian terms as, "what ye sow, so shall ye reap") seems to be relevant.

I was struck by something Malachi had said and I remember reading that under the laws of Karma, that evil acts pursue a soul across time and space until the act is paid and even death cannot abolish a Karmic debt.   Perhaps this is so, I have no evidence but hearsay and I am coming to believe that being alive and aware stands outside reward and punishment, there is no duality here and we are free in one sense.   Perhaps we do live a life infected by a past; the stains and impressions of submerged memory that affects the current and moving present.   Perhaps it does motivate our needs, physical and emotional and spiritual and perhaps it does drive us towards actions that perseverate ad infinitum.   Perhaps an even more distant past, beyond a current life, still affects us subconsciously?   I don't know.

It is a "past-tense" I have only just begun to regard with less mockery and more open-mindedness.

The privilege of knowing Lillibet helped me to see, or at least I believed that I was beginning to "see".

Lillibet: a simple woman with profound knowledge and spiritual awareness. It took a long time to really see her and know what she was all about and how she operated.

I was restless the moment we got back to No. 63.   Thoughts rattled around and around in my head like a stone in a tin can going downhill fast.   I geared my mind to old histories of my sister's disruptive side.

I engaged in a dialogue with my inner self.   It was full of useless anger, hurt and vengefulness against her. Asking myself 'why me?' what had I done to warrant such a devious and evil scheme just to wound me?   I had never, in all our childhood together, had a single negative thought about her.   I had followed her blindly, believed in everything she told me and did exactly what she instructed me to do. But now I had opened a tap that would not close. How could she do this to me?

There was no charity in my thinking - only self-pity.

I neglected to think how she had become this way.

I forced my memory back to that traumatic episode of Mother's death and made myself examine all that I could of that time.   My memory drew out those spiked conversations and arguments between Mother and Father. I remembered then that all the rows were not over another woman but over something to do with Peggy.

After Mother's disappearance I recalled how calm my sister was, while I wrung my hands and wept. I remembered how I was told how silly I was to cry when Mother would soon be back. The long and fairy tale explanations she gave and how she set it all right for me.   I remembered her little confidential, whispered talks with Father, locked in his bedroom so I could not hear.   How she would go into his room at night to comfort him, leaving me alone all night and frightened through the night darkness.

She was so happy those days. I put it down to the wonderful idea of our Mother being happily embraced in some good life somewhere and that she was certain that Mother would come back for us one day.

Peggy changed when Francis appeared on the scene. She became very aggressive and agitated, demanding things done her way and that we were not to pay attention to anything Francis said.

She made Francis's life difficult and often left her crying. Father never interfered, he told Francis that she was just a teenager and would grow up. Of course, she was jealous of Francis. I knew it now. She no longer had Father entirely to herself.

But she had had no need to be jealous of me. Father was never interested in my music as Mother had been. If anything it irritated him. I expect I was a reminder of the wife he had been unhappy with.

Whatever it was that was going on in Peggy's Machiavellian plotting, it had long since been a part of some nightmare gone wrong. It was as if she had become tangled in a giant labyrinth of dark tunnels and had lost all perspective of herself and those around her.

Whilst I raged outwardly at the injustice of her behaviour, I wept for her within.

I knew that she had carried a dark secret all her childhood, on her own, which none of us could face properly.

I started back at college the day after returning to No.63. Lorenzo was away I was told and someone else took me for Flute and Clarinet. I don't remember now which tutor taught what. I tended to play, lost in my own world, taking praise lightly and instruction seriously; making improvements and returning to the story behind the melody.

I was notified by my solicitor that they had dropped the charges against me and I felt a surge of relief, besides the irritation that they had charged me so quickly for Jason's death, without any real evidence other than hearsay. I wondered what had made them change their minds but the worthy Mr. Hooke simply said they were investigating another source. I didn't dare ask but I suspect he knew as much as me at that stage. I was only able to make suppositions, but I had done that already, so mistakenly, over the multi-faced Marcello.

No one called.

I half expected Aunt Sophie or Grandmother to phone to say they had been wrong to condemn me, but there was silence from the outside world. Perhaps they were afraid that I might turn up again and disrupt their world or poison another defenceless dog.

Lillibet said silence is a good thing. As long as there is silence you will be left alone. But silence was only an outer thing, for in my head sounds, old pain of buried thoughts shrieked at me like primal recognitions.

I played longer and longer hours, forgetting to eat and sometimes to sleep but without the music to attach my mind to, the last few days would torment me like a relentless and unbearable ache.

Any time apart from music I spend with Lillibet. I moved my things into the spare bedroom in her flat and stayed there, afraid of the rest of the house and its ghosts. I even longed for a return of one of the personalities. I missed Agatha, her dry comments and her looks of disguised concern.

I pined for Malachi.

Chapter 54

A twist of fate, coincidence, chance, fluke or destiny: perhaps they are all one perhaps they are a part of pre-destiny, I don't know. What made me go downstairs to the basement at a particular time on a particular day can be given any name. I know only that it was pure chance that I discovered Peggy had lost her job. Or, to put more accurately, she had simply not returned to it.

No one knew where she had gone.

I had put off going down to the basement flat to collect some spare violin strings that I kept there. But while I was playing one of my strings snapped and I could not postpone the journey down there any longer.

It was dark. I had left all the curtains, on those windows with that luxury appointed to them, closed. Vestiges of Jason suggested themselves into every inch of space where moving shapes seemed to sketch the air. His smell, his laughter his very essence clung to every fibre and every surface and stayed there.

I thought about his funeral that had still not taken place because of the unnatural circumstances of his death. His body had not yet been released from the pathology lab. I thought of the pain his parents must be going through, waiting for closure.

I found the strings and turned to go out when I noticed an accumulation of mail inside the outer basement door.

Jason had always collected the mail. He was the only one to receive it. Among letters and notifications to him there was one type-written letter addressed to me.

The letter heading bore the name of the law firm Peggy worked for.

'Dear Miss Lockhart,' it began. It must be for Peggy was my first thought, but I read on. My eyes stopped at the line '...failed to return to work and has been out of touch now for over a week.'

The expressions of alarm jumped out at me: "of grave concern" and "that it had been noticed that Miss Lockhart had been unwell for several weeks leading to her disappearance."

I put the letter down; then I picked it up and read it again, slowly, taking in the importance of what was being said. If Peggy was not there, she must still be in England somewhere. According to the date on the letter she had been around for over a month. Where she had been staying all that time and what she had been doing? It was suddenly a frightening prospect.

I took the letter to Lillibet and read it to her. She was silent for a long time.

'Well, what about it Lillibet? Where is she?'

'Your sister, she is in big trouble. She got real mixed up inside and now poison, her own poison, it comes out.'

'Lillibet if you knew all this before, why did you not warn me. Why did you not say something? You could have stopped all this. Jason would still be alive.'

'And who do you think goin to listen to ole Lillibet? Huh? Would you have listened? No. No one was ready for the knowledge, as I said before till you are ready to hear you won't listen. Everyone want proof first. Sometimes proof not available. Same as everyting in life. You listen but you don't hear till you ready.'

I thought of what Malachi had said to me and I knew she was right. You can hold a truth in the palm of your hand and not know it till you have experienced it and even then, you wait for another and another verification.

'Do you know where she is?' I asked.

'She is with her father. He is the one you must look at, but I can't say more. You need to find out for yourself.'

I went down to the flat to find Father's telephone number and rang. Jerry answered the phone.

'Jerry it's Anna. Is my sister Peggy with you?'

She had put the phone down without answering me and I became alarmed. I phoned Father's office and his secretary told me he was visiting their chemical factory that morning and had not returned; would I like to leave a message.

Chemicals - poisons: of course, why had I never thought of this connection before? Things were suddenly beginning to fit together. Surely he had not provided her with the means of destruction? Surely not? Why?

I went back up the stairs to confer with Lillibet. She advised me to contact the police but I could not. It was that old story of needing "proof" that she had referred to.

I thought I had the truth.

What if you think you have found the truth and you are wrong? - without that evidence we can assume wrong. What if all this conjecture was just a badly aimed guess? After all, I had assumed incorrectly before.

I called for a taxi and gave them Father's address. Within an hour of weaving traffic I was outside his house. His car was parked in the front. He must have only recently come home; the bonnet of the car was still warm from the engine.

I knew at once that if my sister was there I would not be welcome. There would be a repeat performance of what happened at Aunt Sophie's.

I remembered noticing the garden gate at the side of the house. I let myself through as silently as I could and slid into the back garden.

It was a Friday evening in early spring. The days were still short enough to forfeit afternoon light and already the borrowed evening lights from outside were glowing. Inside, lights were on and curtains were drawn.

If I was going to see anything it would have to be through a chink in an incompletely drawn curtain or I would have to slide into a back door that might not be locked yet.

The best and only option was the door. I was inside in a moment and found a convenient door to hide behind. There seemed to be no one around.

Then I heard her voice.

'I won't let you do this to me Daddy. You promised. You promised me.'

'Pegs my darling girl, you have grown up now. You have a life of your own. I must have my life to myself now. What has been is over now.'

'But it will never be over for me. I feel dirty because of it. I am emptied because of it. I can't move on. I want to stay where we were. I can't move on.'

'Peggy, I have a new wife now...'

'Another child Father, another child. What is it with you?'

'She is not a child. She is...'

'Is, is, did I hear you say "is". I think you need to speak in the past tense Daddy dearest.'

The pleading voice has changed to her hard brittle voice.

'What do you mean Peggy? What are you trying to tell me? Oh God, not again. No not again. You swore all that stuff was finished. Peggy have you been lying to me again?'

I heard him rush from the room. I heard him shouting out 'Jerry', 'Jerry' over and over.

Peggy had fallen to the floor in the hallway. She was sobbing uncontrollably. He was telephoning from upstairs. He was shouting; 'Ambulance, ambulance for God's sake hurry.'

I slipped outside, back into the dark garden.

I stayed out there under a tree with wide branches so that I would not cause my shadow to give me away, and I watched the house.

The upstairs curtains were still open. I saw two large ambulance medics reach the landing and disappear into a bedroom. They were in there for what seemed a long time. Then I saw movement. A stretcher was being carried back out to the landing.

It disappeared from sight.   Moments passed. The front door was banged shut.

I heard the ambulance drive off with another car following: Father's car.

I let myself back into the house through the unlocked back door. Peggy was sitting at the white kitchen table.   She was very still now.   She had stopped crying.   She looked up and saw me standing in front of her and she smiled.   She did not appear surprised to see me.   She had cropped up unexpectedly in so many places that sudden appearances should be commonplace to her arrangements.

Her eyes had that hollow glazed look of deep pain locked away in some far off recess.   She had become this monster from a kind of love that had brutalized and destroyed her.   It had splintered an inner turmoil embedded in a distasteful and primitive desire that had ripped her conscience apart.   Reality for her had morphed into that subliminal part of her personality, outside consciousness and awareness.

'Hello Annie,' she said.   It was her nice voice.

Her face was swollen from crying.   Her make-up was smudged. Peggy never allowed her make-up to smudge.

Only then did I notice the crimson pool that surrounded her.

She had torn out the veins in both her wrists and the blood was pumping like a burst pipe all over the white floor-tiles.

'God Peggy!   What have you done?'

'Oh don't try to stop me Annie.   You must understand I can't go on.   If you send for an ambulance they will revive me only to put me away for life.   I have poisoned them all Annie.   I did it for Mummy. Mummy knew what we were doing Annie and it killed her,' she said.

The horror of the terrible confession that lay behind her actions, so devoid of moral conscience, impacted upon me like a deadly and inescapable avalanche.

'I thought I loved him Anna. I wanted him all to myself. I thought that was what he wanted.   When I knew it was not, I wanted to destroy him as his kind of love had destroyed me. That is the truly terrible thing about sex.   You can do it without loving or even liking. You do it because it is there to be done and it teaches you to hate and I learned to hate.   I mean really hate.   The feeling was so concentrated, so physical it would make me physically ill.

It was all I thought about when I went to bed at night and when I woke up in the morning.   It spread like a cancer to everything, to everyone I knew.'

It was hard to know quite who she was talking about.   What she was saying was so horrifying, so terrifying, it left me unable to answer or think.

I wondered whatever else he had done to her innocent mind that had brutalized her so.

I knew as she talked that I would not stop her now.

No one would understand this side of her. They would only see the show she would put on in court and judge that. I knew that a life in prison would kill her - slowly. This way, this way was her choice and she would go quickly.

I looked at her sitting there like Titania weaving spells among her pretty fairies, crying for her foundling child. She was fast fading into another world. A world of dreams and fantasies. She was singing a song Mummy had taught us.

'Would you like a nice cup of tea Pegs?' I asked, steadying my voice.

'Oh what a good girl you are my little sister.'

I went to the kettle and switched it on.

I found the best cup and saucer I could find and set a little tray for her. By the time I had brought it to her she was slumped forward and breathing with difficulty.

'Here Pegs, drink this it will do you good.'

'You didn't put any of that white powder in it did you?' she asked looking afraid for a moment.

'No, Pegs. No need for it.'

'Daddy gave it to Mummy that day. He brought a packet of it home from work. He said it would take care of things.

Mummy was in so much pain when we pushed her Pegs. She had to be helped to jump. I saw where he kept it hidden and I took it. He said he wanted it to throw it away after. "The white powder that took care of things." Well, I was the one who had to take care of things. You can see that, can't you? And I worked out how to use it, see?' She held up an arm that was now crimson and the stream flowed back up her arm and circled round the gold charm bracelet that she rattled there.

'You must take it when I am gone. It's yours now.'

She took the cup to her lips, with trembling hands and drank only one small sip.

'Ah,' she said. And the blood spilled over the side of the cup and filled the saucer.

'I would never have let him touch you Annie,' she said. 'I hated you for it later, but I made sure...'

Her voice was slurred and she dropped the cup. I bent down and kissed her forehead.

'I love you Pegs,' I said.

'I know,' she answered. They were her last words before she fell forward onto cup of spilled tea.

I eased her arm to the side with my trembling hands and unclasped the sticky mess of charms that smudged the now coagulating gory blood about the table, smearing its clean, pristine surface. I took it to the sink and ran it beneath the tap.

Amongst the gold trinkets there were five tiny pots whose lids lifted off easily. Four of them had already opened and a small trace of white powder was still inside. The fifth pot was still full. I tore the lid back and washed away all that remained of the venomous white that was there and let the water run till all the blood and powder was gone, down into the protective drain. Then I shook it dry and clasped the last of Mother and my Sister's memory onto my left wrist.

I let myself out of the back door, wiping off any finger-prints that I might have left behind; I slid out into the darkening night. I had learnt only recently the dangers of incriminating evidence.

Then I walked home. It was a long walk.

I was numb.

I kept getting lost, finding myself down strange streets. I would come to for a moment, get my bearing, then walk on, blind to everything but the blank pavement before me, deaf to sound but the echoes of what had passed - taunting and chanting. Its ghosts swirled in mind-teasing patterns about my head.

My whole past had been in limbo, balanced between possibility and fact. Part of me was too sickened to discover what I had forgotten and another part allowed those fragments to storm back into my thoughts.

Our parents' last and terrible argument reconstructed itself vaguely in my mind with words that later resonated a recognition. They were accusing and wounding words spat out in the shock of the moment, untested in their consequence.

Puritanical middle-class views, he'd said.

Incestuous paedophile, she had said.

Lesbian ideals, he defended.

Daddy what is a Lesbian?

Your mother and her simple ideas...

Morning was just peeping over the horizon and those early motorists who broke the day, swept past un-noticed, un-noticing, as I reached No. 63, exhausted and relieved to see its shape in the gloom, a landmark that meant home.

Chapter 55

Funny how wrong the papers are and how assumptions are bred from small information.

The headlines said that a man who had been systematically poisoning all the women in his life over a period of years then callously stood by and watched his daughter bleed to death after cutting her wrists. They told how he had returned from the hospital where his young wife had died of arsenic poisoning. He had made his daughter a cup of tea while she was dying and did nothing to save her.

It appeared that his daughter had written a suicide note which the police found in her handbag later. It explained all the details, how her father had acquired the poison from the chemical company where he worked etc. I forget all the details and complications of the story. I never read them properly.

The man had said nothing to verify his innocence or guilt and was awaiting trial.

I attended three funerals that week.

The police had at last wrapped up the case of Jason's death.

They had got it all wrong of course, but no one came forward to correct their assumed conclusions. It was so convoluted and improbably as to allow it to become credible. The reasons were left for forensic psychologists to postulate over. Psychologists are good at that.

I stood apart from the other mourners and took my place at the back of the church, so that I would not be noticed.

Jason had a large family. They must have loved him very much. The flowers filled the church and spilled out into the church yard.

I felt him there with me, at the back, watching, amused and detached from it. I heard someone say, 'What a waste of a young life.'

I thought of my sister's life. She had never really been a child. Not really.

Hers was the next funeral.

There were no flowers.

I had last seen her when I had to identify her. Someone had brushed her hair into a subdued loose curl about her shoulders. She was lying there in a teasing sleep on a cold gurney, like a beautiful, rigid limbed, white porcelain doll. Her face, drained of blood was like bleached parchment, devoid of life. They had bandaged her blood-dried wrists and her face had been washed clean of smeared make-up. She looked so young, so helpless.

As her next of kin I had to arrange her, "disposal". That's what they called it.

I ordered a cremation.

I asked to see her one last time before they closed her coffin. This time I could not bear to look at her face. I slipped the bracelet back on her wrist. I wanted to make sure it would go with her. Then I went alone to see her humble coffin drawn away behind anonymous curtains.

There was no one else there when she slid through on the grinding conveyor belt. I went round the curtain to follow its progress. Two men lifted it onto a second belt, like the ones that take your luggage through X-ray at the airport. The oven door was waiting like a large yawning mouth. They pressed a button and the coffin moved forward to become swallowed up into the gaping cavern where flames grabbed hold of the wood and bit into it - enveloping the coffin completely and the door was closed up and my beautiful sister was no more.

When it was over, I turned around to walk out of the tiny chapel and saw Aunt Sophie with Ben, standing there. They did not smile, nor did they talk. They turned as I reached them and we went out together.

'There is another truth somewhere,' Aunt said.

'Yes,' I answered. 'But perhaps it is Peggy's and Father's truth. And it seems he is going to keep it to himself and take what is coming to him. I think somehow, that is right.'

'I am sorry,' Sophie said. 'All this weighed heavily upon your shoulders. We were wrong to...'

'Aunt Sophie, I have spent a childhood being shielded from it all, this weight is only small compared to what my sister has carried.'

'I think we should all go home and talk about it,' Ben offered.

'I don't think so,' I replied. 'Peggy spent all her life keeping things secret. This is her private story. Father knows it and he has chosen to be locked away for the rest of his life for it. What is it they say? - "let sleeping dogs lie?"'

I turned away while they were asking me to go back with them, but I could not bear a moment more with them. Hadn't Peggy told me that family were dangerous? Perhaps they weren't, perhaps it was the painful drama of the moment. Perhaps I was over reacting.

They could have made more of an attempt to come to us when Mother died. They might have helped then, but everyone was shouting blame and no one wanted to really know. Knowing now would not bring Peggy back.

I chose not to see them again.

Two days later a white coffin with yellow roses packed into a neat wreath decorated its pure surface. It was a carefully chosen reflection of the young girl it encased. As it too passed through another curtained opening, there was a sigh from those who watched, wanting to keep her back; to give her just a little longer in her brief and eager life.

Jerry's parents looked so young. She had a sister and a brother still in school. Their tears were unguarded and unrestrained. For them bereavement was new and untested. Things should not happen this way.

A photograph of her on her wedding day, (without her groom, naturally) was blown up, life size. She watched us from its gilt frame, posed at the front of the church. She was smiling and happy and trusting.

I took my place at the back again, and no one knew who I was.

Speaking With Strangers

Chapter 56

Autumn was late that year.   Summer seemed determined not to lose its grip.   The days had been hot and stifling. By September when cooler days are looked towards with relief, the heat beat on with persistent disregard.

I hardly noticed it.

I was locked away with my music. I did very little else.

Invitations to play in concerts and recitals were coming through to me all the time. I turned them down saying I was not ready, despite the mass of persuasion from my teachers but emotionally I was not ready to face a crowd.

Lorenzo and Maria came several times to speak with me but I was unable to talk. I could play but I could not talk. Not that idle chatter.   I was brief and I think sometimes I came across as rude but I could not help myself, there was a tangle of emotion that hit each word as it entered my mouth to speak.

I stayed away from everyone.   I even moved back down to the basement flat to avoid Lillibet or any invading personality that might return.

Lillibet had been easy to avoid.   I would not allow myself to think about her or why she too had locked herself away in her apartment, seeing no one.

Jason's room had been cleared of anything that was his by his family.   They had come again after the funeral. Lillibet dealt with them.

They left behind all the photographs he had taken of me.   I was the monster instrumental in his death.   They still hung there, surreal and dreamlike, like those muses of the lower world with their irresistibly sweet music that lap the body and soul into fatal lethargy. I could not take them down. It was as if another side of me was hanging there, taunting me in my blindness.

I closed his door and found a key to lock it.

I locked everything and everyone away that summer - except my music.

I still used the music room.   Somehow the music room had remained sacrosanct, uninfringeable. I became lost there for hours on end and there was no one to break my intense compulsion to lose myself in the folds of perfect sound.

I found a certain release in the drama of Stravinski. I could reach its highs and depths and tortured moments that became surrogate tears for me.

One afternoon, I had come to the end of a piece from Pulcinella, the version for violin, the room was still turning in circles with the power of the sounds. I opened my eyes and my focus converged upon a figure sitting there, and the still and silent face of Agatha stared back at me. I don't remember the details of her now; just that she was sitting quiet and watchful.

Neither of us spoke.

I turned around and put my violin into its case and when I turned back she was gone. She must have closed the door so quietly that I had not even heard her going out.

I went upstairs and knocked on her door. The bolts that had been put there were still shut across from the outside, so she could not have been in there. I went up to see Lillibet, she must be there. There was no sign of Lillibet anywhere. It had been at least two months since I had been up to her flat. All at once the feeling of being alone hit me.

How had I allowed all this time to pass? It was as if I had woken from a very long deep sleep. I felt dazed and little shaken by it. Something was wrong.

For the first time since I had closed myself away, I needed people around me. The urge to see one of them was desperate and disturbing.

I put on a light jacket and went out. Without thinking of direction or purpose I found myself outside the Alberini's door and knocked.

Lorenzo came to the door. He looked tired and drawn.

'Anna,' he said. 'How lovely to see you.'

I smiled and stepped in to the bidding of a sweep of his hand which directed me to the living room. Maria was there with Jacek Lipinski her percussionist friend. They were sitting together on the sofa, their hands locked together. Mrs. Alberini was busy talking and Lillibet was there. They all looked up at me and smiled. Lillibet came up and kissed me saying how pleased she was that I was there. Then they all came up to embrace me and say how pleased they were that I had come.

I knew instinctively that Marcello had gone.

There was a hollow feeling behind their smiles and the house had lost its sparkle but it had also gained a sense of equilibrium.

'What brought you here Anna?' Maria asked as she kissed my cheek.

'Agatha,' I said, 'She has just been to visit me.'

'Who is Agatha?' Jacek asked. 'Is this a member of the family I have not yet met?'

I saw them all look to one another. He does not know about the personalities.

'Agatha is my family,' I answered. 'All I had, but she has gone away now.'

'Ah,' he said, and no one commented.

I did not ask about Marcello. I would hear soon enough.

They were all celebrating Maria's engagement to Jacek. I took a glass of champagne from Lorenzo and slowly my cold heart began to thaw.

Mrs. Alberini was full of confident speculation about an early wedding. She was quite determined it was to be before the summer was quite over.

'Anna, you are to be my bridesmaid.' Maria informed me. There was no question that I could decline. It was spoken as a matter of fact and the champagne going to my head made it seem the nicest thing that I could do.

'That would be lovely,' I said.

Jacek had come from a large family in Poland and they were all to come and stay for the wedding. No one mentioned that No. 63 MacDonald Road would be free for guests but there were plenty of places nearby. Mrs. Alberini had had it all arranged for weeks it seemed.

I had entered a new world, a new time-space. One day followed another, unconnected like soap bubbles rising into the sky, becoming lighter and lighter. I had stepped so neatly, so clearly, away from that old life, so full of the strangers I had known and not known at all. Undisclosed secrets and covet assignations were a thing of the past, nothing mattered any more.

If the Alberini's wanted to keep a family secret, who was I to hinder that? Secrets are sometimes made for leaving that way.

The afternoon stretched into evening. The family were going out for dinner. I got up to go when they went singly to prepare themselves.

'Please join us,' Lorenzo asked. 'It has been so long Anna and the evening will do us all good to have you with us.'

'I need to go home and change first,' I said at once, 'perhaps I can meet you there?'

'Better still, we say a time and we will call for you,' he said.

Lillibet came back with me. She too wanted to dress for dinner. We walked back quietly as the evening was drawing to late summer mellow pastels. She took my hand as we walked and hummed one of her hymns, every now and then breaking out into song with the devout words that went with it.

The house looked bleak as we reached it. No lights in its dark windows. My heart began to sink once more and I began my doubts about going out. Lillibet read my mind.

'You come in front door with Lillibet and put on them lights fast, this house needs smilin' now. None of that back steppin nonsense Miss Violin-player,' she said, and she laughed. It was one of her throaty laughs that hit the soles of her feet and rang out through the top of her head.

The house was different with its lights on. The gloom that shrouded its secrets was dispelled by the simple flick of a switch and at once I was able to discharge my fears by casting a look around at visible emptiness. I went down to the flat while Lillibet went upstairs to her own apartment.

I refused to see the moving shapes that cast themselves before me. I determined to forge ahead into an evening with people who I would rather hide from.

I found a dress that Peggy had bought me. Even though she was no longer able to appear from nowhere, I felt her voice urging me to grow up, stand on my own two feet. That negative aspect of her had died with her and the memory I would always retain of her was the one I had carried from childhood, my protector, my advisor, my champion.

I did my make-up and hair as she would have done, forcing myself to move on and forget.

It's hard to move away from a recent past of loss. The remnant grief attaches itself like sticking bur-weed to clothing and sheds a sombre pallor to every occasion. But that evening something stronger was driving me on.

There had been a faceless concealment behind the family's unbearable lightness of mood. It had unnerved me. I needed to hear about Marcello's passing.

I needed to know before an evening of more of that almost aggressive planning for a future of normality which shut out all those stranger's shadows.

My determination to know spurred me to run upstairs and find Lillibet. She was coming down as I was charging up.

'Lillibet, I have to know. When did he die?'

'His heart. It was his heart,' she said and she sank down on the stair where she stood and wept.

'He was like a young brother, could I even say, a child to me,' she said. 'I loved him and I battled with him. It was the day your sister took her life. God knows how he knew.'

'Which one Lillibet, which one knew?'

'I guess it was Malachi or maybe Agatha. It could have been all of them. I don't know. He wanted to be here to see you when you came back but the heart just would not hold any more. Then when you came in you locked yourself away and none of us could reach you. We were all here for him and we stayed with him. We knew it was his time.   Your music, it crept out into the house and filled it while he was becomin free and his children were gettin free, and so really was his wife.   But my heart, it is so sore for the brother who did not know himself.   I guess he knows now where his pain was comin from.   Now he can understand it more from there and all those others who came and went from him, they too...'

'I find that it's the going on with life that hurts Lillibet.   But the family - they all seem so happy now.'

'Not so much happy.   They can start to live now.   Before, that Maria she loose many boyfriend when they see her Daddy one day a woman, one day a stranger who want to fight them, one day a Daddy.'

'What about Lorenzo?   Did he also lose girl-friends because of his father?   I find it hard to believe, surely...'

'And Lorenzo, he...   and Lorenzo just bin waitin for Miss Violin-girl.   And she can't begin because her sister, she would not let her. Same ting.'   And she laughed, her old belly-laugh, and her tears dried.

I thought of the days that Maria and Lorenzo had both tried to talk to me and I had avoided them so rudely.   They were trying to tell me and I was not ready for hearing.

'I can hardly bear the thought of going out tonight Lillibet.   Can't we make an excuse and stay behind?'

'No, you can't.   They all need you as you need them and slowly we all mend together.   Not this hidin ting anymore.'

The front door was being opened and Lorenzo was calling out to us.   He was transporting us in relays.

The others were already settled at the restaurant waiting for us and all talking at once.   Overlapping conversation was something Jacek was fully conversant with.   Coming from a family of five siblings and two of them musicians like himself, he had not lightly chosen to play percussion.

I wondered how he would have reacted to Miss Constantine or Agatha.   Perhaps it was not worth the risk in finding out as he was making Maria so happy, and, it would appear, her mother - even happier.

The evening continued in the same challenging strain as the afternoon of wedding details and who to invite.

The king was dead.   Long live the king.   Only there was no king to replace him.   Marcello with all his differing 'alters' (as they had referred to them) had died and taken with him all the memories, alive and buried, that haunted all of his family.

An era had finally been laid to rest with all its damaging consequences.   But that somehow was not a complete answer.

Chapter 57

A world of concerts and performances lay before me. I began to attend more of them and I slowly gained the confidence to perform in them myself. The string-quartet that Lorenzo had arranged was becoming very popular and soon I was lost in a world where playing before an audience made little difference to playing in solitude.

Lorenzo was always there with me or in the background. He became that silent talisman that I could not do without.

I was beginning to make a name for myself but without him I could not have dealt with the attention I received. It was an aspect of playing that I found hard to cope with.

There was a kind of irony to how things had turned out. Peggy would have loved the adulation and she had simply faded into oblivion. I would have preferred anonymity and found myself paying the price of success with the uncomfortable glare of publicity.

My friendship with Lorenzo had transformed into a mellow, relaxed adagio of warmth. He was no longer the silent, rigid teacher who did not communicate. We had all those ghosts between us now and they had a way of linking us in an unspoken kind of pact. It was as if his father's death had released a tension in him, allowing him to breathe more freely and feel more comfortable with me.

One day he asked me about the vision I had that day with Agatha.

'I never felt that it was a vision,' I said. 'I saw her clearly and never for one moment assumed that she was not real. But then, all the time I had known her, I had never imagined her as an off-shoot of a disturbed brain. She was always real. She was more real than Marcello, her point of origin. She had opinions and she was able to see things no one else saw. A bit like Lillibet, but different somehow.'

'What was it that you liked about her?' he asked,

'I can't say why I liked her, I just did - unlike Miss Constantine who was easy to imagine as a disturbed consequence; with her it was as if there was a need to vindicate a sense of outrage.'

I pictured her just then, lip curled, eyes steel cold and hard. It was as if adversity had brutalized all that had once been good in her. From that reverie I snapped over to one of Malachi, so opposite, so good and so wise.

'Then, there was Malachi,' I said. 'Where did he come from, surely not the same mind? I simply can't believe that Malachi shared a disturbance that he would not be able to resolve for himself. Malachi was the only one who could understand and discuss the other separate personalities. Surely you must have wondered?'

'We spent our lives wondering. Mother was the one who brought in medical help. When Jacob was alive he would not hear of it. He had an answer of his own about all the personalities. They were a kind of comfort to him, reparation for those he had lost in concentration camps. He said they were the souls of his family returning to him and sometimes it seemed true.'

'Did they have the same names?' I asked.

'No, that's where it flawed. Miss Constantine he believed was an old nurse his family had as children. Well, she would not have spoken English and had some strange Italian name like "Gonsuela," but the character fitted. Agatha, he believed, was a sister, but likewise the language thing did not tie up. His sister was tone deaf and the sound of the violin was agony to her. I can't remember her name. You see nothing quite matched. Someone in Marcello's past had treated him very badly and that person emerged often in a number of guises. Jacob thought they had returned through him because of what they did to him, but I would question why they should. It was all so confusing. Mother said she thought it was all Jacob's wishful thinking, yet sometimes the characters would come out with information that affirmed his beliefs.'

'Perhaps,' I said, 'as Malachi said so often, you were not ready to know or understand the why or what of it all.'

'No, perhaps not. Of course a professional diagnosis led us in the direction of psychosis. A professional mind would never entertain what you are suggesting and we came to believe. You see there was evidence on both sides. On one hand a spirit invasion of separate souls seemed so real and on the other hand, the dissimulation of a disturbed mind creating characters really did seem to be the feasible answer. No one wants to be seen as a pontificator of spiritual clap-trap as it is regarded outwardly. But real proof for either supposition could never be concrete. Where the one ended and the other originated, I really can't give an answer to. Matters of the mind are never absolute. Man has inventiveness, creativity and insight, but it is his capacity for fantasy that leads him astray.

I have spent an entire life wondering. It was your unexpected vision of Agatha appearing before you that has re-opened the issue for me. She had done what none of us could do.'

'What was that?'

'She brought you back to us when you were keen to bury yourself alive in the music room.'   He smiled shyly at me and I returned his smile.

Though we had come a long way towards each other I would content to myself that that was as close an acknowledgement of his feelings towards me as would ever be expressed.   There was still a reserve of distance between us that I accepted would always be there.   That was Lorenzo and I would always be someone who sublimated my feelings.

'And the psychologists, how did they see it?' I asked.

'They looked at his disruptive side.   They were mostly interested in the personalities that wanted to wound and destroy and put them all down to something that happened in his childhood.'

'They would have had a field day with poor Peggy.'

'Yes, I expect they would.   The veiled motive arising from secreted fears or unbearable conscience from a confused child-perspective.'

'I wonder what term they would have used for her?   She never pretended to be anyone but herself but her actions were so incredibly insane.'

I wanted to say "evil" but the term was too harsh for her. I had never seen her as evil and I could hardly think in those terms now. She was more deranged, unstoppable; she had used all the strengths of her personality to carry out tasks that her subconscious angers had dreamt of.

'Dissociative Personality was the term they finally attached to him.   They liked all those heavy "D" words: dissimulation, dissemblance, disguise, deceit, duplicity.   I have them all imprinted in my mind.   The dictionary says: "Dissociated   Personality: the pathological person; to dissociate oneself from, declare oneself unconnected with –   develop more than one centre of consciousness."   But how does one person separate the core of his awareness without being able to connect with another consciousness?'

'It could be said that an actor does it when playing a role.'

'Yes, but the actor has got to be able to construct that character from memory.

The thing with Marcello was, he had no memory that could link each personality and each personality retained their own personal memory.   It is after all, memory that defines us, that makes us what we are.'

'What about those cases where people have lost all past memory and live in a day to day existence of something entirely new each day?'

'Marcello was not without memory. He simply did not remember anything before the time that Jacob found him. I think he knew subconsciously how to block those memories and perhaps they simply surfaced as separate characters.'

There was no answer to the questions we posed and perhaps there would be no understanding of what the answers might have been. But from time to time we would return to the same questions, as if by probing them deeper an answer would be revealed to us.

'As Malachi and Lillibet say, we are not ready for the answers,' he said smiling at me.

Chapter 58

Mrs Alberini was a person with a mission.

She had lived for years with a man who was seldom any part of her life and she had patiently stood in the wings while others gave opinions and marshalled his comings and goings.

She had come from that background and time when marriage was a commitment, to which one was bound for life. As she was certainly living a far more affluent life-style than she would have had she returned to her family home, she had little option but to stay put. Her life had become instead, a dedication to her children and all they did.

If she had loved her husband and mourned his death there was little indication of it by the lack of grief at his passing. Certainly in his wake she became alive with preparations as to what she would and could do with the money that was now available to her. No one cared much about it.

Jacob had left a will leaving everything he had to the care and protection of his adopted son Marcello and at his death only, could it be passed on to the remainder of the family. Lillibet had been already been provided for more than adequately with the added provision that No. 63 MacDonald Road was not to be sold in her life time. Whatever she had been left or given was only ever dipped into to hand on to her many cousins who seemed to creep out of every corner of the globe to become her dearest friend.

She was so good natured that whatever her past had punished her with, she allowed none of it to spoil her present life. She laughed heartily and never once gave a recriminating glance backwards at the family who had once disowned her.

She mended the torn lives of those who came to her to have their fortunes told and sighed and cried with them all.

Lillibet's grief was a private thing as was her life, though she shared and even, it might be said, interfered with the lives of others.

Though she joined in with all the excitement and preparation of the family wedding, this was not so much her time for celebrating as it was for the Alberini family. They had lived so long under the stresses and strains of multiple personalities that had come and gone over the past years, disrupting and destroying any chance of a peaceful life. Now they were free of all that.

This was their time, and you could see it in their faces and their behaviour. Lorenzo was relaxed and no longer that furtive, surreptitious figure who came and went without warning.

Maria was finally getting married. It was something she had speculated over and prayed for since she had dressed her Barbie dolls with bridal clothes and dreamed one day it would be herself. She had reached her thirties and been jilted at every match when they had gone to her home.

Last but not least, was Mrs. Alberini. She was now free of the heavy burden of a commission to guard and care for a husband who had lost his own identity to a series of strangers who passed through him.

I hardly noticed her redecorating plans at No. 63. They went on around me while I single-mindedly came and went, practising, preparing for performance after performance, then simply falling into bed at night into a state of complete exhaustion.

Maria's wedding day arrived and with it a whole new family to meet. Jacek had three brothers, two of them were married. The third was single and a pianist. He had not quite reached concert standard, his brother told us, but he taught at a school in his town. His name was Sergei and he had the bluest eyes I had ever seen and the most charming smile.

Sergei had been staying in London over the school's summer vacation. As he was staying with Jacek, he had been to a few of my solo performances and one of our quartet concerts.

While he was always charming, I could see that he was the sort of man who paid that kind of persistent attention that would not consider "no" as an option.

I had found him a bit disconcerting as there was something about his eagerness that brought to mind Peggy's determination to have a relationship with whomever she chose, at all costs.

The day before the wedding all members of the family from abroad, on both sides, had assembled at various addresses nearby. Mrs. Alberini had finished decorating Agatha's apartment and housed several of them there. I hoped sincerely that I would not be asked to inspect the place. To me it had been desecrated.

Lillibet and I were invited to join the family guests for dinner at the hotel where the wedding would take place the next day. There seemed to be so many of them: Uncles, Aunts, husbands and wives and several of Mrs. Alberini's family out from Italy. It was hard to find anyone who spoke English.

I clung on to Lillibet who had brought two cousins with her. We laughed self-consciously and stuck like glue to each another.

After dinner Maria and Jacek came up to me with brother Sergei in hand and introduced him - again, though I had met him three times before. When I reminded them it was taken in great mirth and excused as excitement over the wedding.

Sergei's English was poor but he managed to convey that he had been waiting to talk to me since I had walked through the door. I felt very flattered but for the remainder of the evening we battled in conversation, talking mostly about music.

Lorenzo was caught in a miasma of adoring aunts and cousins while playing host to the Lipinski family. I glanced in his direction several times but he seemed more than occupied and less concerned about my reluctantly intimate companionship with Sergei.

I managed to break away at last to find Lillibet and beg her to think about our return home. She and Cousin Pearl and Cousin Paulina were very happily engaged in a bottle of Champagne and less keen to go right then and I started to dread the following day.

I finally managed to escape before the intrepid Sergei found me but I had no sooner hailed a taxi than Lillibet came pounding after me. 'Here girl, why you not wait for ole Lillibet.'

'I had enough of Jacek's brother Lillibet. Any longer there and it would have been us getting married tomorrow.' This was followed by loud and boisterous laughter from Lillibet and the cousins, who, worse for wear, were finding it difficult to get into the taxi in one piece.

The next day I took part in Maria's dressing ceremony, with manicurists, hair-dressers and make-up artists. I had never been through such an experience.

Poor Peggy, I thought, she would have loved this.

I was not Maria's only bridesmaid. She had three friends who had been to music college with her and Jacek's two sisters. We all wore the same pink gowns down to the ground. The colour suited all the other five but clashed rather wildly with my red hair, but as no one mentioned it, I allowed myself to blend into the crowd, hoping I would not be noticed; thankful only that Miss Constantine would not be there to point out the flaw in me.

Everything was immaculately organized, with as much emphasis on colour as was possible, from the church to the wedding banquet. Starchily arranged flowers, festooned with matching ribbon, obediently performed their managed shapes to suit each table and the centre isle of the church. Drapes and fairy lights and bunting created a fare-ground of child-magic.

If Jacob had been Jewish there was little sign of it carried forward, as his granddaughter had conformed to Catholicism to suit her new family.

Speeches were led by Lorenzo who spoke quietly about his sister, with the required acknowledgments to her bridesmaids. One solitary glance in my direction and I knew already that he must have noticed how odd I looked. Then, as the speeches continued in a variety of languages, I lost all knowledge of what was being said and continued to agonize over my inelegance and discomfort.

Sergei spent the entire wedding-feast declaring passionate and eternal love to me. If I was looking in any way incompatible with my dress, he had not noticed it. He told me that he had talked hard to his brother to arrange the seating plan that I might be removed from next to Lorenzo and placed next to him at his table and Maria had agreed if it was what I wanted. He had assured her, without my knowledge, that I did.

Later I found Lillibet with Cousin Paulina and Cousin Pearl and tried to lose myself amongst them but Sergei found me and insisted that we dance. I saw Lorenzo pass back and forth across the hall, glance at me, then attend to someone nearby.

I longed for just one small recognition from him.

Sergei, even with his beautiful eyes, was becoming exasperatingly tiresome.

Lillibet and her cousins were having a noisy party of their own from which they needed no other intrusion. Sitting with them was no impediment for the wretched man.

I had to get away. I managed to procure my coat when he had vanished for the moment.

'Lillibet I need to slip away home now,' I said.

'I done think your boyfriend goin to let you,' she said with loud amusement. Her eyes looked in the direction of the bar where Sergei could be seen charging towards us.

'Wait here one minute,' she said and disappeared while Sergei fussed about helping me with my coat saying he was more than ready to take me home.

'Anna,' she called out to me from another door. 'Can you come please?'

Sergei started to come with me.

'Alone!' she called.

Sergei hesitated and said, 'I wait here for you.'

I found myself in a small living room annex to the bridal-hall. Lorenzo was there with Lillibet.

'Now, see here,' she was saying to him. 'Miss Violin-girl stuck now with Mr. Blue eyes and you done notin' to help. What you going to do boy?'

'I don't know,' he answered. 'Maria and Jacek said you... I thought...'

'You know Lorenzo, you don't tink, that your trouble boy. Now she want to go home and she done want that boy goin wid her. You goin help or not?'

'Perhaps if you danced with me?' he suggested.

'That's better,' Lillibet said. 'Here, I take your coat.' She peeled back my coat and thrust me towards Lorenzo.

He took my arm and led me to the packed dance floor where guests were gyrating about in their own particular style of rhythm to the beat of the music.

I felt a flow of relief flood over me as I saw from the corner of an eye Sergey stop and watch. I felt safe at last. Lorenzo's arms were around me touching my hands, holding me and he was moving to the music.

'Thank you,' I said. 'I thought I would never get away from him.'

'And there I was, led to believe you were a designer couple.'

'Heavens Lorenzo, whatever gave you the idea?'

'Well my sister and her new husband for a start and right now, I can feel his eyes burrowing through me from across the room.'

'What can I do to put him off?' I asked, feeling a little desperate.

'A kiss perhaps?'

I raised my face towards him with lips poised and he bent his head and put his lips to mine. I felt them soft and gentle, pressed lightly, then lingeringly, exquisitely - holding me in that wonderful moment.

It was meant to be an innocent kiss, something to show Sergei that I was not interested in him.

But something happened.

A strange and vibrant tingle passed through me as if a current of some wild and magical blend of heartbeat and longing had been released. We stopped dancing, pressing our lips closer and our arms tighter together. His tongue pressed into my mouth and I was lost in an umbilical connection that had crept in beyond words. The world passed around, behind and before us and we were oblivious to the world as sounds and movement pushed and bumped against us.

We had made a separation of duty and obligation that was at once shallow with limited meaning. I was floating, suspended in a pool of light, my world encapsulated in that kiss.

'Anna,' he said, 'Anna, my love.'

Somewhere off - Sergei's voice was talking fast and loud in his language and the bride and groom were trying to calm him down.

People danced round us and laughed and we did not see them, nor did we move from the spot.

Sergei had had far too much to drink and wanted to pick a fight. It seemed ludicrous, laughable. His brother was talking to him as Lorenzo and I were leaving.

Lillibet was still waiting with my coat. We left together with her cousins in a large taxi, crammed in tightly, so that our bodies became enmeshed, throbbing with excitement.

Suddenly everything was enormously funny. We were laughing as if everything had become so easy, so clear: so immensely wonderful.

'About time boy,' said Lillibet.   'About time!'